THE MOURNFUL DEMEANOUR OF
LIEUTENANT BORUVKA

THE MOURNFUL DEMEANOUR OF LIEUTENANT BORUVKA

by

JOSEF SKVORECKY

Translated by
ROSEMARY KAVAN
KACA POLACKOVA
and
GEORGE THEINER

W · W · NORTON & COMPANY
NEW YORK   *LONDON*

Printed in the United States of America.

Library of Congress Cataloging-in-Publication Data
Škvorecký, Josef.
The mournful demeanour of Lieutenant Boruvka.

Translation of: Smutek poručíka Borúvky.
Contents: The supernatural powers of Lieutenant
Boruvka—That sax solo—The scientific method—
[etc.]
I. Title.
PG5038.S527S5513   1987   891.8′635   87-18504

ISBN 0-393-02470-9

W. W. Norton & Company, Inc., 500 Fifth Avenue, New York, N. Y. 10110
W. W. Norton & Company Ltd., 37 Great Russell Street, London WC1B 3NU

1 2 3 4 5 6 7 8 9 0

CONTENTS

I

The Supernatural Powers of Lieutenant Boruvka

T HERE WAS NO talking him out of it. Constable First Class Sintak—the only policeman in the entire land who could boast that rank—was firmly convinced that Lieutenant Boruvka wielded powers that were not entirely in keeping with normal human abilities. But then, Constable First Class Sintak was pushing sixty, and was burdened with the prejudice of religion, though he kept it a secret while on duty. In his native village in the Orlice Hills, where he spent his holidays and took part in the spiritualist séances held in the cottage of a former home weaver by the name of Potesil, he felt no such inhibitions, though, and as far as his superior was concerned, he told all. To Constable First Class Sintak, Lieutenant Boruvka was a wizard.

He proved it, definitely and, in the eyes of Constable First Class Sintak, irrevocably, in the famous Semerak case. That was the case where he arrived late, having spent the previous evening at a class reunion at K., recalling thirty years since graduation. After the elation of the small hours of the night, he fell prey to the inevitable depression, and besides, his alarm clock failed to ring. So early that afternoon, when he arrived at the scene of the crime—a group of isolated bungalows of the sort built before the war by dyed-in-the-wool worker-individualists, at the cost of their entire life's savings—Sergeant Malek was just about through with the case; all he was waiting for was the lab tests.

"That," said the young sergeant to the lieutenant, when he arrived all out of breath, "is the only hitch. From the psychological point of view, you can tell that fellow's a murderer a mile

7

off. But we can't have anybody accusing us of having jumped the gun and made the arrest too soon. Psychologically speaking, he's every inch a murderer, just look at him—and then what happens? It turns out we're all wet, and the public gets all worked up, and when the chief gets through with us, we won't even be fit to pound a beat," declared the sergeant. "No sir, a person has got to have some insurance, and our insurance is science."

While the sergeant was acquainting the lieutenant with his philosophy of criminal investigation, the criminologist of long standing let his mournful baby-blue eyes systematically examine the dismal attic. Hanging by her neck from a rope tied to the middle of the attic ceiling was an old woman in a dirty plaid dress, her grey hair concealing her face. At the height of the lieutenant's belt buckle, the toes of one foot still balanced a worn-down bedroom slipper, while the other foot was bare, and its blackened joints told the lieutenant much of her story. A not very happy story, of what might be called life. On the attic floor, under the corpse, lay the other bedroom slipper, like a sad, deserted little animal. Apart from that, the attic was empty, except for a few musty cupboards and chairs, some flower-pots, a few crates, and a stack of yellowed newspapers, and the lieutenant wondered idly whether he would find, if he were to go through them, reports on the Lindbergh kidnapping, or the Sacco-Vanzetti story. The open sky-light let in the cool breeze of an Indian summer, and for a moment blew the hair out of the dead woman's face. What was revealed there told the lieutenant the rest of the story.

"Suicide?" scoffed the sergeant. "Pooh. Oh yes, it's all just dandy, she had asthma, she had it bad, and she kept threatening that some day she'd hang herself. The neighbours back him up on that. But Joe, look at the strangulation marks. Wait a minute—" He looked around. "We'll get you a chair—Constable, get us a chair—and then you'll take a good look at those marks, Joe."

And while Constable First Class Sintak was obeying orders, Malek kept on talking. He couldn't wait; it was the first case he had ever had all to himself, and he could thank the lieutenant's elation of the previous evening and his unwound alarm clock.

8

He was just quivering to show his boss that he was Johnny-on-the-spot, if not Johnny-a-little-rung-on-the-ladder-below the spot he deserved to be on. And so he continued:

"Everything is just fine. Just fine; the old lady talked about suicide herself. But what about the strangulation marks? They taught us that strangulation marks from hanging slant from chin to nape. And this one has two sets of them. At least I'm willing to bet that's what they are. Just wait till you have a look. It's not too clear, and the rope is still in one set of them, but if you look closely, you can see another one just below the rope. Nobody's going to tell me she jerked her head after she hanged herself! Sintak claims that there's just one set of them, or else that it's double because the old lady tensed her neck muscles, and when they relaxed, she slipped lower in the noose, but I say that's nonsense. And that's why I left her strung up. The doctor wanted to take her down, he said he couldn't be sure of anything until he has her on a table, but I took it on myself. No sir, I said, the lieutenant has to see this just the way it is!"

"Well, thank you for your confidence, Paul," said the embarrassed Lieutenant Boruvka, and his mournful gaze rested on the eager tanned face of the younger policeman. "Of course—"

"That goes without saying, doesn't it?" interrupted Malek. "You're in charge here, and you've got to see it. And in the meantime, take a look at this," he added proudly, and unfolded a piece of paper for the lieutenant to see. "I made a sketch, and a sort of a chart, you see? I remember in your course on Methods of Scientific Investigation, you gave a lecture on that case in Moravia, where it was a chart that you used to analyse the times and the topographical situations, and to put your finger on the murderer."

"Yes," said the lieutenant sombrely, "but..."

"Well, look at it," Malek interrupted him again. "Here you have it black on white, everywhere the murderer, I mean the suspect, says he went, and all of the time and distance factors."

"Yes, but..."

"But first I've got to report on how we managed the investigation." Malek interrupted the old criminologist for the third time, and continued with such enthusiasm that he didn't even register the lieutenant's resigned sigh. Lieutenant Boruvka capitulated.

9

His smooth round forehead crinkled unhappily, and his sad eyes focused on the sergeant's map, painstakingly executed in coloured pencils.

"Old Semerak phoned at a quarter past twelve from the phone booth down the road," explained the sergeant. "At three minutes to one we were here at the scene of the crime. We found everything just the way you see it, we didn't move a thing. Semerak claims that he came home from the tavern at half past midnight, found the place empty, and his wife hanging from this beam in the attic. So he went to phone the police, he says. That in itself is peculiar—home from the tavern at half past twelve and phoning us already at a quarter to one. And the phone booth is a good five minutes' walk from here. That doesn't sound as if he had to look very hard for his wife. It sounds as if he knew just where to find her and went straight up to the attic."

"Certainly," Lieutenant Boruvka made a feeble attempt. "But . . ."

"But let's take a closer look at old Semerak's story." Malek picked up his superior's sentence for him. "He claims to have left the house at six p.m. That's a fact; his neighbour backs him up on that, a fellow by the name of Penkava, a railwayman. He was just arriving home when Semerak was leaving the house. They exchanged a few words, Semerak and Penkava, and what do you think they talked about? The weather! And then he remembered that he'd left his tobacco pouch at home. And what do you think he did?"

The lieutenant shrugged his shoulders. "I don't know. But . . ."

"He called his wife!" declared Malek triumphantly. "He called his wife, instead of going and fetching the tobacco pouch himself. And the two of them bickered back and forth over the fence about where she was supposed to go look for it. You see? Penkava saw her. That's perfect, isn't it?"

"Yes," replied Lieutenant Boruvka in a glum tone.

"That's what I call an alibi," the elated Malek rubbed his hands. "The murderer, I mean the suspect, has a witness to testify that he left the house, one who can swear to the exact time, because Penkava commutes to work, and takes the five forty-five train back every day. And the witness sees his wife too, large as life. And then there are two other witnesses to back up Semerak's story. One of them met him at the crucifix by the road, and the other about a quarter of an hour later at the bus stop. He stopped to chat with both of them, voluntarily—can you imagine that, old Semerak, of his own free will?—and what do you suppose they talked about? The weather again! A fellow who never says an unnecessary word—and I've got witnesses to back that up— suddenly feels the urge to make small talk about the weather. With three consecutive passers-by. The very day his wife hangs herself. That's one thing."

"Yes," said Lieutenant Boruvka, "and—"

"And another thing: he makes sure he leaves the house just when he knows that Penkava always comes home from work, and when he knows for certain that he'll meet him. And he needs to meet him. And not just meet him; he needs Penkava to see his wife, alive, and so, on that particular day, the day his wife does herself in, he forgets his tobacco pouch at home. And he's so lazy that he doesn't bother to go and get it himself; instead he makes his asthmatic old lady run around."

The young sergeant glanced triumphantly at the frail old woman hanging over their heads, and then at the lieutenant.

"Hm," the older man cleared his throat, "your deductions are fine. Hats off to you there. Nobody puts anything over on you. It's just that . . ."

"But that's not all," said Malek hurriedly, "I'll show you a whole lot of weak spots and tangles and discrepancies like that in Semerak's story. Like where he claims that he went to see a certain Barta for some beeswax. That Barta is a well-known beekeeper in these parts, and Semerak keeps bees too. Not very carefully or very successfully, but he keeps them all the same. You can tell if you take a look at the hives in the garden back of the bungalow. Honestly, the only bees that could keep alive in those hives are fourth-rate bees. Bum bees," laughed the sergeant. "Well, anyway, he says he simply went to get some beeswax. Barta and his wife live in a cabin on the edge of the woods about two miles up the road from here. Semerak arrived there at a quarter to seven, stayed there for about three-quarters of an hour, and then he took the path through the woods down to the tavern. Look at the map I sketched. He arrived at the tavern at about a quarter to nine, and by nine o'clock he was sitting at the card table. He played cards till half past eleven, and then he went home. It's two and a half miles from here to the tavern, and it took him an hour. That's all right, all that is just fine."

"But . . ." Lieutenant Boruvka looked away from the dead woman, and his gaze rested on the flushed face of Sergeant Malek again.

"But even if a lot of things are all right in his story—" Malek was quick to pick up where he had left off to take a breath "—some of them just don't stand up. Look here—I have a map of the area he covered."

"Yes, fine," said the lieutenant, "you did a good job here. Still, when . . ."

"You want to see the time chart, don't you? Here it is." He handed the lieutenant another piece of paper. "And here, below it, there's a chart comparing times and distances. Take a look."

Lieutenant Boruvka took a look.

6.00 p.m.—departure from S
6.45 p.m.—arrival at B
7.30 p.m.—departure from B
8.45 p.m.—arrival at T
11.30 p.m.—departure from T
about 40 minutes in men's room
12.10 a.m.—return to S
12.45 a.m.—phoned police
12.57 a.m.—our arrival on the scene.

DISTANCES AND CORRESPONDING TIMES

S—B	1.9 miles—45 minutes' walk
B—T	3.1 miles—1 hour 15 minutes' walk
T—S	2.5 miles—1 hour's walk
B-S-T	4.4 miles—1 hours 45 minutes' walk
T-S-T	5 miles—2 hours' walk
B-S-B-T	6.9 miles—2 hours 45 minutes' walk

"Why did you work out distances B-S-T and B-S-B-T?" asked the lieutenant in spite of himself when he had finished examining the charts.

The sergeant grinned. "I'll tell you. Look, first of all, I'm basing it on the hypothetical assumption that Semerak is a murderer, that is that the old lady didn't hang herself, that Semerak strangled her and strung her up on this beam here."

"But that's . . ."

"I know, that's jumping to conclusions. I can't prove a thing. Not yet, anyway."

"I think . . ."

"But I have very good reason to believe that that's what happened!"

The old criminologist relinquished all hope of getting a word in edgeways. He left it to the young sergeant, who took full advantage of his opportunity.

"All right, then; assuming that Semerak murdered her. His alibi is airtight, on first glance. He left the house at six—a witness saw his wife alive; at twenty past six another witness talked to him at a point about halfway between A and B. At a quarter to seven he arrived at B; here the time is right, because he claims his watch stopped, and he asked Barta what the right time was, and wound up his watch and set it. Barta backs him up there too. We know just when he left Barta's, because Semerak looked at the wall clock, was surprised that it was half past seven already, and even though Barta and his wife tried to get him to stay, he just got up and left."

At that point, the only thing that the lieutenant had the strength to do was to clear his throat, and Malek was off again.

"Let's take another look at beekeeper Barta and his wife before we follow Semerak to the tavern." The young sergeant sounded as if he were giving a lecture in a course for trainee criminologists. The lieutenant let his gaze wander around the bare attic. "There's a number of interesting points there," continued Malek. "First of all, Semerak's interest in the exact time. The day his wife ups and hangs herself, his watch stops, and, besides, that day of all days he has to be at the tavern on time, as if he had heaven knows what kind of an important date there. And it turns out that all he's going to do there is play cards—and he doesn't even have the reputation of being much of a card player. The tavernkeeper says that Semerak isn't a regular at the card table, and when he does join in, he never stays at it for more than an hour. But yesterday of all days, he stayed at it for almost three hours. But back to the

Bartas. His interest in the time there is the first suspicious circumstance. His inconspicuous calling of the witnesses' attention to the time of his arrival and departure. Another interesting thing is the testimony of the beekeeper and his wife. I tried an old trick on them, one I learned from you." Malek smiled, and the round face of the lieutenant was also momentarily illuminated by an embarrassed smile. "I remember," continued Malek, "you told us in a lecture on Interrogation Tactics about the principle of the confrontation of testimony obtained from the separate interrogation of witnesses to the same event—remember? And so . . ."

The lieutenant braced himself for another attempt to put a halt to the flood of words that were pouring out of the sergeant's mouth. "Yes, I do recall lecturing on that. But of course, in this case, you didn't . . ."

His subordinate's enthusiastic eloquence took over again, and the lieutenant gave a weary sigh.

"Wait a minute, you don't know what it was all about," the sergeant said, impatiently. "It was all perfectly simple and straightforward. It was on account of the jacket."

"Jacket?" breathed the lieutenant weakly.

"Yes, jacket. And then—listen to this—his bike!"

A significant silence ensued, and Malek gave a sidelong glance at the lieutenant. The old criminologist read in his look a craving for recognition. Lieutenant Boruvka grew even sadder. He did so like to make people happy . . . So he asked, with an effort at self-control, "His bike?"

"That's right." The sergeant rubbed his hands together. "That's part of the working hypothesis I finally set up. I mean to say that my hypothesis uses the bike as its point of departure. And that's the main reason I drew the map." He tapped the paper that the lieutenant was still holding in his hand. "First of all, the jacket. I asked the Bartas, each one separately, what Semerak had on when he came to see them last night. And now, listen! Barta claims he had a tweed jacket on, and his wife insists that it was a brown corduroy jacket. When I confronted them, they almost had a fist-fight over it. Some couple, those two." The sergeant laughed. "Anybody who wants to get married ought to drop in on those two for a chat. Five'll get you ten he'll stay a confirmed bachelor like me, ha ha ha."

The lieutenant's smile had a sadness about it that his subordinate overlooked.

"They yelled at each other until we just about lost our eardrums and the two of them were both hoarse, and in the middle of it, old lady Barta said, I mean she screamed, 'He had the same brown corduroy jacket on that he had last week when he rode past here on that bike.' So there's another suspicious circumstance for you—a discrepancy between the testimony of two alleged witnesses. Of course the discrepancy by itself doesn't mean much of anything. Men don't usually notice what a person has on. But all the same, what if the whole thing was planned, you understand? What if it was a false alibi? What if Semerak didn't go to the Bartas at all? What if he turned around at the bus stop after he met the witness, went home, did his old lady in, and went to the tavern? I found something that was very suspicious when I investigated the tavern, though, but I'll get to that later. First this: as I was saying, what if they thought up this alibi, but forgot to agree on all the details? You always used to tell us that a false alibi is easy to break down by investigating the details. All I know about all this is thanks to you, Joe."

Once again, the older police officer's countenance assumed a sour smile, and the hand holding the map attempted something that resembled a gesture of rejection. The sergeant responded at once.

"I know it isn't very probable, setting up an alibi for a murder, and doing it with two people at once, and one of them the biggest gossip for miles around. I didn't think much of that theory myself; I'm just telling you about it so that you could follow my thought process right down the line. What's much more interesting is what the beekeeper's wife said about the bike. There wouldn't be anything odd about that; most of the people around here have bicycles. But the hitch is in the fact that Semerak doesn't have a bike. And besides, he denies the encounter with old lady Barta last week."

The sergeant's eyes were pleading for praise. Lieutenant Boruvka cleared his throat. "Yes," he said sombrely, "that's good work as far as deduction is concerned. In other words, the bike led you to the conclusion . . .”

The sergeant, encouraged, launched his explanation with increased verve. “. . . that the time correlations are false. If Semerak had a bicycle hidden somewhere, then the time-table looks entirely different. Look!” He removed another slip of paper from his breast pocket, saying, “I believe in being systematic. Our entire system is based on systematic planning, so we criminologists can’t afford to allow ourselves to be guided by haphazard ideas as they do in detective mysteries.”

The time-table was truly systematic:

DISTANCE AND CORRESPONDING TIMES BY BYCYCLE
B-S-T	4.4 miles—about 20 minutes
T-S-T	5 miles—about 25 minutes
B-S-B-T	6.9 miles—about 45 minutes

AS ABOVE PLUS 20 MINUTES FOR THE CRIME
B-S-T	—about 40 minutes
T-S-T	—about 45 minutes
B-S-B-T	—a little over an hour

Lieutenant Boruvka took a long time to examine the information presented in the sergeant’s precise handwriting. It looked as if he were undergoing some sort of inner struggle. He sighed, cleared his throat again, and asked, “Why did you work out the times for T-S-T, then?”

“Just a minute. I’ll get to that.” The sergeant took the map out of the lieutenant’s hand and indicated point B with his index finger. “Assuming that Semerak had the bike hidden somewhere near the beekeeper’s place—and that is entirely possible, the house is on the edge of the woods, with bushes all around—well, then there are three possibilities. Either he left Barta’s at half past seven, sat on his bike and rode from B to S, home, committed the crime—I give him twenty minutes at the most to do it—and rode the stretch S-T to the tavern. So that B-S-T plus twenty minutes for the murder, that’s about forty minutes. That means he had plenty of time to get rid of the bike somewhere near the tavern, and to show up at the tavern at a quarter to nine.

Lieutenant Boruvka nodded.

"But S-T is a comparatively busy stretch of road that early in the evening. Maybe Semerak didn't dare to risk being seen there, even though it was dark already. He might have taken the much less frequented road back from S to B, and back down the forest path B-T. The stretch B-S-B-T plus twenty minutes for the murder is about sixty-five, seventy minutes. Still plenty of time to make it to the tavern by a quarter to nine."

"Yes," said Lieutenant Boruvka, but he choked on it, and when he had finished coughing, he asked, "But why work out the stretch T-S-T when you say that he was playing cards from a quarter to nine till half past eleven? Besides, I wanted to . . ."

The lieutenant didn't manage to tell the sergeant what it was that he had wanted to do. Malek clutched his sleeve, leaned over to him and breathed his cigarette-flavoured breath excitedly in the lieutenant's face.

"That's just it. He wasn't playing cards all that time," he declared triumphantly. "He spent half an hour or more in the men's room!" The lieutenant's face quivered as if he were in pain. "The witnesses don't agree as to how long it was. We interrogated eight of them, including a couple of kibitzers, the tavern-keeper and his daughter, who's a waitress at the tavern. Semerak claims that it wasn't more than a quarter of an hour. One of the card-players claims that he was gone for almost an hour. It's all a matter of the relativity of the subjective perception of time," said Malek slowly, and he blinked his eyes for emphasis. "If we take an average, it comes to something between half an hour and three-quarters of an hour. And that's enough for the stretch T-S-T plus time for the murder. The road between the tavern and Semerak's place is a new asphalt road, you can take it pretty fast on a bicycle. In any case, Semerak's long stay in the men's room is symptomatic."

"How?" asked the lieutenant uncertainly.

"Symp-to-matic," repeated the sergeant, taking care with each and every consonant. "It either gives him time to murder his wife, if he uses the route T-S-T, or else it proves that shortly before arriving at the tavern, Samerak experienced something that excited his nervous system considerably. Dr Seifert once told us, in a course on Criminal Psychology, that the human organism frequently reacts to sudden excitement by an uncontrollable urge to move the bowels."

"Yes, I know." Lieutenant Boruvka appeared to delve deep into some reminiscence. He had a cool head, and was known to have twisted a loaded pistol barehanded out of a murderer's hand, and when the fellow suddenly pulled a knife on him, to have knocked him down with a single well-aimed blow to the jaw. All the same, though, even Lieutenant Boruvka occasionally experienced sudden excitement, with the accompanying, not particularly pleasant, reaction on the part of the organism. No one knew about these occasions, however. It wasn't on the job that they occurred.

"In words of one syllable," continued Malek, "after he killed his wife, our friend got the runs. But there is where our criminological laboratory comes on the scene, with chemical and biological analyses."

The lieutenant's face twitched. For an instant he was possessed by a fantastic image of some sort of odd laboratory analysis of some very unattractive material. But the sergeant corrected his error almost at once.

"A careful examination of the scene of the—I mean of the men's toilet in the tavern proved that someone had recently climbed in or out of the window, or both. There are a number of items for dactyloscopic examination on the glass of the toilet window," said Malek importantly, and the old criminologist blinked twice. He was used to calling them "fingerprints" himself. But then, the sergeant was a member of a younger, more scientific generation.

"And Semerak has some suspicious abrasions on the palm of his right hand. So I ordered a chemical analysis of the paint on the inside wall under the window, and of the suspect's clothes. We ought to have the outcome of the tests by about four this afternoon. Furthermore I had them fingerprint the suspect and make a comparison with the prints on the window. And finally, I ordered an investigation of the outside wall under the window, in search of human tissue identical with that of the suspect. I also had to order the removal of a sample of skin from Semerak's palm. We had to drive out to the clinic for a dermatome . . ."

"For which?" breathed the lieutenant.

"A dermatome. That's a special kind of dermatological

instrument, a sort of knife that permits the removal of a thin compact layer of surface skin as a sample for comparison."

The lieutenant said wearily, "Yes, but still . . ."

"Still, we ran into more trouble," said Malek. "The stucco under the window was badly weathered, and it was doubtful whether it could be removed and transported to the laboratory without destroying it. So we called in a couple of bricklayers, and they cut the whole area out of the wall and fixed it into a metal frame, in a cement base. We got the frame at the CKD plant, they welded it for us in the workshop on the spot—and so we took a whole chunk of wall over to the lab."

"So the toilet . . ."

"So the toilet," laughed the sergeant, "is temporarily out of order. The tavernkeeper started to give us a hard time about it, but I convinced him when I explained that we're investigating a capital crime, and that all citizens have an obligation towards society—"

"That's all true, but of course . . ."

"—to contribute to the arrest of the murderer. But I must say that, all told, the citizens of the town were much more helpful. You see, in order to confirm my hypothesis, I had to have the bicycle."

The lieutenant's forehead was moist. "Did you find it?"

"Not yet," said the sergeant with an undertone of self-confidence. "But the entire local Youth Union organisation joined in the search. And the principal of the grammar school was more than understanding. The youngsters and the fellows in the diving club are searching the pond." Malek tapped the map. "There are dense reeds on two sides of the pond, and it's up to twelve feet deep in places, but there's a fellow in a diving suit hunting down there."

Lieutenant Boruvka gave something that resembled a sigh. "Listen, Paul, you've got a rare gift for organisation, I know that . . ."

"I know that myself," grinned the sergeant. "I did a real job of organising things here, didn't I? In the meantime, the kids from the grammar school, along with the principal and the teachers, are combing the woods. We'll have that bicycle by nightfall or my name isn't Malek."

19

"That is, unless . . ."

"Don't worry," Malek reassured his superior, who was once again beginning to show signs of nervousness. "Our hypothesis is OK, just wait and see. I have other evidence. In the first place, we found soil and pieces of moss on Semerak's shoes. At first glance, the soil and moss look the same as the stuff under the toilet window. Semerak claims that the same kind of moss grows on the forest path between B and T, where he claims to have walked, from Barta's to the tavern. All right; so we gathered samples of moss from the tavern, and from about fifteen places in the wood where he claims to have walked. We sent it to the Botanical Institute of the Academy of Sciences. The fellows there promised to give us a hand. I spoke to Professor Kavina personally by phone this morning."

There was desperation in Lieutenant Boruvka's glance as it swept the bare attic again, and came to rest on the dead woman's wretched feet. Behind his back, Constable First Class Sintak cleared his throat, and when the two of them turned to face him, they saw that he had a chair in his hand.

"Just a second, Constable. I'll finish giving the lieutenant the background, and then he'll take a look at it himself," said Malek, and he turned back to Lieutenant Boruvka. "Well, and while we were collecting the moss, we looked round for tracks. There's a few places along the path where the ground is moist clay, ideal material for imprints, and sure enough, there were the tracks of at least five different bicycles. I had plaster casts taken of all of them. When we find the *corpus delicti*, we'll make the comparisons, and that'll be first-class proof. All of the tracks were made by old bicycles, with characteristic marks on their tyres."

"Bu . . ." And that was all the old criminologist managed to utter before the sergeant took the floor again.

"Of course, in order to play fair with old Semerak, I had casts made of his shoes as well—I mean, of his footprints—and casts of all the fresh footprints from the forest path. There's an awful lot of them, but since this is a serious crime, we have to set aside all economic considerations."

"We wouldn't really have to, if . . ." Lieutenant Boruvka tried to say.

"If that rascal hadn't thought things out so cleverly that we're

having trouble trying to find proof conclusive enough to arrest
him." Malek was indignant. "But there's no such thing as a
perfect crime, and we have modern science at our beck and call,
and that's a mighty weapon. He can't stand up against science. I
had them bring in the canine squad on the case too," he added.

"The canine squad," repeated the lieutenant dully.

"Yes, Ajax. You know him, don't you? Magnificent beast. A
cross between a dog and a wolf. What a set of teeth! I've never
seen a more magnificent set of teeth in all my life."

"Yes," replied Lieutenant Boruvka grimly. Ajax's magnificent
teeth were not unfamiliar to him. The magnificent beast had
attempted to demonstrate them a short while earlier on the
lieutenant's backside when that rotund officer had been rushing
from the car to the scene of the crime across the courtyard. It had
taken the joint efforts of two experienced members of the canine
squad to calm the beast, who for reasons unknown was excited
to a state of enraged ferocity by the lieutenant's scent.

"We put him on the trail," continued Malek, "and the results
speak for the B-S-B-T alternative, even though there are some
points which need clarification. We'll have to wait for the lab tests
to clear them up for us. Look," and Malek unfolded the map
again, "on the stretch between B and T, the dog lost the scent a
little way past Barta's house, and couldn't find it anywhere in the
woods either. On the stretch B-S, he found it, but he had some
trouble. But on the stretch between the tavern and the house, he
had no trouble at all. What does that prove?" He turned to the
lieutenant with his rhetorical question, but this time the latter was
silent.

"I can see it now, clear as day," declared Malek with characteristic enthusiasm. "A little way beyond the beekeeper's place, old
Semerak climbed on the bike, rode home to S along the route
B-S, twenty minutes later pedalled back along the same stretch
and took the path B-T to the tavern. That means he travelled
the stretch S-B once on foot when he went to Barta's at six
o'clock, and twice by bicycle. All of—" Malek glanced at his
wrist-watch, "—twenty hours have passed since then, and that's
why the dog had trouble finding the trail. Semerak took the
stretch B-T only once, and by bike at that, so it's no wonder that
the dog couldn't find the trail at all. And he did the stretch T-S

on foot, and comparatively recently, less than fifteen hours ago. The trail is still fresh there, and a dog can latch on to it and follow it easily."

"But you mentioned some discrepancies," ventured Lieutenant Boruvka again, and he gave an embarrassed look back at Sintak, who was standing almost at attention, with the chair at his feet, and devouring the sergeant's every word. His years of service in the police force had brought this policeman to a deep respect for superiors, and not even the introduction of "Comradely relations" among members of the force cured him of it. Lieutenant Boruvka cleared his throat as if to say something, but Malek started again before he had a chance to begin.

"It's like this: at the tavern, the dog hesitated. He found the trail all right: he found two trails, one of them led to the tavern door, and the other under the men's room window. Well, that's no tragedy, it just speaks for the T-S-T alternative. The murderer climbed out of the window, and went for the bike that he had left hidden somewhere near the road on the stretch T-S, and then at half past twelve he left the tavern by the door and walked home. The only thing that has me puzzled is the fact that the dog couldn't find the scent on the stretch B-T—unless the murderer hid the bike in the woods near Barta's house, cycled along the stretch B-T, hid it somewhere near the road between S and T so as to have it handy, and waited a while before going to the tavern, so that the times would match, and then took the alternative T-S-T."

"Yet," said Lieutenant Boruvka, "all that is entirely possible, Paul. You really did a lot of work on this case, there's no denying that. But of course . . ."

"Thanks, Joe," said Sergeant Malek, pleased, and then, "Now maybe you could take a look at those strangulation marks. Constable!" He didn't have to say any more, because the constable leapt forward with the chair and set it up at the old lady's feet. "Hop up there and take a good look," Malek encouraged the old criminologist.

Lieutenant Boruvka looked up. Another breeze wafted in through the skylight, and blew the hair out of the bluish face. A glance was enough; the face repeated the life story for the lieutenant. He shivered. "I . . ." he began.

"Go ahead," urged the sergeant. "We're going to have to take her down anyway. She's been up there too long already."

"I . . ." repeated the lieutenant, when the shaky attic quivered with a deafening roar. All three criminologists looked up. Sintak's face showed an expression of respect, Lieutenant Boruvka looked terrified, and Malek smiled with satisfaction.

"Helicopter," he explained. "The major gave his permission. You know," he turned to the lieutenant, "from the air you can see right down to the bottom of the pond. A lot of time saved for the divers. Well, any minute now we can expect word that they have found the bicycle."

"I . . ." said Lieutenant Boruvka, paused, and added determinedly, "I'm not going to climb up there!"

"I know you believe me, Joe," said the sergeant, flattered, "but still . . ."

"No," the lieutenant interposed quickly, "that's not it. I believe you, of course I do. But—I don't have to look. You can go ahead and arrest him," he said mournfully, and added, "for murder."

"Well," smiled Malek, "I'm happy to see that my evidence has convinced you. I did collect quite a bit of information. But I'd just as soon hold off making the arrest until we're certain, until I have at least the bike, the fingerprint and lab test results, and the botanical and dermatological reports. You know how touchy the public is about false arrests and things. In other words, we'll just wait until," and he cleared his throat, "that science of ours gives us irrevocable proof." Another breeze moved the suspended corpse. Or had the lieutenant imagined it? He shivered.

"I don't need proof," he replied. "I *know* he murdered her. Constable—" he turned to Constable First Class Sintak "—would you please go downstairs and have them bring Semerak up here?"

That is how it happened that Constable First Class Sintak didn't hear what Lieutenant Boruvka said to the sergeant. And that is why nobody will ever convince him that the lieutenant's certainty as to the murderer was not a product of his strange and supernatural abilities.

And for that matter, no one ever found out what the lieutenant told the sergeant that afternoon in the dingy attic under the body of the murdered old woman. Lieutenant Boruvka was a soft-hearted soul, and whenever possible, he preferred to conceal circumstances that would cast aspersions on the criminological abilities of his colleagues.

And that is how it happened that the file headed *Semerak* lists as evidence conclusive for the arrest the facts ascertained by Sergeant Paul Malek, in the absence of Lieutenant Boruvka and with the aid of modern science and technology, evidence which finally led the murderer to make a confession.

Two things are certain, however: one of them is the expression of inexpressible sadness on Lieutenant Boruvka's round face when Constable First Class Sintak returned to the attic with the murderer Semerak as he had been asked, and the other is the fact that Sergeant Malek was as red as an overcooked lobster. Sintak didn't know why. He didn't, because he naturally hadn't been able to hear the three questions that the lieutenant had asked the young sergeant in his absence.

The first two: "Didn't you move a thing? Is everything just exactly the way you found it?"

And when the sergeant had looked around that bleak, bare attic, in the middle of which, about a yard above the floor and directly over that single sad, deserted slipper, hung the frail old woman, and when he had replied in the affirmative—that everything was just the way they found it, and that not a thing was touched—then the old criminologist asked, "Then tell me, Paul, how did she get up there all by herself?"

And, with a pudgy finger, he pointed up at the old attic beam, and then, without a word, at the three-foot distance between the old woman's feet and the empty desolate floor, where the breeze was worrying a few shreds of old newspapers and tiny wisps of dust.

II

That Sax Solo

THE BRASS HELD the lead, then they stopped suddenly. The trumpet players rested their instruments on their knees and looked at the singer. It was a pretty view, even from the back. She was standing in front of the microphone, tapping out the rhythm with her foot in its pointed shoe. The rehearsal for the evening performance was drawing to an end.

Then the saxophones fell silent, except for the first tenor. The bass player, a large, gorrilla-like man, looked up in surprise, but the tenor swooped rapidly from high to low in a sobbing solo passage and then came to a sudden stop too. It was obvious to all that the passage was unfinished. The singer looked at the tenor enquiringly. The saxophonist, red in the face, removed the mouthpiece from his lips and broke the silence that had descended by exclaiming loudly and angrily:

"What bloody fool arranged that?"

All faces turned towards the bass player. In his muscular embrace the bass looked more like a cello. His name was Bedrich Polacek, but the band called him Benny. "What's up?" he gulped guiltily.

"What?" asked the saxophonist ironically. "Since when has it been possible to play this on the sax?" He threw the score scornfully at the bass player's feet. Benny picked it up and ran his eye over it. The small, bald band-leader went up to him and looked over his shoulder. He read:

25

The band-leader pointed to the last note and whispered: "A."
The bass player struck his forehead with the palm of his hand.
"Yep. Sorry!" he said. "Sorry! I forgot to give this to the
clarinet. Sorry! Anyone can make a mistake like that."

"Not anyone," came a soft, but audible, remark from the brass
where the band's jokers sat. "Only a lovesick mule!"

The trombonists laughed. Benny's face went scarlet and the
attractive singer's back stiffened. Gustav Randal, the tenor
saxophonist, scowled as he took the corrected score from Benny.
The joke had evidently not been to his taste.

The large hotel clock indicated a quarter past seven when the
waiter placed a plate of Hungarian goulash in front of the singer,
Marie Laurinova, known as Mici.

"I'll get this down and go and change," said Mici to Benny,
sprinkling her plate generously with pepper. "Drop by for me,
love, will you? I've got to take my case downstairs and it's
awfully heavy. You'll give me a hand, won't you?"

Benny growled something in an infatuated tone and laid his
massive paw on Mici's tiny white hand. Gustav Randal got up
from the next table abruptly and left the room without a word.
The girl pretended not to have seen him, and between two
mouthfuls of goulash managed to stroke Benny's heavy hand
and bestow upon him a spectacularly dazzling smile.

"Excuse me," Gustav Randal said to the elderly spinster who
opened the door to him. "Will it disturb you if I play over a
few passages on my saxophone next door?"

The thin spinster, Slavka Matyasova, smiled sweetly.

"Not at all! I shall enjoy listening," she said. "I'm not musical,
but—but anyway it's only a quarter past seven and I don't go
to bed before ten."

"Thank you," said Randal, and without further excuses, he
withdrew into the adjoining room.

Miss Matyasova left her door ajar for a while, then she heaved
a sigh. Randal was a dark, handsome young man with the eyes
of a gipsy. He looked as though he had a wild streak in him.
Miss Matyasova liked to think about wild young men.

She returned to her room, fetched her stockings, which had been hanging in the bathroom to dry, and sat down in an arm-chair by the open French window. It was a warm evening, and the moon was shining. In a moment the sound of a musical instrument emanated from the next room. "So that's the saxophone," she said to herself. She didn't like it. But she was willing to forgive the dark young man more than the weird throbbing which ran up and down and did not seem to her to have any tune.

Randal continued practising the wild passage for about ten minutes. Then suddenly the corridor rang with a deep male bass shouting in despair: "Help! Get a doctor!"

The saxophonist stopped abruptly, like the fall of a guillotine, and Miss Matyasova jumped up from her chair and ran to the door with her heart beating furiously.

Benny Polacek accompanied Mici Laurinova to the door of her room and then went to the second floor to change for the evening performance. His room was in the opposite wing of the hotel which largely catered for foreign guests. He took off his corduroy trousers and polo-necked pullover, and put on a white shirt with a black bow tie, black trousers and a moss-green jacket. This was his working outfit. Then he applied some more hair cream and examined the result in the large mirror on the inside of the wardrobe door. His broad, workman's face was wreathed in a satisfied smile. He took his bass from its canvas cover and left the room with it. He descended to the floor beneath and turned off into the other wing. Along the corridor floated the distant riffs of a tenor sax. Benny's face contorted into a grimace.

He stopped outside door No 118 and knocked. The grimace had given way to an infatuated smile which did not, however, impart to Benny a particularly intelligent mien. There was silence in the room. Benny knocked again. He still got no answer. He grasped the handle and turned it gently. The door opened, showing the light of the chandelier in the gap. Benny straightened his bow tie, flung the door open wide and swaggered in with his bass.

Immediately his jaw dropped and an inarticulate choking sound burst from his lips. An expression of horror spread over his face. He dropped his instrument, went to the doorway and yelled at the top of his powerful voice:

"Help! Get a doctor!"

Lieutenant Boruvka and his team reached the lake-side hotel in the police Volga at twenty minutes to eight. On a bench in front of the hotel two elderly guests were engaged in an argument, obviously unaware of what had happened inside.

"I'm telling you that there've never been any fish here."

"And I'm telling you that a moment ago a carp jumped out of the water over there, all of five kilos!"

"Don't kid me you saw it! You're so shortsighted you can't see an inch in front of your nose."

"I didn't see it, but I heard it! An angler recognises a splash like that a league away!"

Boruvka, who had overheard the conversation from the car, sighed. He got out of the car and walked across the red-carpeted foyer to the staircase.

Mici Laurinova was lying on her stomach on the blue carpet in the middle of the room. She was wearing only a white suspender belt. A dagger with a handle made from a stag's antler was sticking out of her back under her left shoulder blade. The French window leading on to the balcony was open. On the bed lay her short, moss-green evening gown with a daring décolleté, and over the back of a chair hung the flowered silk blouse and white terylene skirt in which Mici had consumed Hungarian goulash half an hour before.

Otherwise the room was tidy. There were no indications that thieves had been there. On a table lay a purse containing 500 crowns. Boruvka turned enquiringly to the doctor, a stout, elderly man who was staying at the hotel to restore his shattered nerves, and was now trembling all over.

"D-death was instantaneous," he quavered. "The d-dagger pierced her heart."

Boruvka looked round at the persons present. He let his gaze rest steadily on Benny Polacek who was sitting, utterly crushed, in the armchair, holding his head in his hands. Then his eyes roved until they alighted on a slight man in a moss-green jacket, who was wiping his sweating bald pate with a purple handkerchief. Boruvka knew him. He was David Golias, familiar to every person of both sexes in the country, except, perhaps, to the congenitally deaf. Lieutenant Boruvka was forty-eight and he had a sixteen-year-old daughter who liked dancing the twist.

"Could I speak to you for a moment," Boruvka paused, then added, "maestro?"

"Certainly, at your service," replied the other, holding out his hand. "Golias. Band leader."

"The rest of you kindly wait outside in the corridor. Let no one leave the hotel," said Boruvka, and when the last of them had gone, he closed the door after them.

"She was a nice girl, a very nice girl, a bit of a minx," the band-leader rambled, mopping his damp crown continually. "She had swing in her bones, you know. And jazz at her finger-tips. We all liked her—"

"Who the most?" the lieutenant interrupted him. Golias reddened all over his forehead which covered more than half of his head. "I mean," added the lieutenant quickly, "was she keeping company with anybody, going steady?"

"Well, you know, in that respect she was, er—" the band-leader was having difficulty in expressing himself "—well, I've heard that she's broken it off with Randal and—"

"What about the man who found her?"

"That's just it." In his agitation the band-leader eased his finger under his collar. "It seems that at this moment she was going out with him. You know, it was difficult to tell with her. She was a very nice girl, but—"

"What do you mean 'at this moment'?"

"I meant—on this tour."

"And how long have you been on this tour?"

The band-leader removed his finger from under his collar, wiped his head and cleared his throat.

"Er—since yesterday evening."

"Yesterday she had a terrific row with Randal," said Benny heavily. "I was waiting for her in front of the house where he was living. It was high time to leave. And then she flew out of the house all red, and he leaned out of the window and bawled—I

29

should say shouted—'I'll settle up with you, you—' and he used a rude word."

"Why did she go to his place?" asked Boruvka considerately.

"To return his presents," replied Benny.

"Presents?"

"She always gave 'em back," said Benny. "So long as they weren't perishable. She was a good kid."

Two huge tears rolled down his massive cheeks.

"And then, you say, you ran for the bus?"

"Yeah."

"And Randal?"

"He pelted up at the last minute. He didn't even have time to knot his tie. The end of his pyjama leg was sticking out of his case, he'd bunged in everything in such a helluva rush," said Benny mournfully.

"Today, when you went with Miss Laurinova to her room, you say you heard the saxophone being played in Randal's room?"

"Yeah."

"When did you first hear it?"

"Er," the bass player wrinkled his brow. "Actually, immediately I went downstairs. Faintly from the distance; but sounds travel in these corridors. It's so quiet everywhere—"

"Did you recognise what he was playing?"

Benny thought hard again.

"Nope, can't say I did. Just jamming, I reckon. I'm not sure. I, you see, er—" Polacek glanced at Boruvka out of the corner of his eye. Then he selected a form of address—like so many before and after him—out of books he had read. "—Inspector, I had my mind on other things. And then the shock—" Fresh tears rolled down his expansive cheeks. "I really can't say."

Boruvka was standing on the balcony of room 116 by the open French window. The balcony stretched along the whole row of rooms on the first floor and was divided by low glass partitions. Miss Matyasova was sitting in an armchair, as white as a sheet. Boruvka looked over the balcony at the lake below. The hotel stood right on the shore, and from the main entrance steps led down to the wharf where boats for hire were moored. A large tranquil moon was mirrored in the lake. It was a balmy late summer night. A light breeze faintly stirred the surface of the water and gently flapped the pale blue curtains at the French window.

Boruvka sighed and turned to Miss Matyasova.

"Do you remember what time he came to your door?"

Miss Matyasova looked at him timidly.

"Yes. It was a few minutes after a quarter past seven. I had just wound my watch up when he knocked."

"When did he start playing the saxophone?"

Miss Matyasova pondered.

"I can't tell you exactly. I went into the bathroom for my stockings and then I sat down here in the armchair, and I had been sitting here for a while when he started."

"Could it have been, let's say, five minutes? Or more? Or less?"

"About five minutes," Miss Matyasova faltered. "Perhaps a bit more."

"Then he played uninterruptedly, didn't he? Until the moment you heard the cry for help?"

"Yes."

"Uninterruptedly? Without a break?"

"Yes. He kept on playing. He always made a short pause and began again. A sort of—a sort of wild trumpeting—up and down—"

"A pause? How long?"

"Oh—five, ten seconds. Maybe a bit longer. But not much."

Lieutenant Boruvka plunged into gloom.

"Would you recognise it, if you were to hear it again?"

Miss Matyasova shook her head.

"I'm sorry, I don't think I would. I haven't got an ear for music, you know, and it didn't have any tune."

"Hm," said the lieutenant in a dissatisfied tone, and became wrapt in thought. Then he thanked Miss Matyasova and left her room.

Malek and Sintak were trying to calm the excited crowd that was still gathered in the corridor in front of room 118. Boruvka sought out the dark-haired young man with the gipsy eyes, who was conversing vehemently with a tall man, holding a trumpet case in his hand.

"Mr Randal, may I trouble you for a moment," he asked.

Randal started and turned to the lieutenant.

"If you don't mind, we'll go to your room. And you too, Mr Golias, if you'd be good enough."

The lieutenant stepped aside and Randal also moved back to make way for the band-leader. The little man bowed to the lieutenant and nervously entered room 117.

The light was on and a golden tenor saxophone lay on the bed. The lieutenant threw a quick glance at Randal. He was wearing his sling. He had on only a white shirt and black bow tie. The green jacket lay on the bed next to the instrument.

"Look, Mr Randal," said the detective, "Miss Laurinova was murdered in the room next to yours. I'd like to know whether you heard any suspicious sounds. A quarrel or blows, footsteps or anything like that."

Randal shook his head.

"No, I didn't hear anything. I was practising here, so I couldn't have heard anything. When you're playing the sax, it fills your head with sound."

"I know," said the lieutenant. "I used to play once, but that's a long time ago. In the army. Only as an amateur, of course."

"Really?" exclaimed Randal.

"An alto," said the lieutenant. "And it rang in my head properly, I can tell you. A tenor must ring even more so. What were you playing, may I ask?"

"I'm writing some clarinet and saxophone études for the State Music Publishing House," replied Randal. "I'm in the middle of a composition and I keep playing it over. You know, so that I can fully exploit all the resources of the instrument."

"Jazz études?"

"Naturally."

"Could you show me a piece?" asked Boruvka. "Just out of interest, you know. After all, I too am a saxophonist."

Randal looked at him uncertainly.

"Sure," he replied coldly. He picked up a black folder with a symbolic drawing of an ancient Greek lyre and handed it to Boruvka. The lieutenant opened it. He scanned the score, full of rhythmic and melodic notations written by an experienced and proficient score writer. The composition bore no title. It was in D flat major with numerous enharmonic changes. The lieutenant read it, trying to imagine playing it on the saxophone. He had not put the instrument to his lips for nearly twenty years, but looking at the passages in semi-quavers and triplets, he saw that he would not have been able to play it even twenty years ago when he had been the first alto saxophonist in the military band.

"It's awfully difficult," he remarked. "Do you really play it?"

The saxophonist's handsome mouth twisted into a slightly scornful smile.

"Of course. If I couldn't play it, I wouldn't write it."

"Are the clarinet études also so difficult? I'm interested, you know. I always used to be a better clarinetist than saxophonist."

"Yes," said Randal. "They are all études for experienced musicians."

Lieutenant Boruvka leafed through the sheets.

"Do you happen to have any with you?"

"No. The clarinet études are in another folder. I didn't bring them with me on this tour."

Boruvka returned to the score.

"You played this, as it is written? In foxtrot tempo?"

"Certainly," replied Randal confidently.

"With five flats? Didn't you transpose it at least into an easier key?"

Randal shook his head.

"It's an étude. It wouldn't make sense to transpose it into an easier key."

Boruvka studied the music again. His face seemed to grow sad. Then he sighed, laid the folder on the table and said:

"That's all for now. You may go on to the stage, Mr Golias. And you too, Mr Randal."

He encountered Sergeant Malek in front of the hotel, near the bench on which the two anglers had been sitting. There was only one now.

"Excuse me," the lieutenant addressed him. "Is it right that someone caught a carp in the lake today?"

"A carp?" the old man curled his lip contemptuously. "You've

33

heard old Svoboda letting his fancy run away with him, haven't you? Saying he heard the splash of a fish this evening. He must have put a few under his belt before that."

"Why couldn't he have heard a fish splash?"

"Because there aren't any fish here. The lake is drained in the winter and the only things that live in it are leeches."

"Aren't eggs put here in the summer?"

"In the summer? You must be crazy!"

Lieutenant Boruvka frowned.

"Thank you," he said and turned back to the hotel.

He borrowed a key to the boats from the janitor, and he and Malek were soon sitting in a boat, rowing on the lake.

The moon and the gold, illuminated hotel windows were reflected in it. The two rowed for a while and then stopped near the shore. Boruvka looked up at the shining façade. He seemed to be counting the windows from left to right, then again from right to left. The riffs of the band sounded from the dance hall.

The lieutenant sighed. He drew a large cylindrical torch from his pocket and submerged it. The water was barely three feet deep—all kinds of objects showed up on the bottom of the lake.

"Row slowly up and down, Pavel," the lieutenant requested his assistant. He lay down on his stomach in the boat and closely examined the bed, slipping away underneath them in the light of the torch. After about half an hour, he found what he was looking for. He took off his jacket, rolled up his shirt sleeve and carefully drew it into the boat.

At eleven o'clock he was already waiting in Randal's room for the tenor saxophonist. He came accompanied by the little band-leader and Sintak. He glanced truculently at Boruvka. Behind him loomed Benny Polacek's huge frame.

Boruvka handed the saxophonist the music folder, asking him sorrowfully:

"Would you be good enough to play that to me. I still can't believe that it could really be played."

The saxophonist put the clarinet he had been carrying on the bed, and with a complacent smile put to his lips the instrument which was hanging round his neck. He glanced at the music. And his courage seemed to evaporate. But he pulled himself together. He passed his fingers up and down the keys several times and then played a note unfalteringly fortissimo. And he continued playing. His fingers flew over the keys.

The lieutenant took the clarinet from the bed and put it to his lips. He removed it again immediately, saying:

"Just a moment, please. Once more from the beginning. Right? I'll count for you."

He tapped his foot rapidly four times, and then simultaneously with the saxophonist played the first note.

An interval of a second could be heard quite distinctly.

They both stopped.

"You're playing a half tone higher," observed the lieutenant gloomily.

"Aha, sorry. I've got this key in my head; I was writing an étude in it this afternoon. I got mixed up."

Lieutenant Boruvka fixed sorrowful eyes upon him.

"So play then!"

Beads of sweat glistened on the saxophonist's forehead. He put the instrument to his lips again. He began. The lieutenant too. This time they were in unison. The lieutenant stopped immediately but followed Randal's performance from the music. Wild syncopated bursts, descending lower and lower—then it stopped, without a proper ending, off key.

The saxophonist sat still; streams of sweat were pouring down his forehead, and his hands holding the saxophone dropped. He glanced at the lieutenant and hung his head.

Boruvka nodded.

"Yes," he said in a terribly sad voice. "You are an excellent player, Mr Randal, but no one has ever played a passage like that on this instrument as long as it has been in existence." He broke off. Benny fidgeted nervously.

"You were in a great hurry yesterday, Mr Randal, so as not to miss the bus. You threw things higgledy-piggledy into your case. One can easily make a mistake. It is particularly easy to confuse folders like this," he pointed to the music folder, "when they look exactly the same and you haven't written a title on them. But there was one thing you did not forget in your haste. This."

The lieutenant bent down and opened the bedside table cupboard. On the lowest shelf was a small battery tape-recorder.

"There's only one tape on it," said Boruvka sorrowfully. "It's a recording of a song by Miss Laurinova. The other tape is here."

He put his hand in his pocket and drew out a spool. The tape hung limply from it; it was wet.

"You know what is on this tape, don't you?"

Randal continued to hang his head.

"This evening you were in a hurry again," the lieutenant went on. "And you made another mistake. You took some music out of your folder without looking at it. Do you know why it was a mistake?"

"Yes," croaked Randal and then, of his own accord, he held out his hands towards the lieutenant.

Sintak, who hadn't followed a thing, clapped the handcuffs on them.

The little band-leader, who was left alone in room 117, had not understood either. Throughout Randal's interrogation he had sweated profusely. Now he drew out his purple handkerchief again, went to the table and looked at the open music. He read it for a moment and suddenly his high forehead beaded with drops of sweat like dew, and the little band-leader mopped them with his purple handkerchief.

For he had read in the fifth line on the paper the following three bars:

III

The Scientific Method

No sooner had they dashed from the stage to the dressing-room in their very negligible costumes than the phone rang. Alena answered it because she was sitting nearest to the phone. A man with a foreign accent asked for Miss Nakoncova. Alena knew the voice well. She put the receiver down on the small table next to the telephone and looked down the dressing-room, full of girls occupied with their diminutive costumes, to the mirror at the far end.

"Ester!" she called. "It's for you."

A pretty petite blonde rose from the small table at the far end of the dressing-room and walked down the room to the phone. Her hand hovered over it.

"Who is it?"

"Him, of course!"

The fair-haired girl, who was about to pick up the receiver, withdrew her hand and said in a muffled voice:

"Tell him I don't want to talk to him."

Alena grimaced and shrugged her shoulders. Then she took up the receiver and said carelessly into the mouthpiece:

"I'm to tell you that she doesn't want to talk to you."

Something fizzled violently in the receiver, like a short circuit. Alena pulled a face at Ester and listened. For a long time. Then she interpreted the content of the fizzling.

"He says that his heart is breaking. If you don't come to the phone, it will go on and on breaking until it cracks in two."

The dancers at the nearest tables, who were listening in, giggled.

"So tell him to go and see a doctor," said Ester icily.

37

"She says you're to go and see a doctor," Alena repeated into the phone.

An electric discharge sounded in the receiver again.

"He says there is no remedy for his illness," said Alena.

The girls chuckled again.

"All right, I'll take it." Assuming a demonstrably bored expression for the benefit of the dressing-room, Ester took the receiver. Alena sat down at her mirror and pricked up her ears. She heard Ester say coldly into the mouthpiece:

"Hullo." And then nothing for a long time, only the unusually loud crackling in the receiver, into which the unknown man—known, however, to her—at the other end of the line was flinging a firework cascade of eloquence. Then Ester muttered impatiently: "Hm, hm," twice and finally burst out resolutely: "No. Don't wait. I don't want you to. I just don't want you to. After the way you behaved yesterday evening, I don't want you to." And again a pause, filled with minor explosions, and finally in a tone which brooked no demur, she stated: "Your idiotic jealousy is getting on my nerves. If you don't believe me, goodbye. Adieu!" Then the receiver clattered as it was replaced vigorously.

In the mirror Alena saw Ester walk haughtily to her dressing table with a graceful swaying of her hips.

The showers resounded with their squeals and chatter to a background of gurgling water and music relayed through amplifiers by the janitor for the refreshment of the girls' minds. The showers were arranged in a row, separated by partitions hung with plastic curtains, behind which were silhouetted naked female figures. The girls chatted to each other through the partitions, shouting to drown the modern mixture of music and mechanical noises, washed their hair and lent each other bars of soap. Slim, firm bodies gleamed enchantingly in the white light, and currents of water carried off the grease-paint and sweat of the dress rehearsal they had just finished.

The lively exchange of soap and other toilet sundries continued amid the babble of voices.

"Girls, which of you has pinched my towel?" shouted a brunette who was standing in front of the end cubicle still clad in her bathrobe. "Alena, was it you?" she asked the natural blonde who was about to refresh her body in the adjacent cubicle.

"What the heck would I be doing with your towel? I've got my own. And it's clean."

"Somebody's nabbed my shampoo, the rotter," sang out a soprano from the cubicle next to Alena's.

"Could I have left it in the dressing-room?" the brunette asked herself aloud.

"Of course, lovelorn!" said Alena.

The brunette flashed her an angry glance and turned to the shower door. Alena saw her pass into the corridor and shut the door behind her. Then the soprano next door called out again:

"Who's borrowed my shampoo, damn it!"

"Shut up, Ester. Here's mine," said Alena and passed a tube of shampoo round the partition to her neighbour.

In the next cubicle Ester Nakoncova, shining like a slim, white seal in her birthday suit, put her head under the shower. She had a lovely long neck. When she bent her head to shampoo her hair, her neck arched in a graceful curve.

Alena drew the curtain, threw off her bathrobe and stood under the stream of lukewarm water.

And then it happened. Actually nothing was heard. The faint crackle was almost drowned in the hissing of the water and the prattle of voices. Alena paid no heed to it, nor to the dull thud which seemed to come from the next cubicle as though something heavy had fallen against the partition.

She noticed something else: the partitions between the cubicles did not reach to the ground—Ester's bare hand appeared under the thin wall which divided her from her neighbour, as though she was groping for something on the floor; then it remained lying still. Alarmed, Alena bent down. It crossed her mind that Ester might have fainted. She took hold of the motionless hand, and the hand hung lifelessly in her own.

Then in the white-tiled groove along which the shower water flowed, a dark red rivulet appeared, as though someone had poured raspberryade into it.

Alena guessed what it was. She dropped Ester's hand and

involuntarily let forth a piercing scream that drowned the melée of voices in the showers.

Someone knocked, and the library door was opened by a young policewoman in an unbecoming sateen overall, with her hair drawn back into a tight, severe knot. She was holding a file under her arm.

"Comrade Bubble?" she asked Boruvka sweetly.

The lieutenant hurriedly pushed his daily crossword puzzle under a thick volume on criminology. He scowled.

"No, Boruvka," he said gloomily.

"Excuse me, comrade lieutenant, but are you in charge of the Vranova case?"

"Yes, I am," said Boruvka even more gloomily.

"Well, they told me that comrade Lieutenant Bubble who is in charge of the Vranova case was working in the library."

"They said 'comrade lieutenant'?"

The policewoman, who had started work that day and whom the lieutenant had not seen before, blushed. Boruvka noticed the attractive curve of her long neck, but that lowered his spirits even further.

"They said 'Bubble', did they?" he sighed.

"Yes," whispered the policewoman.

"Our comrades think they're so funny," observed the lieutenant sadly. "I may look like a bubble but my name is Boruvka."

The girl in the sateen overall gave him a fleeting glance.

"Oh no, you don't!" she said quickly.

Lieutenant Boruvka fixed his mournful eyes upon her.

"I don't know," he said. "You want to work in the criminal investigation bureau? I don't know, I really don't know—with such a poor faculty for observation."

The telephone rang. Boruvka picked up the receiver and listened for a moment. Then he spoke vigorously.

"The Odeon Theatre. All right."

He hung up and without paying any further attention to the scarlet-faced girl, ran out of the room with amazing swiftness, considering his bulk.

The flustered janitor, who was standing in front of the locked door to the showers, stuttered agitatedly:

"I locked them in there comrade—comrade commissar, so that none of them could escape and also so that nothing could be taken out of there, because if—"

"Who came to tell you about the murder?" Boruvka interrupted him.

"Miss Sikorska."

"And where is Miss Sikorska?"

"I locked 'er in there too." The janitor writhed in confusion. "So that—"

"So that, in the meantime, they'd have time to destroy all possible traces while they are running about here and there," said Boruvka, listening to the excited twittering behind the door. "You can unlock it now."

The crestfallen janitor obeyed and Boruvka's team entered the showers.

The room was full of girls in bathrobes, while some had only towels wrapped round them. They began to protest loudly. Boruvka turned a deaf ear to them and strode briskly into the cubicle in which he had glimpsed the murdered girl. She was lying on her stomach and had an ugly wound in the back of her neck. The wound had strangely sharp edges; there was hardly a trace of blood. The water from the shower had washed away the initial flow of blood and the hole was clearly visible.

"Who discovered the body, please?" asked Boruvka politely, glancing obliquely at the row of towel-clad girls. His Adam's apple shot up and down with unwonted energy. A wide-eyed blonde, deathly pale, stepped out of the line.

"I did," she said in a small, faint voice.

"What's your name?"

"Alena Peskova."

Boruvka sighed and said:

"Come with me, please."

"You heard the conversation quite clearly?"

The lieutenant raised questioning eyebrows at Alena.

"I only heard what Ester said," she replied. " 'Your idiotic jealousy is getting on my nerves,' she said. And 'if you don't believe me, goodbye. Adieu!' "

"Adieu," repeated Boruvka thoughtfully.

41

"That's French for goodbye," piped the girl.

Boruvka only frowned. Then he said:

"And before that she said that the person in question should not wait for her, didn't she?"

"Yes."

"Do you know who was calling her?"

Alena lowered her lashes.

"Well—" she said uncertainly.

"Tell me everything," sighed the lieutenant. "Even what might be called gossip."

"Yes." Alena swallowed hard. "It was Alberto Tossi. The Italian pop singer who is at the Vltava restaurant now. Ester was going out with him."

"Hm," said Boruvka. "Do you know whom he was jealous of?"

Alena looked down again. Boruvka waited a moment and then said:

"Even gossip, young lady. That's not camul—cal—that's not slander. Your friend has been murdered."

Alena raised her head and looked at Boruvka with her large black eyes. Boruvka fiddled with his tie awkwardly.

"Well, you know, I don't spread this gossip myself," said the girl. "But it is a public secret. Ester was seen around a lot with the comrade—" she paused for a moment "—the theatre manager."

"Hm," said Boruvka. "I understand. And anyone else?"

"No one else," said Alena more decisively. "Ester wasn't the kind to—er—carry on with men. She was really fond of Tossi; but the manager—well—"

"I understand," the detective repeated quickly. "And was Miss Nakoncova's—how shall I put it—technique good?"

Alena stiffened imperceptibly. "How do you mean?"

"I mean—ahem—as a ballet dancer." He cleared his throat in embarrassment. "As a qualified dancer-artist, I mean. She was supposed to have danced the main solo in this revue, wasn't she?"

"Yes—she was," said Alena flatly.

"She must have been good then, mustn't she?"

Alena's black eyes wandered to the corner of the dressing-room in which he was sitting with the lieutenant. The row of mirrors multiplied the picture of the two: the diffident man in a jacket of somewhat old-fashioned cut and the dainty, fair-haired girl in the bathrobe.

"Actually Ester was a good dancer. Yes, she was," the girl stated not very assuredly.

Boruvka, not taking his eyes off her, asked quietly:

"But?"

"The fact is—" Alena looked at him almost desperately "—well, Zdarska was originally to have danced the solo."

"Why?"

"Because—but this may really be only gossip."

Lieutenant Boruvka grew unusually sad. His round face lengthened and took on a resemblance to a melancholy St Bernard. He asked:

"Was it because Miss Zdarska was the manager's girl friend before Ester?"

The girl nodded. "Yes," she said, adding quickly: "But before that it was supposed to have been Sikorska and before her I don't remember who. So it's most likely only gossip."

"That's for us to verify." Boruvka cleared his throat and changed the subject. "And now describe everything that took place after you discovered what had happened."

"I was terribly shocked."

"Naturally," said Boruvka.

"Naturally," the girl repeated parrot fashion. "And I began to scream. Then the girls all gathered round me and Jana came in from the dressing-room; she was still dry so we sent her for Mr Zahalka—the janitor—"

"Jana?"

"Sikorska. She had left her towel in the dressing-room and had gone to fetch it, and in the meantime—" The girl's voice shook.

"—it happened," Boruvka completed the sentence for her. "Otherwise no one left the showers?"

"No. Mr Zahalka rushed up and locked us all in."

Boruvka gazed at the girl for a long time. She was still pale from shock and was trembling a little. A nostalgic expression crept into the detective's eyes. He sighed:

"Thank you, Miss Peskova," he said, standing up.

Another girl came in. The row of mirrors multiplied the diffident

man and a tall redhead who was obviously waging a losing battle
with the wrinkles which were spreading slowly in a fine network
at the corners of her green eyes.

"Oh the manager," she said in a careless, sing-song voice.
"Mm, he invited me to supper a couple of times. Once to
Hubertus," she reminisced dreamily. "But that's ages ago."

"Weren't you supposed to have danced the main solo?"

The titian-haired girl came out of her dream with a jerk.

"Yeah. It was like this, inspector." She smiled at Boruvka who
involuntarily reached for the knot in his tie. Ascertaining that it
was at half-mast, he adjusted it sheepishly. The redhead's smile
deepened almost imperceptibly.

"Like what?" he asked in an unnatural falsetto.

"The old story. Jana Sikorska went off her nut and dropped
him—"

"Who?" Boruvka's voice again shot up an octave. He cleared
his throat.

"The manager, of course. So he began to make a fuss about me.
You know how it is—I don't have to tell you—" She threw the
lieutenant an emerald glance and his round face flushed a deep
crimson. "One day you're up, the next day you're down," the
girl continued and pulled her chair a little closer to Boruvka's.
"And then Ester came along, and that was that—she got the solo."

"Thank you very much, Miss Zdarska," said Boruvka and
against his will widened the distance between them.

Sergeant Malek picked up a white handkerchief in which lay a
small copper cartridge.

"A seven sixty-five," he said. "It was lying on the floor in front
of the cubicles. The murderer must have been standing directly
opposite the shower where the girl was washing herself."

"Yes," said the elderly Dr Seifert. "From the direction of the
shot we can assume that the girl was standing with her back to
the murderer and the murderer fired horizontally straight into the
nape of her neck. The shot passed through the lower part of her
skull and out through her mouth."

"The weapon hasn't been found yet?"

"No. Comrade Jebava—" the sergeant nodded in the direction
of a stout woman in a dark costume, across whose face flitted the

expression of a hole-in-the-corner abortionist caught *in flagranti* "—conducted a body search of all the ladies before they left the showers. We've combed the dressing-room too. But—" he leaned towards Boruvka "—there's a choice bit of news—do you know, Josef, that they have a miraculous marksman in this theatre?"

Boruvka raised his eyebrows slightly.

"The janitor told me," Malek added.

"Hm," the detective swept the dressing-room with his sad eyes. The disorder left after the search was greater than usual. "Fetch the janitor and tell the com—the ladies that they may get dressed."

"Yes, we 'ave. Mr Krames. 'e sings too, you know." The janitor was only too ready to talk. He assumed a professionally grieved expression. "Imagine, 'e used to shoot at no other than Miss Nakoncova!"

Boruvka's mouth dropped open in surprise.

"Why?"

"It was in 'er contract," said the janitor quickly. "But, mind you, 'e never 'it 'er!"

"Until now," observed Malek sarcastically.

Boruvka threw him an admonitory look. Then he turned to the janitor again.

"Ask Mr Krames to step this way."

A smartly-dressed cowboy appeared in the dressing-room. He was wearing a black sombrero which he removed with a flourish at the door.

"Do you know what *genickschuss* means?" Boruvka addressed him.

The cowboy smiled awkwardly.

"I don't know English, lieutenant. I play the cowboy here and sing Westerns but otherwise I'm from Zizkov. My English is only what I've picked up from Radio Lux."

"*Genickschuss* is a German word," the lieutenant explained to him. "It means a shot through the skull from the nape of the neck."

"Oh. Well, thanks for the information," said the cowboy uncertainly.

45

Boruvka waited, but the cowboy showed no signs of wishing to add anything.

"You're a good shot, aren't you?" the lieutenant asked him.

"Sure. I am that. I was Czechoslovak champion three years ago. I was supposed to have gone to the Olympics. Except—" he stopped short.

"Except what?"

"Oh, nothing. Before that we were in Switzerland. At the European Championships. Well, you know how it is."

"No, I'm afraid I don't," said Boruvka.

"Well—Switzerland is a land of watches," said the cowboy. "I couldn't resist them and so I brought a few back with me. They thought it was too many. So I didn't take part in the Games."

Boruvka frowned. The cowboy avoided his eyes.

"What did you do after that?"

"I was forced to go over to the pros."

"You mean this?"

"Well—this too. I'm also an instructor at the Tesla factory gun club in Vysocany."

"Hm," said the detective, and drew out the handkerchief. He unfolded it and showed the cowboy the cartridge. "What do you say to this?"

"That's from—that's from my colt."

"I also am of that opinion," said Boruvka slowly. Suddenly and unexpectedly he snapped at the cowboy: "What were you doing from the end of the dress rehearsal to the moment the murder was discovered?"

"Lieutenant! I didn't kill her!"

The marksman's eyes bulged and he grabbed the lapels of his jacket. "I was terribly fond of Ester. She came from Zizkov like me! It was me that taught her to shoot!"

"Where? At the Tesla gun club?"

The cowboy looked confused.

"No—here in the theatre," he replied contritely. "Me and the girls formed a sort of—"

"Well?"

"A sort of private gun club—we used the props room—" He looked the lieutenant squarely in the eyes.

"But only with blanks, lieutenant! I always use blanks on

46

stage too. Live ammunition is forbidden in the theatre anyhow."

"I'm aware of that," snapped Boruvka. "But you're not going to tell me that your pistol can't fire live ammunition."

"Sure it can, but on principle I use only blanks on stage."

"Blanks? And what exactly does your turn consist of?"

"Well, it's like this—I sort of shoot at the strings of balloons which hang—er—hung just above Ester's head—"

"How can you pierce the string with blanks?"

The cowboy smiled confidentially.

"Fact is—the whole show's a trick, sir. I can tell you, in a way I have to. You see, the scene-shifter sits back-stage and cuts the strings when I fire—"

"Aha," said Boruvka. "All right, you can go into the next room for the time being."

Malek took the cowboy by the hand and swivelled him round to face the door.

"Have Mr Krames' pistol brought here," Boruvka called after him. "In the meantime, send Miss Peskova in again."

"She was unusually nervous, you say?"

"Yes, she was," Alena nodded. "The boss—the director kept on at her to smile during the shooting stunt, and she just couldn't manage it. So the boss—the director got real mad."

"Why couldn't she manage to smile?"

"Because she was afraid Krames might have loaded the pistol with live bullets by mistake."

"Had that ever happened?"

"No, it hadn't. But this morning he'd said he was going to practise this afternoon and that he'd got some live bullets with him."

"Did he say where?"

Alena nodded.

"Yes. In the spare ammunition box he carries in the pistol case."

The unfortunate cowboy was again sitting in front of Boruvka. The lieutenant took the black case from Malek and opened it. He looked inside and his round face grew sad. He was silent for a moment. Then he said:

"Have you got blanks in the spare ammunition box as well?"

"Er—" The cowboy swallowed. "Er—I was to have gone for a practice at the club after the dress rehearsal, lieutenant, so—"

"So you've got live rounds in it."

"I—er, well—only because—"

"But that's against the law. Live cartridges are supposed to be kept under lock and key."

"And so they are, lieutenant! They're always locked up here!"

"So how come you've got some in your box?"

"Well I—I mean—as an instructor, I've got a key to the lock—"

Krames scratched behind his ear and looked away.

Boruvka cast a mournful glance over the contents of the case. "Hm," he said. "Did you have only the one spare ammunition box with you?"

"Yes, only the one, lieutenant, really! Only the one!"

"That was supposed to last you for the whole practice?"

"Well no—actually—"

The lieutenant nodded sadly.

"A lady-killer, eh? You feel more of a man in the eyes of the ladies when you've got the real stuff on you?"

The cowboy's face turned as red as a beetroot. He croaked:

"Yeah. That's it, lieutenant. Everyone's got his weak spot and I—"

"How many cartridges were there in the box?" Boruvka cut in.

"Six. Ain't they—oh no, don't say they ain't all there?"

The cowboy gazed aghast at the case. But Boruvka was holding it with the open lid towards the marksman so that he could not see inside.

"I don't know," said Boruvka and turned the case towards the cowboy. "But where is the box?" He paused and at the sight of the cowboy's frantic expression, he frowned. "And where is the pistol?"

The velvet cushioned case contained neither weapon nor box. There were only two gaping hollows, the shape of which indicated precisely what had lain there. The cowboy whistled in surprise.

"Wow!" he cried. "I'm in it up to me neck, ain't I, lieutenant?"

"So the case was lying in the basket with the other properties which you had carried off stage?"

The thin props man was standing opposite the crack dectective, blinking nervously.

"Yes, that's wha's usually done, sir—er, prefect." Boruvka, who was accustomed to uninitiated civilians addressing him by a variety of titles, was taken aback by this one. The props man did not notice and continued: "One basket is used to carry fresh props on stage and another to carry 'em off. But before the last scene there is a very short interval. It's a terrific scramble. We couldn't make it. And on top of everything, that Italian bloke was getting under our feet."

"Italian? Mr Tossi?"

"Tossi. Yes, him. He nearly bowled me over. Then the director chucked him out."

Boruvka looked at the fateful basket.

"But you took the pistol case to Krames' dressing-room directly after the dress rehearsal."

"Yes."

"Until then it had been lying in the basket back-stage where anyone could have had access to it?"

"Y—yes."

The lieutenant brooded silently. The props man kept his eyes fixed on Boruvka's face and finally summoned up courage.

"A—am I going to be arrested, prefect?"

"Why?"

"It was negligent of me, I know," said the props man dejectedly. "But as mitigating circumstances I would submit that I have a wife and three children and two more by my first marriage and that the interval is terribly short."

The first suspect dropped out of the game when the Five Lascados, trampoline acrobats, bore witness that from the moment he finished his act until the moment they learned of the murder, he had been playing *marias** with them in the dressing-room. He received this news with grateful relief and unleashed an enthusiastic flood of crocodile tears over the dead dancer, until Boruvka informed him that he would be charged with unlawful possession of live ammunition, which actually made him an involuntary accessory after the fact. The cowboy then focused his emotions on the

* A Czech form of poker.

probable nature of his own immediate future. Boruvka was not entirely satisfied with Krames' alibi. The Five Lascados were taciturn men of indefinite nationality and evasive looks, who made it obvious at first sight that, in conformity with a time-honoured principle, they invariably did the exact opposite of what the police required of them. Boruvka, immersed in cheerless thoughts, made his way to the props room accompanied by the janitor.

On the wall facing them hung a target with traces of many hits. A path led up to it, forged through the bizarre mixture of junk left over from previous programmes and stored for eventual further use. Small copper cartridges were lying about under the target. The lieutenant picked one up and examined it morosely. The janitor, who had remained silent till then, could no longer contain himself. He gave vent to a burst of confidence.

"This place is full of those blessed empties, commissar. As soon as the girls 'ad a free moment, they were in 'ere like wasps round a jam-pot. They were all mad on shooting."

"So they all knew how to handle a pistol?"

"Of course they did. Krames taught them all. Sometimes they 'eld shooting contests 'ere."

"Were the young ladies good shots?"

"Some of them weren't 'arf bad. Miss Peskova was supposed to be the best. Then Dvorakova, Sikorska—and poor Miss Ester. The girls tried to outdo each other in front of that young swank-pot, you know. But I never liked 'im, commissar. There's a queer look on 'is face, like you couldn't trust 'im. I wouldn't mind betting it was 'im that did Miss Ester in."

"Thanks for your verdict," said Boruvka curtly. Then he added in an almost angry tone. "But keep it to yourself. It's a lot of rot."

He strode briskly out of the room, accompanied by the janitor's wondering voice:

"Could I 'ave bin mistaken?"

The lieutenant was ensconced on the *fin de siècle* L-shaped plush sofa in a recess beyond a bend in the corridor which led to the showers, and a brunette in a costume of foreign make was sitting on the other side, fidgeting nervously.

"When you left the shower room, Miss Sikorska, did you see anyone in the corridor?" he asked.

The brunette blinked.

"Yes."

"Who?"

"Mr Tossi."

"What was he doing?"

"Nothing. He was standing here at the corner and he greeted me."

"You know him?"

"Yes."

"Where do you know him from?"

"He was always hanging about at the theatre waiting for Ester," said Sikorska. In the artificial lighting the foreign-made two-piece glistened like a revue costume. Boruvka's eyes wandered from the low neckline to the inviting silvery lap. He took hold of himself.

"When you returned to the showers with your towel, was Mr Tossi still standing there?"

"No, he was no longer standing here at the corner. . . . he was walking along the corridor—"

"In the direction—" Boruvka prompted her. She looked him in the eyes.

"The direction like—like away from the showers."

A mournful shadow crossed the lieutenant's face.

"I see," he said. "Thank you, Miss Sikorska. Kindly remain in the dressing-room for the time being."

"When you and Miss Sikorska ran to the showers, you must have both seen Mr Tossi?"

"Yep, we saw 'im." The janitor nodded. "'e was sitting where you are, on this settee, in this 'ere niche and 'e stood up when we ran past. When I'd locked the girls in there, 'e asked me what was up—"

"What did you tell him?"

"That someone inside 'ad shot Miss Ester." The janitor bit his lip guiltily. "Strewth, I didn't oughta done that, eh?"

"How did Mr Tossi behave?"

"'ow did 'e behave?" Under the pretext of pondering, the janitor stole a glance at Boruvka, and having ascertained that he wasn't going to be reproved for his lack of discretion, he began eagerly: "'e—strewth—I didn't notice, upon me word."

"And then you went to phone for us?"

"That's right."

"Where was Mr Tossi when you returned?"

Something seemed to click in the janitor's mind. His mouth dropped open. "*Hergot!*" he cried. "What d'you know! 'e wasn't there! 'ed 'opped it!"

"I'd just like to clear up a small point, comrade Mara," said Boruvka to the theatre manager. "You claimed you went upstairs to the club after the dress rehearsal. But we have ascertained that at the time the murder was committed you weren't there."

The man sitting on one side of the L-shaped sofa ran his finger nervously inside his collar.

"It's a bit awkward, but—I was in the toilet. That's probably not exactly a watertight alibi."

"If you were there alone, it's no alibi at all," remarked Boruvka gloomily.

"Unfortunately, I was there alone," Mara looked at the lieutenant uncertainly and quickly shifted his gaze. As the detective made no comment, Mara pulled out a handkerchief and blew his nose. "It's terrible," he said. "Such a talented dancer. Who could have done it to her? Everyone must have liked her—"

"You too?"

"Me? Yes, of course. She was a very sweet comrade."

"You called her comrade?"

"Er—no, of course not. I called her Ester."

"Wasn't she your—ahem—" Boruvka cleared his throat, "—your mistress?" and there was a trace of envy in his voice.

"My mistress? I beg your pardon! Who told you that?"

"They're all saying it in the theatre. That's supposed to be why she got that big solo."

"That's slander!" Mara burst out and stopped short. "She didn't get the big solo because she was my—that's ridiculous. I have a wife and children. She got the solo after consultation with the choreographer. I—I—invited her to supper a couple of times. That's probably what caused the tongues to wag. She was a friend of mine."

Boruvka inclined his head and looked at the manager from under his eyebrows.

"Miss Zdarska was also a friend of yours?"

"Zdarska! That—It's all malicious gossip!"

"And what about Miss Sikorska?"

"You believe all this, comrade lieutenant?" Mara laid his hand with its elegant ring on his well-tailored waist-coat in the region of his heart. "It's always said of a theatre manager that he has mistresses in his company. For instance, I put in a good word for Sikorska so that she'd get a part in a film. But no sooner does the manager help someone than people immediately interpret it in the worst sense."

"It would be only human," said the detective darkly. "Among so many beautiful—" he stopped and looked round desperately. "I could do with a cup of black coffee."

Mara responded readily.

"May I offer you some upstairs in my office?"

Boruvka got to his feet.

"Thank you. We'll arrange a little confrontation over coffee. Pavel," he turned to Malek, "ask Miss Peskova, Miss Zdarska and Miss Sikorska and also Mr—that wizard shot, the props man and the janitor to come with us. And also the director. The others may go home."

"*Hergot!*" the janitor swore. "Someone's gone and left the bloomin' lift stuck on the seventh floor!"

The group were standing in front of the lift shaft, the opening of which was covered by an ornate *fin de siècle* lattice, dominated by an ugly cast-iron statue of Eros. The lift was situated in the middle of the corridor next to the staircase.

"If you wouldn't mind walking up, comrade," said Mara.

"Where is your office?"

"On the sixth floor."

"Hm. Wouldn't there be any coffee lower down?"

"Comrade Mara," the janitor piped up, "I could fetch the key from the service lift. We could use that."

"That's true," said Mara. "Pop off and get it."

The janitor ran upstairs and disappeared.

"Haven't you located Mr Tossi yet?" Boruvka turned to Sintak.

Sintak clicked his heels.

"Not yet," he answered briskly. "No one has seen him leave the building though."

"But there's a passage upstairs," Malek interrupted him, "and the building is connected with the adjacent ones on nearly all floors. It's no problem to make a getaway from here."

"Hm," murmured Boruvka. He gazed at the bend in the corridor round which a small group of titivated dancers were coming into view. All dressed up, they were just leaving the dressing-room, as Boruvka had permitted. They were reluctant to leave the theatre. When they saw Boruvka, they stopped, a little out of countenance.

The janitor dashed downstairs holding a key in his hand.

"'ere I am, we can go. The service lift is at the back round the corner on the other side, comrade commissar. Behind the gents' dressing-room."

The lieutenant strode forward and the whole group moved after him. The janitor hopped along beside him with alacrity.

"That lift's locked, you see," he explained. "So that if—" At that moment the lights went out and the basement corridor was plunged into pitch blackness. The girls shrieked. The atmosphere of murder was still too vivid and the sudden darkness had scared them.

"Zahalka!" Mara cried in an angry baritone. "What the hell—heck is going on?"

"A fuse, I should think, sir. I'll fix it." The janitor spoke out of the darkness.

The clamour of female voices had died down so that Mara's sudden yell of pain, followed by a girl's terrified scream, were all the more clearly heard. Confusion reigned once more.

The darkness was penetrated by a beam of light. Sintak had taken his torch out of his brief-case. As he quickly flashed the torch over the corridor, frightened faces appeared one after the other, each for a second like a procession of spirits. The beam stopped at the figure of Mara. He was sitting on the floor, and blood was spurting out of a wound in his temple. Next to him Alena Peskova was getting up from the floor and a little way off, by the lift lattice near the foot of the stairs, Jana Sikorska was struggling to her feet.

54

"Some wretch turned off the main switch. It's here, round the corner—"

Boruvka's gaze rested on the two girls, who were brushing themselves down and straightening their skirts.

"Someone bumped into me!" cried Alena.

"Me too. I fell against the lattice," said Jana rubbing her elbow.

"Didn't you hear footsteps?" asked Alena. "As though someone was running upstairs."

Malek and Sintak mounted the stairs quickly. They disappeared from view and the tramp of their feet resounded in the now quiet corridor. Then they died away. Voices were raised, somebody was protesting. Then again the echo of footsteps and protests. Malek's head appeared above the ornate lattice.

"We've got Tossi, Josef!"

Then another, dark head came into sight, as though cut out of an Italian film.

It looked down at Boruvka with a wry expression, and said: *"Buona sera!"*

Boruvka looked gloomily at the elegant, olive-skinned young man with sparkling eyes. The handsome Italian was sitting on the edge of the plush sofa and gesticulating with his hands.

"I didn't turn ze lights off! As I was going downstairs it went dark. Of its own accord. Quite wizout me!"

The lieutenant nodded.

"Why did you run away from here when you heard what had happened in the shower?"

"I got ze feeling in me of—horror—fear or what you zay. I zought zat I vould be suspiceeous."

"Why did you come back then?"

"Because I zought zat if I go I shall be even more suspiceeouser. She was my beloved!"

A crystal clear drop of sweat ran down Tossi's tanned forehead.

"How did things stand between you exactly?" asked Boruvka.

"I loved Ester." Tossi indicated himself and then pointed his finger in a vague direction. "Ester loved me. Our love was beyond the grave. And I shall be unhappy to my grave."

"But," said Boruvka, "we have ascertained that Miss Nakoncova broke it off with you."

"Viz me? Broke it off? Nevair! Ve vair two pizhons, pidzins, no, doves!"

"Really?"

Tossi raised his hand to swear an oath.

"I did not mortify her, tenente!"

"No, you didn't do that," said Boruvka slowly and stepped towards the dressing-room door. "Miss Peskova, could you come here for a moment?"

Alena entered, wearing a somewhat crumpled plastic raincoat. She looked at Tossi with respect.

"Would you kindly repeat what you heard Miss Ester tell Mr Tossi over the phone."

" 'Your idiotic jealousy is getting on my nerves,' " the girl recited as though she had learnt it by heart. " 'And if you don't believe me, goodbye. Adieu!' "

The spark-emitting Italian leapt up as though he had been ejected from the sofa by a catapult.

"Miss Peskova! Zat is lying! Such enormous lying, Miss Peskova!"

"The others heard it too. They can bear me out."

They did so.

"But it isn't true, Miss Zdarska! You misheard!" Tossi tried to stick to his guns, and when Sikorska reiterated that they had all heard it in the dressing-room, he exploded: "Jana! How can you zay such a perfidy. It was only such an angry love. As you zay, she who is not loved—no! If she is not enraged, she is not in love!"

"Look here." Boruvka laid his hand on Tossi's shoulder and the latter stiffened instantly. But only for a moment. "You claim that you were sitting here on the couch all the time while you were waiting for Miss Ester. And that no one except Miss Sikorska went into or came out of the showers."

"Not a single soul," declared the Italian firmly.

The lieutenant turned to the brunette with the glistening costume, saying:

"Kindly repeat what you saw when you left the showers and before you entered the cloakroom—and afterwards, when you returned from the showers again."

"If you vould speak more slowly, I don't understand," begged Tossi.

"I'm addressing Miss Sikorska," stated Boruvka coldly.

Sikorska looked Tossi up and down with a spiteful glint in her eyes and said calmly:

"When I stepped into the corridor from the showers, Mr Tossi was standing over there in the corner and he greeted me."

Tossi nodded in confirmation.

"But you said you were sitting here," put in the detective.

"Like glued," declared Tossi categorically. Then realisation dawned and he threw up his hands. "I mean, no I vasn't! I vasn't sitting always! I vas agitated. I valked along ze corridor, up and down, down and up!"

"So, were you sitting or walking?" the lieutenant snapped at him.

"A moment I sat, a moment I valked," cried Tossi desperately. "Vhen I sat, I sat glued, vhen I valked, I valked like crazed."

"When you greeted Miss Sikorska, were you walking or sitting?"

"No! I zen valked from the doorr up to the corner and back from the corner to the doorr."

The lieutenant signed to the brunette in the imported costume.

"When you returned from the showers, where was Mr Tossi?"

"Mr Tossi was walking quickly along the corridor away from the showers," answered the girl promptly.

"Not quickly!" Tossi objected violently. "Not quickly, Jana! Slowly! Dragging one foot, dragging ze ozzer foot!"

Sikorska shrugged her shoulders.

"It seemed quick to me."

"But I alvays valk qvickly! Vhen I valk slowly it's like vhen ozzers valk qvickly!"

"Well," said Boruvka in a funereal voice. "We won't lomog— logum—dispute about the relative velocities of movement. The fact is that you were going from the showers towards this part of the corridor."

"Zat is a fact," affirmed Tossi. "It is not a fact zat I vas valking qvickly! It is a fact zat I vas valking slowly. As slow as a," he gesticulated, "zat teeny weeny animal—snile!"

"Snail," Boruvka corrected him. "So come along with us!"

"Mara is all right." Dr. Seifert wiped his hands on a

bloodstained towel. "It's only a superficial wound. Not a fractured skull as I had feared."

"And the weapon?" Boruvka screwed up his eyes.

"An object with sharp edges."

"Could it have been the butt of a pistol?"

"Yes, it could. Any kind of metal object."

"Hm," sighed the detective. "But Tossi hasn't got a pistol on him and no bloodstained object has been found on anyone else."

At seven in the evening it was still a complete mystery. Boruvka was sitting in his study with Malek. They were silent, waiting for the routine result of the autopsy and the equally dull ballistic report. From time to time one or other of them thought aloud.

"Everything points to Tossi," Malek mused, running his pencil over the plan of the theatre basement, which he had drawn. "The shot must have been fired by someone who got into the shower from outside through the door and fled after the deed. No one in the showers had a weapon. They couldn't have thrown it out either, because there are no windows. And Tossi says that no one besides Sikorska left or entered the room. That of course is a bit puzzling because that makes Tossi the only one who could have got in unnoticed. In that case, why did he admit that at the critical moment he was pacing up and down the corridor? Of course, on the other hand, he couldn't very well deny it because Sikorska saw him."

"He could have. It was his word against hers," Boruvka remarked. "But he ran away and then came back. You think, perhaps, so that he might—let us say out of jealousy—bump off Mara in front of about ten witnesses?"

Malek said nothing, but his imagination continued to work, for a moment later he burst out:

"Perhaps it wasn't jealousy. Or not only jealousy. Maybe Mara knows more than he says and Tossi knew that he knows."

"For heaven's sake, Pavel," said Boruvka wearily. "Don't end up by making a spy case out of this. You know how that annoys me!"

"Oh no," said Malek quickly. "But a jealous man does not think logically and is capable of anything. I don't mean espionage," he hastened to add, "but a reckless act."

The phone rang. Boruvka picked up the receiver and immediately began writhing as though under torture. "Yes, Lucinka," he cooed in an incongruously honeyed tone, and his habitually sad face assumed an expression verging on absolute despair. A voice prattled piercingly in the receiver. Malek grinned. Like all of the lieutenant's colleagues, he knew Mrs Boruvkova's voice very well.

"I'm on a case, Lucinka, you see," cooed the lieutenant, and continued for about five minutes to make in a similar tone weak sugary, and slightly inarticulate sounds. At one point he exclaimed in consternation: "What? A'D' did you say? I'll talk to her. Tell her to come to the phone." Boruvka's hunted expression gave way to the severe, frowning countenance of an implacable father, which made a very amateurish impression. "What's this I hear, Zuzana?" he said and got no further because he was silenced by another, higher pitched and perhaps even more rapid flow of speech. "All right, all right. But it's a good thing that Mr Lavecky is strict," was all he managed to get in before he was forced to listen again After a while something evidently provoked him, for he exclaimed: "What? Tonda Spacek? That parachutist? But he nearly failed in maths! He's swotted it up since, has he? I only hope he has!" And again he listened, then finally he gave his daughter permission to turn for assistance in a difficult piece of algebra homework to a young man whom Boruvka characterised scornfully as a "parachutist". The line was again dominated by Mrs Boruvkova's voice and when the lieutenant had assured her innumerable times that he would be home as soon as he could make it, he managed, after a clear twenty-two minutes—the sergeant malignantly timed it with his stopwatch—to put down the receiver.

Boruvka sank on to a chair and mopped his forehead with his handkerchief.

"Our showers aren't working yet, are they Pavel?"

"No, they've been put into the repairs and maintenance plan for the next quarter."

"I'll pop next door then," said the exhausted detective. "I can't think straight any longer."

There was a crush at the public baths next to the police station. The sight of the queuing crowd plunged Boruvka into melancholy, and his spirits sank even lower when a beautiful, slim young woman in an elegant gown and a becoming hat attempted to strike up an acquaintanceship by making eyes at him.

At least it seemed to Boruvka that she was trying to flirt with him. As soon as the girl saw him, she nodded and flashed him a dazzling smile. But the lieutenant's gloomy face remained coldly grave. The girl's smile flickered uncertainly; in the end she buried herself in a woman's magazine which she was holding upside down.

Boruvka too became uncertain. It was many years since he had been the object of a pretty, unknown girl's attention, and he had a feeling that he'd seen the lovely coquette before. He tried to get a proper look at her undetected but he kept meeting her eyes as she stole a glance at him and smiled encouragingly. After several such encounters, he gave up.

His peace of mind had been shaken, though; he tried to marshal the facts in the case of the murdered dancer, but the lovely, delicate face of the girl reading a magazine upside down persistently intruded upon his thoughts. Perhaps his odd behaviour in the cubicle later could be explained by this unusual uneasiness.

He took off his hat, loosened his tie and contemplated the white wall behind which water was burbling in the next cubicle. The unknown, yet vaguely familiar, girl must be undressing there. Boruvka had noticed her final attempt at making overtures to him as they were simultaneously entering adjacent cubicles.

The partition was made of plastic material and the lieutenant's eye was caught by something shining in it. He went closer and discovered that an unknown hand had recently drilled a hole in it, the purpose of which was not open to doubt.

Such things happen in public baths. But it was not a usual occurrence for an officer of the security force, a criminologist of unblemished reputation and the father of a teenage daughter to use such a hole for the very purpose for which it had been created. But Boruvka did just that.

An attractive female figure with water pouring over it was shaped in a cloud of steam. Boruvka traced the outline from the knees, visible above the edge of the bath, over the soft line of the thighs and buttocks up the graceful curve of the back to the neck. The girl was washing her hair under the shower. Her head was bent over her chest and the swanlike arch of the long neck was very aesthetic.

Beads of sweat stood out on Boruvka's forehead and his mouth dropped open in an unbecoming and almost lascivious gape. Not because it had dawned on him that the naked flirt in the next cubicle was a civilian, flesh-and-blood replica of the new police-woman in the sateen overall, whose powers of observation he had questioned in the morning. Not at all.

But he did something that one would hardly have expected from a senior detective. He took a felt-tipped pen from his trouser-pocket and on the white wall of the cubicle rapidly executed two sketches which, with the best will in the world, one could not have described as entirely moral.

One indicated—rather primitively—a naked girl standing stiffly to attention like a soldier. An arrow pierced her head horizontally from the nape of the neck through the mouth. The second, equally primitive, drawing was also of a naked girl standing erect but with her head on its long, swanlike neck inclined toward her bosom. An arrow passed through the nape of her neck and out at her mouth. But it was pointing obliquely downward.

The detective gazed for a moment at these somewhat indecent drawings. Then, as though in a trance, he jammed his hat on his head and shot out of the door.

As he ran along the corridor, the indignant voice of the attendant, who had just entered the vacant cubicle, floated after him.

But Boruvka ignored it.

He did not stop until he reached the janitor's desk at the Odeon Theatre, where the evening performance was drawing to an end. The night watchman, whom Boruvka had not met, was on duty.

"The key to the lift," he demanded without wasting words.

"The lift is open, comrade—major."

"I mean the service lift, the one that is usually kept locked."

The watchman, regarding Boruvka with suspicion, took a key down from a hook next to the small window and handed it to him.

"Shall I go with you?" he asked.

"No, there's no need," barked Boruvka and dashed over to the lift on the other side of the foyer.

Owing to the size of his horizontal dimensions, the lieutenant was averse to walking, especially up or downstairs. Therefore, he found it worthwhile to take the lift in order to descend one storey from the foyer on the ground floor to the corridor in the basement. It was indeed worthwhile.

After about five seconds, the lift stopped at the bottom. Boruvka noticed that the cast-iron Eros dominating the ornate lattice was gazing at him through the glass door. Instead of looking out over the corridor, Eros was facing the lift. Boruvka opened the glass door and stretched out his hand to the statue. It wobbled. When he tried to lift it, it came away easily from the worn vertical support. He took a good look at the decrepit bust in his hand, and sighed mournfully.

Eros had a dark spot on the back of his head. Boruvka scraped a little piece off with his nail, and his experienced eye recognised dried blood. He replaced the figure carefully on the shaky support, and then walked along the corridor to the door of the women's dressing room. It was not locked. He went inside and looked round. At the far end of the room he saw another door. He passed through the dressing-room and seized the handle. But this door was secured.

He looked round in perplexity, and met the suspicious gaze of an elderly woman in a shiny overall who was just entering with a load of silk costumes.

"Lieutenant Boruvka," he introduced himself. "Do you happen to have a key to this door?"

The woman measured him with a far from amiable look, deposited the basket of costumes on the nearest dressing table and silently took down a large key from a nail in the wall.

"Here y'are," she growled. "The door's locked because the men's dressing-room is on the other side and the fellows used to come barging in here."

The sound of applause descended from above, followed by a babble of voices. The stairs rang with the pattering of women's feet. The performance was over. As the lieutenant opened the door and began to shut it behind him, he caught a glimpse of the first dancer—in a very scanty costume—hurrying into the dressing room with the others jostling behind her. He pushed the door to, put the key in his pocket and looked round. Opposite him he saw a door with the notice "Gentlemen's Dressing-Room". To the right in the end wall of the corridor was the gate to the service lift. Three men in white T-shirts appeared round the bend. Boruvka turned to the lift door, feeling in his pocket. He found the two keys and drew them both out. He could hardly believe his eyes. On his palm lay two large keys of identical size and shape. He examined them carefully, one after the other, then tried to open the lift with one. It worked. But he did not enter the lift. Instead, he locked it again and tried the other key.

It also worked.

The lieutenant groaned faintly. He did not lock the door for the second time. He hopped into the lift, shutting the door after him.

He pondered for a moment gloomily, then concentrated his attention on the inside of the cabin. It was a primitive, old-fashioned piece of equipment, consisting merely of a boarded floor and a balustrade barely waist high. The cabin was suspended from four metal rods and had a wooden ceiling. It did not work on a push button. It was operated by a lever. An antique. It had one advantage: it could be stopped anywhere between storeys.

Boruvka gazed glumly at the chipped walls on three sides. Steps resounded beyond the door and the last wave of applause echoed from above. The lieutenant sighed and seized the lever. The lift started to move slowly.

The dilapidated walls of the shaft slipped slowly away as the open cabin bore the detective aloft to the higher floors. Here and there age-old indecent inscriptions and drawings similar to those the lieutenant had scrawled in the public baths were engraved in the ancient plaster. Boruvka scrutinised the drawings.

Suddenly, as though something had startled him out of his wits, he pulled the lever vigorously and the lift stopped. The lieutenant carefully moved the lever in the opposite direction and the cabin began to descend slowly. He stopped it again almost immediately. In the wall of the shaft on his right was a round aperture about a foot and a half in diameter, covered on the far side by horizontal metal strips, reminiscent of plate armour. At some time the vanes of a ventilator must have been there, but now only the broken frame remained. Otherwise, the hole was empty.

Empty except for a small copper cartridge lying in the dip of the circle.

Boruvka wrapped it carefully in his handkerchief. It was a replica of the cartridge that Malek had held in his handkerchief that afternoon. Boruvka leaned into the opening and raised one of the metal strips. From his bird's eye view, he saw an interesting sight: a row of shower cubicles in which girls were washing themselves, their bodies silhouetted against the plastic curtains. Fair and dark heads were visible over the top of the curtains.

The lieutenant's expression, albeit fixed, held no trace of lascivity. His eyes filled with immense sadness.

He released the strip and, sighing mournfully, sat down on the small seat in the corner of the lift. He thought hard.

Then he suddenly leapt up, leaned out of the cabin and groped above the wooden ceiling. A wave of despair swept over his face. He drew his hand back and in his dirty palm he held a black 7.65 calibre revolver.

"I dunno why that lift's locked," said the night watchman. "It's an order. Probably for safety reasons. It's an old boneshaker. But I dunno exactly. I'm new 'ere."

"Is Mr Zahalka on the phone?" asked Boruvka impatiently.

"Yes. 'is son's a doctor and—"

"Hand me the phone." Boruvka reached over the janitor's desk for the phone. "What is his number?"

The watchman told him.

There was no answer for some time. The chorus girls began to trickle past the desk. Some of them were being met by smartly dressed young men. Boruvka followed them with his eyes and waited. Finally, a sleepy voice mumbled something into the receiver at the other end.

"Comrade Zahalka?" asked the lieutenant, and when the sleepy voice had confirmed this, he continued:

"Do you remember when we were walking towards the service lift before the lights went out, you were going to tell me something. About the lift, I mean. Why it had to be kept locked or something."

"Oh yeah, that's right," the remote voice crackled. "Yeah, and then we didn't get around to it, did we? That's the way it often is. When the comrade manager got bashed, I forgot all about it in the cufuffle."

The Scientific Method

"Tell me now," said the detective, his voice quavering almost imperceptibly.

"Well it's like this," said the janitor, and began to narrate a long story. The lieutenant listened in silence. His eyes followed the slim, beautiful girls who were filing past him from the basement staircase. They bade the watchman goodnight politely, cast curious glances at the lieutenant's face and then donned sweet smiles with which they tripped towards their respective escorts. The lieutenant stood alone, as though forgotten, and as he watched that procession of almost mythical beauties, he grew sadder and sadder.

The janitor told him:

"We 'ad an assistant director, you know, a Mr Novacek, a pimply youth, and I noticed that evenin' after evenin' when the performance was over, 'e was getting into the service lift. It seemed odd to me that 'e didn't go by the ordinary lift, which was much more comfortable. Suddenly the thought 'it me, what was 'e opening it with, if the key was 'anging up in me cubby 'ole. So I keeps me eyes on 'im, and what do you think, comrade commissar? 'e was opening the lift door with the key from the gents' dressin'-room. I tried it out meself then, and the keys was exactly the same!"

"From the men's dressing-room?" exclaimed Boruvka incredulously.

"Yeah," said the janitor mysteriously. "Well, I thought it funny what 'e was up to, so once when Novacek 'ad the flu, I took the service lift meself after the performance, and what d'you think, comrade commissar, from one side you can see through the old ventilator 'ole—" the janitor stopped short; there was silence for a moment, then he shrieked, making the membrane in the receiver crackle: "Jesus Maria!"

"I know," said Boruvka darkly. "Into the ladies' showers. Who knew about this? Try to remember."

"Jesus Maria!" repeated the janitor, then he calmed down. "No one at first. Then later on everyone. I didn't tell no one, except the comrade manager, and 'e ordered me to change the lock. Well, of course, then everyone noticed it. I 'ad a bright idea that saved us a lock. I swopped over the locks from the gents' and ladies' dressing-rooms. Let the girls go and look at

65

each other, see?" The janitor chuckled gleefully. "The comrade manager approved," he added quickly. "And that young fellah, that Novacek, got the sack. Not only because of what I've told you. But the girls complained that 'e was pesterin' them and things kept disappearin'."

The lieutenant was no longer listening. A mournful shadow darkened his face, and he again resembled a sad St Bernard. Beautiful girls were still flashing past the janitor's desk, hurrying into the night life of the metropolis. .

A particularly beautiful, dark-haired girl, wearing a white costume with a large turquoise brooch in the lapel appeared. There was no one waiting for her. Boruvka replaced the receiver and leaned over the janitor's desk. "Miss Sikorska!" he called quietly. "Would you step this way for a moment, please."

The girl started, her large black eyes dilated, she swayed and when the alert detective caught her in his arms, she had already lost consciousness.

Perhaps Boruvka had a cold; if not, it was a tear that dropped on the turquoise brooch.

"Removing the revolver from the properties basket presented no problem," the detective dictated to the young policewoman who—back again in her sateen overall with her hair wound into a strictly businesslike knot—was typing his report on the completed investigations.

"My deduction was as follows: the shot was fired through the empty ventilation aperture from the service lift. This could be opened with the key from the ladies' dressing-room where Sikorska was at the time of the murder. As far as motive is concerned: I noticed that Tossi addressed all the girls as 'Miss' with their respective surnames, but he called Sikorska 'Jana'. According to Peskova's testimony, Sikorska dropped the manager of her own accord. Why should she break off a relationship that was so advantageous to her? Only because she had fallen in love with another man. And that was, as she herself admits, Tossi. When a new dancer, Ester Nakoncova, joined the company, two things happened: she found favour in the manager's eyes and Tossi too fell in love with her and deserted Sikorska. The motive, then, was jealousy. And now, regarding cartridges: one was found in the showers, the second by me in the ventilation aperture, but only one bullet was found at the scene of the crime. The explanation is this: Sikorska wanted to create the impression that the shot had been fired from the showers, therefore she took an empty cartridge from the properties room where a large quantity were lying about after the shooting practice carried out by Krames there, and threw it into the place of the murder before her departure from the dressing-room. After firing, she did not notice in her agitation that the cartridge from the used bullet had got stuck in the ventilation aperture, the said cartridge being found there by me."

"Er—" the policewoman who had been squirming strangely, spoke up"—excuse me, comrade lieutenant, but wouldn't 'where I found it' sound better?"

"Do you think so?" asked the detective, frowning.

"Definitely," replied the girl.

"Where I found it then," Boruvka continued. "The circumstances of the murder are also explained by the later attack on Mara in the basement corridor. When Sikorska realised that the janitor was about to tell me the story of assistant director Novacek, she was afraid lest the possibilities of the lift shaft be discovered by me—"

"That I would discover—" piped up the policewoman quietly.

"That I would discover the possibilities of the lift shaft, so while the janitor went to fetch the key, she quickly devised a plan. Unobserved, she switched off the electricity at the main which is located round the corner at the foot of the staircase. She groped in the darkness for the statue of Eros—we found out that most of the dancers knew about the statue and that it had served them for various jokes—and struck the nearest person, accidentally bumping into Alena Peskova as she did so. Then in the darkness she felt for the support and replaced the bust on the lattice—or that took place during the excitement occasioned by the appearance of Tossi—back to front."

The girl squirmed again but she controlled herself. "This all had one motive," Boruvka continued. "Sikorska did not intend to murder her former lover Mara; she merely wanted confusion to be caused by the darkness and thereby the attention to be diverted of the police from—"

"So that the attention of the police should be diverted from—" the policewoman put in, unable to restrain herself any longer.

"So that the attention of the police should be diverted from Zahalka and so that he should forget his original intention concerning the relating of instructions concerning the replacement— simply that the lift keys were to be changed. Put it in your own way as regards style." Boruvka broke off and looked over the policewoman's shoulder at the typewritten page. It was a good report on a closed case. He had reason to be satisfied with it. Then he noticed the girl's long, graceful neck and realised that he had omitted one factor from his report—a factor that had played an extremely important role in the discovery of the murderer. Again he looked at the girl's long neck and decided that he had better omit any reference to that specific factor.

The girl typed the last sentence and turned to the detective with shining eyes.

"That was wonderful, comrade lieutenant!" she cried enthusiastically. "Your reasoning! Sherlock Holmes and all those fictional detectives aren't a patch on you. You work on purely scientific lines."

"Ahem," Boruvka cleared his throat. "You shouldn't underestimate Sherlock Holmes. For his time he employed a relatively scientific approach—"

"Oh yes," the girl broke in. "But he was always helped by some fluke, whereas you have a system. A consistent, rigorously applied scientific *method*!"

Boruvka cleared his throat again.

Malek entered the office and concluded from the crimson flush on Boruvka's face that he had disturbed the detective of hitherto unimpeachable reputation in doings which had no connection with police duties, and definitely did not befit the father of a teenage daughter.

He therefore apologised curtly and, walking backwards, withdrew rapidly from the room. In the depths of his heart he felt towards the lieutenant and the girl a bitterness which later turned to anger. And no one ever succeeded in persuading him that— from the point of view of staff relations—what had occurred in the lieutenant's office had been absolutely beyond reproach.

68

IV

Death on Needlepoint

PATERA DISAPPEARED IN the mist beyond the rock edge. Bartos saw the rope slide through the safety loop on the "hourglass", felt it tighten on his chest. The light breeze cooled his perspiring forehead. A thin mist streamed among the summits like smoke from some gigantic cigarette.

Then he heard Patera's voice:

"O.K. I'm pulling."

Cautiously he got up from his squatting position on the ledge, turned, and reached for the first handhold.

"I'm coming!" he shouted up into the mist as, with slightly numb fingers, he groped for the next hold.

"A bit more to the left," advised Jirina next to him, and Bartos obeyed without a word.

He saw her some twelve feet below when he secured his rope to the snap link on the "hourglass" above the ledge leading to the rock edge where a little while ago Patera had vanished and where in a moment or two he himself would lose sight of Jirina. He looked down at her. Beneath yawned a sixty-foot precipice, showing the distance they had already covered in their ascent. It was not his habit to break the rules in this way, but just now he had simply been unable to resist the temptation. Jirina did not look up at him. Of course not; after all they were "on the rope" where nothing mattered but the task in hand, which had to be given complete and undivided attention. People linked by the line in this way depended on one another for their survival.

He negotiated the ledge round the corner of the rock. Now came the most difficult part of the whole ascent of Needlepoint: the large overhang just beneath the summit. Only the rope remained to link him with his two companions, neither of whom he was able to see. As carefully as he knew how, he shuffled his way underneath the bulging sandstone almost a hundred feet above the ground. He was conscious of a fleeting fear that Jirina was paying out the line that stretched from a knot on her bosom to another on his chest too rapidly; the line did not seem sufficiently taut; but he rejected the thought as soon as it came to him, dismissing it as a symptom of the anxiety known even to the most experienced climber on so tricky an ascent. He hauled himself cautiously up.

He had just reached the critical point and was hanging in the air, suspended on three points of balance: his two big toes in the canvas shoes, and the fingers of his left hand gripping a slight crevice on the edge of the overhang. With his right he explored the rock face in the hope of finding a secure grip that would enable him to pull himself up and over the jutting rock.

It was then that he felt—this time it was quite unmistakable, nothing to do with fear—that the rope by which Patera was holding him from above was not taut.

"Tony!" he shouted. "Tony! Haul me up!"

But the tension did not increase, the rope remained slack.

"You asleep, Tony, damn it?" he yelled up into the mist, pressing himself against the smooth, bulging rock face. He was aware of the terrible strain which his own weight exerted on the two fingertips clutching the shallow hand-hold.

Then he felt a genuine tremor of fear, as the rope he could just see disappearing into the thin mist above his head began to trickle slowly down the overhang and to collect in a disordered tangle on his chest.

"Hey Tony!" he shouted desperately. "What's the matter with you? Are you mad?"

No reply. Only the rope kept quietly slithering down, piling right up to his chin.

"Jirina, hold me!" he shouted to the girl below. He did not hear any reply. Not that there was any need for her to reply—it was enough for him to feel the slight tug of the rope which, round the corner of the rock, passed through the safety loop in the "hourglass". But he felt nothing of the sort, and he could not turn round to look to make sure that the rope was really taut, so perhaps it was again just an illusion created by fear.

That other rope, gathering in folds against his chest, was no illusion, though. He gave way to panic as he suddenly grasped the incredible explanation.

"Tony!" he cried out in a strained voice. "For God's sake, man, stop fooling about! You can't do this to me!"

Nothing. Only the rope stopped coming down; but it remained slack. Drenched with a cold sweat, Bartos shut his eyes and summoned up all his energy and will-power. He thought he must surely dislocate his right arm as he clutched an uncertain hold, impossibly far away. Feeling something akin to despair he edged his right foot towards a narrow cleft. Then he cautiously brought over his left hand. By means of a desperately risky "eagle" technique he inched his way across the most hazardous part of the ascent.

At last he managed to grip a hand-hold above the overhang. Tensing himself, he exerted all his remaining strength and swung himself to safety over the rock edge. There, on the top of Needlepoint, he remained lying, quite spent, his face against the rough, weathered surface of the sandstone cap.

When he had recovered his breath he raised his head—and his whole body quivered as though he had just received an electric shock.

On the bare summit of the rock, surrounded on every side by a wide and very deep precipice, sat Tony Patera, strangely contorted, his face between his knees, and with the carved handle of a bowie-knife protruding from his back.

Bartos recognised his own knife, which he had that morning, before they set out on the ascent, left in the tent back in camp.

Lieutenant Boruvka looked round with sad eyes from the bare top of Needlepoint, on which he was herded in close company with the dead man, with Bartos, and with a girl who he had found out was called Jirina Fikotova. The mist had disappeared, so that they could see the whitish summits of the other rocks, pointing up towards the grey sky.

"So you say that when you recovered from the shock you

asked Miss Fikotova to climb up to where you were, and you called Mr Malat?"

"Yes," said Bartos, speaking in a constrained voice. "I thought I'd better stay here, at the scene of the crime, so that everything could be reconstructed just as it happened. *I* didn't kill him."

"But it *is* your knife?"

Bartos shrugged his shoulders and wiped a forehead that still glistened with perspiration.

"I left it in the tent this morning. The murderer could easily have taken it."

Lieutenant Boruvka looked cautiously down to the bottom of the rock where, in the shadow of some fir-trees, he could see his men, who had not been able to accompany him to the top, as there simply was not enough space on Needlepoint. A few minutes ago he had laboriously (for in those far-off days when he had undergone his gymnastic training, mountaineering had not been included in the curriculum) been hauled up here at the end of a rope by these two, one of whom was a murderer. He was not sure yet which one.

The lieutenant thought about it, but the effort seemed futile.

"What happened then?" he therefore asked.

"Frank, Mr Malat that is, came running out of the wood over there, to the Lookout. Our tents are just a little way beyond that. I told him to go and fetch you."

Boruvka looked in the direction in which Bartos was pointing. Some ten yards from the summit of Needlepoint and a little above it there protruded from the sheer rock face a sharp spur on which Sergeant Sintak was at that moment standing, gazing down at them. The spur was perhaps seven or eight yards above the top of Needlepoint, forming part of a standstone barrier which ran along the length of the precipice and could easily be ascended from the North by forest paths. Of all the rocks that rose from the bottom of the precipice, the spur of the Lookout was closest to Needlepoint but even this was fantastically far away and too high up. No one, reflected Lieutenant Boruvka, could have jumped here this way. That would be a superhuman feat.

He turned back to face Bartos.

"Still, it looks pretty bad for you, doesn't it, seeing it was done with your knife."

"Maybe it does," replied Bartos, his manner curiously calm. "But I didn't kill him, just the same. I'm not crazy, you know."

Lieutenant Boruvka gave him a sad look.

"No—but under the circumstances you were the only one who *could* have killed him," he said.

"So you say that when you heard Bartos calling, you stopped collecting firewood and ran to the Lookout?"

Lieutenant Boruvka was looking thoughtfully at a very ugly man with a hook nose, who was sitting on a bunk opposite him, wearing a pair of badly worn plus-fours with leather patches on the knees.

It was dark inside the tent, and the rain beat a tattoo on the taut canvas.

"That's right," said Malat. "It's less than fifty yards from here to the Lookout."

"What did you see when you got there?" As he spoke the lieutenant made a mental inventory of the tent, which seemed to contain nothing that was superfluous.

His interest was aroused by a large, twisted coil of ordinary thin rope that lay on the bunk. He could not have said why.

"All three of them were on top of Needlepoint," said Malat. "First of all I thought that perhaps one of them had been taken ill and couldn't get down. Then . . ."

"Yes?" Lieutenant Boruvka prompted him.

"Then Jirina called out to say that I should fetch the police because some one had—because Tony was dead."

Malat hung his head and looked at the ground.

"I see," said Lieutenant Boruvka. "What's this rope for?"

"We hang our things up on it to dry. You get wet pretty often in this weather."

Lieutenant Boruvka ran a hand across his forehead. "Listen, would it have been possible for some one to climb to the top of Needlepoint earlier this morning, wait up there for Patera, kill him, and then get down on the other side?" Malat shook his head.

"Possible, yes, but who could have done it? We're all alone

73

here. No one else got off the train when we arrived yesterday, and there have been no cars either. And in any case they'd have been bound to see him from the Lookout as they walked to the foot of Needlepoint."

"Well, how about someone jumping from the Lookout to the summit of Needlepoint?"

"Out of the question," replied Malat firmly. "And even if this *were* possible, how would he have got back? The difference in height is some ten yards, you know."

"So it is," said Lieutenant Boruvka, his eyes again wandering to the coil of rope as he conjured up a mental picture of Needlepoint, the Lookout, and the precipice underneath them. His head swam slightly. "So it is," he repeated. "Quite out of the question." Something occurred to him, but he at first did not feel like saying it out loud. Then he thought better of it:

"And—what if someone threw that knife?"

He read ridicule in the other's eyes.

"Well," said the ugly mountaineer, "all I can say is I wish I knew how to do it. I'd make a great living travelling with a circus."

Lieutenant Boruvka felt ashamed of his notion and pretended to be lost in thought.

That it was nonsense he reassured himself a few minutes later, standing on the Lookout with Bartos. The summit of Needlepoint was terrifyingly far away, and below that yawned a precipice of almost ninety feet. Sprouting out of it were the black crowns of tall fir-trees.

The lieutenant came out of his reverie—this time he was not merely feigning thought—to ask:

"You and Patera were good friends, I take it?"

Bartos did not reply.

"That's what you said, isn't it?"

Bartos raised his head and looked Boruvka full in the eyes.

"Look here, lieutenant, you're bound to find out anyway, so I might as well tell you myself."

Boruvka nodded encouragement.

"We *used* to be good friends. Until Jirina started coming with us. Understand me?"

The criminologist nodded once more. Then he asked softly:
"Do you realise that you're handing me a perfect motive
for the murder?"

"Sure," replied Bartos. "But I'm not such a fool. If I'd
wanted to kill Patera, I'd have pushed him off a rock so it
would look like an accident. I had lots of opportunity, you
know."

"No doubt. But it's always a trifle suspicious if an experienced
climber just falls off a mountain."

Bartos grinned.

"Isn't it a damned sight more suspicious if you find him with
a knife in his back at the top of Needlepoint, where he couldn't
have been reached by anyone unseen?"

"You're right there," admitted Lieutenant Boruvka, and fell
silent. Then he added: "And of course this is bound to confuse
the police investigating the crime. Maybe that's just what the
murderer counted on."

"Well, you see, I on the other hand thought..." Bartos
stopped.

"Yes, what did you think?"

"Well, when Tony stopped hauling me up, it occurred to
me..."

"Yes, go on?"

"It occurred to me that perhaps he meant to kill *me*. That
he had cut the rope and would then pretend that it had split. I
completely lost my nerve. It even seemed to me for a moment
that Jirina had stopped holding me. I called out to her and..."

"And what about her? *Was* she holding you?"

"Yes. At least, I think so."

"You mean to say you're not sure?"

"That's something you can't tell for certain. I couldn't see her."

"How was she supposed to be holding you? From below?
Surely that's impossible?"

"No, it isn't. It's done through the loop in the 'hourglass'.
If something had happened, I'd have been left hanging on the
loop."

"Can't such a loop give way?"

"Hardly," replied Bartos. "And if it did..." He broke off,

and then continued: "Do you realise what would have happened?"

"What?"

Bartos made a face.

"Think!"

The lieutenant thought. He looked sadly into Bartos's eyes.

"Miss Fikotova would have been in danger of crashing with you, is that it?"

"Exactly. That's why I at once dismissed the idea that Patera might be trying to do away with me. Why should he have put *her* in danger as well?"

"Provided," said the criminologist darkly, "she was really holding you, of course. Provided she had not monkeyed about with the rope she was securing you with—hadn't untied it or something like that."

Bartos tried to say something but only managed to grunt. He cleared his throat and tried again.

"Why should she have done that?"

"That's more than I know," said Lieutenant Boruvka bitterly. "But perhaps *you* might know why."

Bartos gulped, and lowered his eyes. Boruvka stepped forwards, right to the edge of the rock, and looked down. Though he did not suffer from vertigo, the sight of the tops of the tall trees deep down in that horrible abyss made him feel slightly queasy.

"What's this?" he asked, pointing to a metal ring sticking out of the tip of the rocky spur they were standing on.

Bartos glanced down.

"That's a piton. You pass the rope through it and ..."

Bartos broke off and looked at Boruvka.

"Yes, what is it?"

"Nothing," replied Bartos quickly. "You pass the rope through it, throw the rope down, and lower yourself on it. It just occurred to me that I wouldn't have expected to find one here."

"Why not?"

"Well, this is an outlying rock. Even if someone wanted to climb it—and as far as I know no one ever does—he wouldn't have to let himself down by the rope. You can get down by the path through the woods there. See it?"

He pointed. Some fifteen yards below, Boruvka saw the zig-zag line of the path Bartos had mentioned.

"Perhaps someone was practising here before going on to something more difficult," the lieutenant suggested.

"That might explain it," agreed Bartos. "Except that this isn't exactly an ideal rock for practice purposes. You see, here the rope's going to hang straight down."

"Does that matter?"

"No, it doesn't. But it isn't typical. In this kind of descent you've got to learn to push yourself off from the rock with your legs. And that's something you can't do here."

Lieutenant Boruvka thought about this for a little. The stout police photographer Kana was laboriously going about his business on top of Needlepoint, where he had been transported by two members of the local mountaineering club, recruited by Boruvka's team to aid them in their work of investigation. The two young men were now suspended on their ropes below the summit, one on either side, to give the photographer more room on top as he went about his job of photographing the body. The sight of the two youths "sitting" there in mid-air, their feet just touching the edge of a small plateau under the top of the tall rock formation, was a fantastic one. Lieutenant Boruvka felt he was dreaming all this—it was only a dream and he must wake soon, because he was damned if he saw how Bartos could have done the murder. Or the girl, for that matter. He raised his field-glasses and examined the smooth grey walls of Needlepoint, his eyes coming to rest a little way below the top.

"Couldn't someone climb up from this side?" he asked.

"From the western side you mean?" said Bartos, and shook his head. "You think that while we were climbing the eastern wall the murderer could've—no. That's quite out of the question."

"Why not?"

"It just isn't humanly possible, that's all. The rock here is almost thirty feet high, it's completely smooth, and worse still, it overhangs slightly. To get up this way, you'd have to keep putting in cleats every half a yard or so. And that's not moun-taineering, that's acrobacy. And anyway, I don't see any cleats there, do you?"

"No, I don't see any either," replied the lieutenant. "Now tell me, when someone climbs up the other side, can you see them from here?"

"No, you can't."

"And they can't see us?"

"No. They'd climb up the eastern wall all the way, and that prevents them from seeing anything on this side."

"Ah." Boruvka again scanned the wall with his field-glasses. "And what's that?" he asked. "It looks like a little sandstone pillar—"

"Where? You mean above the ledge? That's the 'hourglass', so-called. You find formations like that everywhere in sandstone. Supposed to be caused by whirlpools when the region was still under the sea. They're ideal for safety purposes."

Lieutenant Boruvka took another careful look at the "hour-glass" on Needlepoint. The thoughts it conjured up were of diluvial seas and of huge prehistoric reptiles looking like the Loch Ness monster—but then he forced himself to leave the realm of fantasy and return to reality. This, however, seemed any-thing but real. The "hourglass" was immediately below the top of the rock face, and below it he saw a horizontal fissure which Bartos had described as "the ledge".

"So you say it's impossible to climb up to the 'hourglass' from this side?" Boruvka enquired cunningly.

"Definitely."

"And couldn't one," the lieutenant went on, squinting at his companion, "somehow negotiate the rock by that ledge from the eastern side and make one's way over here?"

Bartos gave him a swift look.

"You mean traverse from the eastern face to the western?"

"I suppose that *is* what I meant, only put more expertly."

Bartos thought about it. The lieutenant's notion seemed to surprise him. His face registered his astonishment, then a hint of terror.

"I've certainly never heard of anyone attempting it," he said when he had recovered a little. "That ledge—I don't know this for sure, but I don't think it goes all the way round—"

"You're not sure, though? That means it isn't out of the question, then?

"It would be terribly risky. And on her own . . . ."

78

He stopped.

"What did you want to say?"

"Nothing," said Bartos hastily. "Look, Lieutenant, these are rocks for training purposes. Every possible way of getting up them has been tried."

"Has it?" Boruvka saw that Bartos was struggling against some incredible suspicion the policeman's questions had instilled in his mind. Although he knew what that suspicion was, the lieutenant only asked:

"That means, I suppose—" he broke off, and Bartos caught his breath,"—that Mr Malat, for instance, knows all of them?"

Evidently relieved, Bartos almost smiled as he made his reply: "Malat? That's more than I know. But even if we were to admit that some acrobat might conceivably have climbed Needle-point up the western face—" now he was smiling quite definitely, "—it most certainly wasn't Malat."

"Oh, and why not?"

"Because Malat is just about the most incompetent climber who ever held a rope," Bartos explained eagerly. "A rock in the third category is just about all he can manage. And even then we've practically got to haul him up ourselves."

"Why does he come on these expeditions, in that case?"

Bartos made a grimace, then shrugged.

"Why indeed? Something must attract him, I suppose. But it's not the rocks."

Lieutenant Boruvka gave Bartos such a penetrating look that the young mountaineer again lost his composure.

"I'm not thinking of the western face," Boruvka said at last. "I thought that perhaps Malat could've climbed up the eastern wall behind you when you were negotiating that last tricky bit. You yourself said that a climber doesn't look back, so you wouldn't have seen him. Then he could have gone along the ledge to the "hourglass" on the western side and—"

Bartos shook his head resolutely.

"But it *is* possible? In theory?"

"No, not even theoretically. Because, you see, to get to that ledge you'd have to start off from the shelf from which we set out for that last overhang below the summit. And Jirina was sitting there, securing me. Malat would have had to wait for her to turn the corner, and by that time I was on top. And I'd found Patera, and he was dead."

Boruvka thought hard. He was not so naive as to imagine that someone could really have followed the first three climbers without being seen, but he had his reason for asking the question. The same reason that now made him ask:

"How long did that last bit take you? I mean from the moment you lost sight of Miss Fikotova until you reached the top and found the body?"

Bartos again seemed to crumble inside.

"I—I couldn't really say. I just lost my nerve."

"At least approximately?"

"No, I simply don't know. It seemed ages, but I guess it couldn't have been more than a few minutes."

Lieutenant Boruvka leaned closer to him and said significantly:

"Long enough, though, for someone to traverse from the eastern to the western side?"

Whereupon Bartos blanched and hung his head.

"So you were going up Needlepoint without Mr Malat because it was too difficult a climb for him, is that it?"

"That's it," replied Miss Fikotova. "Frankie's a hopeless ninny."

"Do you often leave him behind in the camp to cook lunch?"

"More or less always." Miss Fikotova laughed. "He's certainly a better cook than mountaineer, and none of us find it much fun to do the easy climbs *he*'s capable of."

Boruvka took a look round the girl's tent, which was a shambles. Miss Fikotova herself, however, was faultlessly groomed and made up. Though still wearing her "mountain" pants, she had found time to attend to her face, and her mascaraed eyes regarded the benevolent lieutenant coldly.

"I understand that the murdered man was in love with you," he said.

The girl shrugged her shoulders.

"Yes, he was."

She did not seem much moved by Patera's demise.

"And Mr Bartos?"

Again she shrugged.

"It's hardly my fault, is it? It's not against the law."

"No, it isn't. Not in the legal sense," said the Lieutenant bitterly. "And what about Mr Malat?"

The black eyes of the icy beauty facing him met his uncomprehendingly.

"What about him?"

"Was he in love with you as well?"

The girl lifted her eyebrows.

"Frank?" She paused, then went on slowly. "Well, if you mean was he bothering me all the time, then the answer is yes. Only I . . ."

"You didn't love him?"

"No, of course not."

"And did you love Bartos?"

The girl dropped her eyes. After a moment's silence she said: "I wasn't sure. But I didn't find him disagreeable."

"And what about Patera?"

No reply.

"You didn't find *him* disagreeable either, is that it?"

She threw up her head, and her platinum hair fell across her eyes.

"It's just that I wasn't able to make up my mind, that's all. That happens sometimes, doesn't it? Hasn't it ever happened to you?"

Boruvka looked away, thinking guiltily that *his* moments of indecision did not spring from dilemmas such as these.

"Did this lead to any unpleasantness between Bartos and Patera?" he asked.

"If you're trying to find out whether they quarrelled on my account," she said calmly, "the answer is they did." Then she added virtuously: "I was terribly unhappy about it. I didn't know what to do."

"But the three of you still went on climbing dangerous rocks together."

"When you're climbing you forget all personal differences," said Miss Fikotova, as if reciting from a mountain-climber's manual.

"In that case, why didn't you reply when Mr Bartos called

out to ask whether you were holding him?" Lieutenant Boruvka asked slyly.

The blonde beauty seemed startled.

"How did you know that?"

"He told me."

Regaining her cool manner, Miss Fikotova gave Boruvka an arrogant look.

"I was holding him, that's all. Every beginner can tell you you're not supposed to talk up in the rocks. No more than is absolutely necessary."

"I see," said Lieutenant Boruvka. "How long, would you say, did Mr Bartos take over that last bit to the top of Needlepoint?"

"Terribly long. I got awfully nervous by the time he got there."

"How long, exactly? Five minutes?"

"Oh, at least that. More like ten. Of course you lose your sense of time in such situations."

She seems too eager by half to tell, thought Boruvka. He did not like it, nor did he like the way she offered this very damaging information, which Bartos had been careful to withhold. He frowned, thinking once more that all this was only a dream, that he would never find out how the thing had really happened. Nevertheless, he decided to try shock tactics.

"And how long does it take to undo the knot of the rope with which you were holding Bartos?"

Miss Fikotova was either a very self-possessed young lady, or she failed to grasp the drift of his question.

"That's done in a jiffy," she replied. "Why do you ask?"

"Because I want to know," said Boruvka, and since the girl still did not seem to understand, he went on: "Listen, do you know beforehand when you arrive here which of the rocks you're going to climb on any particular day?"

"Usually we do," she said. "Not always."

"Did you know you were going to do Needlepoint today?"

"Oh yes, we knew that all right. We'd originally meant to climb this one *last* Sunday, but at the last moment Tony—that is, Mr Patera—couldn't come, and so—"

"How long beforehand did you know?"

"Well, Needlepoint happens to be one of the most difficult," the girl explained. "It's in the fifth category. We had it in mind all through the summer."

"I see," said the lieutenant, changing the subject abruptly. "Oh, and something else. Did those two know about Malat?"

Again Miss Fikotova did not seem to understand his meaning. Only this time Boruvka did not believe her.

"Did they know what?"

"That he was—as you put it—bothering you?"

"Of course; everybody knew that," she replied with a trace of contempt in her voice. "But no one took Frankie seriously."

"They didn't quarrel with *him*, then?"

"Goodness, of course not! Quarrel with Frankie?!"

She pronounced the name in a way that brought back to Boruvka memories of himself and a similar blonde in the far-off days of his boyhood. He had been a shy Fourth Former, and the girl had treated him with exactly the same kind of disdain—and he had not forgotten it to this day.

"Everybody made fun of him," she added.

"Patera and Bartos too?"

"They most of all. They really gave him a bad time."

"And you?" Lieutenant Boruvka asked softly.

The light was bad inside the tent, but he thought he could see her face turning a little darker.

Then she shrugged her shoulders once more, and her lips twisted disdainfully.

"There's no law against that, either."

"No," replied Boruvka mournfully. "Unfortunately there isn't."

"But why?" Sergeant Malek asked him insistently. Lieutenant Boruvka sank heavily on to a large boulder in the shade formed on the bottom of the precipice by the tall sandstone rocks.

"That I don't know as yet," he replied. "So far we only know that she could have done it, and we know *how* she could have done it. As soon as Bartos was out of sight, she untied the rope by which she was holding him, crossed over to the western face, got up on top via the 'hourglass', killed Patera, and returned to her original place."

"Yes, but why?"

Malek almost shouted the question this time.

"For the time being we must be satisfied with answering two questions: Who? and How?"

"But in Bartos's case we can answer all three," the Sergeant reminded him. "Including the question 'Why?' And in every case the answer is a more acceptable one than where the girl's concerned."

"But the snag is that taken together, the three make nonsense," Lieutenant Boruvka retorted, bending his head backwards and looking up at the top of Needlepoint. There, above the summit, a large bird was circling in the air. As Boruvka watched, it alighted on the fateful ledge and sat there, majestically oblivious of the human activity below.

"Why nonsense?" Malek asked irritably.

"Well," replied Lieutenant Boruvka, "surely he wouldn't rely on us crossing him off as a suspect just because he happened to be the most suspicious character around. We're not in a detective story, you know."

"Aren't we?" said the Sergeant brusquely, also looking up at the sky, which was beginning to turn blue. The mist and the clouds were gradually dispersing. "I almost feel as if we were." After a pause he went on: "But in any case—this girl Fikotova would have to have some kind of motive. And she hasn't . . ."

"Perhaps she has, only we don't know what it is. Who can tell, with women . . ."

Malek gave him a searching look, and the lieutenant added quickly:

"It must've been a very complicated triangle. Someone ought to help us unravel it." He sighed. "All right, let them send Malat to me."

Boruvka gazed for a long time at the ugly young man before saying:

"Look, Mr Malat, you know that those two—the murdered man and Bartos—were rivals."

"You mean because of Jirina?" Malat asked calmly.

"Yes, that's right. Can you tell me which one she preferred?"

"I really couldn't say." Boruvka thought the other man had

84

frowned at the question. "I think she played around with both of them, actually."

"And what about *them*—Bartos and Patera, I mean—didn't they also have, ahem, other irons in the fire, so to speak?"

"I don't know. It's possible."

"Why do you say that?"

"Patera was very much a ladies' man."

Was he right in thinking he detected a shadow of envy in Malat's words? Lieutenant Boruvka was not sure.

"And what about Bartos?" he asked.

"Maybe he too. I don't know. I didn't pry into their private affairs."

"But you wouldn't rule out the possibility? In Bartos's case?"

Malat thought about this.

"I'd say it was more likely with Patera."

"He was more of a Don Juan, was he?"

"It's not that. Bartos showed more interest in her."

The dark young man's voice now carried a distinct tinge of melancholy.

"And did it perhaps strike you that as a result she was more interested in Patera?" Boruvka asked quickly.

"Maybe," replied Malat cautiously. "All I can say is that as I see it she had both of them in tow."

"Yes, that's what you said. And Patera probably had other women as well."

Malat looked up sharply.

"I didn't say that!"

"Not in so many words, but you didn't rule out the possibility."

"No, I guess not."

"Thank you. You can go back to your tent," said Lieutenant Boruvka lugubriously, turning his back on the young man.

Then he issued a number of rather complicated orders and in about an hour he was again standing on the rock known as the Lookout, at the side of the cool platinum blonde who, even in her patched "mountain" pants, caused his throat to contract a little. Below them, standing on top of Needlepoint, was Sergeant Malek, a stop-watch in hand. And next to him squatted two lads from the local mountaineering club, ropes slung across their shoulders as they prepared to haul up someone who could not be seen from the Lookout.

"The chap on the left," said Boruvka sombrely, "is securing the man who's going to climb up via that large overhang under the summit—the way Bartos came. The other one is securing the fellow who—" Boruvka paused.

"Yes?" said the girl. "Who represents me, is that it?"

Lieutenant Boruvka looked her squarely in the face.

"That's right," he confirmed, and then called out to Sergeant Malek: "Take it away!"

Malek shouted into the void below:

"Ready?"

And from far down came a duo of voices:

"Ready."

The girl seemed quite calm as she watched these preparations, only the muscles in her smooth cheeks grew a little tauter.

"All right, then, get ready—get set—go!" ordered Malek, as if he were the starter in a running contest, and he pressed his stop-watch. The lieutenant glanced at the blonde.

"The first chap's taking Bartos's route—now he's probably turned the corner, so that he can't see you—that is, he can't see the fellow who's acting you. But we'll soon be able to see—"

He broke off.

For the first time the beautiful blonde gave signs of unease.

"What shall we see?" she asked.

"You'll see," Lieutenant Boruvka permitted himself the pun as he raised the unnecessary field-glasses to his eyes. The distance was not such as to require them. But the field-glasses were not altogether superfluous. They hid his eyes and he was able to observe his companion surreptitiously.

She stood there, tense, her eyes fixed on the rock, not understanding what it was all about. Or she pretended not to understand. Yet when a moment later her face assumed a horrified expression, Boruvka felt she was not acting.

"But this—" she said, her voice the merest whisper, "this—"

The lieutenant laid aside his field-glasses. He did not need them to see the young fellow from the mountaineering club as he skilfully and without any apparent difficulty traversed the southern face towards the 'hourglass'.

86

"Why would I've done it?" the girl wanted to know, having at last found her voice.

"I've no idea," replied Lieutenant Boruvka. "I don't pretend to be an expert on feminine motives."

"I had no motive whatsoever," the girl retorted. "Masculine or feminine."

The young man had by this time reached the western side.

"My God!" the girl exclaimed. "And why would I have done it here, of all places? Taking such a risk! When I could easily have put something in his tea in the camp—"

"Maybe it wasn't as risky as all that. Look!"

She looked.

The young climber caught hold of the "hourglass" and quite effortlessly swung himself up to the summit of Needlepoint. There he made an amateurish gesture to indicate stabbing.

Sergeant Malek glanced at his stop-watch and turned towards the Lookout.

"Two minutes seventeen seconds!" he shouted triumphantly.

"How did it go?" Boruvka called out to the young mountaineer.

"Fine. It could be done quite easily even without the rope."

"And what about the other chap?" Boruvka asked the Sergeant.

Malek leaned carefully over the edge of the rock.

"He's about half-way up," he said. "He has still not got past the overhang."

"And *he* knows we're securing him," the lieutenant pointed out, turning to the girl.

Her face was white, paler than her beautiful platinum hair.

"Two minutes seventeen seconds to get there, a few seconds to commit the murder, two minutes seventeen back. And the other fellow is still only half-way. Not quite half-way."

"But why?" she demanded. "Tell me why?"

They led her away, slightly hysterical now and no longer so beautiful, and Boruvka gave himself up to thought. Once again he let his eyes rove round the rocky formations, silent, mysterious, and slightly sinister. The men on top of Needlepoint were beginning their downward journey. The sun was slowly sinking in the west, illuminating the weird scene with a light that was reminiscent of the red colour of blood.

And once more it came to Lieutenant Boruvka that this must surely be a dream.

He was not happy about the case. Although everything seemed to fit in the way they had reconstructed it, he was not happy. He turned round. On the other side of the Lookout another, taller rock towered like a warning finger raised towards the reddening sky.

Or like an exclamation-mark with a red point, turned upside down, Boruvka thought.

The idea that came to him the next moment startled him considerably. It seemed as if things were beginning to fall into place, like a complicated jigsaw puzzle. But it was still very confused, he could not be sure. . . .

He turned round again and shouted:

"Bring Bartos up here!"

"What's this, can you tell me?" he asked, pointing to the upturned exclamation-mark.

"That?" said Bartos dully. "Why, that's the Cone. First category."

"What's that?"

"The rocks are classified according to the degree of difficulty in climbing them. The first category is the easiest. You can do them without any special equipment, just as tourists."

"You don't say! But it's so high!"

"That's nothing to do with height," Bartos informed him drily, a touch of contempt in his voice.

"And can you get down from the Cone without any equipment too?"

"Why, sure you could. But it's better to use a rope. There's a clamp there, can you see it?" Bartos stopped speaking, then went on suddenly: "Listen. Lieutenant, I'm sure Jirina didn't do it. I—"

"Well, why don't we go and take a look up there," Boruvka interrupted him. "Do you think I can manage it? I used to be pretty good at sports in my time, but . . ."

"Oh, *anyone* can climb the Cone," said Bartos impatiently. "But Jirina—"

Lieutenant Boruvka was not listening any more. He was striding energetically down from the Lookout.

It soon became clear that Bartos had spoken the truth. On the
western side of the Cone there was a steep but negotiable footpath. They reached the top a little out of breath. The view of
Needlepoint from here was slightly unreal. The rock seemed
to be crouching expectantly behind the threatening pinnacle of
the Lookout. The summit of Needlepoint was blood red. But
that was only a trick of the light caused by the setting
sun.

Looking across at Needlepoint, Lieutenant Boruvka could make
out the ledge, as well as the formation Bartos has described as
the "hourglass". And he could also see clearly, against the pink
and blue eastern sky, the black ring of the clamp which someone, contrary to logic, had fixed to the farthest protrusion of the
Lookout.

"Now show me how to rope down," demanded the lieutenant,
taking from his shoulder the rope they had brought with them.
Following Bartos's instructions he passed the rope through the
clamp and then wound it round his right thigh and over his left
shoulder. Taking up a sitting position on the rope he gingerly
but, in view of his stout figure, quite adroitly lowered himself
over the rounded edge of the rock. It was not particularly difficult. Using his feet to push himself off from the rock face, he
started his descent. Every time he swung out away from the
rock he descended a few more inches, and he managed to describe quite a large arc in the air. He was aware of an illogical
feeling of safety and absolute freedom. But he knew this was
only a typical piece of self-delusion well known to mountain
climbers. When he was a little distance below the top of the
Cone he glanced across at Needlepoint. And though he had fully
expected to see what he saw there, he was so startled by it that
he slipped down the rope much too fast all the way to the bottom,
scorching the palms of his hands.

He spent the following half hour in the police car, talking to
one of the lads from the mountaineering club, before sending
Sergeant Malek to the tent, where the police had Bartos and
Malat under surveillance, to fetch the coil of cord he had seen

lying on the bunk. Then he and the young mountaineer vanished in the rocky maze.

They were gone quite a long time, and Lieutenant Boruvka returned alone. Pushing his head inside the tent, he said peremptorily:

"Come with me!"

The girl, Bartos and Malat came out of the tent accompanied by two constables and set off down the path in the lieutenant's wake. The path led through a thick fir wood, coming out some fifty yards on to a rocky plateau where the Lookout projected out of the dark forest, towering above the beautifully-coloured evening landscape. There, above the rocky summits, they stopped. Sergeant Sintak, who had been waiting among the bushes, came out to join them.

"Look down there," Lieutenant Boruvka bade them, pointing down into the chasm. A rope was hanging from the piton fixed to the projecting rock, reaching some fifteen yards below to the path which zigzagged its way down the steep slope below the Lookout, to the foot of the Cone and then to the bottom of the precipice. Standing on the path by the end of the rope was the young man from the mountaineering club looking up at them expectantly.

Lieutenant Boruvka turned back to the little group behind him, scanning its members with a sorrowful look.

"Watch carefully," he said. "I know who killed Antonin Patera. And I know *how* Patera was killed."

The three young people stiffened, their eyes wide with horror.

"And saddest of all," the Lieutenant went on, "I know *why* he was killed. Now watch."

He leaned over the edge of the rock and called out to the young man below.

"All right, you can start."

All of them looked down now, tense with expectation. The young man bent down and, with the cord Boruvka had found in the tent, tied together the two ends of the rope. Then he strode quickly away to the foot of the Cone, disappearing from view behind the sandstone pillar. He had kept the other end of the cord in his hand and thus pulled the rope behind him as he walked.

"This murder," Boruvka continued mournfully, "was done by someone who wanted to prove several things at once. To himself, as well as to others."

He broke off, and there was a silence. No one had the nerve to ask for an explanation of this somewhat cryptic remark.

"That lad from the local club is at this moment ascending the western face of the Cone," the lieutenant went on. "It's a very easy climb. In ten minutes at the outside we'll see him over there." And he pointed to the bare top of the rock.

The young man did it in eight. He stood there on the smooth, rounded summit of the Cone, the silhouette of his figure against the sun making him look like some ancient falcon hunter or dragon slayer, and he started making curious motions with his hands, as if he were pulling something up. Before long they could all see what it was. The ends of the rope suspended from the piton on the Lookout were slowly crawling up the side of the Cone towards the young climber as he hauled in the cord he had taken with him on the ascent.

Having got the rope up, he untied the cord and pushed the large, tangled coil in his pocket. The small group of people standing on the Lookout heard his voice, weakened by the distance and the depth of the precipice.

"All right?"

Lieutenant Boruvka only gestured with his hand, and the astonished group was treated to a fantastic sight.

The young climber took a deep breath and, exerting all his strength, jumped upwards. In the air he drew up his legs and then thrust them violently forward. He passed the edge of the Cone and, his body describing a mighty arc, shot by under the Lookout. They all turned quickly round. The young man appeared on the eastern side, a long way below. Then he soared up again, to land on the edge a few inches below the summit of Needlepoint, where he seemed to find a firm handhold. And finally he attached his rope to whatever it was that he had gripped.

Only Lieutenant Boruvka knew that it was the rock formation which climbers called the "hourglass".

Only Lieutenant Boruvka and the murderer.

"Whoever managed to do this," Boruvka told them, "proved

to himself that he was no ninny. Sometimes such a proof can have great value for an individual. A greater value even than human life. Or at least," he added gloomily, "than someone else's life."

By now the young climber had settled himself comfortably on top of Needlepoint, his head provided with a red halo by the last rays of the setting sun.

"In particular the life of someone who was making his own a little hell. Someone who kept wounding his male vanity, and doing it in front of the woman he loved."

His three listeners seemed to have stopped breathing. The lieutenant was gazing over their heads into the distance, his face having acquired a pink tinge.

"There were two such people. And then it occurred to him that he could perhaps kill two flies with one blow. All he had to do was to kill one of them under circumstances that pointed to the other as the murderer, virtually excluding anyone else from suspicion. Like this, he would in fact do away with both of them, for the other would go to the gallows."

He paused, glancing across at Needlepoint. The young climber was now again standing on the ledge under the "hourglass". He took the rope in his hands and pushed away from the rock. For a few seconds he swung to and fro in the air like a living pendulum; when the swinging motion had almost ceased he slid nimbly down the rope and, coming to rest on the footpath below the Lookout, started removing the rope from the piton that held it fast.

Lieutenant Boruvka sighed. The rope slipped down and with a gentle hiss fell on the path at the young man's feet. Boruvka turned back to the three young mountaineers.

"It was all terribly risky, but he was willing to take that risk. He simply had to do it in order to regain the self-confidence he'd lost on account of the woman he was in love with."

Again he broke off, gazing with narrowed eyes at his three companions.

Two of them turned horrified eyes upon the third. Upon the small, dark, ugly young man.

"Isn't that the way it happened, Frank Malat?" Lieutenant Boruvka asked softly.

But Frank Malat did not reply. He leapt past the police officer to the edge of the rock and, with a horrible cry, jumped off into the abyss.

When a little later the police were picking up his shattered body down below, it occurred to Sergeant Sintak that it was strange that Lieutenant Boruvka, well known for his great presence of mind, had not tried to prevent Malat from taking that fatal leap.

And as he looked at the lieutenant now, it even seemed as if he were not particularly remorseful about it.

Sergeant Malek, on the other hand, was.

"I'll never forgive myself as long as I live!" he declared as they were driven away from the scene of the crime, the police car threading its way along the tortuous road between the tall rocks that threw dark shadows like those of medieval castles out of some fairy tale. "I'll never forgive myself for not watching him more carefully."

"Not me," said Lieutenant Boruvka.

"How can you be so callous, Joe?" Malek looked at him in surprise.

"On the contrary," said the lieutenant. "He would have been hanged in any case. Like this he's got it over and done with. Without the long waiting and the fear—"

"But, for God's sake, the man was a murderer!" exclaimed the Sergeant. "Surely he deserved to suffer a little."

"You think so?" Boruvka asked mysteriously, and Malek was completely at a loss to understand him. "I'd say there was someone else here who deserved it more."

They drove on in silence for a few minutes. The tall black castles had filled the little valley with twilight, and Sergeant Sintak, who was behind the wheel, switched on his headlights. The rocks all around them now looked like the scenery in a puppet-theatre.

"You know, the whole thing seems more like a dream," meditated Malek, and his words reminded the Lieutenant of his own reflections earlier in the day. "I've never known a case like this."

A smile crossed Lieutenant Boruvka's gloomy face.

"I guess you don't read detective stories, Paul," he said. "If you did, you'd know that this was nothing out of the ordinary. It's just a variation of the Locked Room Mystery."

"Of what? Locked room? What on earth are you talking about?"

"No, I know there was no locked room in our case. But we did have a place which the murderer couldn't have reached and from which he couldn't have escaped. And yet he did get there, and he did get away from it. Just like a murderer who leaves the corpse in a room that's locked on the inside."

Sergeant Malek shook his head.

"The things these scoundrels think up!"

"Detective-story writers you mean?" asked Lieutenant Boruvka slyly.

"No, I mean murderers!" Sergeant Malek retorted with some heat.

V

Whose Deduction?

L IEUTENANT BORUVKA WAS sitting at his office desk, gazing glumly out of the window at the dilapidated façade of the little old church in the narrow street opposite the back of the police station. A fresh early spring day was dying dimly away and in a niche in the church façade, where a sparrow family was building a nest, crouched a plaster St Sidonius. The statue and the lieutenant frowned at each other; the statue because the *fin de siècle* stucco artist had not been able to make him otherwise, the lieutenant because the saint had aroused in him uncomfortable moral misgivings

Not that the lieutenant was a religious man—he knew that the misshapen statue in the plaster cloak was an imaginary effigy of the Clermont-Ferrand bishop only because the inscription under it, standing out in relief, was visible from a distance. In his early youth he had attended instruction in religious knowledge and there a terribly dignified gentleman, Mr Meloun, had hammered the ten commandments into his round head. The little Father was awesome, of course, only in the eyes of the humble schoolboy. In reality he was a kindly man who came from Olesnice and even at the grammar school at K. had not lost his dialect, his habit of wearing long under-wear sticking out at the ankles even in the hottest summer and his exceptionally naive Catholic faith. He too had a round head, like his name and similar to that of the terrified sinner in the front row, who was later to become a detective. When he described sins and their commensurate infernal penalties, he rolled his eyes under their bushy brows in so blood-curdling a manner that subconscious taboos haunted his listener long after he had ceased to believe the beautiful folk tale about an innocent virgin, a good-hearted foster-father and a charitable

95

friend of ruffians, fishermen and prostitutes. A subconscious awareness that certain things were simply not done. Sometimes this had thwarted the lieutenant's own interests; but if it had been to his own disadvantage, others had invariably benefited.

Now, however, on this capricious spring evening, when a hint of lilac was perfuming the air from the Vltava, and the metropolis was humming with the life of its night clubs, pubs and theatres, Boruvka was about to do something that was not done. He intended to phone his wife and tell her that he would not be in for supper and would be home very late because he was going to a performance given by the Slovak Folk Song and Dance Ensemble then appearing in Prague. The cymbalist in the company was an old army friend of his, and after the show they would go somewhere for a beer—probably to Flek's.

In actual fact he was contemplating spending the time in quite a different manner. At 7.30—it was now seven—he intended to be at a particular wine tavern in the Old Town to meet the young policewoman who, unknowingly, had helped to solve the case of the murdered dancer at the Odeon Theatre. At the same time—and if she did not know this, she must at least have sensed it—she had affected his peace of mind in a most peculiar way. It seemed peculiar only to the lieutenant, of course. Otherwise, it was manifested in quite normal symptoms: every now and then his round face would assume the vacuous expression of a dreaming somnambulist, and he now on principle dictated to the policewoman various reports and announcements which he had always tapped out on the typewriter himself.

While dictating he would throw in an occasional sentence that had nothing to do with the matter in hand. To do this, he had to summon up all his—in other situations considerable—stock of courage. "Do you like working here?" he once asked her, for example, in the middle of a report about a man who had tried to poison his wife with sleeping tablets but fortunately in his agitation had given her a laxative by mistake. And if that sentence sounded innocent enough, the statement: "That hairstyle suits you, you should always wear it!" was a demonstration of bravery to the point of heroism. The lieutenant had paled, then reddened at his own audacity.

This had a significant—nay fateful—consequence, as it transpired much later. The hairstyle, a large, monstrously beautiful chignon (stuffed with a foam ring, of which the unsophisticated lieutenant was unaware) worn on the nape of the neck, became a permanent adornment on the girl's head—although until then she had worn an austere, smooth, businesslike style. She continued to wear it despite the fact that Sergeant Malek was transformed into a sworn enemy of the chignon. He exerted by no means inconsiderable efforts to persuade the policewoman that the old straight style suited the shape of her face far better. But his eloquence—of which, unlike Boruvka in his dealings with women, he had an abundance—was powerless against the lieutenant's single, diffident sentence: "That hairstyle suits you, you should always wear it!"

The girl did not wear the chignon in order to curry favour with her superior. True, its function was persuasive, but the hoped-for effect was entirely divorced from his office, and in this respect it was quite successful, as it turned out. It was slightly absurd and everyone at the police station, except Malek, joked about it. But that is the way of the world, and the lieutenat as he ruminated uneasily, face to face with the plaster saint, involuntarily recalled a sentence by a classical poet, which merged from the débris of his long forgotten Latin, and he experienced a moment—a very brief moment—when he saw things in their true light. The sentence ran: *Sic visum Veneri, cui placet impares formas atque animos sub iuga aenea saevo mittere cum ioco.* Rendered into a Czech translation, called in the time described in the historical writings of the scholarly teacher Jaroslav Zak* a "crib", it read: Thus was Venus seized with a whim, delighting in a cruel jest, uniting incompatible bodies and souls by common bonds.

Thirty years had elapsed since then, and now the lieutenant was pricked by a guilty conscience *ante factum*. The nearest he had got so far to sinning against the sixth commandment was another passage, inserted in a report on a woman who, unfortunately, had not mistaken a laxative for barbiturates, worded:

"Ahem. What are you doing this evening? Would you care—er

* Jaroslav Zak: a grammar school master famous in the thirties for his humorous stories about teachers and pupils.

—to have dinner with me? It would give us a chance to—er—well, have a little chat."

Its effect had been instantaneous and unequivocal.

So now Boruvka was sitting plagued with a butterfly stomach, premature pangs of conscience and various complexes about his age, and the frowning countenance of St Sidonius, which altogether added up to a state called voluptuous ecstasy. His hand was creeping irreversibly towards the telephone. It touched the receiver and hesitated. At that moment the cool breeze bore to the lieutenant's window the sinful voice of a saxophone from a record being played in the vicinity. The detective's heart contracted with banal, primeval desire and he lifted the receiver.

He did not dial the number, however. Before he could insert his finger in the dial, a woman's voice sounded in the receiver, uttering words which, formed by feminine lips, always excited erotic sensations in the lieutenant. Boruvka succumbed to the nation-wide indifference to propriety, combined with a technical hitch, known as a crossed line, and instead of hanging up, listened in. His eyes wandered to the saint and it seemed to him that that ancient worthy pulled a wry face. But he was not superstitious. He scowled at the battered bishop and pricked up his ears:

"I can't wait till they phone, Sidi! I'm off to the theatre. It's seven o'clock. I'll have to go."

A man's voice said impatiently:

"Don't be daft, girl. How else can I fix it?"

"But can't you understand? I have to be there. Ask every hour if the car has been found. I—"

Something crackled in the receiver; a blow sounded. The voice cried out in terror:

"Sidi! Sidi! He's here! He had a key! Sidi, help! He'll murder me! Si—"

The line was cut off. Boruvka was already on his feet, and his forehead was covered with beads of sweat.

Then he sat down and slowly replaced the receiver. Another ingredient had been added to the turmoil of his thoughts and self-reproaches. Senseless, he told himself. What can I do? A crossed line could not be checked at the post office. She could have phoned from any number within the Prague telephone area and she had not said anything by which he could establish her whereabouts. I'll have to wait, he thought cynically—and unbeknown to him this subconsciously swayed his mind in the opposite direction—until the man with the key kills her. Then I'll be called in, I'll discover clues, I'll follow them up, apprehend—

Had she really not said anything that would set him on the right track? Boruvka was on the verge of lifting the receiver in order to carry out his original intention, but he replaced it again. There were two clues, after all: the man was called Sidi and the girl was getting ready to leave for the theatre where she "had to be". Who "has to be" at a theatre? He put a rhetorical question to himself. In the first place, one would assume, an actress.

He glanced at his watch. Seven five. It was ten minutes to the Tomcat wine tavern. Suddenly a third fact sprang to his mind. The unknown woman had spoken Slovak.

SLUK!*

He looked at his watch again and hesitated. His inner eye mirrored the apple of temptation in the shape of a seductive, chestnut-coloured chignon on a swan-like neck. If he took a taxi, he could still make both. Or should he wash his hands of the whole affair? A voice that was not his own whispered in Boruvka's ear. The woman could have been exaggerating. A man came to slap her face for some undoubtedly justified reason and—

But he had been investigating murders for a good few years and he knew that in matters of life and death it was better to be a thousand times too zealous than once to turn a deaf ear.

The voice had not been his; he did not recognise it. He seized his hat and coat, threw an angry glance at the saint who was again looking as inscrutable as a sphinx, and tore out of his office.

He reached the theatre at seven fourteen, and his police credentials immediately secured him entrance to the dressing-room.

The air was bristling with nervous tension, which convinced Boruvka of the correctness of his deduction.

"Is someone missing?" he asked the agitated artistic director.

* The Slovak Folk Song and Dance Ensemble.

99

He had just offended his friend, the cymbalist, by cutting short his expressions of joy at their reunion. But he really had no time.

"Yes. You know about it, comrade lieutenant?" asked the director in amazement, and led Boruvka into a small office which was almost entirely taken up by a desk strewn with papers.

"Yes. The name?"

"Pavol Rohac."

"What?"

"Rohac. Pavol."

"Aren't you a woman short?"

"No. The women are all here. Rohac is missing. Without him we can't do the Brigands' Dance. And that's our big number, comrade!"

Boruvka was once again strongly tempted to drop the whole thing. In his heart he was already feeling ashamed of his deduction. What had he actually deduced? That some Slovak girl had to go to a theatre, of which there were probably thirty in Prague, and that a Slovak folk song and dance company happened to be performing in Prague? He looked at his watch again. Seven seventeen. He could still make it.

"We phoned him," the distraught director continued. "He left a number with Jozka and the name of the girl, saying he'd be there this afternoon and evening—"

"Yes?" prompted Boruvka, interested in spite of himself.

"A Vera Selucka. We phoned but we must have got the wrong number. A fellow answered but when we said we wanted to talk to Mr Rohac, he lost his head and banged down the receiver. When I dialled again, he slammed down the receiver as soon as he had picked it up."

Boruvka frowned. Automatically he looked at his watch, asking: "What number was it?"

"Half a sec, I wrote it down on the blotting pad." The director turned and leaned over the table. The blotting paper with something written on it was lying on the table in front of an empty chair.

"Seven, eight, eight, three, two, six," he read out with difficulty, while Boruvka jotted it down in his notebook and added to it the name of Vera Selucka.

In the public call box opposite the stage doorman's desk in the theatre he dialled directory enquiries. He did not wish to involve himself in the case within the artistic director's earshot, because he was determined that in five minutes at the latest he would be sitting in the intimately cosy wine tavern awaiting the advent of his opportunity to sin, the first in eighteen years of marriage. At the same time he wanted to have a clear conscience.

"Hullo!" answered the vexed voice of the telephonist on duty.

Boruvka pressed the button and said, "Would you mind telling me the address of a subscriber whose number is—"

"Hullo," repeated the vexed voice even more surlily.

Boruvka quickly pressed the button a second time.

"Hullo," he cried. "Can you hear me?"

"Hurry up! Say what you want!" The girl, who plainly regarded any kind of enquiry as an intolerable nuisance, waited a moment and as Boruvka banged the coin box furiously, hung up. Only then did Boruvka notice that an unknown public-spirited person had scratched on the paint of the coin box: Watch out! It doesn't work, but it steals! He swore, ran out of the call box, glanced at his watch, and cursing afresh burst into the adjacent call box. There the whole procedure was repeated, and when the girl finally began to dictate, Boruvka, crushed by the arrogance of her tone, wrote the name down quickly in his notebook—Dr Radegast Tejlibenovsky. He wasn't sure whether he had caught it correctly, but he hadn't the nerve to ask the girl again, and anyway he had his work cut out to scribble down the address rattled off in a half-mumble between her teeth: Dejvice, Podbaba, Okrouhla 6. He dashed out of the box, pulled up, paused irresolutely, then spun round like lightning and shot back into the box. He dialled Dr Tejlibenovsky's number, but there was no answer. With the receiver to his ear, Boruvka watched the march of the second-hand impatiently, muttering under his breath a certain obscene word several times in quick succession. On the dirty, scrawled-over wall of the call box a vision of the young policewoman appeared, entering the Tomcat tavern, looking round, searching for him, a lecher at the next table watching her with a leer—and now she was sitting in the corner, poor thing, telling the over-alacritous waiter that she would wait for a little while, that she was expecting someone . . .

He realised that Dr Tejlibenovsky's phone was still ringing in an empty flat, and hung up angrily.

He flung himself out of the call box.

He returned to it immediately, turned the pages of the directory frenziedly and dialled a number.

"The Tomcat tavern? Would you mind asking Comrade—Miss—" when he uttered the girl's name, he felt a stab in his heart, "—to come to the phone, please."

He waited a moment. Then his eardrums were caressed by a well-known velvety voice.

"I must apologise, comrade," he stuttered. "Something—something's cropped up. No, no, don't go home. I'll be a little late—if you'd wait for me . . . No, order dinner. I'll have something later—I'll be along in about half an hour—an hour at the latest. Yes, it's a murder, or rather a suspicion—well, I must take a look at it. You'll wait for me, won't you?" he pleaded and into his voice crept a note of anxiety incommensurate with the misfortune represented by a young female member of the police force not waiting in a wine tavern for one of her superior officers.

The girl heard it quite unmistakably.

"I'll wait for you, comrade lieutenant," she purred as softly as a kitten. "Don't worry!"

The lieutenant hung up, and despite the fact that somewhere someone—perhaps Dr Tejlibenovsky in Podbaba—had murdered a Vera Selucka, his face was wreathed in a blissful smile.

He quickly straightened his face, ran out of the theatre and called a taxi.

He reached Okrouhla Street at seven forty-two and absent-mindedly paid the taxi driver and let him go. At seven forty-three he was ringing the bell at the garden gate of a super modern villa, bearing a brass plate inscribed with the words

Dr Radegast Tejlibenovsky
Professor at the Academy of Arts

The villa, standing on its own on a hill top, commanded a view of the Dejvice valley over the roofs of other villas lower down the road.

Whose Deduction?

No one answered. The wide window on the ground floor mirrored the scene behind the lieutenant: a distant panorama of Prague with a red star shining on the International Hotel and a honey-yellow moon in its spring fulness.

Boruvka pressed the button once more impatiently, looked at his watch and grasped the handle.

The gate was open.

He walked quickly towards the house door, crunching over the small white stones on the path. In the silence of the residential district the noise sounded like gunshots. He found that the front door was ajar. He knocked, there was no answer. He entered.

It was dark inside. He took his torch out of his pocket and flashed the beam over the walls of the hall. They were hung with pictures—or had been until recently. Now there remained only lighter patches on the distemper.

Boruvka was overpowered by an intuitive premonition. He looked round and saw an open door leading into a room. He went in. It was a large ground floor salon with the wide window which from the outside mirrored the sea of lights. Only now did Boruvka observe that it too was open a crack.

And he noticed further light patches on the walls. He noticed the glass-doored sideboard yawning with emptiness. He noted the heavy Persian carpet which was lying rolled up by the wall. His eyes took in the statues, heaped up in the middle of the table, from which chairs were missing. Either Dr Tejlibenovsky was moving, or—and where was Vera Selucka? He left the room quickly and went upstairs. He looked into several rooms, which showed no preparations for moving house, but there was no sign of any Vera, dead or alive, or of a struggle.

Boruvka returned to the landing and was about to go downstairs—a further nervous glance at his watch had shown him that it was eight o'clock—when at that moment it crossed his mind that he had forgotten to phone his wife. He looked round. There was a telephone on a table in the corner above the staircase. He picked up the receiver and dialled.

"Boruvkova," snapped an impatient voice at the other end of the line.

"It's me, Lucinka," cooed the lieutenant. "Don't hold dinner for me, there's a good girl. I have a sudden case—"

"Where are you, for heaven's sake? I've been phoning the office for half an hour. Come home straight away! Instead of going to her piano lesson, Zuzka went to the cinema with that flashy character, that Spacek. I happened to go there too, and copped them myself. So come home and have it out with her. She's getting beyond me."

Mrs Boruvkova's energetic tone belied her professed defeatism. The lieutenant adopted an impotently threatening tone:

"What? Tell her she's got it coming to her. I'll give her—"

What he'd give her he left unsaid. Cautious steps scrunched up the path to the main entrance, and the door was opened softly. The lieutenant hung up and crouched down behind the bannisters.

The man who entered was evidently not Dr Tejlibenovsky. He did not switch on the light, but crossed the hall as noiselessly as a cat and disappeared into the large ground floor room. He was carrying a cabin trunk. The next minute a suspicious clinking sound emanated from the salon. The lieutenant straightened up and saw through the window in the hall a white Volga drawn up in front of the villa. It gleamed phosphorescently in the nocturnal darkness, through which the radiance of the city rose from the valley to meet the dewy stars.

The lieutenant slipped his hand under his armpit and drew out his revolver. Then he crept on tiptoe downstairs and looked into the large room through the open door. A man was standing by the table, taking the statues one by one from the pile on the top, and putting them hurriedly into the cabin trunk. He was wearing white suede gloves. The wide-open window silhouetted another man who was commenting on the activity of the one busy with the case.

"For Gawd's sake, watch it, Tonda! Don't smash a bloody thing!"

The lieutenant sighed quietly but did nothing. Scowling, he watched the man who had finished packing the statues and was looking round. The lieutenant followed his gaze so that he too let his eyes rest upon a decorative pedestal made of wood inlay in the corner of the room. The pedestal supported a gilded wooden figure which gleamed in the diffused light.

The man stood looking at the statue as though mesmerised.

"What are you gawping at, Tonda?" cried the voice from the window.

"At that over there. Shall I take it?"

"What is it?"

"I dunno. A saint or sump'n, I reckon."

"Is it bronze?"

"No, gilded wood."

"Sod it."

"You bloody fool, it may have great artistic value."

"Sod artistic value. Shove over the case and grab the carpet."

The man with the case did not stir. He gazed at the statue in fascination.

"Get a move on! The case!"

Only then did he move. He shut the case, lifted it and with an effort hoisted it on to the window sill. The man outside the window heaved it out and disappeared. Steps crunched over the path and then a car door clicked.

The man who had remained in the room turned and bent over the rolled carpet. But he straightened up again, his attention riveted by the dully gleaming statue. He walked over to it. In the light of the moon it looked as though the two, statue and man, were gazing into each other's eyes. Boruvka hardly dared to breathe. The scene reminded him of something; he couldn't recall what. At that moment the man made up his mind and reached for the statue.

At that moment Lieutenant Boruvka also made up his mind. He strode resolutely into the room, switched on his torch and aiming his pistol at the man, ordered him sternly:

"Put up your hands!"

The man swung round, holding the gilded statue in his right hand. Blinded, he blinked at the light and raised the hand with the statue and the other, empty one, above his head. The lieutenant advancing towards him, stepped on something which on the parquet floor denuded of carpet slipped away from under his feet. He lost his balance and sprawled out on the floor.

The man took advantage of this. Not to fall upon Boruvka in the best gangster fashion, but to dive for the window. He swung his legs over the sill and disappeared into the starry night, taking the statue with him.

Boruvka sprang to his feet and with one bound was beside the window. In the moonlight he saw the fleeing figure distinctly. The man was streaking towards the garden gate, and the golden statue in his hand was describing sparkling curves, reminiscent of Ptolemy's epicycles.

"Lojza! Start her up!" he yelled.

Boruvka slowly raised his pistol, half closing his left eye. The fugitive fluttered in the V of the backsight as though pinned to the black foresight. A strange pity touched the lieutenant's heart. Dr Tejlibenovsky's villa was enveloped in a beautiful, humid spring night. Treacherous, phantasmal and fraught with folly. The fugitive ran up to the car and jumped in. Boruvka waited until the car started moving. Then he fired. He aimed at the tyres.

He fired only once because the car turned sharply behind the hedge and was lost to view. Boruvka did not want to shoot blindly, for there were human beings in the car.

When the car with the intruders had disappeared, the detective sighed and looked at his watch. It was clearly all a mistake, he thought with relief, and the best thing to do would be to forget about Vera Selucka. I'll report this to the station from the phone upstairs, wait until the comrades arrive, and I'll be at the Tomcat by nine o'clock at the latest. In his stomach a tremor of anxiety blended with a feeling of deliverance in a heterogeneous mixture. Maybe she was still waiting—but perhaps she had already left.

He looked out of the window again, sighing. He was filled with pleasurable excitement. The next minute he frowned. Below, in the street skirting the garden suburb, the white Volga had appeared: it was careering drunkenly down the road into the valley. The lieutenant discovered to his displeasure that visibility from Dr Tejlibenovsky's window was unnecessarily good, and that the road, down which the car with the thieves was zigzagging, curved along the side of the huge natural amphitheatre clearly lit by the moon, and vanished near the grammar school. There was nothing for it but to obey the voice of duty and follow the beams from the headlights until they disappeared from sight. It seemed to take ages. He looked at his watch and subconsciously regretted that he had fired at all, even if only at the tyres. In the meantime, the Volga was meandering slowly and wantonly, its path traceable against the dark background of the villas.

Boruvka scowled and swore under his breath. The car had stopped. Its lights were switched off and in the ensuing darkness it whitened like an outsize phantom.

The lieutenant was caught in a fresh dilemma. The thieves had obviously overlooked the fact that they could be seen from the scene of their crime. Boruvka had the chance to act quickly and effectively. And the girl in the meantime—perhaps at least she had ordered dinner. . . . With rising irritation, he realised that he was a pitiable victim of a sense of duty. He had known it for a long time, but as long as his duty had clashed with his presence at the family hearth, it had not bothered him. Now he was annoyed because he could not sit in the Tomcat wine tavern. And also because he wanted to sit in the Tomcat wine tavern. Suddenly it began to annoy him that he was supposed to be sitting there. Unaccountably, he felt a twinge of something akin to inexplicable hatred towards the young policewoman. He didn't know why. Was it because she had destroyed his peace of mind and shaken the foundations of the world which, like every man, he had laboriously built up; because he wanted her and was afraid of her and of the consequences of the things for which he longed? He shook his head, muttered a four-letter word, glanced desperately at his watch, and leapt out of the window with remarkable agility for one of his bulk.

Outside, in the fresh air of the spring night, burdened with transgressions against divine commandments and articles of the penal code, he mercifully succumbed to the hunter's instinct. He pressed his hands to his chest and set off at a gallop along the road leading in a wide sweep into the valley.

He reached the white Volga very short of breath. It was empty, the door was open and the key was in the ignition. He bent down to look at the rear tyre. It was punctured and the rim of the wheel was nearly flush with the road. The lieutenant derived little satisfaction from his direct hit.

He straightened up and looked at the house. It was a tall, two-storey villa divided into flats. The first floor windows shone with light, and in the distance incensed voices were raised in dispute.

Boruvka went up to the garden gate and examined the cards showing the names of the inhabitants. He stiffened. A visiting card inserted in the middle slot bore the name:

ANTONIN SELUCKY
Representative of the State Insurance Company
Tel. 788329

He felt as though an immaterial finger had touched something inside him, his soul or his conscience, had tickled him mockingly and pointed to the number. He quickly drew his notebook out of his pocket. Yes. There it was: Vera Selucka, 788326. The last digit did not tally.

He recalled that the artistic director of the Slovak Folk Song and Dance Ensemble had dictated the number, leaning across the table. He had read it from the blotting paper—upside-down! Nothing would have been simpler than to mistake a nine for six.

A coincidence?

Coincidence? An alien voice taunted him. Boruvka pulled a wry face and examined the front of the villa. He thought he glimpsed a figure, lurking on the first-floor balcony, its back pressed against the wall next to one of the windows from which light was streaming.

Without further ado, he ran into the house and raced up to the first floor. He stopped outside the door bearing an identical visiting card to the one at the side of the gate. There could be no mistake. A man and a woman were quarrelling inside the flat. But—when he put his ear to the door— he recognised that they were arguing in Czech.

Notwithstanding, he rang the bell.

The door was opened by a man in a violent temper, braces and an open stiff white collar of a kind the lieutenant had not seen on a living person for at least twenty years.

This made him notice all the more the smart, light brown, man's coat made of polyvinyl, indubitably a foreign product, which was hanging on the hallstand next to a black, man's coat with raglan sleeves and a velvet collar.

"What do you want?" the man snarled at him.

108

"I'm sorry to trouble you," said the lieutenant showing his credentials.

"Aha!" This seemed to suit the man's book. "The police! Who are you looking for?"

"I'm on the track of two thieves. They left their car standing outside your house—"

"Two?" the man interrupted him. "I hope only one has been here. I hope!" he turned menacingly to someone inside the room and then back to the lieutenant. "Come in."

Boruvka followed him into the room. The French window obviously led on to the balcony; the couch in the corner was occupied by a pretty, tearful woman of about thirty-five. She did not look up at Boruvka.

"We've had a thief here!" the man in braces raged. "A stealer of chastity. A wife-stealer!"

"I'm looking for stealers of art objects," remarked the detective quietly.

"To the devil with them!" the man exploded. "Vera! Look at the inspector!"

The woman did not raise her head.

"You're ashamed, aren't you? Ashamed! But you weren't ashamed before!"

Boruvka bowed politely in the direction of the silent woman. "Lieutenant Boruvka."

"Vera Selucka." The man spoke for her in a mocking voice. "Mrs Vera Selucka. My wife. My wife and—a tart!"

The woman shuddered. Boruvka's gaze fell on a large ashtray with three cigarette ends.

"Yes! And clever too!" fumed the gentleman in braces. "I can't help thinking, inspector, that it's like a French farce. I set off on a business trip—I miss the train—the next one doesn't leave till the morning. I return home—everything is as it should be here. Except," he bawled, "except that my powers of observation had not been reckoned with! An insurance broker has to be sharp! He must have eyes everywhere! He must notice every trifle! Look here!" He seized the ashtray so violently that the stubs nearly fell out of it. "I don't smoke. She says she smoked them herself. But she hasn't got the paper packet from them. She says she flushed it down the lavatory. Ha! Ha! The only thing is the lavatory doesn't flush, inspector. I tried it. It doesn't flush! And there's no bucket there. Oh no! No fucking bastard is going to fool me. Nothing escapes me."

He turned to the woman and yelled:

"Who did you have here, you whore?"

The woman looked up for the first time. She cast a side glance at the French window but the sharp-eyed gentleman did not notice. She had blue eyes, reddened round the pupils.

"No one," she whispered.

"Don't lie! I'm too sharp for you to wriggle out of this. I notice every detail! Even such a trifle as three cigarette ends in the ashtray!" the gentleman roared.

The woman cast another glance in the direction of the French window, and the lieutenant thought it strange that for all his powers of observation the man had overlooked the polyvinyl coat in the hall—for he was sure that a wearer of braces and stiff white collars could not be the owner of a polyvinyl overcoat.

Eyeing the pot-bellied husband, beside himself with rage, Boruvka felt sorry for the tearful woman. Again the finger prodded him in the chest. He remembered the girl waiting in the wine tavern and hoped fervently that she had left.

"Might I trouble you to go down with me and identify the car?" he asked.

"Of course!" cried Selucky vehemently. "*I* respect the law. *I* fulfil my obligations! Civil and matrimonial! Get up!" he ordered the woman rudely, and when she had risen to her feet, he pushed her roughly into the hall so that she tripped over the door sill. The lieutenant pitied her again; then he felt ashamed of his compassion, but quickly placed himself between the gentleman and the polyvinyl coat.

It wasn't necessary however. The sharp-sighted husband was afflicted with blindness in his newly inflated jealousy.

"I don't know it!" he declared brusquely in front of the villa. "I've never seen it before. No one round here has a car like that. Not like that. I'd know because I handle all the insurance round here."

While the lady was examining it, Boruvka looked cautiously over her head at the balcony. Light was still streaming from the window, but the figure had vanished. Boruvka frowned. He accompanied the couple back upstairs but when the gentleman in braces had unlocked the door, he drew back.

"Thank you for your co-operation. I won't come in. I have finished actually. Goodbye."

Before the sharp-eyed Selucky shut the door, prior to indulging in a further bout of bullying, Boruvka noticed that the polyvinyl coat had disappeared from the hallstand.

He stood in front of the villa and gazed down at the town. He drew a deep breath and looked at his watch. Eight forty-five. Shouldn't he really wash his hands of the whole affair? The woman—she wasn't Vera Selucka—had already been murdered God knew where. He sighed. Cut up in polythene bags perhaps and the murderer was throwing them into litter bins, Neruda style.* Poor woman; but what could he do for her? He knew nothing about her except that she was Slovak. His line of reasoning leading to SLUK, and all his other deductions, had proved false. He could have been sitting in the wine tavern all this time. Why the devil did he have to get involved in such a crazy nocturnal hunt?

Why the devil?

The devil?

He shook his head and he did not know how far the devil was to blame and how far he was himself. And what exactly did he want or not want, anyway? Suddenly he felt that the only thing he wanted was never to have started anything with the policewoman.

Stairs inside the villa creaked under footsteps, as he had expected. He bent down quickly and climbed into the back of the Volga. He peeped over the edge of the window and saw a fair-haired young man furtively leaving the villa. He was dressed in the light brown overcoat which had been hanging in the flat of the eagle-eyed Selucky.

The young man looked round on all sides and glanced at his watch; then the Volga caught his eye. Boruvka crouched down on the floor. He felt the car bounce slightly as someone dropped into the front seat and slammed the door. The ignition key was turned,

---

* A reference to a short story written by Jan Neruda (1834–91), a leading Czech classical poet and author.

the engine growled then started up. The driver changed gear and the Volga moved forward.

Boruvka hurriedly sat up to warn the driver about the deflated tyre, and caught sight of his round face in the mirror. The driver did too. Startled out of his wits, he wrenched the steering wheel frenziedly. The car skidded, street lamps whizzed wildly past the window, there was a screech, probably of brakes, and Boruvka was thrown into the back seat. The front wheels ran into something hard and unyielding, the car leapt into the air, then came a thud and a crash and suddenly everything went quiet. The lieutenant sat up and saw the man at the wheel trying frantically and fruitlessly to open the door. His efforts were in vain because the car was wedged between the two concrete posts of a front garden gate. The two men were virtually imprisoned.

"Stop trying; you won't make it in time for the Brigands' Dance anyway, comrade Rohac," remarked the lieutenant calmly.

The fair-haired young man's eyes popped out of his head.

"Which one are you?" he gasped. "Mr Blatny? No—Mr Matejka?"

"No," said the detective gloomily. "You haven't had anything to do with my wife. She's Italian and therefore an ardent Catholic. She has strict moral principles and wouldn't be taken in by a womaniser like you—" He bit off his words, for the immaterial finger had again brushed his conscience. "Ahem," he cleared his throat and added weakly: "And that sort of thing."

"Do you mind telling me who you are?"

"Lieutenant Boruvka," said the detective. "Is this your car?"

Rohac writhed in embarrassment.

"No," he replied. "But I didn't want to pinch it, lieutenant. I just wanted to get to the theatre in time for the interval at all cost. In time for the Brigands' Dance."

Boruvka looked a his watch. Eight fifty-two.

"What time is the interval?"

"Nine o'clock. It lasts a quarter of an hour. I could still make it, lieutenant!"

His attractive eyes pleaded eloquently.

"All right," said the lieutenant. "If you can get out of here, run along. And drop in on us tomorrow."

"I won't let you down," gulped the young man gratefully, and began turning down the window. An idea occurred to Boruvka.

"Listen, is there a Sidi in your company?"

"Mr Sidi?"

"No, no. A Christian name Sidi."

"We don't have any Arabs in our company, lieutenant."

"I don't know about an Arab." The lieutenant was recalling other things. "Simply Sidi."

"Sidi, Sidi," mumbled the young man agitatedly, his attention on the window. "Sidi, Sidi, Sidi—"

"Oh, get along!"

"Thanks a lot, lieutenant," the young man sang out, and began to squeeze agilely through the open window. Boruvka became wrapt in thought.

"Come on out! We're waiting for you!" cried a grating voice which Boruvka recognised unmistakably as that of a uniformed official. The dancer moaned:

"But captain! I didn't do anythin'! It's an accident!"

"Yeah" said the voice. "It is. And this car is stolen"

"But I didn't pinch it!"

"No, you were driving it back to the owner, I suppose."

Boruvka looked out of the window and saw two members of the police force. One of them had an open notebook and was studying the car's registration number. Then he snapped the notebook shut and exclaimed curtly:

"Let's go! Is there anyone else there?"

"Me," said Boruvka, sticking his round head out of the window.

"Yes, comrade lieutenant," said the thin sergeant in a shabby room of the police station at the corner of the street. "That car was stolen in Zizkov at five-thirty this afternoon—"

"So I can prove I didn't pinch it!" burst out the young man who had been peeping over the partition at the wall clock. The hands were moving inexorably towards nine. Boruvka looked at him.

"Can you?" he asked almost reproachfully.

Rohac scratched behind his ear.

"Actually, I can't," he said despairingly. "It—I could, but

consideration for a certain lady prevents me. Unless the lieutenant could vouch for me . . ."

Boruvka waved his hand.

"Let him go. I know him. He'll have to pay for the damage to the car, that's why you'd better let him go—so that he'll have something to pay for it with."

Calling out his thanks, the young man made off rapidly.

"Who is the owner?" asked the lieutenant.

"A," the thin sergeant consulted the report book, "Zdenek Farkas, address V mlazi 3, Zizkov. He's on the phone. We'll give him a blow and tell him his car's been found."

The sergeant dialled a number and waited. Boruvka noted gloomily the posters adorning the empty office. They were left-overs from the personality cult of the fifties. The room was not exactly spick and span, but Boruvka didn't notice that. He became engrossed in his private thoughts, admitting to himself that he hoped the policewoman would lose patience. He realised with relief that it was highly probable she had given up. But even while his guilty conscience was eased, a feeling of regret and a gnawing sadness reminded him that if she did not hold out, a chance would be lost for ever. Maybe the last. And again Boruvka did not know what he really wanted.

The sergeant was still waiting with the receiver at his ear. The office door opened and the early spring scent of awakening trees and a fat policeman were wafted in. He was dragging a very large case.

Boruvka kept his thoughts to himself when he saw the case. He recognised it as the piece of luggage into which the thief had packed the loot from Dr Tejlibenovsky's villa.

"Look Vasek," gasped the fat policeman. "Look what I've got! But they gave me the slip!"

"He's not answering," said the sergeant irritably. "He was told to stay put, but now there's no answer."

"Phew!" gasped the fat policeman. "What a weight" With Boruvka's help, he heaved the case on to the counter. The lieutenant looked at it as though he couldn't believe his own eyes.

"I was walking along with Jarda, Vasek," the corpulent policeman continued breathlessly, removing his cap, "and two

young fellahs are coming towards us with this case. You bet I
sized them up straight away. And I was right. As soon as I
stopped them and said: 'Your documents, please,' they lost their
nerve and scrammed. Jarda chased them, but we didn't catch 'em.
Well, perhaps there's something in the case."

Boruvka was silent with amazement, and when the fat policeman opened the case, he blinked and rubbed his eyes.

The case was full of statues made of bronze, alabaster, marble,
fired clay and plaster, and on top lay a gilded figure depicting a
bearded man in a flowing Baroque cloak.

Boruvka rubbed his eyes once more and blinked again.

The pedestal bore the clearly legible inscription:

ST SIDONIUS

For the second time that evening the crack detective had
encountered the little-known saint.

"Well, I never!" exclaimed the fat, purple-faced policeman.
"They must have robbed a museum somewhere!"

"There's no answer," said the sergeant, and hung up. "What
have you got? Smugglers?" he asked hopefully.

"Smugglers, my foot! A coupla kids. Flashy jerks. They were
in a blue funk. Yep," the rotund policeman began to rummage
among the statues. "But they were professionals. When we
copped 'em, they were both wearing gloves. So there won't be
any fingerprints on these here gimgaws. Hey!" he cried with
sudden enthusiasm, taking a white alabaster statue out of the
case. "Hey, look Vasek! Nice goings on, eh?"

Boruvka had retained enough of his classical education to
recognise the wife of the Spartan king Tyndareus, reclining in
the embrace of Zeus who cunningly transformed himself into a
swan for the occasion.

An idea began to germinate in his mind.

"Could it be a penal offence, keeping such bits of perversion
at home?" asked the fat policeman dreamily, but his attention
was soon attracted by something else.

"Or this—quite something, isn't it?" he picked up a statue.
"Must be Franta Jerabek, Vasek, remember? Remember—at
swimming instruction." The fat policeman guffawed, and the thin
sergeant looked at the statue with interest. It portrayed Priapus,

the ancient Greek God of Fertility. It could not have resembled the legendary Jerabek in anything but its copulatory organ. It had no other distinguishing feature.

The lieutenant's head was buzzing with amorphous thoughts —he could not yet give them shape—but they were beginning to link up in a chain of deduction.

He examined the wooden statue of the saint which the pot-bellied policeman had laid aside as being of absolutely no interest.

Then he glanced at the report book on the counter.

SANCTUS SIDONIUS

That was a Latin name.

ZD. FARKAS

That was a Slovak name.

The educated lieutenant knew that until fairly recently Latin had been the official language in Slovakia.

"Zd" was an abbreviation for the Christian name "Zdenek". "Zdenek" was the Czech form of the Latin "Sidonius". As the latter was an inconveniently long, old-fashioned name with a suffix which evoked atonement and prayer rather than billing and cooing, why shouldn't a mistress shorten it to the honeyed "Sidi"?

Sidi who was to "ask every hour whether the car had been found"?

That's what I call deduction, thought Boruvka.

"Oh, yes, as I was saying, they were whippersnappers, but they were working with gloves on," sighed the corpulent policeman, putting on his cap. "Young but pros!"

Boruvka felt inside the case thoughtfully. The two policemen had taken out all the statues and stood them in a row on the counter. The case was lined with brown paper. Boruvka removed it and turned it over. On the other side a clumsy hand had written an address in indelible pencil:

Alois Broda Esq.,
Praha—Zizkov,
Na Majzlovce 7,
3rd floor across the courtyard

"They were not pros," said Boruvka sadly.

*　　*　　*

116

Whose Deduction?

He was taken to Zizkov in a police car. As the two policemen chatted excitedly the whole way, he had no time to probe his own problem. But it was still fermenting at the back of his mind.

He got out at the corner of Na Majzlovce and while the other two banged on the heavy outer door of the dingy block of flats which feigned to be dead and deserted, he turned round the corner into V zavetri Street and strode quickly over the moonlit stretch of waste land strewn with tins, paper and condoms towards a few houses standing on their own at the top of a hill, which together formed the street called V mlazi. It was nearly half past nine, and the lieutenant surmised with relief and regret that the policewoman would not wait any longer than two hours.

Number 3 was a poor working-class house with a window on either side of the door. It was dark inside, but when the lieutenant drew nearer, he noticed a small light moving inside. It was not difficult to look in through the ground-floor window. When he did so, he grew very sad, for a melancholy sight met his eyes.

He saw a small but cosy room with surprisingly modern furniture, which was revealed bit by bit by the beam of a pocket torch. When his eyes grew accustomed to the darkness, he made out a person bound and gagged lying on a couch by the wall and another sitting in an armchair. The one in the armchair was a man, the one on the couch—judging by the nylon-clad leg glistening when the torchlight fell on it—was a woman. The room was being searched by another man who was not wasting time clearing up after himself. At that moment he was going through the contents of a chest of drawers. In the moonlight white, pink and pale blue clouds of dainty women's underwear were flying through the air like large butterflies, as the man tossed them on to the floor.

The large mantel clock on the light oak chest of drawers indicated a quarter to ten.

Boruvka sighed, stepped back from the window and looked round. The house was surrounded by a garden with a low fence. This did not represent a serious obstacle. Boruvka climbed over it nimbly and found himself at the back entrance. He turned the handle and the door moved. The windowless corridor exuded a chill dampness.

He too took out his torch and entered cautiously. He stopped at the door on the right and peered through the key-hole. The intruder's back, bent over the chest of drawers, was in his line of vision. This suited the lieutenant. He slipped his hand under his arm and drew out—for the second time that evening—a flat pistol. He turned the handle and flung open the door. The man spun round and was blinded by the beam of light.

"Hands up!" cried Boruvka reluctantly.

This man, however, more closely resembled a big-time Chicago gangster. He hurled himself violently at the lieutenant who, as usual, had not the heart to shoot. Therefore a tussle ensued.

The struggle did not last long. The man was strong, but he had not learnt the basic jujitsu holds, and so he was no match for Boruvka, who had once earned his living as a physical training instructor. When he had tied his assailant's hands behind his back with the cord of a man's silk dressing-gown lying on the floor, he turned the light on and went over to the couch to perform a more pleasant duty: that of liberating the woman who had been assaulted. His pleasure was enhanced by the discovery that she was a comely young girl endowed with the kind of generous curves which can be resisted—sometimes—only after three score years and ten.

He untied her, tenderly removed the gag from her mouth and smiled.

"Thank you very much," she said in melodious Slovak, and Boruvka turned to the man in the armchair.

He was a scrawny, sparrow-like little man. The lieutenant soon relieved him of his bonds and as he straightened up, everything went dark in front of his eyes, and red and green stars leapt out of the blackness. He turned round with difficulty. Behind him stood the girl armed with a rolling pin, her arm raised to deliver another blow.

This too was no problem for the crack detective, although he had been taken unawares. He caught the girl by her slim arm and gently twisted the weapon from her grasp. He was seized by the throat from behind and a puny fist hammered on his head. This, however, produced nothing more than two tiny green stars. The lieutenant took a judo hold and flung the little pip-squeak forward over his shoulder on to the floor, where he remained inert.

Boruvka stepped back.

"Take it easy!" he said soothingly. "What are you playing at, citizens?"

He looked round at the gathering, but all three preserved a deep, hostile silence. Previously they had been at daggers drawn, now they had joined forces against the law in true gangster fashion.

"Well," sighed the lieutenant, "let's take things in order."

At ten-thirty, after a complicated and unsavoury investigation, he knew everything. It was a sordid case of blackmail. The trap was one which cried to high heaven in its transparency, and yet intelligent people fell into it again and again and probably always would, as victims of the painful delusion which lack of self-discipline combined with certain glandular activity defines as that phenomenon romantically described by the troubadours of long ago as love.

The man who had tried to turn the comfortable little dwelling into as big a shambles as possible was a high-ranking ministerial official whose career was at a turning point. The outcome depended upon the result of his feverish search. His prospects should have been excellent, for he had married into the family of a highly respected and even more highly placed state functionary. since he was far from incapable, possessed a passable origin and applied above average assiduity, it could not be said that his rapid rise was due only to wire-pulling. But his prospects could equally well have plummeted to zero, or at least have taken on a far less rosy hue; for the daughter of the highly placed functionary was extremely jealous. The woman graced with intoxicating physical charms, who had attempted to fell the lieutenant with a rolling pin, had in her possession certain letters written by the ministerial official that winter when he had been convinced that those shapely curves were vital to his existence. On the advice of Sidi Farkas, the woman had decided to put the letters to advantageous use: Mr Farkas, although almost devoid of any kind of shape, wielded over her an irresistible and inexplicable power. In despair the official had resorted to force. Sidi had made an abortive attempt to come to her aid, having guessed immediately whom she had referred to in the telephone conversation over-heard by Boruvka on a crossed line. Believing Boruvka to be one of their victims, or possibly another blackmailer, but in any case an enemy, the two of them had tried to get rid of him as soon as he had freed them from their humiliating situation.

By ten thirty the lieutenant had wormed out the whole story. At ten forty he made his way back over the moonlit waste land strewn with tins, papers and condoms, carrying the fateful letters in his pocket, resolved to destroy them in his office. He was also reflecting gloomily on the moral and practical advantages of conjugal fidelity.

He reached his office at eleven o'clock and opened the window. The moon, to which atmospheric elements had imparted a greenish hue, hung over the pantile roofs of the now silent town and illuminated the time-scarred façade of the little church and the hoary figure of the plaster saint.

Boruvka sighed, brooding over the girl with the attractive chignon and the swanlike neck; and over his quarrelsome wife to whom he had been faithful for eighteen years. He gave a thought too to Vera Selucka and the ministerial official whom he had just saved from the consequences of compromising infidelity.

He sighed again. His thoughts returned to the girl with the swanlike neck and a wave of deliverance mixed with regret swept over him. It was eleven o'clock. She must have had the sense to go home, he thought sadly and yet with relief. But it turned out that the girl had no sense. When Boruvka dialled the Tom-cat's number, he did not need to describe her in detail.

"Yes, the young lady is still waiting for you!" said the charac-teristically foxy voice of a waiter. "One moment, please!"

In that one moment Boruvka relived his whole life. And for no particular reason a heavy weight of fear and anxiety descended upon him. He didn't know exactly what he was afraid of.

"Comrade lieutenant?" The voice at the other end of the line was like an idealised shawm playing poetical metaphors.

"Yes," he answered hoarsely.

"I thought you weren't coming," said the girl quietly. She

paused. Boruvka heard his heart beating. Then artfully, compellingly, seductively, like a kitten or a snake, she said: "Come!"

"I—" croaked the lieutenant. He looked desperately out of the window, and was stunned with such regret, such fear and such longing for his lost peace of mind—guilty conscience or faint-heartedness—he didn't know which—that he became tongue-tied. When, after a pause, the girl whispered softly: "Hullo?" he took the cowardly way out and hung up.

Looking out of the window, his eye fell on the weather-beaten saint. Boruvka scowled at him. Go to Jericho, he growled under his breath. You're the last one to understand! You and your ten commandments! He stood up, resolved to terminate all entanglements. From now on the relationship between him and the young policewoman would be ruled by strictly official courtesy.

And he would dismiss it from his mind.

With a tinge of pride he recalled how little he had had to go on at the beginning of that crazy evening, what scant information he had had at his disposal, and how his fantastic deduction had guided him to success—and, it occurred to him, back to burdensome fidelity. He shook himself.

He looked out of the window again, and frowned. He had had another hallucination. He could have sworn that the plaster statue had leered at him lewdly.

Hell, he said to himself, whose deduction was it really?

VI

The Case of the Horizontal Trajectory

"REPORT ON THE Clarification of the Case of the Horizontal Trajectory." Lieutenant Boruvka, who had a fondness for flowery titles, was dictating to the young policewoman with the massive chignon at the nape of her neck. "On the morning of May twentieth, nineteen—"

"Lieutenant, sir—"

"Well, what is it?"

"Excuse me, sir, but how do you spell horizontal?"

"You ought to know that," said the lieutenant rudely. His churlishness was an effort to cover up a variety of conscience pangs which he felt in connection with this particular policewoman, and a recent evening when he, a married man, had made a date with her, only to stand her up in favour of an interesting murder case. "Didn't you take a secretarial course?"

"Yes, but—"

"Then write it right."

"Yes, sir. But horizontal—"

The lieutenant slammed his note-pad abruptly on to the desk top, and substituted a note of unpleasant sarcasm for the rudeness in his tone: "You know what! Look it up in the dictionary. And now, let's go on."

The policewoman bowed her head on her long graceful neck, and concentrated on the typewriter keyboard. The lieutenant felt a twinge of pain somewhere near his heart, and that might explain the blast in his voice as he continued: "On the morning of May twentieth at seven twenty-five a.m., Mrs Barbara Potesil telephoned the station to report a murder committed at number thirty-two Neruda Street. The victim was found, by the officers arriving on the scene, recumbent in bed with a pointed object sticking out of the left eye of the head resting on the right ear in a position perpendicular to the axis of the body, and its handle pointing at the window."

"I don't understand," squeaked the policewoman.

"Do you want me to say it in French?" growled the lieutenant. "The old woman was flat on her back, her head was turned to the right, with something like a dagger in her eye, that's all. What's so hard to understand about that?"

But when he recalled the scene, he had to admit that he was not being too clear. It wasn't even a dagger, really, that was stuck in the wrinkled old woman's right eye, and so the lieutenant barked at the policewoman to insert a footnote to the effect that a drawing of the murder weapon was attached. Later on, he made the drawing himself.

And then, with his eyes half-shut, he recalled the situation as he had seen it.

The old woman lay stretched out straight as a string precisely in the middle of the big double bed, with a thin little pillow under her head. Behind her, hanging over the head of the bed, within the reach of the bony hands, was a push-button switch on a cord. The handle of the odd weapon was pointed like a terrible index finger, directly at the window of the house across narrow old Neruda Street. In that window stood a bearded old man, observing the activity of the police officers with curiosity. The room—it was a spacious room on the third floor of a narrow eighteenth-century house—was full of antique furniture and all sorts of knick-knacks, lamps, candlesticks, vases, reminiscent more of the storeroom of an antique shop than a bedroom. There was a sourish smell in the air, in spite of the wide-open window.

"So this is the way you found her, professor?" Lieutenant Boruvka asked the long-legged man with the disconcerted expression who was standing behind him.

"Yes, that's right. My sister-in-law brought her breakfast up for her, but she didn't respond to the knocking. The door was locked on the inside, and we were afraid that something had—had happened during the night. It's possible, you know, she was eighty-five—and—well, my sister-in-law didn't know what to do, she was so upset—so I sent her for our neighbour, and when he came, we broke down the door and—"

He nodded his head towards the old carved door, now hanging crookedly from its hinges.

"And then you sent your sister-in-law to phone for us. You didn't touch anything?"

"Not a thing. Our neighbour was here all along, weren't you, Mr Kemmer?"

A grey-haired man in a striped shirt, who had been standing to one side, nodded his head. "I didn't want to leave the professor here by himself," he said.

"You didn't open that window?"

"No. Mother always slept with the window open, from spring till autumn. She believed in fresh air," said the professor.

"And always flat on her back like this?"

"Just like that. She used to say that sleeping on your left side puts pressure on your heart, and sleeping on your right puts pressure on your liver. And that a person should always sleep with as little as possible under his head."

"So you might say that she was fussy?"

The professor—his name was Peter Potesil—smiled sadly. "In some things, she was extremely fastidious. I should say that she kept to a very strict regimen."

"And it paid off," sounded from behind them. Unasked, a thin woman, who had perhaps once been handsome, spoke up. "Eighty-five. That's an age we'll never live to see."

Sergeant Malek turned to her sharply. "What makes you think so?" he asked dangerously.

"For heaven's sake, the worries, the rush—she lived a calm life. Nothing was allowed to disturb her comfort!"

"Barbara!" Another man, resembling the professor but not quite so tall rebuked her. "She isn't alive any more—"

"No, let her go on," the sergeant broke in. "This is an official interrogation. What is it you were saying, ma'am?"

The woman made a face. "Take a look at this apartment," she said, and there was hatred in her voice. "Two little cubby-holes, a dining-room and this room, big as it is. This was hers—and the cubby-holes were ours. And Paul and I have three little children and Peter and Mary have two. And we weren't even allowed to use the dining-room for a living-room, she was used to having dinner there, she was used to sitting around there afternoons.

What's the use of talking. It's just as simple as that—old people are sometimes unbearable."

Malek gave the lieutenant a meaningful glance. The lieutenant returned it. The case was beginning to be clear. Far too clear. The only thing that wasn't clear was the locked door.

"Let's go over it again," sighed the lieutenant. "You, professor, your wife and two children live in the little room facing the courtyard, and you, doctor, your wife and three children in the larger room facing out into the street. And your mother lived here in this big room."

"Yes," nodded Dr Paul Potesil, and swallowed.

"Hm," said the lieutenant. He looked around the room. It was a high-ceilinged room in an old-fashioned house, and from the dirty ceiling hung a variety of cobwebs and antique chandeliers.

There were bronze lamps and candlesticks on the tables and stands, and dusty alabaster statuettes, a pendulum clock stood on top of the secretaire, and a numer of old paintings hung on the walls. A storeroom. The man in the window opposite was leaning out and staring shamelessly across the street.

"Hm," repeated the lieutenant. "Who was the last one to see the victim alive?"

It turned out that it was Dr Potesil. About nine o'clock in the evening, he brought her a glass of milk. That glass of milk was part of the old lady's daily health regimen, and the two families alternated regularly in carrying it out. Dr Potesil placed the glass of milk on the table by his mother's bed, and left. He heard her lock the door behind him—as usual—and turn the key a second time as was her habit. Then he retired to the pub on the corner. For some time now, he had found evenings at home unbearable. Lieutenant Boruvka understood.

"So the last person to see her was you. The rest of the family saw her last at dinner?"

"No," volunteered Professor Potesil. "When she went to her room after dinner, I went to the kitchen for a glass of water, and she called me to her room."

"What for?"

"No real reason, actually. She told me some sort of crazy, mixed-up story about how the children had hidden her eye-glasses somewhere, and how the colonel had put them up to it, and then she gave me a lecture on rearing children."

"And then you left, and afterwards your brother went in with her glass of milk?"

"That's right."

"Hm," growled the lieutenant again, and fixed his gaze on the bearded man in the house across the street. Was it the lieutenant's imagination, or had the fellow really grinned at him?

"One more thing," the lieutenant turned to the neighbour in the striped shirt. "When you broke down the door this morning, was the light in the room off or was it on?"

"It was off." The witness was certain. "We didn't touch a thing, and certainly not the light switch."

The lieutenant cast another look at the inquisitive fellow with the beard across the way.

"Who's that?" he asked the professor.

"That's the colonel," he replied with a smile. "The one who is supposed to put my children up to all kinds of mischief. He's retired, and staying with his widowed daughter across the street. He and my mother used to have terrible arguments."

Malek and the lieutenant exchanged glances.

"Arguments! What about? You mean they used to visit each other?"

"No, they would just argue from window to window," said the professor with just the slightest indication of a smile on his lips. "And what they argued about, heaven knows. Probably out of boredom. For that matter, ask the colonel yourself."

Malek gave the lieutenant another significant look.

"Yes, we'll do that," said the lieutenant. "We'll just do that. And now would you all go into the next room, please?"

"It is perfectly obvious," declared Malek, once the door had closed behind them. "The old battle-axe was taking up space in the apartment, and they needed to get rid of her. And they set it up so it would look as if the old man across the street did it: the room locked on the inside, the murder weapon ideal for throwing—did you notice the heavy lead front end, streamlined, and the dural-aluminium rear? Why it's just as if it were copied from a game of darts. Only lethal. And arguments across the street—"

"But the room really was locked on the inside," the lieutenant interrupted him softly.

"That's their story."

"And the neighbour's."

"Look Joe," grinned Malek, "if we take them in one by one, and try a little cross-examination, I bet we'll put an end to the locked room. They had a deal on with the neighbour."

"I don't know," said Lieutenant Boruvka. "Well, have him come in here."

"Yes indeed, the door was locked," nodded the man with the grey hair. "I looked through the key hole myself and saw the key on the inside before we knocked down the door."

All of a sudden, the sergeant wheeled on him: "You're lying! How could the door be locked on the inside if somebody murdered her in there?"

"Don't raise your voice at me, officer," said the man in the striped shirt calmly. "And take a look out of the window. Maybe somebody could have climbed along the ledge."

Malek flushed and looked at the lieutenant uncertainly. The lieutenant nodded. Malek went to the window and leaned out.

"The doctor's wife asked me to help them with the door. I can't help it, it was really locked."

Malek returned from the window looking rebellious. "Perfectly smooth wall," he said. "Nearest window three yards away. Do you think a fly could have done it?"

"That's up to you to find out," the neighbour cut across the sergeant. "All I can do is swear that the door was locked and the bolt was shot."

Both of the policemen turned inadvertently to the massive carved door. There it was, hanging by a single screw, the bolt proving that the door had been locked on the inside.

"Could it really have been the colonel across the way?" wondered Malek. "But could a person have thrown it all that way? And with an aim like that? No, somebody's trying to make fun of us."

"It doesn't seem like fun to me," growled Lieutenant Boruvka, and he looked at the dead woman. "But to throw this all the way across the street..." He weighed the murder weapon in his hand. Dr Seifert had removed it from the victim's eye, and now it was carefully wrapped in a napkin. "... that's something I find pretty hard to believe. Unless—" he stopped in midsentence. The sergeant, irritated, urged him to finish it.

"Unless what?"

"Have you read 'The Aluminium Dagger' by Austin Freeman?"

"Oh no," grimaced the sergeant, "not another detective mystery."

"Oh, yes, another one. The situation was just like this one, and the murderer shot an aluminium dagger across the street out of an old musket."

"For crying out loud!"

Lieutenant Boruvka sighed. "I don't know what you mean. But we'll go and take a look at the colonel."

The bearded man was overjoyed at the arrival of the police. "Come in, do come in, gentlemen. I'm at your service, indeed I am. So you say somebody went and murdered the old crone, did they? Serves her right. He should have done it long ago."

"It isn't nice to talk like that," frowned the lieutenant.

"Nice, Shmice, she was a crotchety old hag and it serves her right."

"You hated her," asked Malek foxily.

The old man wrinkled his nose, and his face, or what could be seen of his face beyond the borders of his full tangled beard, lit up with a joyous smile. "Am I a suspect?" he asked with unconcealed delight. "Am I really suspected of murder?"

"I didn't say anything of the kind," said the Lieutenant Boruvka.

"But I had a reason to kill her," the old man insisted. "I wanted to kill her any number of times. You see that shotgun?" He pointed at a beautiful old double-barrelled shotgun hanging on the wall. "Many's the time I had a longing to load 'er up and—"

"When was the last time you saw her alive?" the lieutenant interrupted him.

The old man squinted cunningly. "Why, before I murdered her," he said.

"And when was that?"

"Last night," he said with alacrity. "I just got back from watching TV—my daughter has the TV set in the kitchen next door—and what do you know?—the light was on across the street. The old battle-axe was standing by the door with her son, the tall one, and she was talking at him hard. Then he went out. The old crone pottered around the room a little; that's when I took the shotgun down off the wall—." The old man rubbed his hands, and his eyes were shining. "But that's when the other son came in my sights; he had some milk for her or something. Anyway, so I had to wait a while until she drank it up. But I had my shotgun loaded here on the windowsill. Well, and then the old crone got into bed—" the old man's cheeks were blazing with excitement "—I took aim, and just when I had her monkey face in the sights, she turned her head and looked right at me with those stingy eyes of hers. And that's what she shouldn't have done, gentlemen. I might have changed my mind, but when I saw the old skinflint look me straight in the eye, well—" the old man indicated the motion with his index finger "—I pulled the trigger, and that was that!"

Sergeant Malek approached the old man, who stretched out his wrists eagerly.

"That's it, handcuffs, and make it snappy. And will you walk me through the Old Town on foot? So everybody sees me?" he asked hopefully. "Do you think the evening paper will—"

The sergeant, fascinated, actually reached into his pocket.

"Just a minute, Paul," murmured the lieutenant, and looked sombrely at the old man. "Tell me one thing, Colonel, if you shot her with your shotgun, how did you turn off the light in her bedroom?"

The bearded man looked at the old criminologist, disappointed, and the smile slowly faded. "Well, what do you know?" he said regretfully. "That's something I didn't think of. Well, you know how it is, General; every murderer makes a mistake somewhere."

But the lieutenant couldn't get rid of the idea of the miracle shot, and so, before he went to lunch, he borrowed a text on ballistics from the station library. Back at his desk, he opened it hopefully. But right on the first page, he found the words, "With x and y as the vertical and horizontal axes respectively,

129

co-ordinates for the points determining the parabolic trajectory of a missile in a vacuum as follows:

$$X^{(0)} = v_0 \cdot \cos \psi \cdot t$$
$$Y^{(0)} = v_0 \cdot \sin \psi \cdot t - \frac{G}{2} t^2 \text{ ”}$$

So, disappointed, he closed the book, and went home for lunch. At home, after an unpleasant exchange over school work with his daughter Zuzana, he began to think. Then, as a punishment for his daughter, who had an afternoon lesson in reparatory mathematics, he gave her the following problem to solve there: How much atmospheric pressure would it take to expel a missile weighing half a kilogram from a muzzle with a diameter of 21.6 millimetres, in order that it attain a velocity of 6 metres per second at a distance of 12 metres.

Zuzana, unversed in mathematics, and thus incapable of judging whether the problem was easy or hard, took off for her reparatory maths lesson, under the guidance of Paul Lavecky, D.Sc. She didn't have the slightest idea that her father was relying less on her mathematical talent than on the effective assistance of the said learned gentleman.

All of the data concerning the weight and diameter of the death weapon, and its velocity upon impact, had been obtained by the lieutenant at the police laboratory earlier that day.

"Nonsense," said Dr Seifert. "It hit the head fairly slowly, five or six metres per second at the very most. Otherwise that old skull would have looked a whole lot different, if a bomb like that had hit it any faster. It'd be shattered to bits. No, Joe, somebody must have simply tossed it."

"Besides," said Dr Hejda, the police lab chemist, "There aren't any traces of gunpowder on it."

The lieutenant looked at him timidly. "And what if—you know the way suicides do it sometimes—what if he poured water in the barrel first—then the traces of explosive—"

"Nonsense," the ballistics expert Jandacek interrupted him. "If you want to shoot a missile that weighs over a pound, you need a small cannon, and not a shotgun. The calibre is all right, but I'm telling you, it'd have to have been a cannon. A shotgun wouldn't have been able to take it."

The lieutenant didn't let himself be put off. "Or—that would eliminate traces of gunpowder—something—in the order of an airgun—"

He didn't finish saying what he had started. Jandacek burst out laughing, and, from his sitting position on the edge of the lieutenant's desk, he fell across it on to his back.

"Great jumping Jehosephat," he bubbled. "Never, I say never, say that aloud. Particularly not in front of the chief. Or else he'll send you to keep an eye on pickpockets in the White Swan department store, if nothing worse."

The blushing lieutenant stopped asking questions. It was all nonsense. He added to the conversation that had just taken place the absurd mystery of the light in the old lady's bedroom: how could the murderer have turned it off when—according to the testimony of Dr Potesil and that of the prison-hungry colonel—it had been on. And nobody could hit a target like that in the dark. It must be nonsense, somebody is making fun of us, the lieutenant thought to himself in the words of Sergeant Malek. This case belongs among my fantastic cases, the ones that nobody believes when I tell them, rather than in the station files.

But on the other hand, there were certain things that appeared to confirm the lieutenant's ballistic hypothesis. The locked door, and the concierge's testimony that at about nine o'clock she had heard a bang that shook the old house in Neruda Street, a report that sounded, in retrospect, for all the world like a gunshot. A noise that a number of other perfectly reliable witnesses had also heard. But it might, the lieutenant told himself, have been the back-fire of one of the cars which, mounting the steep old-fashioned street, had to be given plenty of throttle.

When Zuzana had left for her reparatory maths lesson, the lieutenant settled down in the chair at his desk with a painful sigh. Nothing could be done for the present but meditate and wait for the final results of the autopsy and the lab tests. And the lieutenant preferred to meditate at home. He leaned back comfortably in his chair, closed his eyes, folded his hands behind his head, and turned his face towards the ceiling. On the inside of his eyelids, he projected the odd store-room with the spartan sleeping facilities in the midst of it, several bronze candelabras hanging from the ceiling, statuettes of alabaster shepherdesses. He could see the wrinkled old face with the handle of the curious weapon sticking up out of one eye, the face contorted in a death cramp. He shivered. It was like the dust-jacket on an American murder mystery. And the handle of the weapon pointing straight out of the window . . .

Suddenly he opened his eyes and stared at the abstract painting on the ceiling, the result of an absent-minded bather on the floor above who had left the bath-water running. He closed his eyes again, opened them, then he humped out of his chair and pounced on Zuzana's bookshelf in the corner of the room. Once long ago, in a praiseworthy attempt at being educational, he had hung a portrait of Comenius over the bookcase, which had more recently been joined by the photograph of another man with a beard, this time a much younger one, holding a banjo. Lieutenant Boruvka dug about furiously among his daughter's school-books until he found what he was looking for. It was a book covered with wrapping paper, which in turn was covered with monstrous little drawings, and incomprehensible notes like "At five, you know where!" or "Right?" (in an unfamiliar handwriting); "Right" (Zuzana's handwriting); "That's great!" (the former handwriting); "Isn't it?" (Zuzana's hand again). Almost lost among the scrolls and scribbles was the book's title, *Second Year Physics*. The lieutenant took it to his desk and flipped the pages until something caught his eye. He pulled up a note-pad, picked up a pencil and within the course of the next hour, filled the page with the unclear calculation shown opposite.

He had just come up with a ten-mile altitude, and crossed it out disgustedly, when Zuzana arrived home from her maths lesson.

"Did you do the problem I gave you?" he asked in a severe a tone as he could muster. Zuzana pursed her lips.

"No, Daddy," she replied.

"And why not, pray?"

"We had the principal teaching us today, because Professor Lavecky had to miss class on account of a voluntary brigade. And the principal said," she explained, "that although he is

$$v = g \cdot t$$
$$6 = 9{,}8 \cdot t$$
$$t = \frac{6}{9{,}8}$$

$$6 = \text{----}$$
$$9{,}8 = \frac{6}{t}$$

$$t = 9{,}8 \cdot 6$$
$$\underline{t = 58{,}8}$$

$$s = \frac{1}{2} g \cdot \frac{q^2}{9{,}8} t^2$$

$$s = 4{,}9 \cdot 58{,}8^2$$

$$58{,}8 \cdot 58{,}8$$
$$2940$$
$$5504$$
$$5504$$
$$\overline{35\,\cancel{3}4\,4}$$

$$s = 354554{,}4 \cdot 4{,}9$$
$$151\,62176$$
$$31909896$$
$$\overline{18{,}353{,}165\,m = 18{,}353\,km}$$

z ~~cujleа 18 km~~ ? ? ?

aware of the fact that the science of ballistics is near and dear to you as a criminologist, nonetheless, he as a teacher has an obligation to guide us towards the idea of peaceful co-existence among all the nations of the world, and so he thinks that it would not be proper to teach us mathematics on problems of ballistics."

"Is that what he said?" asked the lieutenant pointedly. He wondered whether that intolerant choleric individual hadn't fallen victim to the attack of pacifism only after he had looked up the equations:

$$x^{(\circ)} = v_0 \cdot \cos \psi \cdot t \text{ and } y^{(\circ)} = v_0 \cdot \sin \psi \cdot t - \frac{G}{2} t^2.$$

He didn't say it aloud, though, and continued interrogating his daughter.

"What did you cover today?"

"Equations in one unknown."

"How did you do?"

"Not bad," said Zuzana, and looked her father straight in the eye.

"Well, we'll see how you did," said her father ominously. "Sit down and take a pencil and a piece of paper. And now, write. From what altitude—"

"But Daddy, I wanted to watch TV. There's a programme with—"

"Quiet, sit down and write!"

"But Daddy—"

"No TV until you work out a problem," decided her father. "We'll soon find out whether or not you know anything about equations with one unknown. Write!"

"But—"

"YOU HEARD ME!" roared Lieutenant Boruvka in a mighty voice. The unusually forcible volume surprised Zuzana to the point of making her sit down obediently at her desk in the corner, and, with a tearful look at the bearded banjo player, take down what her father dictated: "From what altitude must an object weighing 500 grammes fall in order to achieve an impact velocity of six metres per second. Got it?"

"Yes, Daddy," whined Zuzana.

"Now work it out. I'll go in the other room and watch TV so you couldn't say that I was in your way here."

That last sentence was not quite honest. His departure for the other room was based on a plan founded on the full knowledge of Zuzana's psyche, particularly where problems in mathematics were concerned.

The room with the TV was empty. Mrs Boruvkova was out with Joey at a party, and when the lieutenant had shut the door behind him, he remained standing there with an ear laid quietly to its painted surface. His calculations had been correct —not the ones on paper, resulting in 18 kilometres, but the ones concerning his daughter's activity within the ensuing minutes.

A soft sound could be heard through the door, resembling the whirring given off by an old pendulum clock when you are winding it. It sounded six consecutive times, each time lasting less than a second. There was a brief silence, and then Zuzana could be heard, speaking softly.

"Oliver? Hi!—Say, he gave me a problem to work—that's right, a maths problem—he says I can't watch TV until I do it— but Oliver, Ollie, say you're a pal—it's nothing at all for you—all right, thanks, grab a pencil and some paper, and hurry up, he's next door gawking at that blonde blues singer of his."

Behind the door, "he" bridled at the mention of the blues singer. He had hoped that his interest in TV programmes in which the said blonde performed had gone unnoticed by his daughter. Apparently it hadn't.

"All right, are you ready?—then take it down: from what altitude must an object weighing 500 grammes fall—" dictated Zuzana in a soft voice, and the lieutenant listened. Under different circumstances, he would have taken drastic steps against this underhand manner of obtaining knowledge, but this time . . .

"What?" he heard her say, "what do you say?—the weight is unnecessary? The formula for free fall is the same regardless of mass? Well, you know him. He's forgotten his multiplication tables already. He doesn't need them for those murderers of his."

Behind the door, the lieutenant blushed a little, and went to sit down in the armchair in front of the TV set. He sat there for a good quarter of an hour and forgot to turn it on. Then he heard the sounds reminiscent of the winding of an old cuckoo clock again, and Zuzana speaking in a quiet voice again. Then there was a long silence, interrupted only by the scratching of a blunt pencil on a pad of paper. "Thanks, Ollie, you're a darling!" she whispered finally, and then there was a silence following the tinkle of the phone being hung up. The lieutenant, engrossed in thought, wondered morbidly how he must appear to his daughter, and realised that he must seem like an old man, and that that undoubtedly is the way he appears to another young woman, not too many years older than Zuzana and possessing a regal chignon—he was rescued from these unpleasant thoughts by the squeak of the door and Zuzana's voice, the soft one that she used for wheedling: "I've got it, Daddy."

"You have? Well, all right, let's see!" He almost ripped the paper out of her hand, and immersed himself in the calculations.

"Can I turn it on now? The answer is right," purred Zuzana.

Her father nodded absent-mindedly. When Zuzana flicked the switch on the TV set and settled down blissfully on the hassock beside her father's armchair, the lieutenant got up and walked, with the air of a sleepwalker, to his study.

There, he placed the sheet of paper on his desk under the lamp.

$$N = g \cdot \ell$$

In Zuzana's neat handwriting, the computations started in the same way his had, and then they continued as shown opposite.

The lieutenant stared for a long time at the result, so very different from the one he had arrived at, and he growled reluctantly, "That could be right."

His eyes grew sadder. In the hallway, he put on his raincoat and hat, and he left the apartment in a hurry. As he shut the door, he could hear the bearded banjo player insisting that the yellow rose of Texas was the only girl for him, in Czech. But not even this encouraging statement succeeded in cheering him up.

Constable First Class Sintak opened the door to the apartment in Neruda Street for the lieutenant, and saluted respectfully.

$$g = 9,8 \; m/sec^2$$

$$G = 9,8 \; p$$

$$h = \frac{G}{9,8} = 0,612$$

$$600 : 98 = 0,612$$
$$120$$
$$22$$

$$s = \frac{1}{2} g \cdot h^2$$

$$h^2 = 0,612 \cdot 0,612 = 0,375$$

$$0,612 \cdot 0,612$$
$$3672$$
$$1224$$
$$0,374544$$

$$s = 0,5 \cdot 9,8 \cdot 0,375 = 1,83 \; m$$

$$0,375 \cdot 9,8$$
$$3375$$
$$3000$$
$$36750$$

$$s = 1,83 \; m$$

"Have you come to make an arrest, Lieutenant?" he asked, gravely.

"Maybe," replied the lieutenant, and disappeared behind the door of the room where the dead old woman had been found that morning.

He turned the light switch by the door, and looked around. One of the chandeliers, refurbished as an electric light fixture, had been turned on. It was the big one in the centre of the room, over the round polished dining-table. The old lady had apparently had a weakness for chandeliers—there were all of five of them hanging from the ceiling of the room.

One of them hung directly over the bed.

Lieutenant Boruvka sighed and approached the bed. He stood

there for a while, staring at it, and thinking about something. Then he looked up at the ceiling, and the heavy bronze chandelier hanging over the bed. It had two arms with light bulbs attached, and above them was a sort of a stand, displaying the figurine of some classic god or other. Maybe it was Mercury. The lieutenant didn't know, didn't really care.

His hand went out slowly to the push-button switch on a cord hanging over the head of the bed, within the reach of the person lying in bed.

He pressed it, and both arms lit up. The little god glowed.

For some time the lieutenant gazed at that vestige of the late Baroque period, electrified for the twentieth century. The electric cord wound around the shiny rod that supported the stand with the little god. He couldn't take his eyes off it. Several times he made a motion as if he wanted to climb up on to the bed, but each time he changed his mind again. The round face expressed something akin to inner suffering. It seemed that Lieutenant Boruvka was afraid of something. Perhaps it was the disappointment he would feel if the fantastic thing he had tricked his daughter's classmate into figuring out for him proved wrong. Or rather, if it proved correct.

Finally, he took courage. He switched off the light, took off his shoes, and climbed on to the bed. When he straightened up, the cowlick on top of his head touched the bottom part of the chandelier, where there was a bronze rosette. Once again, he became thoughtful, and once again he stared at the rosette, but it was not with admiration, although it was a beautiful asymmetrical work, with the face of a cherub in the middle.

He reached up, touched the cherub inquisitively with his forefinger, carefully; then with thumb and forefinger, he grasped its little bronze nose, and pulled.

The cherub tipped open. It was fastened on one side to the lower part of the chandelier with a spring that obviously did not date back to the Baroque period. And above it, at the base of the shiny rod that supported the god's stand, gaped a round hole reminiscent of the bore of a 12-gauge shotgun.

The lieutenant's expression grew even more mournful. He reached up and twisted the statuette of the god.

It turned. It was fastened to the stand with a screw. He

removed it carefully, and found that it was hollow, and that its hollow had concealed two fat coils that gave off a coppery sheen in the fading light of evening.

The contemptuous opinion of his daughter to the contrary, the lieutenant still recalled enough elementary physics to recognise an electromagnet when he saw it.

"The electromagnet was placed inside the chandelier," he dictated with despicable superciliousness to the young police-woman, "parenthesis 'drawing attached' end parenthesis—here is the drawing."

He tossed his drawing of the chandelier on to the desk in front of the girl at the typewriter.

He allowed a pause long enough for her to admire his drawing abilities to the full, and then he went on dictating: "All right then, the electromagnet was placed inside the chandelier by Professor Potesil, who, as we determined, is a professor of physics. He also fastened the spring on to the cherub. He had plenty of opportunity to do so, as, according to the previous testimony of Mrs Barbara Potesil, she was in the habit of spending her afternoon in the dining-room."

"Who was?" asked the policewoman.

"The victim, naturally. And thus the bedroom was empty. Potesil, moreover, admits that earlier that evening he had entered the bedroom of the victim—wait a minute, put victim-to-be or something like that, but make sure it doesn't look sloppy—and loosened the light bulbs in the chandelier. He had determined earlier by means of experiments conducted at times when the old woman had retired to the dining-room during the daytime that the mouth of the rod in the chandelier opens directly over the pillow where the old woman, who was generally known to be extremely fastidious, was in the habit of placing her head when she—"

"Full stop?" suggested the policewoman.

"All right," replied the lieutenant, irritated. "Put a full stop after 'head'. And let's get going. After dinner of the fateful day, the professor followed the old woman out of the dining-room, and upon determining that the chandelier over the bed didn't work—"

"Who, lieutenant? The professor or the old woman?"

"The old woman of course. He knew it! Anyway, when she determined that the light didn't work, she called the professor into her room. He tightened the two light bulbs, which lit up, and simultaneously covertly slipped the projectile into the tube. The electromagnet, which was connected to the regular electrical circuit by means of the cord to the switch that controlled the light, but insulated from the bulbs, of course, the electromagnet held the murder weapon in the tube by means of the iron plate affixed to the end of it by means of a screw that—"

"Full stop?" asked the policewoman.

"Full stop," growled Lieutenant Boruvka. "When subsequently the subsequently murdered—no, wait a minute—when subsequently the later victim—the late victim no, that's not it, put: Later when the old woman went to bed, and reached behind her by memory for the switch and turned off the light, the power supply to the electromagnet was interrupted which caused the projectile to be released, opening the hole covered by the cherub by its own weight—" The lieutenant paused, sensing a misplaced qualifying clause, and then, quickly, said, "—full stop."

"The projectile, released, fell on to the victim's head at a velocity of six metres per second. In view of the sharpness of the point and the weight of the weapon, and the age of the victim parenthesis eight-five years and seven months end parenthesis the impact was fatal. The weight of the handle turned the victim's head to the right and made it appear that the weapon had been thrown through the open window. Furthermore the professor knew that the murdered woman—no, put that his victim was in the habit of getting up after his brother and his wife—no, better put down between his and wife—else put the wife first, in front of the brother, that's it, like this: after his wife and his brother left the apartment; and so he was counting on the crime being discovered by his sister-in-law when she brought the old woman breakfast. In order to make sure of another non-partisan witness, he had the unsuspecting neighbour called to help break down the door to the locked room.

The lieutenant gave a satisfied pause, and looked over the policewoman's shoulder. He intentionally ignored the long, lovely neck and the chignon.

"There," he said. "And at the end, put Motive with a capital

M, colon, the crisis produced by the housing shortage in the family of Professor Potesil and Doctor Potesil, his brother."

Lieutenant Boruvka sat back, musing over the argument that he and the sergeant had had over that. Sergeant Malek known as an inveterate supporter of capital punishment and famous for being indomitable with regard to murderers, had softened up when analysing this case, and had said:

"You know, Joe, it's a nasty business, it really is. But I sort of feel for them. The old gal was as old as Methuselah, no earthly good to anybody at all. There's a housing shortage, and what does an old woman like that need all that room for? And those people lived like sardines."

Surprisingly the lieutenant, an out-and-out opponent of capital punishment, and a collector of extenuating circumstances of all varieties, frowned.

"But they were people," he said, "not sardines."

"Exactly," said Malek, significantly.

"Exactly," said Lieutenant Boruvka, equally significantly.

Malek thought that his superior was voicing agreement. But the lieutenant was possessed by the idea of how he would be treated, as the possessor of a three-roomed apartment, where with some small interruptions he had already spent eighteen years of his life—no matter what kind of a life, it was a life, and that was what mattered—and how long had that fussy old woman lived in that store-room of hers? How would he be treated when he was really old, and no earthly use to anybody at all—

"Was there anything else, lieutenant?" He heard the velvety and somewhat stiff voice of the policewoman.

He immediately assumed a disgruntled frown.

"No, give it here. Let me see."

He took the sheets of paper from her, and they seemed to be typed with heavier strokes than usual. He glanced at the title: Report on the Classification of the Case of the Vertical Trajectory.

He was furious.

"Why did you put vertical? I remember quite clearly dictating horizontal?"

The policewoman, offended, tossed her head on her lovely long neck, and said, "You know what, lieutenant? Look up horizontal in the dictionary."

VII

A Tried and Proven Method

IT WAS MID-OCTOBER, the off-season. A lone car, red with a white roof, was crawling along the asphalt road leading from San Candida to Cortina. The Dolomite valley was filled with a phantom steaming sea of thick autumnal mist which crept right up to the edge of the road. The car stopped, a man in an anorak got out and opened the bonnet. A young girl in clinging trousers and a mohair sweater scrambled out of the other side. The man began tinkering furiously with the engine. The girl stepped to the verge, adopted a graceful stance with legs astride, and fell into a reverie. Opposite her a rugged rock, a stark mountain crest, loomed out of the surging, vaporous whiteness like a Gothic cathedral carved by Salvador Dali; a spray of sunbeams, straggling through a rent in the grey autumnal clouds, played upon it. The sinister, gilded Dragon's Peak with its twin towers, rising out of the grey-black mist alternately resembled a mythical castle in an Arthurian legend, the abode of redoubtable knights and sorcerers in league with the devil. Gazing at the phantom, the girl sighed, awed by the presence of something older and more wondrous than the things of this world to which she was accustomed. She was a slim but not skinny girl with a mop of blonde hair and light green eyes, in which the golden Dragon was mirrored in miniature. The chilly breeze blew the golden curls from her forehead; she sighed again. The man under the bonnet swore immorally.

In the summer and winter seasons endless columns of cars streamed along the road, but now it was deserted. Near to the spot where the red car had stopped a narrow but negotiable path turned off with a sign that read: HOTEL NESTE DI

142

FALCONE 4 km. The path ran along the mountain side, then cut through a saddle, after which it ascended a steep incline for about fifty yards and then zigzagged sharply down into the valley.

The red car began free-wheeling slowly down the slope, engulfed in the peak-ringed silence. The only sound was the occasional grinding of brakes on the precipitous parts. The car carefully skirted a cliff jutting out at a menacing angle, and descended to the lowest point of the saddle. There it stopped again, and to an observer stationed above the leaden clouds it would have looked like a red strawberry below the radiant orange-gold pinnacle of this surrealistic cathedral. Or like a ruby-red drop of blood under a flaming torch with a backcloth of dark, overcast sky.

If the heavenly spectator had moved earthwards, he would have heard exasperated voices.

A girl's voice:

"Now we *are* in the soup!"

A man's voice:

"I didn't want to take this path anyway. Driving with a disengaged clutch is always risky."

"But that's your fault, Daddy. That's you all over."

"What do you mean, me all over? I can't be expected to think of everything, Zuzana."

The man took off his hat and an unruly tuft of hair stood up on his round head.

He was Lieutenant Josef Boruvka and with him was his seventeen-year-old daughter Zuzana.

His present plight was due to Zuzana's lust for foreign fields. In order to turn this desire to educational advantage, he had promised that if her school report turned out well, they would spend a holiday together in Italy, the home of her mother's family. He had, however, committed a fateful error: he had neglected to define the term "turn out well"; consequently, after a hard struggle with his wife and daughter, he had been compelled to keep his promise, although the report had comprised an abundance of Cs, two Ds—for maths and physics—and As for singing and physical training. Zuzana interpreted the phrase "turn out well" as "not to fail" and explained away the Ds for maths and physics as the result of refusing to flirt with the teacher, Pavel Lavecky, D.Sc.

Lieutenant Boruvka took himself off gloomily to the Cedok travel agency. There had been a time when he too had longed—in vain; such was the nature of the time—for foreign lands. Now, however, he had reached the age when a comfortable armchair in front of the goggle box—his substitute for tranquillisers—was more attractive. Visualising lumpy beds in cheap hotels and other hardships of foreign travel, he strode through the Prague streets in summer bloom, mentally calculating the amount that would be left in the family savings book after he had paid Cedok the cost of Zuzana's academic success. At the bottom of his heart he hoped that the foreign currency quota for that year would already have been exhausted. But the highest hopes are wont to be dashed. There still remained the prospect that the formalities would not be completed in time, or that as a communist policeman he would be refused an Italian visa, in conformity with some politico-bureaucratic caprice. But everything went without a hitch and in the spirit of international understanding. Barely four months had elapsed since handing in the applications, and there were the passports.

The lieutenant made a final bid: it was nearly the middle of October and Zuzana's term had commenced. She was in her matriculation year, he tried to explain to his wife. She would be away for a fortnight and as a result she would fail her finals. He met with no support even on the part of the headmistress, whom he had secretly regarded as his last resort. Well, said that lady, it is the last school year, but Italy is a historical country, Zuzana will absorb many new impressions, and they will be useful to her in both history and geography, at which she does not exactly shine. Therefore, despite his efforts, so untypical of a Czechoslovak citizen, Lieutenant Boruvka was now sitting with his daughter Zuzana in his red Felicia under the Dragon's blazing crags and, regardless of his daughter's teenage presence, was swearing angrily and not altogether blamelessly.

Actually, he was no longer sitting and cursing fate. The fact that the Felicia had not conquered that fifty-yard ascent in the saddle was due to Boruvka's absent-mindedness. The crack detective had toothcombed the car as though for a major expedition and had virtually spent the last two days before their departure flat on his back, but in the excitement of approaching the Italian border he had forgotten to fill up, and so below the peak the car had refused to render further service. At Zuzana's suggestion they had pushed it on to the path leading to the Neste di Falcone hotel where, according to the sign, a petrol pump was located, but they had not reckoned with a trap in the shape of a mountain saddle.

So now they were climbing the winding path on foot, and suddenly they were swallowed up by the thick grey-white mist which filled the whole valley.

Zuzana walked ahead, Boruvka, shivering slightly in his thin anorak (he had worn it for sunny Italy), plodded behind. In the mist the familiar features of Zuzana's figure merged into a universal outline, symbolic of young womanhood. A pleasant memory disentangled itself from the detective's gloomy meditations; the image of another, similar figure belonging to another girl, also dear to him, though in a different way, to whom he was just as gruff, though in a different manner, as he was to his daughter. But that girl was a long way off, the lieutenant's legs were aching, the mist made him gasp for breath, the stony path was torture to walk on. He stumbled, sighed, shook his head to drive out the cheerless thoughts and looked about him. In the thick grey-white mush a quirk of nature had formed a strange funnel into which a stream of sunlight was pouring like syrupy lemonade and dripping over into the abyss below the winding path. Zuzana stopped and looked down into the diluted gold, then cried:

"Oh, Daddy! Look!"

The lieutenant was moved by Zuzana's unsuspected feeling for natural beauty; she had hitherto appreciated only the beauty —to him incomprehensible—of the bedlam raised by the school beat group, The Backside Slappers, but now the magic of primeval nature had evidently touched even her electrophonicised heart. Boruvka stepped to the edge of the precipice and looked down. The light fell obliquely on to the pale gold sand deposited on a plateau about sixty feet below them.

145

"It is beautiful," he agreed "It's a pity your mother isn't here with us."

But Zuzana shook her head impatiently.

"No, not that! Look! Down there! The footprints!" She pointed to the stretch of sand.

Boruvka looked in the direction she had indicated. The smooth sandy surface was disturbed as though a struggle had taken place there. Fresh, clearly outlined prints of large men's shoes led from the spot into the mist. But the lieutenant was on holiday and intended to remain on holiday.

"Yes, yes," he muttered testily. "Someone tripped over and then got up and walked on."

Zuzana was dumbfounded.

"But, Daddy, don't tell me you can't see it?"

"Of course I can see it," growled Boruvka. "Why don't you just concentrate on the beauty around us? You may never come here again."

"But where did he come from?" wailed Zuzana in despair.

"Who?"

"Whoever it was had a fight down there and walked on."

Boruvka's mind jerked into attentiveness. A cogent question. The footprints led away from the scene of the struggle and there was only one set. No track led to the spot. The sand all around was absolutely smooth. The lieutenant rebelled inwardly.

"What's it got to do with me?" he asked brusquely. "Has a crime been committed? No. Besides, I'm on holiday!"

Zuzana curled her lip.

"You sound like the commissioner in Capek's story," she snorted. "How do you know a crime hasn't been committed here?"

"Which story?"

"Oh, the one about the footmarks."

The lieutenant vaguely recollected having read that Capek story a long time ago. It poked fun at his profession and that had annoyed him. Besides, the story lacked an ending, the origin of the mysterious footmarks was never disclosed; he had put the book aside in disgust and had never returned to it. Then a lecturer at the general studies course for members of the force had quoted the story as an illustration of Capek's non-materialistic philosophy and leanings toward mysticism. Quite rightly. The lieutenant liked mysteries, but only solved ones. He gazed keenly at the footprints, frowning.

"So what?" he exclaimed. "They'll be all round the rock, they'd be visible if it weren't for this mist. A mountaineer probably let himself down there or jumped . . ."

At that moment the atmospheric phenomenon ceased to exist for the breeze veiled the disquieting sight in mist.

"Or it was a fata morgana," added Boruvka and felt that he had explained the matter satisfactorily, rationally and logically as befitted a member of a force working on scientific lines. The footmarks in that metaphysical Capek story could probably be explained by something like that. If I were to write detective stories, he thought to himself, I would never leave the reader at sea.

But the holiday soon came to an abrupt end. They had covered about half a mile; the mist had lifted a little, but it still hung over the path like the ceiling of a low cave—and Zuzana suddenly shrieked in horror and pointed a slim, rather grubby finger in front of her. There, under the thin, whirling wisps of vapour, a short distance from the stony path it lay. Boruvka furrowed his brow in dismay. It was the body of a woman, lying on her back with her mouth wide open and eyes staring at the illuminated summit of the Dragon, shining through the mist like a ghostly lantern.

Zuzana was shaking with fright—it was her first real corpse. Boruvka inspected the unknown woman despondently. He found that the back of her head was lying in a pool of blood not yet dried. There was also a small bruise of blood on the temple, caused by a blow with a blunt instrument, the lieutenant's experienced eye told him. The woman was dressed in black skiing trousers and a thick sweater, over which she was wearing an anorak of soft and obviously expensive leather. She was aged about forty, pretty and well-groomed, and looked as though she had never lacked for anything. Several large diamonds sparkled on her fingers with their pink-lacquered nails. The lieutenant felt her pulse but her hand was already cold; there was no trace of a heart-beat. Boruvka, an old hand at his job, automatically rejected the possibility of assault and robbery.

"Da-daddy, come away from here!" begged Zuzana, white-faced, her teeth chattering. "Come away! It's horrible!"

"It is," agreed the crack detective. "This would have to happen to me! Well, we'll report it at the hotel and be on our way. Come along."

But he knew—and he was annoyed with himself for it—that he would have no peace and that he would not stir from the hotel until he had discovered who had murdered the woman with the diamonds. For Lieutenant Boruvka—unlike the metaphysical humanist to whom the future prospects of life and society were obscure—never left the reader at sea.

A little farther on, the road forked, and at the intersection stood a signpost with two arms. The left-hand one read CASTELL GIORNO 3 km, and the right-hand one HOTEL NESTE DI FALCONE 1 km. They quickened their pace; Zuzana was driven by fear and the lieutenant was impelled by a sense of duty. In less than a quarter of an hour they reached the hotel.

It was a luxurious mountain hotel with a dance floor on the terrace, now empty and deserted, an indoor car park and freshly painted green shutters, most of which were latched. They glistened in the mist like a chromolithographic picture on the wrapping of Swiss chocolate. Father and daughter passed through the glass-covered verandah into the plush and chrome hall. Not a soul was about; the reception desk was empty and its telephone was off the receiver. Silence reigned and a faint aroma of coffee pervaded the air. Unoccupied leather chairs gleamed in the tobacco-brown half-light of the foyer, and a solitary key hung from a row of hooks on a board behind the reception desk.

Zuzana, trembling, pressed close to the lieutenant.

"It's eerie here, Daddy. Perhaps—perhaps they've all been murdered!"

Instead of a reply, somewhere in the entrails of the hotel a vacuum cleaner hummed. Boruvka coughed diffidently. The sound rang, echoed faintly and then died away in the corridors panelled with stained wood.

The lieutenant coughed again and called softly:

"Hullo there!"

No answer.

"You give them a shout, Zuzana," he pleaded.

"I'm afraid!"

"Oh go on! You've got me with you," Boruvka reassured her owlishly, and crossed over to the fireplace. No flames were burning in the hearth, but a poker was leaning against the side. The lieutenant seized it, prepared for every eventuality.

Zuzana, emboldened by this show of resolution, cupped her hands to her mouth and shouted in a high, quavering voice: "Hullo!"

In the upper regions someone was galvanised into action. Heavy footsteps thumped overhead and a man's voice cried: "*Ja, ich geh schon, gnäd'ge Frau!*"

A ruddy black-moustached face, topped by a bald dome appeared above the banisters. It registered surprise.

"*Ja?*" asked the owner of the face almost rudely. "*Sie wünschen?*"

Boruvka mobilised his once excellent German: "*Eine Frau liegt auf dem Wege—unweit von dem Hotel.*"

"*Eine Frau?*" The man twitched with horror. "*Die gnädige Frau Winterbourne?*"

"*Ich weiss nicht,*" said Boruvka. "*Sie ist tot.*"

The man turned pale and reeled.

"*Tot?*" he shrieked. "*Alice tot?*"

"*Ja,*" said Boruvka. "*Er-ermordet.*"

The man clutched his chest in the region of his heart and with an anguished cry toppled down the stairs like a felled tree.

Upstairs the patter of women's feet resounded and a maid hurried over the coconut matting.

"Does this often happen?" asked Boruvka kneeling down beside the unconscious man.

"No," she answered also in German. They were in a region of border disputes and permanent bilingualism. The lieutenant glanced at her sharply because her tone struck him as cold. She was a pretty, dark-haired girl, and her manner was disproportionately calm. She began gently to slap the face of the man with the brigand-like moustache.

"So why do you think he fainted?"

Without looking at him, the girl replied coolly:

"He was in love with Mrs Winterbourne."

"Now wait a minute," said Boruvka. "How do you know that Mrs Winterbourne—"

"I heard you upstairs," said the maid. "It was to be expected."

"What?"

The girl shrugged her shoulders.

"That the gentleman—that this gentleman would faint" Boruvka pressed her, "or that someone would murder Mrs Winterbourne?"

The girl grimaced.

"Rather that someone would murder Mrs Winterbourne."

"Who?"

"Him." The girl tossed her head in the direction of the man who was slowly regaining consciousness. "Signor Faggioti. The padrone."

When the hotel proprietor finally came round and at the lieutenant's instructions went to phone the police, an unformed question was plaguing Boruvka's mind. The padrone spluttered agitatedly into the receiver, and the lieutenant's mournful gaze wandered from the man's ruddy face to the trim maid's immobile, waxen features. It seemed to him that the wide, attractive mouth was curved in a contemptuous—or ironical?—smile. But he couldn't be sure.

"Why was the telephone off the receiver?" he asked the proprietor as soon as he had finished speaking.

"Why? Yes, why, for heaven's sake?" He wrinkled his brow. "Oh, I know. This morning I wanted to phone Savini. He's a friend of mine from Castell Giorno. The number was engaged. I put the receiver down on the desk—then I forgot about it—"

"And what did you do?"

"When?"

"After you'd forgotten about the receiver?"

The padrone, gazing into space, sank down slowly and wearily as though something was weighing him down. But what? the lieutenant asked himself. What could be weighing him down? Perhaps the fact that he could not invent an answer on the spur of the moment.

"Why do you want to know? Who are you, anyway?"

Boruvka blushed faintly.

"I'm a member of the criminal investigation department," he said. "On holiday. But you'd better tell me everything. That is if you want Mrs Winterbourne's murderer to be found quickly."

It was some time before the padrone spoke.

"I took the Winterbournes' breakfast into the dining-room and then left. I went for a walk. I returned five minutes ago."

He went on: "Yes, at the moment they are the only guests at the hotel. I let them stay here only because Mr Winterbourne is a friend of Professor Skeet's up at the observatory. Yes, there is an observatory at the top of Dragon's Peak. What? No, it isn't because of Mrs Winterbourne that I let them stay here. Well, perhaps—partly. One can't help doing what Alice sets—set her heart on." Boruvka noticed that the hotelier's dark eyes were shining and an inexplicable sadness enveloped him. "It's the off-season now. The hotel is being done up, the staff are on vacation. But the Winterbournes are more like my own private guests. I cook for them personally—and for myself and Carla. Such a terrible thing!" he gave a sob. "I still can't believe it!"

"Where is Mr Winterbourne now?"

"I don't know. They said they were going to Castell Giorno after breakfast."

"What time did they have breakfast?"

Faggioti looked at the clock on the wall behind the reception desk. The hands indicated ten o'clock.

"Just before nine."

Boruvka became lost in thought, then he asked:

"The way to Castell Giorno from here would be by the path that turns off the road above this hotel?"

"No. Well, you could take that way, but it's hard going, up a steep track. They always went down from the hotel. Along the road. Like for a constitutional."

"But she—" Boruvka stopped short. He recalled the dead woman who was lying on the flat boulder between the fork and the saddle where according to Faggioti's story she should not have been. He did not tell the proprietor so, however. Instead, he asked:

"How far is it to Castell Giorno?"

"About four miles. But it's easy going. And they always used to take a taxi back."

A tear rolled down Faggioti's cheek.

"Hm," said Boruvka. "And where is Mr Winterbourne now?"

The hotelier wiped away the tear and snapped:

"I told you, I don't know! I don't keep a check on him."

He sobbed hysterically: "Mr Winterbourne can go to the devil!"

The maid led Boruvka into Mrs Winterbourne's bedroom, into which a cold, white light was falling. It flowed over the oval dressing-table mirror, the battery of bottles, jars and other items for the preservation of beauty. But Boruvka was not interested in these. His attention was attracted by another assortment of bottles, vials and tubes on her bedside table and—as he discovered when he opened them—inside the drawers. These—he ascertained at a glance—served to preserve something more important.

"Yes," said the maid carelessly. "She always had a tableful of those. Mr Winterbourne used to bring them from the town. She was supposed to be ill."

"Do you know what was the matter with her?" Boruvka picked up one of the boxes. The name did not mean anything to him, but the word "barbiturate" occurred in the chemical composition.

"No, I don't," replied the maid.

"Mr Winterbourne never spoke about it?"

"Yes, he did. To the padrone."

"And the padrone?"

The maid frowned. Or had Boruvka only imagined it? He was holding another box in his hand. Open. Nearly empty. Only two small ampules, containing a colourless liquid, remained. Among the foreign words indicating the chemical composition, Boruvka recognised the word "morphine."

"Well?" he prompted. "The padrone never said anything?"

The maid looked down, then she tossed her head and gazed out of the window at the mist.

"Yes, he did," she replied icily and with something akin to

satisfaction. "He said she was seriously ill. That she would not live longer than two or three years."

"I learnt it from Dr Benito," sniffed the proprietor. "Madonna mia, I couldn't stand it! She moaned with pain—sometimes in the night. It was terrible! Terrible! Poor lady! So young! So beautiful. And such suffering!"

He wiped his eyes with a large handkerchief and burst into tears again.

"Pull yourself together," Boruvka urged him gravely. "You were alone on this walk?"

"Yes," the padrone hiccoughed.

"Which direction did you take from the hotel? Did you go up by the path or down by the road?"

"Up," replied the proprietor. He looked round nervously then riveted his gaze on the maid who was sitting in one of the four leather armchairs in the foyer. Zuzana was huddled in the second, quiet as a church mouse and quivering like an aspen; in the third Boruvka was rubbing his hands. Not with glee. With the cold. Faggioti occupied the fourth.

"You didn't meet anyone?"

"No."

"And no one met you?"

"No, no one."

"So that means," Boruvka enunciated slowly, "that you have no witnesses?"

"Witnesses? Why? What do I need witnesses for? You don't think—good God—you surely don't think—"

"I don't think anything," Boruvka rejoined. "But the facts don't quite tally. Perhaps there is an explanation. You said that the Winterbournes went down by the road. But Mrs Winterbourne is lying on the upper road. The one you took."

"Madonna mia!" the padrone wailed. "But I—I only went a little way along it! Only a tiny way! I turned off immediately behind the hotel to the bench, to a bench from which there is a view of the valley. I sat down there—"

"In this cold?"

"Yes, I don't mind the cold. I'm hardened to it. And I remained sitting there for a while. Carla!" he turned abruptly to the maid.

"You must have seen me! On the bench. I was watching you hang the covers from Alice's—from Mrs Winterbourne's bed over the window-sill. I saw you! I waved to you! You must have seen me!"

Boruvka observed the maid. She remained silent, but lashed Faggioti with her dark, derisive eyes. Then she drawled:

"I didn't see you, padrone. It was misty."

"Yes," put in the lieutenant. "How could you see the young lady at the window through the mist?"

Faggioti's chin quivered.

"B-but," he stuttered. "But I didn't kill her! He did! He did!"

"Who?"

"Winterbourne," sobbed the padrone.

"What makes you think so?"

"They quarrelled a lot lately."

"What about?"

"That—that woman at the observatory!"

Before Boruvka could discover more about the inhabitants of the observatory, heavy boots clumped over the verandah and a sun-tanned young man in the uniform of the mountain police force entered the hall.

"Murder?" the young carabiniere repeated eagerly. "Why didn't you say so over the phone? You should have reported it immediately. If it's murder, the superintendent must come from town. Where's the phone? I'll report it to him at once! It's my duty! Why didn't you tell me straight off that it was murder?"

In spite of his brown Italian complexion, the carabiniere spoke German.

"I didn't have the courage," whispered the padrone. "I just couldn't get the word out."

"I thought someone on your staff had stolen something," the carabiniere grumbled. "I'm not competent to deal with this. Where is that phone of yours?"

He looked round, and strode resolutely to the reception desk. Boruvka heaved himself to his feet and followed him briskly.

"How long will it take the superintendent to get here?"

"About half an hour. Or nearly three-quarters. Why?"

"Nothing. It's just that I'd prefer the investigations to begin now," replied Boruvka. He was pondering whether Faggioti was really such a sensitive soul that he couldn't call a spade a spade, or whether he had employed a ruse to delay the arrival of experts for some reason or another.

"And who exactly are you?" the carabiniere regarded him with distrust.

"A tourist."

"He's a policeman!" the hotelier blurted out. "On holiday."

That was the last thing the carabiniere had expected.

"A policeman?"

"Yes. But a foreign one," Boruvka interpolated quickly.

The carabiniere let his hand, which had been hovering over the telephone, drop.

"On holiday?" His voice was heavy with suspicion. "Now? And here?"

"Yes. My application for a passport wasn't granted in time. I wanted to come in the summer, but—"

"What wasn't granted in time?"

"My application. For an exit permit. In my passport."

"And when did you hand it in?"

"In June."

The lieutenant was beginning to perspire. The carabiniere did not take his eyes off him.

"It's now October," he observed significantly and dialled a number.

The matter of Boruvka's passport seemed to intrigue the carabiniere more than the circumstances of the murder. It soon became clear why.

"When did you apply for that passport?" he asked about twenty minutes later when they were standing in a solemn semicircle round the corpse.

"In June."

"And you say it was you who discovered the dead woman?"

"Yes."

"And that you ran out of petrol up there on the road because you had forgotten to fill up your tank?"

"Yes."

"And you free-wheeled downhill and got stuck in the saddle?"

"I can prove it," said Boruvka weakly. "The car is standing there."

"That," the carabiniere laid significant stress on the word, and his eyes bulged at Boruvka, "I can believe. And you say you came here as tourists?"

"Yes."

"Now. In October?"

"I told you that it took a long time—"

"*Was erzählen Sie mir da für Märchen!*" the carabiniere roared all of a sudden in a rich tenor. "You say June—and it's now October! Don't tell me it takes as long as that to arrange things for a policeman. For some other people perhaps. People who have connections with the police, but of a different sort!"

"But you don't understand—"

"*Mir scheint Sie sind höchstenst verdächtig!*" The carabiniere glanced angrily at the corpse and then threw a distrustful look at Zuzana. She, fortunately, had not understood a word because she spent her optional German lessons answering numerous love letters of which, naturally, her father was ignorant.

"Where exactly are you from?" barked the carabiniere.

"Czechoslovakia," breathed the detective.

The olive-skinned young man performed a neat little turn straight out of an operetta. He hooked his thumbs into his belt, swayed backwards and forwards on his heels, opened his wide mouth and whistled.

"*Ach so!*" He turned to Faggioti. "This lady, I believe, was a citizen of the United States of America?"

"*Jawohl, Fritz.*"

"I'm beginning to see it all!" cried the carabiniere, glaring at Boruvka with incontrovertible suspicion. "So, you're a policeman, eh? A communist policeman!"

"I'm a non-Party man," gulped Boruvka.

"Ha! A secret serviceman!"

"I beg your pardon, I'm from the criminal investigation department," protested Boruvka, but the man in uniform had his own opinion on this subject.

"An agent," he declared. "A communist agent! And Madame Winterbourne was a rich American lady. Evidently the daughter

times the other chap had used a pistol. That was why his nerves had snapped.

"That's nonsense," he reiterated. "For heaven's sake! Suicide! I've seen a good few suicides made to look like murders, but—"

"Eyes, brain, deduction," repeated the superintendent cuttingly, and pointed upwards at the sky. "Look!"

Boruvka leaned back until his spine nearly cracked. He was not aware of it; the pain was drowned by a fresh flood of sweat. For in the meantime the mist had dispersed and the sunshine had spread from the Dragon's summit to its slopes and to another stone tower on the far side of the valley. From it, at a height of about one thousand feet directly above the spot where they were standing two thick cables were suspended.

Boruvka went red and then paled.

"It was misty," he whispered. "They—they were concealed from view."

Winterbourne spoke calmly, and again not a muscle of his face moved:

"In the morning we had originally intended to walk to Castell Giorno. Then Alice changed her mind. On misty days, such as today, she used to like to take the cable car to the observatory. It's nearly always sunny up there, and the sun did her good. Also she enjoyed looking down on the sea of mist. But as I had to go to Giorno today—we were expecting a parcel of vital medicaments, and we often used to walk to the post office for the exercise—I rang from the station for them to switch on the motor, then I helped Alice into the cable car and waited for it to start moving. Afterwards I took the road to Giorno and just before I reached the village I met the superintendent. He told me the dreadful news. God, when I think that only two hours," he looked at his wristwatch, "not quite two hours ago I saw her alive—I glimpsed her beloved face for the last time when I closed the cable car door for her. But I am to blame." He dropped his head but did not raise his voice. "I ought never to have let her go alone. I knew she was contemplating something like this."

"Has my esteemed colleague any questions?" Bramante turned to Boruvka. "But, please, no punching."

The lieutenant controlled himself. In his heart he genuinely detested the superintendent; Bramante had insulted his powers of reasoning and, what was worse, his professional honour, his feelings and his vague but benevolent political outlook. He overcame his loathing, however, and said:

"If you don't mind, I have. I should like to know—if it was suicide—how that bruise on the left temple is to be accounted for?"

Bramante was momentarily thrown into confusion, and his face darkened. He peered at Winterbourne who answered evenly:

"Alice slipped this morning and hit her head on the banister. Miss Carla saw her, didn't you?"

The dark-eyed maid nodded.

She smiled at Winterbourne—or did Boruvka only imagine it?

"Yes," she confirmed. "She hit her head on the banister. I helped her to her feet."

"Poor lady!" sobbed the padrone. "Such agony—and now this."

Bramante regained his aplomb and cast a derisive eye at the lieutenant.

"Where is the cable car operated from?" asked Boruvka, ignoring the Italian policeman's look.

"From the main station at the top of the Dragon," Winterbourne explained quietly. "The station is on the east side of the rock; it is not visible from the observatory, but the bell rings in the observatory as well. So it isn't necessary for someone to be on duty at the station. The caretaker or one of the Skeets comes from the observatory and switches on the motor."

"So anybody can ring from the bottom?"

"No, not anybody. Only someone who has the key to the cable car."

"And you have?"

"Yes. Skeet is an old friend of mine. And of Alice's."

"So you rang in the morning?"

"Yes, I rang. I helped Alice into the cable car, I waited for the signal from the top that the motor was about to be switched on, I shut the door after Alice and Alice rang again. The car moved off. I stood looking at it for a time and then I set off for Castell Giorno."

Boruvka looked up at the cables. They were about one thousand feet up, or more. The valley was narrow, certainly not more than half a mile wide. He contemplated the thick wires that curved in a majestic arc above them.

"Hm," he said. "Did anyone meet you on the way to Castell Giorno? I mean before Superintendent Bramante?"

"Yes. About a mile and a half from the village the signor carabiniere passed me on his motor bike."

The olive-skinned young man nodded.

"Right," said Boruvka and thought hard. They were all silent. "But tell me," he continued, "if she jumped out of the car while it was on its way up, the car must have arrived at the top empty. And that was two hours ago. How come that the people up there did not think it strange? Why didn't they phone the hotel? Or come down?"

Winterbourne shrugged his shoulders. Boruvka turned to the hotel proprietor.

"Don't you know?"

Faggioti cast an oblique glance, black with hatred, at Winterbourne.

"How should I know?" he asked angrily.

"That's what I don't know," said Boruvka, catching sight of a figure that had appeared on the path from the hotel. A short, square man in mountaineering breeches and studded boots was striding rapidly towards the group.

"Who is that?" asked Boruvka.

The superintendent looked round at the newcomer.

"I think we shall learn why the people in the observatory were not surprised at the open car," he said. "That's the caretaker."

"No. I was working in the store. I was unpacking tins of food from a crate, I didn't hear the bell," said the caretaker. "Mrs Skeet went to the station."

"Didn't it seem odd to her that the car was empty when it arrived?"

"She thought it was a joke," replied the caretaker.

"But the door must have been open?"

"Yes, it was. That's why Mrs Skeet thought that Mr Winterbourne had played a trick on her. He'd done it once before."

Boruvka turned to the Englishman without a word.

"It wasn't a joke that time," said Winterbourne. "Alice and I had really intended to go up. But at the last minute we changed our minds; we forgot to ring the bell and jumped out of the car. Then it was too late to do anything about it. The car was on the move and it was hauled up to the top empty."

"I see." Boruvka turned back to the caretaker. "What made you come down if you thought it was a joke?"

"Because the professor was perturbed and sent me. He tried to phone first but the hotel number was engaged all the time."

Boruvka looked sharply at Faggioti. He recalled the telephone on the reception desk. The telephone that was off the receiver. The hotel proprietor was gazing sadly at the dead woman and tears were rolling down his cheeks.

Inside the cable car Boruvka's attention was caught by the seat. The car was small (it served the needs of the observatory only) and had recently been spruced up. The windows sparkled like crystal, the brass handles shone like gold. The seat, too, had been freshly painted; it extended along the whole of the rear wall and was on a hinge. When the lieutenant tipped it up, it struck him that the space underneath was large enough to conceal an adult.

They did not take advantage of this space on the way up. All four of them—Boruvka, Bramante, the caretaker and Zuzana, who was afraid to stay down below with strange people whose language she did not understand—squeezed into the car with its seat down. To avoid the Italian detective's ironical eye, Boruvka gazed out of the window, holding Zuzana's hand.

The wild mountainous scenery slowly slipped away beneath them. At first the ground was only a short distance below the car, then it suddenly dropped into a deep abyss as they passed over the fateful valley. They saw the path, the plateau, the stretch of sand. Then the hairpin bends came into view and they passed over the saddle and saw the red Felicia like a drop of blood on a grey carpet. They gradually drew near to the top of Dragon's Peak.

It loomed in front of them menacingly, deeply cleft into twin architectonic structures deformed by a monstrous paroxysm. Zuzana squeezed her father's hand and caught her breath.

But Boruvka was oblivious to the formidable beauties of nature. "What is this for?"

He pointed to a red button on the wall.

"A signal to press if one wants to go up."

"There's no other way of ringing the bell?"

"No. Only here from the car. And only if one has the key."

The car sailed through a thin cloud and ascended into clear, bright sunshine. In the east at the rim of the brilliant, intensely blue sky the orange, white and yellow crests of the distant range stretched like stone lacework above Cortino d'Ampezzo. The car was in the shadow of the Dragon which rose between it and the sun.

"The car's very spick and span," remarked Boruvka. "Do you often clean it up?"

"Not really," replied the caretaker. "But it's the off-season now. During the season friends of the professor's come to see him from time to time. When things slacken off I do up the cable car."

"You did it up fairly recently, didn't you?"

"The day before yesterday," said the caretaker. "The paint on the seat is barely dry."

Boruvka involuntarily rose from the seat.

"Don't worry. In our country," Bramante stressed, "paint dries quickly."

"Paint, yes." Boruvka looked the superintendent sadly in the eyes. He turned to the caretaker.

"When was Mrs Winterbourne last up at the observatory?"

"When?" the caretaker reflected. "Just a minute. No one used the cable car yesterday, and the day before I painted it. Yeah, that's it. Three days ago."

They were quite close to the summit. The station into which the cable disappeared was drawing rapidly near. Next to it stood a robust, bare-headed man with white hair and a beard. The fierce wind which here, at a height of nearly ten thousand feet, probably never abated ruffled his silvery mane.

When the car stopped and the superintendent opened the door, the old man started and asked anxiously:

"Superintendent Bramante? What's happened?"

Bramante shook his head sorrowfully:

"It wasn't a joke, professor."

"Oh God" cried the other. "Alice—"

"Yes, she put an end to it herself."

The old man said nothing. He looked towards the rock. Boruvka looked also and noticed something that momentarily drove other thoughts out of his head. They were joined by a girl in skiing trousers and a short, rust-coloured fur. She had red hair and blue eyes, she could have been about twenty-five and was the type of young woman who forced the lieutenant to talk about the weather.

"Audrey," said the old man, his voice breaking, "Alice—has committed suicide."

"Oh!" said the girl, expressing conventional sympathy in an unfeeling tone. "That's too bad."

In the observatory living-room Boruvka saw that the professor was not old at all. He was fifty at the most; the impression of a venerable patriarch was due to his silvery beard and Einstein-like mane. The redhead turned out to be his wife.

"I was very fond of Alice. She was a rare and sweet woman who suffered cruelly. Cancer of the stomach," he sighed. "And she knew it. She was too intelligent to be kept in the dark."

"She was already married when you met her, or did you know her before?" asked Boruvka.

"Well," the professor hesitated, glancing at his wife.

"It's all right, Johnny," she nodded. "Tell him."

The professor sighed.

"I met her at the same time as Winterbourne during the war. He and I served together with the commandos and Alice, well," he sighed in a truly British fashion, "I think James and I might have been called rivals. She came to England with the American Women's Auxiliary Corps. And, well, she—er—chose James. We all remained the best of friends."

There was a short silence. Boruvka reflected on the mysteries of the British character which he had always regarded as an invention of humorous writers. The professor and his wife sat motionless with dead-pan faces, their serenity undisturbed by the shadow of the dead woman.

At least outwardly.

"Did they often come here?" Boruvka asked at length.

"Only during the last two years. I suggested it to them. Alice liked it here."

"I don't blame her," said the detective, staring out of the window. The white sea was spreading again, its surface rippling with clouds, from which scattered grey and orange pinnacles protruded. "It's beautiful here. One would never have believed. . ."

The lieutenant did not finish his sentence. He was plunged in thought.

"And you," he asked Audrey Skeet when he was alone with her in her room, "were you fond of her, too?"

Audrey looked him squarely in the eyes. Hers were as blue as his own. Boruvka could not withstand such an identical gaze; he blinked.

"No," she said, "I didn't like her. I had no reason to, had I?"

"No, I don't think you had," Boruvka agreed. "When the cable car reached the top, were you alone at the station?"

"Yes."

"The car arrived with the door open?"

"Yes, I thought that Jimmy had played a joke on me again."

"Jimmy?"

"Mr Winterbourne."

"Aha. Neither the caretaker nor your husband was there?"

"No. My husband was in the observatory and the caretaker was busy in the storeroom, emptying crates or something, I think."

"What did you do when the car came up empty?"

"I told you, I thought it was a joke. I was rattled. I went into the kitchen to do the washing up. You can't entice a maid up here. Here the wife has to cope with everything."

The sarcasm was not levelled at Boruvka this time. At whom, then, the lieutenant wondered.

"And then?"

"About half an hour later my husband came into the kitchen. I told him."

"What?"

"About the empty cable car and Jimmy's practical joke. But he was worried, he tried to phone the hotel—"

"—and the number was engaged. I know that."

"So what else would you like to know if you know that?"

The lieutenant stared out of the window. A large, shiny bird was darting among the puffs of cloud.

"So you didn't like Mrs Winterbourne," remarked Boruvka. "And what about Mr Winterbourne?"

He studied her face. A vicious light glinted in her eyes.

"What do you mean?"

"I was thinking," Boruvka followed the flight of the bird which with primeval assurance was gliding above the tops of the crags, its grey breast turned to the sun, "I was thinking you may have disliked Mrs Winterbourne because your husband once wanted to marry her or—there could have been another reason."

"You think too much," snapped the beautiful young woman. "All policemen do. I didn't like her simply because she wasn't the type I find congenial."

"Forgive me." Boruvka watched the bird until it disappeared among the peaks. Then he tried another tack:

"The cable car can be operated only from here, from the station?"

"Yes," the girl thought for a moment, then she contorted her lips. "It can't be operated from inside the car, if that's what you were thinking."

"Yes, that's exactly what I was thinking," said Boruvka quietly. "How long would it take from here to the hotel on foot?" he demanded.

"On foot? Why on earth do you think we have a cable car?"

"Hm. So, walking is out of the question. The cable car is the only way."

"Well, if you were a mountaineer," the girl sneered, "you could descend by a rope from the eastern wall down to the path."

"Aha."

"But you'd have to have a rope or borrow one from the caretaker."

"A rope. Of course. I have one in the shed." The caretaker seemed surprised at the question.

"Are you sure it's there?"

"Yeah. Come and see."

The rope was there, hanging on a hook in the shed built on to the observatory tower. Boruvka looked round. He noticed that the shed was not visible either from the store or from the station.

"You were alone in the store?" he asked. "Professor Skeet was not there with you?"

"What would he be doing there? He was in the observatory."

"Why were you unpacking tins of food on this particular day? Had the kitchen stock run out or something?"

"I suppose it had. I don't know. Mrs Skeet told me to. She does the cooking."

The lieutenant pondered. Then he said:

"Very well. How long were you working in the storeroom?"

"Until the professor came and told me to go down."

"So when the bell buzzed, which you didn't hear in the storeroom, Mrs Skeet went to the station, and from that moment you three did not see each other for at least half an hour?"

"You're right. We didn't."

"That's interesting," observed Boruvka. "Thank you."

While Boruvka was conducting his investigations, Bramante and Professor Skeet, with Mrs Winterbourne's tragic decease as an excuse, had pitched into a large bottle of Scotch. When Boruvka entered the room, the spirit level had sunk considerably and the Italian policeman's black eyes were swimming in tears like olives in oil.

The lieutenant's arrival cheered him up.

"What can I do for my Czechoslovak colleague?" he asked gaily. "Arrest someone? Punch someone on the nose?"

"As you think fit," said Boruvka coldly. "I'll be satisfied if you'll kindly take impressions of the fingerprints in the cable car and compare them with those of Professor Skeet and his wife, the caretaker, Mr Winterbourne and Mr Faggioti."

Bramante tapped his forehead.

"Oho! The eyes missed the big thing—now they want to catch up on trivialities. Why fingerprints?"

"I'd deem it a favour if you'd do as I ask."

"I get it. In your country everyone suspicious. All persons

suspicious. People may do only what is ordered. Here—what is allowed. No one suspicious. Without cause we don't take fingerprints. And I—" he spread out his hands and shrugged his shoulders in a theatrical manner "—I have no grounds for suspecting either the professor, or Mrs Skeet, or Mr Faggioti, or Mr Winterbourne. I suspect only the deceased," he chortled. "And do you know what of?"

Boruvka regarded his Italian colleague with distaste. During fifteen years of contact with cadavers he had not managed to acquire such a thick skin.

"I know," he said glumly. "Of suicide."

"Correct!" exclaimed Bramante. "And you—of murder! But I have no reason to suspect the living. Only the dead."

An idea hit Boruvka like a blow on the head.

"Do you know what? Have only the deceased's fingerprints taken."

This amused the superintendent.

"My esteemed colleague wishes to indict the dead? My colleague wants to convict the corpse of suicide?"

"No," retorted Boruvka icily. "Of murder."

This produced a fresh and even heartier burst of merriment.

"But in our country fingerprinting's had it. In your country —not yet. In backward countries murderers are still stupid— they don't wear gloves. Mrs Winterbourne is from the United States. Mrs Winterbourne wasn't wearing gloves. So Mrs Winterbourne cannot be a murderer. In civilised countries, my dear colleague, murderers wear gloves!"

A melancholy shadow clouded Boruvka's round face.

"Yes," he said. "That's the whole point. They wear gloves."

Later the lieutenant sought a map in the hotel. The padrone, sighing heavily, rummaged in his desk for some time, and finally dug out an old, large-scale physical map; Boruvka had rejected coloured advertising maps dotted with hotels, forest fauna and ski jumps. He took the map and retired to his room where he sat the whole afternoon, racking his brains over it. Zuzana, unusually quiet, was curled up in the armchair by the window, looking out. She did not dare to disturb her father. This was the first time she had exhibited deference towards the lieutenant, he noted with satisfaction.

It was growing dark and Boruvka was still hunched over his map. He was no longer studying it, though, having forgotten to switch on the lamp. The opaque light of the early autumn dusk fell upon his dishevelled hair which assumed a rose tinge reflected from the mountain tops, glowing in the sunset. Then darkness closed in and only Zuzana's fluffy head was silhouetted in the window. At the summit of the Dragon shone a lone light like an unusually bright evening star. The observatory.

The lieutenant stood up and went over to the window. He laid a plump hand on his daughter's shoulder. Zuzana turned her light green eyes upon him.

"Have you got it, Daddy?"

"No, I haven't," replied Boruvka glumly. "I think I know what happened, but one thing just doesn't fit in."

"What?"

"Oh—" The lieutenant waved his hand and was about to enlarge his point, but pulled himself up. "Look, Zuzana, you know very well I never discuss my work with you. Ask me about anything else you like, but you are too young for things like this."

"But Daddy," Zuzana snuggled up to her father, "we discovered this corpse together, so I've got something to do with this case, haven't I? And I—"

She stopped short.

"You what?" Boruvka prompted anxiously. His ear was too well attuned to the nuances of Zuzana's tone not to guess that she was concealing from him something which she was loath to admit.

"Nothing."

"What do you mean, nothing? It sounds as though there was quite definitely something."

"You'll be cross, Daddy."

"If it's wrong, I shall be," he declared sternly, but spoilt the effect by adding: "You know how cross I get when you do something that isn't nice."

And as Zuzana knew exactly how cross her father used to get, she replied carelessly:

"I only wanted to tell you that in any case I read the reports that you bring home and go over at night. Like that case before we came here about the fourteen murders committed out of carnal lust—"

"Zuzana," wailed the detective, "that's an official secret! And in any case it's definitely not for children!"

"I didn't talk to Pepik about it!" Zuzana snorted, not classifying herself, of course, in the same category as her ten-year-old brother. "And I'm only telling you so that you'll see I'm no starry-eyed innocent. For instance, I know how that senior clerk at the savings bank on Wenceslas Square cut up his wife into little pieces and incinerated her in the kitchen stove. You all thought she'd fled abroad and didn't even search—"

"Now wait a minute," groaned Boruvka. "Let's get this straight! We convicted him in the end."

"Yeah. But if he hadn't gone and got an appendicitis and yapped when they put him to sleep, you wouldn't—"

"We would have got him, appendix or no appendix! We—"

"Oh, I know Daddy." Zuzana pressed herself even closer to her father, and he did not see the mischievous lights in her green feline eyes. "I know how cleverly you unmasked that Vinohrady murderer who suffered from necrophilia and killed his wife and afterwards used her—"

"For heaven's sake, child," yelled the lieutenant desperately, administering himself a mental kick in the pants for his domestic negligence. "Stop it! Stop it! It looks as though it will be simpler if I just tell you how this case is taking shape."

He crossed to the table and switched on the lamp. "Look." He spread the map over the table, took a notebook out of his open case and quickly sketched a plan.

"Mrs Winterbourne," he began to explain, "according to my Italian colleague, committed suicide. If I know anything about suicides, I know this: a lady, and by all accounts a pampered lady, who has a bedside table full of drugs, doesn't jump out of a cable car. A lady like that who has experienced pain won't risk being maimed. A lady like that—"

"—will take a lethal dose of barbiturates," Zuzana completed the sentence for him.

Surprised at her expert terminology, the lieutenant discarded his oratorical manner.

"Of course," he said. "So I think someone threw her out of the cable car."

"But how?"

"That's the point—how? Whichever way I look at it the murderer couldn't have brought it off alone. He must have had an accomplice."

"But Daddy!"

"Yes, yes. That doesn't make sense either. For murder, people hire professional criminals—"

"Or when a young husband wants to get rid of his father-in-law, like—"

"Quite," cut in Boruvka. "But let's concentrate on our own case. Someone must have thrown her out of the car, but he had to get out of it himself without being seen by anyone at the top. Otherwise he'd have needed an accomplice. At first I thought the car could be operated from the inside, that Winterbourne could have entered with his wife, stopped the cable car, thrown her out, returned to base and sent the car up again."

"But they would still have noticed that from the top."

"Correct. That's why I discounted that version. But there's an alternative. Listen: the cable car was operated by Mrs Skeet. In the morning she told the caretaker to unpack tins of food in the storeroom, thus ensuring that he wouldn't hear the bell. Do you follow me?"

"Sure," said Zuzana. "It's as clear as daylight. Mrs Skeet is good-looking, and so is Mr Winterbourne—only Mrs Skeet is married, isn't she?"

"Well," said Boruvka, "I really don't know whether I ought to discuss such things with you, Zuzana, but in real life, you know—"

"Yeah! I've got it! Mrs Winterbourne got wind of it! And she threatened Mr Winterbourne that she'd alter her will. She must have made a will, if she knew she was going to die soon. And that didn't suit Mr Winterbourne . . ."

"That's about the gist of it," agreed the lieutenant gloomily. "You seem well versed in these matters, although I—"

But Zuzana was not interested in her father's ideas on her ideas on life. She was consumed with the ardour of the detective:

"So Mr Winterbourne threw Mrs Winterbourne out of the cable car, signalled Mrs Skeet who stopped the car and sent it back in the opposite direction. Mr Winterbourne got out at the bottom and skedaddled to Giorna!"

"Yes. That's a feasible solution. But we'd have to prove it. If Bramante would only let me take impressions of all the fingerprints . . ." The lieutenant became immersed in gloom, and at that moment the telephone rang.

Boruvka picked up the receiver. The voice travelling over a distance was distorted by the phone but Boruvka recognised it as Bramante's. The superintendent had dropped his broken German, and all traces of irony and alcoholic joviality had vanished. He said soberly: "Permit me to offer my apologies. Please don't be offended at my ill-chosen jokes."

"My pleasure," returned Boruvka, as no other German phrase came to his mind. "What have you found out?" He listened attentively to the thin voice crackling down the line and his grave face grew even more gloomy. At last he hung up and turned to Zuzana whose eager gaze was riveted upon him.

"They've taken fingerprint impressions," he said. "There are several fingerprints on the door handle. They are very clear because the caretaker polished it not long ago." He paused. "Mrs Winterbourne's fingerprints are not among them."

"But that means," Zuzana sighed, "that Mrs Winterbourne didn't go up by the cable car at all. She wasn't wearing gloves and so she would have—"

"Yes," Boruvka nodded. "Or she did go by the car, and the murderer was wearing gloves."

A funereal silence reigned in the room.

"Or perhaps he wasn't. He may have relied on there being a lot of other fingerprints on the handle. He stunned her with a blow on the temple, where she had knocked herself in the morning, opened the door and threw her out. He must have relied on the fingerprints. In his agitation he wouldn't have noticed that the car had been cleaned up—"

"Winterbourne!" cried Zuzana.

"Maybe. Superintendent Bramante is coming here to take the fingerprints of Mr Winterbourne and the hotel proprietor and also of the three up at the observatory."

"Why them?"

"Because there are other possibilities. All of them, unfortunately, presuppose the co-operation of at least two confederates. For instance: two of the three at the observatory could have struck a bargain. While the cable car was ascending and for nearly half an hour afterwards their movements were concealed from one another. This has been confirmed by both the caretaker and Mrs Skeet. One of the malefactors must have been Mrs Skeet, the other either her husband or the caretaker. I can't pretend to divine their reasons. But, Zuzana, if I were to tell you the incredible motives for murder—"

"Like that member of the works guard who was only four feet ten inches tall and shot that lathe-turner who he didn't know from Adam, and only because he spotted him in a clinch with a girl he didn't know either—"

"Yes and others," Boruvka broke in. "In short, people commit murder for the slimmest of reasons if they only have the chance. So, let's consider this: Mrs Winterbourne arrived at the top, one of the conspirators stunned her, was transported part of the way back, threw her out, was brought back to the station, and then Mrs Skeet told us she thought it was a joke. That's one way it could have been worked. In any case the murderer counted on the police swallowing the suicide hypothesis. Everyone knew that Mrs Winterbourne was incurably sick."

He fell silent. Zuzana hardly dared to breathe. He went on:

"Then there's a third possibility. But that's too fantastic."

"Oh go on, tell me, Daddy. Remember how that ballet dancer fired a shot through the—"

"—ventilator shaft. Yes, I remember. I am peculiarly lucky as regards extraordinary cases. They don't seem to fall to the other comrades in the police force. They get a straightforward blow with a hammer and—"

"Yes, like—"

"Quite," the lieutenant cut in, preferring to preserve some

illusions on the extent of Zuzana's knowledge rather than confirm the appalling truth. "But this is the most fabulous I have ever come across."

"So spill it, Daddy."

"Do you remember the Prachov case?" He stopped short. "Actually, I've never mentioned that to you—"

"When the murderer swung from one rock to another on a rope? Oooh!" Zuzana clapped her hand to her mouth. "You're thinking about—the footprints! The track like in that Capek story!"

Boruvka nodded and bent over the map, Zuzana's fluffy head next to his. "The stretch of sand is at the eastern foot of the Dragon. One could rope down there. Now picture the seat in the cable car. There's enough room for a man to crouch under it."

"Aaaah!" Zuzana clapped her hand to her mouth again.

"And Faggioti says that he served the Winterbournes breakfast and then went for a walk. Before they went out, see. And he took the phone off the receiver. Then he tries to kid us that he had nothing better to do in this cold weather than look through the window at the maid. Bosh! The maid denied it anyway."

"But she's got it in for him."

"Very perceptive of you." The lieutenant praised her. "And why? Because Faggioti was obviously having an affair with her. Until Mrs Winterbourne turned up. Then he fell in love with her and the maid was inflamed with jealous hatred."

"You think she did it?"

The lieutenant turned this suggestion over but shook his head immediately. "No, she couldn't have done. But Faggioti could have."

"But why him—aha! Mrs Winterbourne didn't want to have it off with him!"

"What a way to talk!" Boruvka gasped. "What does it mean— have it off with?"

"Well, it means—"

"I know very well what it means! But such an expression on the lips of a young girl—"

A lecture ensued on the type of vocabulary befitting a young girl. This was akin to the parlour language of sequestered young ladies of the late nineteenth century. When Zuzana had dutifully heard her father out, she took up the thread again.

"So you think he crawled under the seat, having left the receiver off so that no one would be able to phone him from the observatory and he would have an alibi. He threw her out on the way up, hid under the seat again and when Mrs Skeet went into the kitchen, he crawled out—and he had a rope with him under the seat—or he borrowed the one from the caretaker—how long is it?"

"Fantastic, eh?" Boruvka sighed. "Almost absurd. Of course, one could rope down in several leaps if one knew the terrain."

"But weren't the footprints a long way from the rock?"

"I don't know. We'll have to go and look there tomorrow when there's no mist."

"Perhaps he only swung down part of the way and then jumped. People can jump from a terrific height. Like Olda—"

She stopped short.

The lieutenant was on the scent, however.

"Which Olda? That yob from the Armed Forces Auxiliary Society? Spacek or something?"

"Mm, him," mumbled Zuzana, caught out.

"The one I forbade you to have any dealings with—"

"Yes him. I said it was Olda Spacek. And I don't have any dealings with him. Only—Oh, Daddy!" Zuzana suddenly squealed so shrilly that the lieutenant spun round like greased lighting with his fists up. But there was no one standing behind him. He turned back to his daughter who was gulping like a fish out of water. When she had recovered herself, words began to trickle out unsteadily: "Daddy, listen—"

Boruvka listened intently for some time. A wind had sprung up outside; it had drawn a black curtain of cloud across the bright star of the observatory; it whistled, howled and raged. Notwithstanding, when Zuzana had finished speaking, Boruvka set out with her into the dark night.

They returned in two hours. But they did not stay for long. From the foyer Boruvka phoned the observatory to ask Skeet whether he might visit him. Then he headed for the cable car with Zuzana, and together they ascended the Dragon through the squally night, dark as a sea of ink. As they approached the peak, high above the clouds, it glistened in the white moonlight like a spectre in a nightmare. For a moment it seemed to the lieutenant, pressing his nose against the cold window pane, that it was really only a vision in a terrible and phantasmagoric dream, a dream that, nevertheless, contained a certain logic, to an awareness of which he had been brought by his daughter Zuzana's forbidden but perhaps only platonic relationship with a certain young man.

Superintendent Bramante reached the hotel shortly after Boruvka and Zuzana had set off on their mysterious nocturnal jaunt. With a lack of consideration, unusual in so charming an Italian policeman, he woke up Winterbourne and Faggioti and took impressions of their fingerprints. For good measure, he took the maid's too, then he climbed into his car and drove fast through the rising wind along the road via Castell Giorno to the town.

An hour after leaving the hotel, Zuzana and Boruvka returned by the cable car, accompanied by the white-haired astronomer; then all three again plunged into the nocturnal shadows. They took the path from the hotel and at the fork mounted the steep track to Castell Giorno.

When Bramante, glum, confused and rubbing the sleep out of his eyes, appeared at eight in the morning, all three were waiting for him in the hall. Faggioti, Winterbourne and the frosty-faced maid were sitting with them. Bramante took Boruvka aside and informed him in a low voice:

"We've compared the fingerprints. Those on the outside handle are the caretaker's, Mrs Skeet's and mine, and on the inside the caretaker's and mine."

"And Winterbourne's?"

"Winterbourne's are not there. There is only one set of unidentified fingerprints. They are probably yours—if you would allow us later—to complete the record."

"It won't be necessary," stated Boruvka flatly. "The murderer was from a civilised country. He worked with gloves on."

They made their way to the spot where Mrs Winterbourne had been found lying dead the day before. All of them, that is, except Skeet whom Boruvka—for reasons known only to the two of them—and Zuzana, of course—had left at the hotel.

It was a beautiful autumnal day in the Dolomites. The incandescent sun shone like a large and distant magnesium light, and under the orange fire-breathing Dragon's Peak Boruvka expounded his original hypotheses about the murder to the assembled group.

"But," he concluded, "they all presupposed the existence of an accomplice. Except the last variation—entailing concealment under the seat and roping down, which could have been carried out by Mr Faggioti."

The hotelier protested plaintively as he had done several times during Boruvka's exposition.

"Don't excite yourself," the lieutenant soothed him. "Then my daughter gave me an idea—and I recalled a number of clues that confirmed its correctness. In the first place," he looked at Winterbourne: the Englishman preserved his unruffled English calm, "the cable car had arrived empty at the station once before. Mrs Skeet regarded it as a poor joke. You explained that you had jumped out of the cable car and hadn't had time to give the signal."

"That is what happened," Winterbourne affirmed.

"Hmm. We discovered the second clue last night behind a boulder near the steep footpath which is not negotiable by car but which forms a short cut to Castell Giorno for a walker. So that he can run into a carabiniere half a mile from the village at a time which would correspond to a leisurely stroll along the road from the hotel. . . ."

Bramante started violently and stared at Winterbourne with his eyes popping out of his head.

Winterbourne nodded wordlessly.

"The third clue," Boruvka went on, "is your friend Professor Skeet, with whom you served during the war. With the commandos, if I am not mistaken?"

"You are not mistaken." Winterbourne spoke in the same impassive manner.

"This friend of yours, Skeet," the lieutenant continued, "is now entering the cable car and giving the signal to his wife at the top. Mrs Skeet is switching the motor on. In a moment we shall see the car."

He fell silent. The whole group turned their eyes on the mountain opposite the Dragon, where a tall pylon towered. A light, cool breeze was blowing, the sky was a deep ultramarine, as clear as if it had been swept after the night's gale. From a height—or from a distance—the throbbing of an engine could be heard. Perhaps, though, it was only an illusion.

But the red splotch which appeared from behind the pylon was no hallucination. Suspended from two cables, it moved at a terrific height above the valley.

"Observe carefully," said Boruvka in a subdued voice.

They watched the cable car draw near; it was directly overhead. A dark spot separated from it. Some of the group cried out in horror. It was a human body, and it was falling straight towards them.

Boruvka scanned the semi-circle of faces. Only two expressed unconcern: Zuzana's and Winterbourne's. But Boruvka discerned a fundamental difference in the kind of equanimity. Zuzana was genuinely unperturbed. Winterbourne was exercising self-control.

Boruvka watched the falling body. It was no longer dropping headlong. It was suspended in the air; above it, against the blue backcloth, a large white flower had blossomed, a flower that resembled a gigantic mountain snowdrop with its corolla turned earthwards, and it was floating slowly towards the sandy patch below the Dragon.

At the sight of it Boruvka's expression saddened. He faced Winterbourne. Bramante watched him closely. The muscles in Winterbourne's face tensed, his grey eyes gazed steadily into the lieutenant's, then slid to the superintendent and back to Boruvka.

"Yes," said Winterbourne dispassionately. "That's how I did it." Back in Prague some time later, this was translated by Zuzana into ungrammatical Czech for the benefit of Oldrich Spacek, the rather flashy young man from the parachute section of the Armed Forces Auxiliary Association: "Yes, in this way did I do it."

VIII

Falling Light

T H E R A Y S O F the October Italian sun were agreeably warming Lieutenant Boruvka's rotund figure, but he was not in a contented frame of mind. He was sitting on a striped deckchair on the beach, remarkably like a bubble with a dishevelled tuft on the crown of his head, and gloomily watching his daughter Zuzana romping with two gentlemen. Zuzana was wearing a scandalously skimpy bikini, the existence of which she had successfully concealed from her father as far as Venice. The older of the two gentlemen was dressed in Bermudas and a shirt imprinted with the titles of yellow journals of various countries. The younger man sported turquoise trunks. A red-and-white striped ball was floating between them and Zuzana to the accompaniment of peals of tinkling, girlish laughter. Lieutenant Boruvka was thinking that the behaviour of the two gentlemen, particularly the older one who had long since passed the prime of life and could easily have been Zuzana's grandfather, was somewhat improper. He was convinced that similar thoughts were passing through the mind of the young and extraordinarily attractive lady seated in the chair next to him, whom he tried from time to time to entertain with broken English comments on the weather. For the lady was the wife of the frisky patriarch in Bermudas.

Lieutenant Boruvka and his daughter were spending a few days of their Italian holiday as guests of this lady and her husband, Signor Greffi. Greffi was Mrs Winterbourne's cousin, and in gratitude to the lieutenant for unmasking his cousin's murderer (Winterbourne had murdered his wife—without Mrs Skeet's knowledge—because he was afraid Mrs Winterbourne might alter her will), he had invited father and daughter to his

179

Venice residence. He was, like so many other Venetian settlers, a citizen of the United States which he had been obliged to leave, after twenty years of fruitful business transactions, for reasons never fully divulged. The detailed character of his American commercial dealings remained undivulged in Italy: ill-natured (and impecunious) countrymen hinted at Greffi's connections with a certain organisation in Chicago, Illinois, which dealt in arms rather than commerce, but no one dared to state this publicly. One thing was certain: the high-spirited and spry old gentleman had money, and this he displayed very ostentatiously to his Czechoslovak guests. In addition he had a son, a handsome, strapping young man, by his first wife. His son's predilection (and mainly lack of talent) for gambling had caused him recently to suspend the latter's allowance and circulate an announcement to all well-known European money-lenders, repudiating responsibility for his son's financial liabilities. Finally, he owned a still beautiful palace on the Canale Grande and a wife, the second chronologically, who could have been not only his daughter, but the daughter of the much younger Boruvka. Therefore, the lieutenant repeated to himself, this lady could not be enjoying the spectacle of her husband outdoing in high jinks the young man in turquoise trunks, who was the son of Signor Alfieri, a friend of Greffi's.

The sun was sinking slowly towards the spires of St Mark's, and Boruvka stood up with the intention of informing Signor Greffi that the wind blowing from the sea was rather cool. His attention was caught by another sight on the beach. A very fat man in white trousers, a very fat young lady in a two-piece swimsuit, a very pretty, curvaceous woman of about thirty and a muscular young Apollo resembling Alfieri in the contrast between physical beauty and the insipid mental fluid he exuded, were all chasing a sturdy little boy. The youngster was holding a hideous doll with ginger hair in one hand and a bottle of French cognac in the other, and was shrieking like a vocally well-equipped baboon. So far the little boy had successfully evaded his pursuers; whenever he gained ground or improved his position, he tipped up the bottle with a mischievous grin.

Lieutenant Boruvka sighed and tried to tell his neighbour that he had a son of the same age. The signora nodded, smiled and remarked that she, too, was of the opinion that it would rain during the night. The lieutenant turned his attention gloomily to the unfolding drama; in the meantime, Zuzana and the two merry gentlemen with the coloured ball had joined in the chase. In the end the boy was caught and handed over to his parents for chastisement. They were the fat gentleman and the beautiful, curvaceous lady.

They were conveyed from the Lido by gondola. Before they reached Greffi's residence, the boy had been rebuked several times without effect. He and his parents, as well as the plump young lady, Isabella di Campiano, who was engaged to the young Marcello Greffi, were all staying at the Greffi palace as guests of the rich Italian American. The little boy's name was Cesare Farina and his misdemeanours that day included pouring his morning cocoa into the fountain pool in the ceremonial hall of the Greffi palace, placing a drawing pin on Isabella's chair, tying the bell which was rung to summon the inhabitants to meals to the tail of his mother's Boston terrier Einstein, stealing a bottle of French cognac which his father, a big businessman, had hidden under his deckchair, and consuming its contents without permission, biting a young Czech lady's finger, when she caught him, so that it bled, bursting (in revenge) the red-and-white striped ball (which had earned Boruvka's secret approval because this had put a stop to Zuzana's flirting with the old gentleman in the Bermudas and the young man in the turquoise trunks), and finally throwing an ugly doll, a souvenir of the kind that were then a craze in Venice, into the murky water of the canal in front of the palace. The doll sank slowly into the depths, accompanied by a resounding slap which the boy received on his cheek, for the fat Farina could no longer restrain his pedagogic instincts. The doll's hideous face turned twice below the surface and then it got caught up in an undercurrent and was dragged down out of sight to an outburst of extraordinary grief on the part of the boy who now belatedly regretted his act. Immediately afterwards the gondola drew alongside the steps to the Greffi palace where the obliging major-domo helped an unsteady lieutenant on to relatively firm ground.

*   *   *

Farina immediately repented of his impulsive and cruel action, the boy's incredible roars having obviously rent his paternal heart. During the two hours which elapsed between the guests' arrival from the Lido and the ceremonial dinner, Cesare managed to fall into the fountain basin so that he had to be taken upstairs and changed into dry clothes. Nevertheless, Farina stroked his head good-naturedly at the table and Cesare even had a new trendy doll, uglier than the first, on his lap, in place of the one which had sunk into the dark waters of the Canale Grande. And as though that were not enough as a bribe to secure forgiveness, the solicitous businessman fed his son the choicest dainties from the richly laden table, at which Cesare pointed his sticky fingers, being too short to reach them. Boruvka pondered on the strange methods of rearing children in Italy.

That evening the dinner was particularly ostentatious. Greffi's best friend Alfieri and his son and their guests, a Signor De Cervi and his wife, whom Greffi had known in America, were present. But Zuzana Boruvkova was the hit of the evening—in the light of the expensive candles she radiated a blonde, feline charm which, as everyone knows, no Italian can resist and vice versa. Her foreign charisma was enhanced by the elegance of her short skin-tight evening dress which Czechoslovak women call "a nice little thing" and which Mrs Boruvkova had made with such consummate skill that even the sophisticated Signora Farina thought it was a Schiaparelli creation.

Lieutenant Boruvka was not exactly overjoyed at his daughter's social success. He was filled with misgivings connected with the person of the young man whose turquoise trunks had been exchanged for a sort of naval uniform, and particularly with the person of the old gentleman, dressed now in a white dinner jacket instead of Bermuda shorts, but prancing round Zuzana no less persistently. Boruvka's English conversation was therefore more chaotic than usual. He failed to find the proper expressions for such pleasantries as that the dining hall was agreeably cool, which he had intended to declare to Signora De Cervi, or that it was usually cold in Czechoslovakia at that time of the year, which piece of information he had intended to impart to Farina, or that the climate was altogether milder in Italy than in his country (remark designated for Signorina di Campiano); he did not even manage to communicate one of his five observations concerning barometric recordings, with which he had hoped to hold the attention of the extraordinarily attractive Signora Greffi. When he overheard this beautiful lady chide someone—obviously her frolicsome husband—behind the folding screen for something of which Boruvka caught only a snatch, sounding roughly like "coketria con regatsa cheko", he abandoned further conversational ventures and sat down gloomily on the edge of the large basin in the middle of the hall, in which the fountain was bubbling soothingly, and looked up at the glass ceiling. The proud owner of the palace had informed him in the afternoon that it was called falling light in English and that it was one of the classical features of Venetian palace architecture. And so he gazed glumly at the classical feature, and a silver star winked at him coquettishly through the glass.

He was distracted from his reverie by a furious quarrel which drowned the restful gurgle of the fountain. He stood up and looked towards the tables at the other end of the hall. Greffi senior and De Cervi were facing each other like two cocks, purple in the face, and both bowing deeply. They remained in that incredibly deep bow not because the laws of gravity had ceased to apply to them, but because the arms of each of them were held by two other gentlemen, Greffi's by his son and Farina, De Cervi's by Alfieri and the cheerful major-domo who in this situation, however, wore a grave expression.

On a couch in the corner lay Isabella di Campiano in a faint, attended by a trio of ladies. Cesare was hopping about between the two red-faced rivals, laughing at both of them indiscriminately. Zuzana and Alfredo Alfieri were standing in embarrassed silence a short distance away and the air was thick with loud and undubitably pithy words which Boruvka did not understand.

He did not even try and there was no chance of having them translated. The evening went flat after the temperamental display by the two former Chicago businessmen, and Boruvka was glad of this; he sighed with relief when he had taken Zuzana off to the safety of the luxurious guest suite before she could vanish into one of the palace's nooks and crannies with one of the fiery gentlemen who lived there.

The Mournful Demeanour of Lieutenant Boruvka

An infuriated voice could still be heard shouting outside, and when the lieutenant leaned out of his first floor window, he saw a gondola disappearing in the distance; Alfieri, restrained by his son, was waving his fist threateningly at the second floor windows of the Greffi *palazzo*. And from above Greffi's no less impassioned voice rang out in the mild, starry night and ricocheted off the coloured façades of the palaces along the canal. The reflections of the lanterns swinging from the prows of the quietly dreaming, phantom floating black gondolas danced over the rippling surface of the water. Boruvka pulled down the Venetian blinds, lay down under the silken canopy and tried to fall asleep. Without success. Loud snores emitted by Isabella di Campiano penetrated the thick stone wall and persisted interminably.

They were not the only sounds to disturb the nocturnal peace of the old house: the fountain splashed faintly in the quietness of the hall and keys grated in locks—the old major-domo was conscientiously securing all the entrances and shutters of the Greffi residence.

A desperate cry aroused the sleeping—and waking—inhabitants of the old palace. "Help!" cried a man at the top of his voice and a slapping sound of hurried steps echoed over the marble staircases.

Boruvka—who was not the only wakeful guest—jumped up. Zuzana was sleeping the sound sleep of a seventeen-year-old. Boruvka opened the door carefully and slid into the corridor dimly lit by candles. A very fat gentleman in a flowing dressing-gown was running towards him, shouting lustily, and every step sounded like a pistol shot because the gentleman's chubby feet were encased in heelless bedroom slippers.

Boruvka asked, or so he thought, in English: "What's happened?" The fat man stopped short, rolled terrified eyes at the lieutenant and declared defensively: "No, no! You're wrong! I didn't kill him!"

It soon became necessary to awaken Zuzana. The lieutenant had to, like it or not, but he conscientiously compelled her to wrap a white bathrobe round her coquettish pyjamas with three-quarter trousers. In the English which she had partly picked up at school but mostly acquired from industrious study of lyrics from Radio Luxemburg, Zuzana finally liberated him from linguistic isolation. The lieutenant had probably never been more grateful to her in his life, because the behaviour of the horror-struck fat gentleman at three o'clock in the morning had begun to interest him exceedingly.

He did not need Zuzana's English—at least not at the beginning —in order to ascertain what had happened. This was clear at first glance when he entered Greffi's second-floor room to which the trembling Farina led him by the hand. The old gentleman who had been frolicking in so sprightly a manner that very afternoon would frolic no more. He was lying on the floor in the middle of a bedroom furnished in the most exclusive Venetian style— apart from the fact that he did not share it with his wife. A short while before he had exchanged the white dinner jacket for lemon pyjamas and a bright green dressing-gown. His eyes were staring wildly at the ceiling covered with gold stucco, and his blue swollen tongue was stuck out at the Venetian chandelier.

"I went—I went to my wife," Farina spluttered and Zuzana translated as best she could, "and I thought I heard Signor Greffi choking. Perhaps I should have entered but natural discretion prevented me. When I returned, I knocked again, and again no one opened the door. I summoned up my courage then—and went in—and—"

Boruvka bent over the dead man. His neck showed clear imprints of fingers. Very strong, powerful fingers. They had dug into the old man's throat with such force that the mark left by them had turned black immediately. A man's handiwork, the lieutenant said to himself, and looked around him. The carpet was awry and a wet towel which had obviously been dropped by the murdered man—because the door to the bathroom was open and water was still running in the bathroom—testified to a struggle. Yes, the deed of a man, Boruvka repeated.

One other door in the room was open: it was a low metal gate with a bolt that could be manipulated only from the inside. Beyond it the light from the chandelier fell on a narrow winding staircase.

*   *   *

185

"Where does this lead to?" Boruvka asked the major-domo.

"To the hall," replied the dignified old man.

He was in control of himself but it could be seen that the fate of his fun-loving master had touched him deeply.

"The one with the fountain?"

"Yes."

"Is it always wide open?"

"No. The master always used to shut it from the inside. And bolt it."

Boruvka looked round again. There were no further signs of disorder in the bedroom. The old gentleman's bedclothes were turned back but the bed had not been slept in. A lamp was burning at the head-rest of a large armchair in the corner. A map, writing paper, a pen and an open tube were lying on the table in front of it. Boruvka picked up the tube. It contained sleeping pills.

He turned and went into the bathroom. Water was still gurgling from the tap. He turned it off thoughtfully. Something crunched underneath his foot. He stooped down and picked up a splinter of glass. He looked round keenly. A pool of water was lying on the marble floor and in it were pieces of shattered glass.

He straightened up and looked reflectively at Farina.

"Well, I didn't actually go to my wife," the fat man babbled in confusion. "I don't usually go to her, but—I couldn't sleep—I had drunk a lot of wine. I'm sure you understand, it arouses desire even if I can no longer—I knocked at her door, but she didn't reply—the door was locked—I went on knocking for a while—then I assumed that she was tired and had fallen asleep, and I went back to my room."

"And on the way you heard Greffi moaning?"

"No, not yet. Er—when I returned to my bedroom, I looked out of the window for a while and then—well—I felt the need to relieve myself. I went into the corridor again and walked back, and then just as I was turning the corner—"

Farina stopped short.

"You heard it?"

"No, not yet. I saw—it isn't very well lit there—but as I was turning the corner, I glimpsed a figure at the other end of the corridor just before it disappeared round the next corner into the corridor leading to Signor Greffi's room."

"Did you recognise who it was?"

"It was a man," said Farina evasively.

"Who was it?"

"I couldn't swear to it—"

"You don't need to. Who do you think it was?"

"I think it was Signor Greffi."

"Greffi? That would mean that just before the murder he went somewhere—"

"No, no, no!" Farina flapped his pudgy hands. "Not *old* Signor Greffi, *young* Signor Greffi!"

The lieutenant looked at the corpse of the old man, at the waxen neck with its ugly black finger marks. The finger marks of a young, strong man.

"And then?" he asked.

"Then I turned round the second corner, and as I passed Signor Greffi's door, I heard that choking sound. I knocked on the door as I told you—but it was quiet inside. I proceeded to the toilet. There I turned everything over in my mind. I decided that Signor Greffi must be feeling bad—may be, God forbid, it was a heart attack!—," the fat Farina clutched his heart fearfully, "—and when he did not answer my second knock . . ." His voice died away and he nodded in the direction of the corpse.

Boruvka dismissed Farina and glanced anxiously at Zuzana. But her experience in the Dolomites seemed to have toughened her. She was bending curiously over the black marks left by the strangler and it occurred to her father that the profession of detective would be a lesser threat to his daughter's virtue than that of a film star, which Zuzana was bent on pursuing, and that it was after all a better paid job. Therefore he addressed the major-domo through Zuzana:

"Did you lock up the house for the night."

"Yes, sir."

"Is it possible for someone to get in from outside or to escape from inside?"

"That is out of the question, sir. The house has only two entrances; both are locked and I am the only one to possess keys, sir. I locked up, sir, even the smoking room, from which there is access to the terrace, because I had left the doors to the terrace open to air the smoking room. I always do that when we have a big party, sir. And as far as windows on the ground floor are concerned, they all have bars. The attic is permanently locked and is opened only if something is required from it."

"Did you hear anything suspicious?"

"No, sir."

The lieutenant looked round the bedroom once more and went over to the window. The shutters were open. The lieutenant looked out. Below him black wavelets glistened in the deserted canal and the lights on the mooring posts gleamed dully. Three gondolas moored outside the Greffi palace bobbed up and down. The lieutenant looked to the right at the neighbouring house. No, no one could have climbed over from there; the façade was quite smooth, void of sculptures or any kind of ornamentation, and the nearest window was a good fifteen feet away. It was the same on the other side. He looked across the canal with hope but this was soon dashed. Directly opposite the palace stood a large church. The chance that the nocturnal tragedy in Greffi's bedroom could have been witnessed was exceedingly remote.

He turned back to the major-domo.

"Look, what were Greffi and De Cervi arguing about today?"

"It is an old dispute, sir," replied the major-domo drily. "It dates back to the days when the master ran a business in Chicago, sir."

"A dispute about what?"

"About a wreath, sir."

"A wreath?"

"A funeral wreath, sir. The master laid a very expensive wreath on the coffin of his business friend, a Mr Dilling. The most expensive of all wreaths, sir. But Signor De Cervi denies him this honour and claims that the most expensive wreath came from him. It's ridiculous, of course, sir."

"It is. Over such a trifle—"

"I didn't mean it like that, sir. The claim that Signor De Cervi's wreath cost more than the master's is ridiculous. Signor De Cervi's firm was much smaller than ours. His losses were barely six people a year, sir. Whereas we recorded, if I am not mistaken, thirty-two dead and twenty injured in 1927, sir!"

"Aha," said the lieutenant and did not pursue the dispute between the two businessmen any further. He thought hard. The major-domo waited for a moment, motionless, and then he coughed and said:

"Pardon me, sir—"

"Yes."

"Have you any suspicions, sir?"

Boruvka looked at him sharply.

"What do you think?" he asked. "It couldn't have been a woman—apart from a professional wrestler. Signor Greffi was—despite his age—a very vigorous man, and look at that imprint. It wasn't Signor Farina—for one thing, he would have kept quiet about it, and for another thing, he is too hefty—I don't mean brawny, you understand. I mean—" and when Zuzana had explained this to the major-domo, he replied:

"I understand, sir. You meant it euphemistically."

"Something like that," said Boruvka. "Then there's young Greffi—he and Farina are the only two men in the whole house who can be taken into account because it certainly wasn't me."

The major-domo coughed. He seemed to be offended.

"You don't regard me as a man, sir?"

"But of course I do," the lieutenant hurriedly covered up. "But in any decent murder case the murderer is never one of the servants. That simply isn't done."

"Thank you, sir," said the major-domo with relief. "That means then—?"

"Yes. Send Marcello Greffi to me and call the police. But leave the house locked for the time being."

"So you admit that it was you whom Signor Farina saw in the corridor?" Boruvka asked the dark-haired young man with the insipid face a moment later. Young Greffi, clad in a flowered dressing-gown, was blinking nervously.

"Yes, it was me. I couldn't sleep."

"So you walked up and down the corridor?"

"No, I was returning—"

The young man bit off the end of the sentence in a way that aroused Boruvka's suspicions.

"From your father's room?" he suggested.

"No. From—I was in the smoking room. I smoked a cigarette to calm my nerves."

"Why did you need to calm your nerves?"

"Not exactly to calm my nerves. To—well, simply I felt like a smoke—"

"You don't smoke in your bedroom?"

"No. Actually sometimes I do—but sometimes I don't—"

"Sometimes you do and sometimes you don't," repeated Boruvka scornfully. "And what made you feel like going down to the smoking room for a cigarette at three o'clock today of all days?"

"I don't know. I just felt like it. It was a cool, that is warm night—" The young man floundered in obvious confusion.

"It was a cool night," stated the lieutenant in English, and then had the following sentence translated: "Tell me, where did you get the key to the smoking room door from?"

"The key? Why a key?"

Without a word Boruvka went to the door, opened it and looked out. The major-domo was surrounded by a circle of guests in brightly coloured night attire, drinking in every word he said, their heads inclined towards the servant's lips. As soon as the lieutenant opened the door, they moved away from him guiltily.

Boruvka invited the major-domo into the bedroom again and asked:

"Did you open the smoking room for Signor Greffi during the night?"

"No, sir."

"What have you to say to that?" The lieutenant turned to Greffi.

"I—I . . . only that the smoking room was open."

"We can go and see—"

"No. Oh no!" Greffi exclaimed. "I believe you."

"You do?" Boruvka drawled. "But I don't believe you. Where were you?" he asked and nodded to the major-domo to withdraw.

Young Greffi replied unhappily:

"In the corridor. I was walking up and down the corridor—and—smoking—"

He obviously realised how unconvincing his statement

sounded. His hand involuntarily flew to his throat and rubbed his Adam's apple. The lieutenant frowned.

"Have you any debts?" he barked at the young man sharply.

Greffi started, gazed steadily at Boruvka and nodded.

"Your father's possessions fall to you under his will?"

"Only half. His wife gets the other half."

Young Greffi held out his hands imploringly.

"I didn't kill him! It comes to quite a lot. But I didn't kill him! I thought that it was too risky—I'd be the first to be suspected—I mean—," he corrected himself quickly, "I never contemplated anything like that! I'm not a murderer!"

Boruvka looked at him gloomily.

"Really?" he asked. "So where were you during the night?"

Before young Greffi could reply, there was a knock at the door.

"Signor tenente," whispered the plump Isabella di Campiano. "I must tell you something. Something important—" she turned to cast an adoring look at Greffi "—and very private!"

Boruvka nodded his round head and Greffi thankfully withdrew.

"Signore!" The young lady clasped her hands to her magnificent bosom, as though in prayer. The lieutenant noticed her hands; like everything else about her, they exceeded the average feminine dimensions.

"Signore!" cried the young lady piteously. "You suspect my fiancé of patricide—"

"Of what?" asked Zuzana.

"I know." Isabella flung her arms wide in an adjuratory gesture, and her broad palms reminded Boruvka of those of a man from Stehovice, who had covered his mother-in-law's mouth with them so effectively that he was still mining ore in the Pribram mines.

"What do you know?" he asked.

"That you think Marcello murdered his father. The majordomo said so. But he didn't murder him! I can prove it!"

"How?"

"He was with me! The whole night! Until the moment that Signor Farina's shouts awoke us!" Isabella bowed her head. "I beg of you to exercise discretion. This is very embarrassing for me—but do not think badly of me—we have been engaged for five years..." She blushed and her voice died away. The lieutenant contemplated her sadly. He was thinking about something. First of all about the sounds which had disturbed the nocturnal peace of the palace, the grating of keys, the gurgling of the fountain, and also about the buxom young lady's loud breathing. About what young Greffi had been doing next to her when sounds so unlike human ones had kept the lieutenant awake from half-past twelve when he had lain down until three o'clock when he had unwillingly got out of bed.

And then he pondered what young Greffi had really been doing.

A pale, opaque light begun to appear outside the bedroom window and picked out the haloes of cream-coloured saints on the façade of the church opposite. Day was beginning to break. An idea occurred to Boruvka.

He assured Isabella that she might rest easy on that score, and politely piloted her through the door. He did not invite anyone to come in. He took a sheet of writing paper and a pencil from Greffi's desk and—with his idea in mind—rapidly sketched a plan of the second floor of the ancient palace.

He sat musing over the plan and running his finger over it here and there. Zuzana wanted to know why he was doing this, to which he snapped that she was too young to be told. He suddenly leapt up and went into the corridor.

The consternated guests chattering in the corridor fell silent and six pairs of eyes were fixed on Boruvka. One pair reflected an uneasy conscience.

He mustered his command of English and with great mental exertion addressed the curvaceous lady in a Chinese dressing-gown.

"Signora—would you mind coming with me—into your bedroom."

"Yes," said Signora Farina, "Luigi has already phoned for the police."

Zuzana had to intervene again, even if she was too young.

In the lady's bedroom Boruvka changed his mind, ordered Zuzana to wait there, and pulled the beautiful Signora Farina through the sliding doors into the adjacent room where her naughty little boy was sleeping sweetly, clutching the ugly doll to his chest. Einstein, the Boston, crawled out sleepily from under the boy's bed and gazed at Boruvka in surprise.

Boruvka again mustered his English and enunciated very slowly:

"The murderer—Marcello Greffi!"

The beautiful woman turned pale.

"Why are you telling me?"

The lieutenant wrinkled his brow and with great effort got a few more words out:

"Don't you know?"

At that moment he resembled the Boston terrier: like the dog's face, the lieutenant's too expressed profound sadness. Signora Farina bowed her head.

"Yes," she said quietly. "I know. He was here with me."

Cesare tossed on his bed and the monstrous-looking doll fell on to the thick carpet. Boruvka picked it up. It was damp; the boy had probably been holding it when he fell into the fountain before supper. One fiendish glass eye gleamed at the lieutenant like an opal.

"Yes, I was with her," mumbled Marcello. "Would you please keep it dark?"

Instead of replying, Boruvka asked, "When did you leave her?"

"Someone knocked at the door—she—she was afraid it was her husband—"

"Thank you, you may go," said the lieutenant. He had expected that sentence and now he knew that the curvaceous lady, unlike Isabella di Campiano, was speaking the truth.

But who, then, had murdered the spry old gentleman if Marcello was the only man in the palace who had the necessary physique?

Could he have accomplished it in the brief, tense interval between the moment Farina had glimpsed him in the corridor and Farina's return from the toilet when he had knocked at Greffi's door for the second time?

That did not seem very likely to Boruvka.

* * *

193

He ordered everyone to go to their rooms and he and his daughter withdrew to their allotted suite. It was growing lighter outside. On the façade of the church opposite not only the haloes glowed but the saints themselves were high-lighted against the honey-coloured shadow above the canal in all the yellow gold beauty of the dawn. The first motor boats laden with milk, bread and fruit were racing along the canal. In a window of the palace next to the church, a sleek, glossy black cat was meticulously performing its morning toilet.

Boruvka had the feeling that he had forgotten something. He didn't know what. A faint, cold trace of something seen and assimilated which had not yet reached conscious level was pressing uncomfortably on the deeper layers of his mind. He began to recite a meaningless string of words under his breath. Not altogether meaningless. Once, a long time ago, at a course in psychology, a degenerate scientist, Freud, had been mentioned, and the shining example of some academician's slobbering dogs had been held up in opposition. Boruvka had behaved precisely in accordance with the law of dialectics concerning contradictions and had scoured the criminological library for *An Introduction to Psychoanalysis*. It had provided many moments of secret amazement, for it had made him aware of the innermost workings of his mind torn by so many obscure currents, and there he had read, too, of forgotten things being recalled by the method of association.

Therefore he now glanced gloomily at his daughter who, worn out by a host of impressions, had fallen asleep on her bed, and muttered:

"Zuzana—Zuzana—little girl—doll—little boy—little boy—doll—ah!"

With this theatrical shout, he shot off the couch.

Zuzana woke up.

Rubbing her eyes, she mumbled:

"What is it, Daddy?"

"Nothing! Wait here for me!"

And he dashed madly out of the bedroom.

He rushed into the nursery and made for Cesare's bed. Signora Farina who was resting in the adjoining room, draped picturesquely over a Renaissance armchair, started out of her doze and groaned:

"Haven't you done enough? What else do you want?"

"Yes. Police comes," muttered Boruvka somnambulistically.

He seized the ugly doll and the surroundings ceased to exist for him. He thought back intensely. No, he hadn't scrutinised the doll closely at supper—but the original one, the one that had sunk into the canal, that one, had had only one eye like this one!

He turned round—the doll fell from his grasp—and he tore out of the room like one possessed.

He ran along the corridor and disappeared through the door of the murdered man's bedroom. He bent down, picked up the wet towel from the floor and ran into the bathroom.

It had pink tiles and two towels were hanging on the chrome towel rail. They had pink and white stripes. But the towel in his hand had pale green spots.

Again Boruvka turned round as though he were sleepwalking and tore out of the door like a madman.

"Zuzana!" he called impatiently from the doorway of his room. "Zuzana, change into your—"

Young Greffi, listening eagerly round the corner, did not hear what the lieutenant had ordered his daughter to change into because the detective slammed the door behind him. In any case, even if he had heard, he would not have understood. Boruvka had been speaking to his daughter in Czech.

Half an hour later a policeman, his face crumpled with sleep, arrived. The corpulent captain saw a man with a round face and a dishevelled tuft of hair sitting on the edge of the fountain in the hall and a young girl in a white bathrobe. The man was looking thoughtfully at a small Boston terrier in front of him, which looked extraordinarily like him, while the pink-tinged "falling light" was pouring down on all three of them from the glass ceiling above. The captain riveted his gaze on the slim attractive leg which the unbuttoned bathrobe revealed from well above the knee. The leg was bare and gleamed rosily in the half-light. And as the stalwart detective followed the direction of his gaze to the girl's leg, it escaped the captain that she was wearing, quite illogically, a bathing cap on her head.

Eventually, he learned that the round-faced man was the communist colleague of recent fame, and therefore raised no objection to his leaving the Greffi palace for a short time. Shortly afterwards, the gossiping gondoliers watched a very melancholic lieutenant battling with the long oar of a black gondola and doggedly guiding the gilded prow towards the rising sun, against whose fiery ball an Alfieri palace was magnificently silhouetted.

The oar must have been dirty because the first thing the lieutenant requested of the half-awake major-domo was to wash his hands. The major-domo led him into the marble bathroom and went to awaken his masters as ordered.

The desire to wash his hands, strangely enough, left Boruvka once he was in the bathroom. When the major-domo returned to announce that the guest was awaited in the hall, he caught the detective gazing sadly at two white towels with pale green spots hanging on the towel rail. He looked as though he was hypnotising them or, vice versa, as though the pale green spots, the same colour as his daughter's eyes, were hypnotising him.

Alfieri senior was crushed by the news, but the sprightly deceased's former colleague was even more deeply moved. De Cervi raised his long hands to heaven and his bony fingers began to tear the remains of once luxuriant hair. "My God! My God!" he cried despairingly. "Holy Joseph! All the saints! It can't be true!"

The lieutenant coolly left him to the care of his wife, who preserved a dignified composure both then and later, when they were all stepping into the gondola and the detective lost his balance. His Italian trip almost ended in disaster because the detective could swim only the few strokes necessary to gain the general physical fitness badge. De Cervi, whom he caught hold of at the last minute and who as a result fell into the canal instead of him, could not, it transpired, swim at all. The bald head disappeared immediately and only a column of bubbles indicated that even under water the pious gentleman had not ceased to call upon heaven. Fortunately, the major-domo did not lose his presence of mind and fished out his sinking master with the oar. The gondola's departure was delayed until the shaken De Cervi had changed into dry clothes.

In the large hall all those who had feasted there the evening before were gathered round the rectangular basin. The only one missing was the elderly gentleman who the day before had been prancing about after a ball; on the other hand their numbers had been swelled by the corpulent captain and his entourage. He was not looking very pleased. A cursory examination had not revealed anything of any consequence and so he threw ill-tempered looks at Boruvka, Signora Farina and Marcello Greffi.

"No," said Boruvka gloomily, as though reading his thoughts. "Signor Marcello did not murder his father. You know that already."

As the captain transferred his gaze to the fourth, Farina, the lieutenant added quickly:

"As I know who the murderer is, Signor Marcello will not require an alibi. Therefore, I would request you not to record it in the file. We are gentlemen, after all."

Farina, fortunately, did not follow this; he was too worked up. His wife shot the lieutenant a grateful look—but met reproachful, melancholy eyes.

"All the doors were secured from inside by a key or a bolt; the ground floor windows are barred; it is impossible to climb into this building from a neighbouring one," said Boruvka. "The typical mystery of the locked room. But all possible solutions of that mystery have been exhausted, so our solution will necessarily be one of them. The murderer," he continued, "must have been a man. A man of strong physique. There is only one of that description in the palace. But, as you know, he did not commit the murder." The company held their breath. The Boston terrier opened its mouth and stuck out a pink tongue.

"Therefore, it must have been someone who got in here from outside," Boruvka went on. "With your permission I'll interrupt my exposition for a moment and send my daughter outside for something."

He nodded. Zuzana—still in her white bathrobe—got up and

gracefully left by the main entrance. The captain watched her in wonderment.

"What for—?" he began, but Boruvka silenced him with a wave of his hand. The hall was as silent as the grave, and the "falling light", pale and cold, lit the pool. The fountain had been turned off; not a ripple disturbed the surface, as smooth as glass and covered with rainbow-coloured patches of grease.

The lieutenant turned slowly and ostentatiously towards the basin. This seemed to act as a signal to all the others. The semi-circle moved and the greasy surface shining some distance below the level of the floor became the focus of many eyes.

Something moved below the surface. Something long and white broken by two narrow red stripes and ending in a red bobble. Then the surface started rippling and at the edge of the basin a slim, but not thin, girl in a diminutive bikini and a red bathing hat bobbed up and removed the diver's goggles she had been wearing.

Although the corpulent captain's attention had not been drawn in the first place to the girl's face, he recognised her as the Czech detective's daughter.

Among the gathering someone groaned. It was Alfredo Alfieri and he began to tear his hair in the manner of Signor De Cervi.

The girl in the red bikini grew sad like Lieutenant Boruvka.

"Yes," Boruvka told his daughter in a slurred voice some days later when he was steering the red Felicia in dangerous zigzags along the deserted road through the Dolomites, this time in the opposite direction. "Yes. It was the doll that gave me the idea. Cesare dropped it into the canal in front of the palace and no one fished it out for him. And yet he had it with him that night —and it was wet! Cesare had fallen into the fountain before supper. That made me think there might be a connection between the fountain and the canal. Then you tried it out."

"Yes," hiccoughed Zuzana. The lieutenant, protected by the liberalism of the Italian law, had bought a bottle of Chianti on the way, and Zuzana was prescribing herself generous doses of this beverage, which the lieutenant fondly assumed she was imbibing for the first time. Still less did he realise that, unlike at home, here Zuzana was drinking to drown her sorrow. "An

—an elephant could've swum through," she said with another hiccough, adding, "if, of course, it could swim."

"Then it all began to fall into place of its own accord. The wet towel in the old man's bedroom didn't match the towels in the bathroom. But they had similar ones in the bathroom at Alfieri's. Someone from Alfieri's house had had it with him—most likely in a polythene bag—so that he could dry himself thoroughly when he climbed out of the basin. He didn't want to leave wet traces. And then, during the struggle with the old man, he dropped it on the floor. When Farina knocked, he lost his head and bolted. It couldn't have been old De Cervi because he can't swim. That's why I threw him into the water—to find out."

He lapsed into silence; somehow he wasn't managing to keep the car on the right-hand side of the road divided by two thick white lines.

"I found the polythene bag on young Alfieri, tied round his waist with a piece of string. During the struggle, the old man tore it with his ring and the towel fell out. It's funny, the significance of a remark of Mrs Greffi's, which I had overheard behind the folding screen, dawned on me only long afterwards."

"What was it?" hiccoughed Zuzana.

"She was reproaching someone for flirting with that Czech girl—and she meant you—" Boruvka added, instilling a note of sternness into his voice. "And she was right! The way you were carrying on on the beach, Zuzana! That was for the last time! And I don't want to see that swimsuit on you ever again!"

"It was only for Italy," said Zuzana sadly. "And I couldn't help their bothering me."

Boruvka was about to remark cuttingly that their bothering hadn't bothered her unduly, but he swallowed it. "I thought," he said, "that Mrs Greffi was telling her husband off, and at heart I approved. But then—" the lieutenant broke off gloomily— "then I realised that she had been speaking to Alfredo Alfieri. He was her lover," he said lugubriously, "and as divorce isn't possible in Italy, he decided for—murder."

They drove in silence for a while. Felicia stoutly conquered the steep incline.

"Who would have thought it of him?" the lieutenant mused. "From the outset I found him rather likeable—except, of course, the way he carried on with you—and then he turns out to be an ordinary, beastly murderer!"

He was silent. The gold serrated edges of the mountains above Cortina loomed up out of the autumnal haze.

"Maybe he wasn't that bad," whispered Zuzana. "And he must have been terribly in love with her, if because of her—" her voice broke. The sharp-eyed Boruvka flashed a glance at his daughter. Zuzana's green eyes were swimming in tears. She sighed.

"He was a murderer," repeated the detective in a hard voice. But Zuzana appeared not to have heard him.

"Do you think—do you think, Daddy," she asked with a sob, "that they'll hang him?"

The lieutenant took his eyes off the road again and glanced obliquely at his daughter. Hot tears were trickling down her round cheeks, leaving glistening trails. The last time Boruvka had seen his daughter cry like that was when he had forbidden her to go out with a certain young parachutist. He frowned, fixing his gaze gloomily on the grey roadway, and resolved to be severe. But, as it had done so many times before, his soft heart lost the great but vain struggle over his daughter's moral education.

"No," he growled, "unfortunately, they definitely will not. In Italy they don't hang people for crimes of passion."

He screwed up his eyes and studied fixedly the road racing away under the wheels, so that he should not see Zuzana's green eyes turned on him with hope and gratitude.

IX

Aristotelian Logic

I T W A S T H E season of spring fashions. Mrs Lucie Boruvkova
had had a little item made for her daughter Zuzana at Rosenblum's. This time it was a floral blouse and—as in preceding
years—the two hundred crowns which she had paid to the highly
skilled staff of this reputed establishment were to prove a good
investment.

Mrs Boruvkova was a dressmaker herself. She had not got
a diploma but she had an unusual flair. The cocktail dress which
she had run up for Zuzana the year before had been taken for
a Schiaparelli model among the wealthy Italian nobility. A
similar creation made up secretly (her husband did not know about
it; like many a Czech woman she earned an untaxed income on
the side) for the wife of a French diplomat posted in Prague was
hailed as the latest Dior line at the Cannes film festival.

Every talent, however, requires inspiration, and for this reason
Mrs Boruvkova expended a few hundred crowns on the services
of the Rosenblum salon. The salon held private shows for its
customers. There one could see what was not displayed at the
large-scale fashion shows held for the ordinary public in the
Lucerna Hall. These private shows affected Mrs Boruvkova's
creative ability like fantasy-freeing marijuana. One could also see
the prettiest models there, which was the reason why Lieutenant
Boruvka attended the shows.

This time, too, he was sitting in the front row, lapping up the
exclusive spectacle with ostentatious indifference. At the corner
of the stage, immediately above him, stood a woman whose
dimensions would be described in fashion magazines as "outsize". Every now and again she threw an eloquent glance at the
lieutenant, but he did not notice it. He did not pay any attention

either to her expert commentary addressed to the female public and characterised by the peculiar application of a linguistic law, as yet unknown to science, by which under certain circumstances all substantives changed into their diminutives. For this stout lady things like "dress", "skirt", "blouse", "stockings", "shoes", and even "husband" and "man" did not exist in their natural starkness but only qualified as "an exquisite little dress", "a fetching little skirt", "a dinky little blouse", "sheer little stockings", "dainty little shoes", "darling little husband" and "dear little man".

A similar law affects, for example, the language of waiters, but Boruvka had never thought about it. His attention was devoted entirely to the exquisite little dresses or rather the charming little girls who modelled them either as a full-time or part-time profession.

He was not the only one: the audience at this show of exclusively women's fashions comprised a surprising number of males and only a few of them were "darling little husbands". The majority were "dear little men" of a different type and different relationship to the lovely little ladies they were accompanying.

One was sitting next to the lieutenant. Strangely enough he was alone and the diminutive absolutely did not suit him. He was over six feet tall and more than three feet broad. Although this was extremely unusual, Boruvka noticed him only when the giant blocked his view for a moment and trod on his foot, after having been called to the telephone by the janitor during the bikini display. This gave the detective the chance to estimate his weight as about thirteen stone. All this turned out to be not entirely wasted.

No sooner had he regained a view of the stage, where a delicious brunette in a two-piece sunbathing set was just turning round, when the stout lady smiled at him so significantly that Mrs Boruvkova noticed it. The lady quickly directed her gaze to the hall and announced that the models would now present a few little things for swimming. "The first item," she said, "is a two-piece swimsuit made of pink ruched tulle, particularly suitable for very young girls."

The lieutenant swallowed hard with excitement, felt a disapproving wriggle next to him and therefore feigned a bored yawn. The intimate music, flowing from concealed amplifiers, switched to a languorous slow rock and the hall grew hushed in anticipation of the little two-piece item. But nothing came. The stout lady protracted her smile professionally, but underneath traces of anger and impatience began to show through. The intimate music continued to play, the velvet curtain from behind which the models emerged remained drawn. A low whispering of perturbed voices merged with the music. The smile on the lips of the stout lady gradually faded, and Mrs Boruvkova began to converse quietly with Zuzana. "I crave your indulgence for a moment," twittered the stout lady. She threw the lieutenant an apologetic look and disappeared behind the velvet curtain. The buzz in the hall grew louder.

A minute passed, two, three minutes. Only the music, the languorous slow rock, went on playing uninterruptedly. Boruvka fidgeted impatiently in his seat.

At last the velvet curtain was drawn back, but to his disappointment instead of a young girl in a bikini, the face of the stout lady appeared. And it was not wreathed in a professional smile. It exuded horror.

She nodded at the lieutenant and when Boruvka had first of all looked round twice to see whom she meant, she hissed:

"Inspector—could you step this way for a little second?"

The detective scrambled up on to the stage and disappeared behind the folds of the curtain in dead silence. In a moment he re-appeared, coughed and addressed the silent gathering:

"You are requested not to leave the room. Would you all please remain where you are."

In the small room to which he then withdrew the murdered girl was stretched out under the mirror. She was lying on her stomach, wearing a two-piece swimsuit of pink ruched tulle and the handle of a knife of the kind sold in sports shops was sticking out of her back below her left shoulder blade. A mauve handkerchief wrapped round the handle reached as far as the girl's back and was partly saturated with blood. In spite of this the white monogram JN showed up in the corner.

The scene of the tragedy was separated from the rest of the room by rough cloth curtains attached at both top and bottom on two sides; behind these were other similarly improvised changing rooms; on the remaining two sides the curtains hung freely, giving access on the left to the dressing-room behind the stage and on the right to the workroom.

In the dressing-room the stout lady was waiting for the lieutenant, together with the chief designer, two tailors, a hairdresser, the five remaining models and six dressers. Long rows of dresses on hangers extended along the two lateral walls and across the middle, while the velvet curtain filled the whole of one side. The workroom on the right was empty during the fashion show because all hands were fully occupied backstage.

The lieutenant looked gloomily round the cubicle, resembling a beach cabin. Then he turned abruptly and entered the dressing-room.

"Where is your phone?"

The stout lady stepped forward.

"Come with me. We have one in the office but the one in the corridor is the nearest."

She stalked along the stage in front of the lieutenant, stopped after the last cubicle, drew back the curtain, holding it for Boruvka. The detective passed through and found himself in the workroom. To the right was a wall with a door which the lady opened. Directly opposite the door on a shelf fixed to the wall was a telephone. While the lieutenant was using it, he noticed that on that side the door had no handle but only a small knob and therefore could not be opened from there without a key.

A little later he was sitting in the office of Dagmar Kralova, the manageress, and ignoring the ardent glances she was showering upon him. The interest of this lady of his own age depressed rather than inflamed him, and he waited impatiently for the arrival of his colleagues.

"I am sure, inspector, that I shall be able to be of great assistance to you in discovering the murderer. As this salon employs mostly women, I think I can say that I know my employees very well. Nothing escapes my intuition."

"I usually rely rather on logic," remarked Boruvka.

"But this, I believe, is a somewhat unusual case, even for you. I follow your work, you have no idea how closely!"

"How?"

The lady put a plump little hand to her mouth.

"I probably shouldn't say this, but you won't report me, will you? My sister's husband is a judge and she lends me—but her husband doesn't know—*The Criminologist's Journal.* It gives great prominence to your splendid achievements."

"*The Criminologist's Journal* is not a book of detective stories," observed Borukva sternly. "And it is not a magazine intended for the public."

"I know," said the lady, laying her plump little hand on Boruvka's. "Anyway, I can assist not only with feminine intuition but also with your masculine logic. Listen! Are you listening?"

The lieutenant nodded. He had a plan of the Rosenblum salon in front of him and while the lady was talking he studied it.

"Marcela could have been murdered only by someone who was in the dressing-room or workroom," she whispered in a conspiratorial manner. "It is actually one large room, divided provisionally by the models' cubicles and hangings. After the show all this is cleared away, leaving only the one workroom which has two doors. One at the back leading to the rear staircase, and that was shut. The other is the one we went through to telephone in the corridor. And it—"

"Yes," Boruvka interrupted. "It can't be opened from the corridor. Who has a key to this door and who has a key to the door at the back?"

"I have," said the lady with a smile. "Several of the workroom employees also have a key to the door leading to the rear staircase. Not the office staff, mind you. But they were all in the dressing-room at the critical moment. You can imagine that during the show they have their hands full and they have no time to notice what the others are doing. Each model—there are six altogether—has a dresser at her disposal to help her undress and dress so that everything goes smoothly. The girls change in the cubicles. In some salons," she said in a scandalised tone, "in some salons the girls change in front of the male employees, but I don't allow that here. That's why I had the temporary cubicles arranged, even if it does complicate the running of a show."

"Elsewhere, ahem," the lieutenant cleared his throat, "the ladies don't find that embarrassing?"

Kralova smiled tolerantly at the lieutenant's naïveté. "Some of them don't. But I don't allow it here in my establishment. Partly for moral reasons," she said severely, "partly for a special reason —and I think this played an important role in the case. But first of all I'll describe to you the arrangements during a fashion show."

Boruvka nodded and followed her finger as it pointed to different parts of the plan:

"It's like this: the model leaves the stage here, goes into her cubicle where the dresser is waiting for her with another outfit. She helps her to undress, then to dress and carries off the outfit that has been displayed to one of the three rows of hangers here." She indicated three criss-crossed lines, two along the lateral walls of the dressing-room and one across the middle. "The model in the meantime finishes getting into her costume—she puts on her little hat, pulls on her little shoes or draws on her little gloves— and then she goes out of the cubicle into the dressing-room where one of the designers checks her over and a hairdresser fixes her hair. She is then ready to pass in front of a second curtain here on to the stage. Everything must go as smoothly as clockwork. So you see—", she leaned towards Boruvka confidentially, "—that no one has time to bother about anyone else unless it is part of his job."

"Certainly," said the lieutenant. "But the girl—Marcela—was changing into her swimsuit at the time of the murder—"

"Yes—and that is why she was in the cubicle alone longer than the others. She had to strip to—," the lady blushed, "—that is she had to strip completely and she did not need the help of a dresser for that or to put on her swimsuit. This fact is very important for my—what do you call it?—deduction? Or is there another word?"

"Deduction," said Boruvka coldly. "And what is your deduction?"

"Someone—", Dagmar Kralova raised her voice significantly, "—someone knew that Marcela would be in the cubicle alone for some time. That someone obviously knew the programme of the show. Ergo: it must have been a workroom employee.

Ergo: he must have been in the dressing-room at the critical moment—"

"H'm."

"But there everyone is engrossed in his job! A person could leave there only if his work was not connected directly with helping the models to change, or with clearing away the clothes or doing the models' hair or giving them a final run-over. He could pass through this curtained partition into the workroom," she pointed to the sketch, "go round the cubicles and enter any one he chose from the rear."

The lady assumed a mysterious expression and, to his acute discomfort, laid her fleshy hand on the back of Boruvka's again. "And now we come to the main reason why I don't want my models to change in the men's presence. We have a head designer, a real expert, in the fullest sense of the word. He has worked in Vienna, London and Paris, even at Dior's. But as regards character," she pursed her lips primly, "he is a terrible philanderer—an extremely fickle, yet jealous, philanderer at that. He won't leave any woman alone, even when she's dressed, let alone if he sees her only in her little undies."

"Really?" exclaimed Boruvka expectantly.

"Yes, really. Several of the girls have had scenes with him, some right here on the premises. That's why—and I'm sure you appreciate this—I insist on these cubicles at all times and under all circumstances. And now—listen carefully: this designer—his name is Fendrych—to put it mildly, had been interested in Marcela for some time. But Marcela wasn't the least bit interested in him, you know."

"I know. That is, I didn't know," said the lieutenant gloomily.

At that moment the door opened to reveal a glum-looking Sergeant Malek who had just arrived with Boruvka's team.

Malek's surliness surprised the lieutenant. The sergeant was usually in a good humour over every nice new murder. Altogether his attitude towards his work was entirely constructive, as all his testimonials confirmed. Hence Boruvka's astonishment. But he soon saw the reason for Malek's ill-humour. It was written on the face of another member of the team, brought along in case body searches of the salon's female staff should be necessary. It was the young policewoman with the majestic chignon. Her expression indicated that she had been offended. She was substituting for comrade Jebava who had gone on maternity leave. Boruvka had not sought a replacement in time, and so the policewoman, who until then had filled only a junior position, consisting mostly of typing, had been given an unexpected chance. No one, not even Boruvka, knew how ardently she had longed for such an opportunity, and how mistaken Malek had been when he had tried to put his arm round her waist in the police car.

Since that day, about a year ago, when she had joined the homicide squad, Malek had waged a continual offensive. The girl's magnificent and awe-inspiring chignon was, however, a monument to his failure. She stuck to it stubbornly, although the sergeant consistently made fun of it. It had adorned or disfigured —according to taste—her head since that moonstruck moment a long time ago when Boruvka had allowed his thoughts to wander, forgotten what he was dictating and had declared awkwardly:

"That hairstyle suits you, comrade. You should always wear it."

Such trifles sometimes play a decisive role in a person's fate. She wore it, even if the lieutenant—since his crazy adventure with a little known saint one crazy spring night which she had spent alone at the Tomcat—had not uttered a single sentence of a similar nature, and had restricted his relationship with her to dictating bombastic reports, interlarded with an exceptional quantity of passive constructions and other Germanisms. Now she appeared in the doorway wearing a smart, high-necked black blouse with white buttons and fixed her beautifully made-up eyes on Boruvka. Perhaps it was the eyes in their wistful frame or the chignon or the black blouse with the white buttons—the lieutenant had fought desperately to combat his critical age for so long and now he had lost the struggle: for the moment she opened the door until the end of the case of the murdered model his brain was veiled in a thick fog. And so the girl's first essay at fieldwork became a case in which Boruvka displayed what was for him unprecedented and therefore astounding lack of ability. He was not yet aware of this. With the air of a fascist dictator he strode off to the scene of the crime.

*   *   *

Examination of the place brought the usual kind of results: ascertainment that death had been instantaneous, the tip of the knife having penetrated straight to the girl's heart. The blow had been dealt with great force, evidently by the hand of a man of physical vigour. There were no fingerprints on the handle because the murderer had had the forethought to wind round it a mauve handkerchief which he had then incredibly—either in a state of panic or because he was feeble-minded—left at the scene of the crime, despite the fact that it bore the monogram JN.

The murdered girl's handbag revealed the usual contents: an address book with an average number of addresses, mostly men's, a lipstick, powder compact, a tin of black shoe-polish with a small brush for applying to the eyelashes, a small bottle of Chanel perfume, a silk handkerchief, a purse containing twelve crowns seventy-five hellers, a bunch of keys on a ring, one separate key, an opened packet of American mint-flavoured Chicletts chewing gum, a cigarette lighter and a packet of Partyzan cigarettes, a tube of tablets, the medicinal purpose of which the old police doctor Seifert whispered in Boruvka's ear, and finally a love letter of a rather peculiar nature:

Marcelka don't be mad at me I could kick meself your Pepa*

From this the lieutenant judged astutely that the writer was a man and not a very well educated one at that.

"What is Mr Fendrych's Christian name?" he asked.

"Josef," replied the lady promptly, looking over Boruvka's shoulder at the letter. She nodded significantly.

"Send him to me upstairs," said the lieutenant and withdrew to the manageress's office.

The mental fog was already having an effect: at that moment he had no doubts that he would shortly make an arrest.

Fendrych was a gentleman classified by fashion magazines in the same category as amply-proportioned ladies. Apart from that he was very bald and had wet, lascivious lips. Apart from that he was quaking with fear. "What have I done?" he asked in a baffled, helpless manner. "I was just having a drink—"

"Of what?" barked Boruvka, while the policewoman pounced simultaneously, asking:

* Diminutive of Josef (trans.).

"Where?"

The lieutenant looked at her reprovingly. He disliked any interference with his interrogation. His mental fog was thickening.

"Beer," squeaked Fendrych in terror. "Actually in the corner by the dress rail," he politely amplified his statement. "I had a bottle hidden there."

"Have you any witnesses?"

"N-no, I shouldn't think so. There's always a dickens of a rush when there's a show on, comrade. But I don't need witnesses. I hadn't any motive. I didn't start anything with Marcelka—"

"You can hardly make a virtue of that, can you?" put in the policewoman quickly.

Boruvka growled his dissatisfaction.

"What do you mean—miss?" asked Fendrych faintly.

"I mean," the policewoman began, but Boruvka interrupted her in a raised voice:

"The young lady—the young comrade means that you had been pestering the murdered woman for some time. That you had threatened her—" he said curtly.

The policewoman thrust the letter found in Marcela's handbag under his nose and snapped assiduously:

"And what is this?"

The man looked at it and a weight was visibly lifted from his mind.

"You think that note was from me?"

"Who else?"

"I don't know, but I'd say it was from that boxer."

"What boxer?" chorused Boruvka and the policewoman, and looked at each other. The lieutenant sourly, the policewoman with an apologetic smile.

"That heavyweight champion. Nesetril. He was sitting in the front row during the show. Right next to you, comrade—comrade prefect."

"Comrade," croaked Boruvka with odious arrogance while they were waiting for the boxer, "kindly refrain from interfering in my investigations."

"I only wanted to help," said the girl humbly. "I read in the handbook for members of the police force that cross-examination is usually the most effective kind of interrogation."

"I have Sergeant Malek for cross-examinations when I need them. You," said Boruvka condescendingly, "will be used for some less exacting job if the occasion arises."

The policewoman hung her head and the beautiful, glossy chignon shone in front of his eyes. He frowned and ordered Sintak to go and see why it was taking so long to fetch Nesetril.

When they finally brought him in—he was a head and shoulders taller than the stalwart Malek—the boxer behaved in a strange manner. Boruvka stood up to dispel his feeling of physical inferiority and asked the seated giant abruptly:

"Have you had an affair with Marcela Linhartova?"

The large man, whose face registered no sign of emotion, replied calmly:

"Yeah. I'm still having one."

He screwed up a large green handkerchief in his hand and then laid it on the table in front of him. The monogram JN gleamed whitely on it.

Boruvka looked at Malek. Malek shook his head and shouted roughly at the boxer:

"You're not! Marcela Linhartova has just been murdered!"

If he was counting on the psychological effect of this callous tactic, the result exceeded his expectations. The boxer's jaw dropped, his eyes closed, leaving his face void of any identifiable expression, and he slumped to the floor like a sack of potatoes.

"That's as good as a confession," observed Malek cynically, while the policewoman bent over the unconscious colossus.

"He murdered her?" exclaimed Sintak incredulously.

"Yes," said Boruvka, "maybe."

The policewoman raised her eyes to his. "Oh no," she said. "He didn't murder her. He was just very much in love with her."

This irritated Boruvka. He bleated:

"That's enough, comrade! Keep your opinions to yourself! I told you not to meddle in our interrogations."

"But I—"

Something inexplicable, which he did not understand himself,

enraged Boruvka to the highest degree. Without knowing exactly
how it happened, he resorted to his most repelling tone and to the
command which he had never used during nearly eighteen years
of service in the force:

"That's an order!"

The policewoman stood to attention. The white buttons on her
bosom shone and a tear oozed out of the corner of one immacu-
lately made-up eye.

"Very good, comrade lieutenant."

"You may leave. You may help the others write down a list of
objects found on or near the victim at the scene of the crime."

The regulation "Very good, comrade" was a barely articulate
whisper.

Sergeant Malek glanced at the lieutenant, grinning oddly. Then
he turned eagerly to watch the slim figure in the black blouse
go out of the room.

The boxer on the floor sat up and Boruvka, almost beside
himself with rage, browbeat him relentlessly.

What he ascertained made him even more furious, partly
because it proved that the policewoman had been right.

For the boxer—however much circumstantial evidence pointed
to the contrary—could not have been the murderer of the unfortunate model. Yes, he'd been going out with her and had had
sexual intercourse with her, he replied frankly to the lieutenant's
question. Yes, the mauve handkerchief with the initials JN was
his; he didn't know how it had got into the cubicle. He must
have lost it or lent it to Marcela; she was always forgetting her
own and borrowing his. Anyway, it had been a gift from her.
She'd had the monogram embroidered on it for him. Of course,
they'd quarrelled sometimes but he'd never laid hands on her.
He knew he might have hurt her. He could not always keep his
enormous strength under control. He was Czechoslovak heavyweight champion and was going to take part in the Olympic
Games in the autumn. What had happened during the show?
Well, the janitor called him to the telephone. He didn't know
who phoned him. When he took up the receiver, yes the one in
the recess in the corridor, no one answered. So he waited and
waited—how long? He didn't know but it seemed like ages. He

was curious to know who could be calling him. He kept repeating Hullo! hullo! And then the caller hung up. No, he didn't say anything, he just hung up. He stood there for about another minute, repeating Hullo! Why? Oh, simply to make sure. Yes, yes, the inspector was right, it was pointless, but it didn't occur to him then. Things never did until some time later.

Then he returned to the hall and was told that he was not to leave, so he stayed. He didn't go away.

The boxer's evidence was confirmed for the most part. The janitor hadn't exactly seen him while he was phoning—the phone was not visible from his desk—and also he hadn't heard very much. At the beginning, yes. He'd said Hullo! hullo! several times, but he kept on repeating it so the janitor had stopped listening. Whether he stopped saying Hullo! he didn't know. He thought so, he had an idea there was silence for a long time there, but the loudspeaker was going from the hall, the janitor had listened to the music until the murmuring started in the hall and he went to see—

"Was Nesetril standing by the telephone all this time?"

"I suppose so," said the janitor uncertainly. "He must've. He didn't go past me at any rate. He came into the hall. I was already there. He came back after I did."

In spite of the janitor's vagueness, Boruvka regarded this point of his testimony as proved in essentials, like all the others.

Except one.

Jarmila Hezounkova, the dead girl's best friend, mentioned that Marcela had complained about the boxer. She'd said he was jealous, quarrelsome and, though he wanted to sleep with her all the time, kept postponing the wedding. Once she came to a rehearsal with a monocle, that is a black eye, and after a lot of prompting she confided to Jarmila that Pepa had done it because something had got into her eye in the street and Pepa thought she was winking at that pop singer Matuska who happened to be passing by.

The boxer denied his authorship; according to him the bruise round Marcela's eye was caused by her having "fallen on her eye". But he couldn't remember why or where or how, so that, as far as Boruvka was concerned, he had as good as confessed.

This meant—in Boruvka's view—that his claim to never having laid hands on Marcela did not hold water.

Nesetril admitted shilly-shallying over the wedding, but he explained that he had wanted first of all to win the Olympic Gold Medal and "bring it to Marcela as a sorta weddin' present". The lieutenant looked sceptical at this, especially when the boxer tried to substantiate this story by the assertion that "marital duties ain't fittin' durin' tough trainin'." How is it then that during your intensive training you continually prevailed upon the deceased to fulfil pre-marital duties, as Miss Hezounkova has testified, asked Boruvka sarcastically. Nesetril, incapable of a subtle lie, simply denied Hezounkova's unattestable statement, hung his head, thus—in the lieutenant's view—confessing to this aggravating circumstance as well.

Notwithstanding, it was impossible to pin the murder on the boxer yet. The door dividing the telephone recess from the workroom could not be opened without a key. And a key had not been found either on the boxer, or any of the spectators, nor had one been revealed by a cursory search of all the rooms. Only the janitor, the manageress and the chief designer possessed one.

It was not possible to pin the murder on the chief designer either; he had produced two witnesses in the meantime. Both these witnesses of the female sex averred that at the critical time they had noticed the designer taking a pull at a bottle that had been standing on the floor behind the dress rail. One of the witnesses was a hunchbacked dressmaker, the other was a pretty, young model with a slightly Japanese touch about her. Neither of them impressed Boruvka as a thoroughly convincing witness and the contrast they presented seemed too striking, but there was no way of proving perjury against them. Therefore he returned to the question of how the pugilist had acquired a key to the workroom.

He drew a blank and this annoyed him. He again vented his spleen on the policewoman. They finished their work in the salon late in the evening and were descending the stairs from the first floor when the unfortunate girl asked the janitor off her own bat:

"Where do those stairs lead, comrade?" pointing to a narrow staircase which led into the foyer of a block of flats on the other side opposite the main staircase and disappeared behind the public call box.

"Upstairs into the next building."

"Don't they lead—?" the policewoman began, but Boruvka was seized with such a fit of almost military apoplexy that he recovered from it only on the pavement in front of the building.

In the murdered girl's one-room flat the first thing that met their eyes was a large mourning card leaning against the mirror on the dressing table. It was written in German and informed all friends and acquaintances that Mr Anton Streytschek, owner of a sugar refinery, had died in Vienna at the age of sixty. The announcement was made by the employees of his factory, not the bereaved family as was usual. Why the model had displayed this card was not clear. At least not to the lieutenant whose mental fog had turned into a London smog. Sergeant Malek hazarded a guess at a foreign tourist whom, as he expressed it, the deceased had "picked up somewhere in the Yalta hotel".

Otherwise, the only suspicious objects in the flat were further love letters from the boxer, mostly written on odd scraps of paper and full of grammatical and spelling mistakes. The boxer evidently felt the need to correspond only when he had quarrelled with his sweetheart. He was probably not a unique exception in this respect, nevertheless one of the letters made the investigators sit up. It read:

Marcela if you do that agin I swear I'll do you in Pepa

The word "swear" had been spelt "sware" and then corrected.

The sergeant whistled and gave Boruvka a significant look. Boruvka returned an equally significant one. The policewoman, whose cheeks were aflame with the fervour of detection, forgot herself once more and burst out:

"That doesn't mean a thing. He definitely did not kill her."

Boruvka switched from odious arrogance to slimy irony:

"To what, may I ask, do we owe this degree of certainty? To feminine astuteness or feminine stupidity?"

The eagerness faded from her face, she swallowed hard and gasped for breath. Her cheeks reddened and her eyes glistened with tears, then she hardened herself to do something she had never managed to do in her relationship with her superior. She took offence.

"If that's what you wish to call it, comrade Lieutenant Boruvka, the answer is yes," she replied stiffly. "But I can see it on his face with that flattened nose—"

"Excellent observation!" cried Boruvka with an unpleasant laugh. "You don't miss anything, not even the fact that a boxer has a flattened nose!"

"While we are on the subject of noses," retorted the girl, "I read in the Medilek file—"

"That's quite irrelevant," the lieutenant cut her short. He did not like to recall the Medilek case. For three days and three nights he had interrogated an almost deaf old-age pensioner who swore that he knew nothing about the corpse of the woman who occupied the adjacent flat in a small suburban house. The corpse had been discovered by workmen who used to pass the house on their way to work every day and had smelt the foul odour emanating from the house. When the lieutenant reached the scene of the crime, he had nearly fainted from the stench; the corpse was in an advanced stage of decomposition. The deaf old man asserted that he knew nothing about the deceased, that it had seemed odd to him that he hadn't heard the radio next door, but he had put it down to his deafness. After a three-day interrogation during which the lieutenant had employed all his assiduously acquired subtleties of cross-examination, he finally mentioned the reek; no one could have remained oblivious of that! He had saved this until the end as a trump card and expected the old man, faced with this piece of cast-iron logic, to confess abjectly. He was mistaken. The old man grimaced, pointed to his large, bulbous nose and declared: "I lost my sense of smell when I was fifteen!" and produced a medical certificate to substantiate this statement. It was afterwards ascertained that the old girl had been murdered by a door-to-door haberdashery salesman.

For this reason the lieutenant protested violently against reference to the Medilek case in connection with the boxer's nose, and felt a fresh wave of hatred sweep over him, mixed with admiration for white buttons.

"Simply," the policewoman continued flintily, "I can see even by his nose that he is a good-natured man, and secondly: had he really intended to murder her, he wouldn't have written to her—that is, if the murder was not premeditated and this one clearly was. And if he had really written to her, he wouldn't have said that he was going to kill her."

Boruvka could not manage any more than a needling:

"How do you know?"

"I just do," snapped the girl. "Maybe from personal experience."

"You have committed a murder?"

"Not yet," she said and bestowed a piercingly eloquent look upon the lieutenant.

In a flash of awareness the detective realised why he hated her so fiercely. It had a lot to do with dialectics. Frowning, he hurriedly returned to the boxer's love letters.

He found nothing in them to modify his view of the case. There remained only to discover how the boxer had obtained a key to the workroom, and where he had hidden it after the murder.

While they were sitting at the round table and pondering over the outpourings of the simple but obviously passionate soul, the investigations took an unexpected turn.

Sintak led into the room a man who announced that he had learnt of what had happened and wished to volunteer some evidence that probably had a bearing on the case.

It had. It appeared that a violent quarrel had broken out in the model's flat on the evening before the murder. So violent that the witness, who lived in the flat above, had had to bang on the floor several times with a broom handle to make them argue more quietly. It was impossible to make out what the dispute was about, but it must have been serious because they were screeching like baboons.

"Did you recognise who was there?"

"Miss Linhartova's young man, Mr Nesetril," replied the witness promptly. "That heavyweight champion."

"We know," the lieutenant interrupted him. "And who else?"

"Her cousin, Professor Linhart."

* * *

Once more that evening the young policewoman attempted to fan the embers of detection and thus to illuminate the lieutenant's vexatious mental fog. She had been insulted but she felt sad at the thought that perhaps never again would an atmosphere of tender colleagueship—so dear to her—prevail between her superior and herself, and so she controlled her emotions. While they were driving to the police station engrossed in their own thoughts, she said in the melting, unprofessional tone which Boruvka, too, recalled with nostalgia:

"Comrade lieutenant, permit me one question."

And because he remembered that tone so well, and because he was plagued by regrets, he snapped with odious arrogance:

"What do you want now?"

"I think it would be a good idea," said the girl humbly, "to take fingerprint impressions from the telephone in the foyer under the Rosenblum salon."

Her respectful manner irritated the lieutenant even more and he switched from odious arrogance to slimy irony:

"And why, may I ask? You—you Holmes in skirts!"

At this the patience of this very patient girl ran out.

"For no good reason," she snapped. "Just out of feminine stupidity!"

And she swore a sacred oath that she'd never meddle in the case again.

At least not so that the lieutenant would find out.

A confrontation between the model's lover and her cousin, arranged late that night, only confirmed Boruvka's suspicions. He therefore issued strict orders to continue the search for the hypothetical key and extend it to the ventilation and sewerage systems.

The confrontation resembled David and Goliath in the physical sense and vice versa in the intellectual sense. Linhart was small, irascible and shrewd; the heavyweight champion weighed a good third more than the professor but exhibited no traces of anything that with the best will in the world could be described as astuteness.

The dispute of the previous evening had arisen because the model had complained to Linhart of her fiancé's boorish behaviour and particularly of his postponement of the wedding.

Nesetril again denied this and offered a not very credible explanation, but as the professor's evidence tallied with Hezounkova's testimony, his word could not be doubted.

The professor had invited the boxer to the girl's flat for a chat. He felt called upon to protect her interests as she had no parents. When he had quietly reproached his cousin-to-be with these other faults, the latter had flown into a rage commensurate with the truth of the reproaches, denied the use of violence in words and immediately confirmed it by deeds: the model had been about to mention something, and with one prod of his little finger he had pushed her on to the couch. He had explained the postponement of the wedding with the story about the Olympic Gold Medal as a wedding present.

And then it came: the bride had retorted venomously that the medal would serve as a christening present, for she had learnt at the health centre that day that she was expecting a baby. This news strangely did not bring the athlete to his knees tearfully begging forgiveness and promising to phone the town hall to book the nearest date. Instead, he had worked himself into an even greater fury and accused his fiancée of frequent and promiscuous infidelity. At this point the man above had used the broom for the first time. Although nurturing prudent respect for the physique of his relative's suitor, Linhart had dared to raise his voice in defence of her honour, but all he had accomplished was that the boxer had raised his voice, too—the neighbour had banged on the floor again—and seized the professor by the throat with such force that he had left bruises on it, which the scholar readily showed the investigators. He had tried to call for help and had already given himself up for lost when the third thudding above them had saved him. The boxer cooled off a little, flung the professor on to the couch next to the girl and left in a huff. It had taken the professor till midnight to calm his cousin who was afflicted by a strong attack of nerves and nearly fainted.

The boxer admitted all this contritely. He only added that on the way home he had suffered pangs of remorse and had phoned his sweetheart all the next day, but she had refused to answer the phone and so in despair he had gone to the fashion show, to which the janitor, knowing nothing, had admitted him as a favour. He wanted a reconciliation to be crowned by a binding date for the wedding which he had booked at the Old Town Hall that afternoon.

In the morning the lieutenant checked that the boxer had spoken the truth on that point at least. Sergeant Malek however explained the wedding date to the boxer's disadvantage. The date, as well as the mysterious telephone call (obviously planned by the boxer) were mere attempts to establish a psychological and practical alibi, and Malek considered them to be further proof of subtle premeditation. In the sergeant's judgment Nesetril was not such a dope as he looked. After protracted but hazy consideration, Boruvka concurred with him.

The policewoman no longer attempted to interfere.

At least not so that the lieutenant would find out.

The fog did not lift even at night. Boruvka spent the night in vigilance, alternated with erotic dreams, the subject of which was certainly not the stout lady who entered his office the following day at about eleven o'clock. He greeted her politely but not very cordially.

"Dear inspector!" she twittered and the lieutenant was enveloped in a cloud of perfume as though a procession of Muscovite tourists had just passed through his office. "You won't be angry, will you, if I take the liberty of criticising you a teeny bit?"

"Go ahead," said Boruvka curtly.

"You disbelieving Thomas!" the lady wagged her finger at him. "Fendrych is still at large!"

"Which Fendrych?" he asked blankly, because for the past half hour his mind had been occupied with things other than the murder.

"Oh, you will have your little joke! *Our* Fendrych, of course! Our chief designer!"

"H'm, him," Boruvka frowned. "He has an alibi. He was seen drinking beer at the time of the murder."

"Don't tell me you believe the testimony of that poor Bozenka Smetanova? Oh dear inspector—why that's a clear case of platonic love! Bozenka, poor thing, worships him! She'd put her hand in the fire for him. That, in my view, is no alibi!"

"Independently of her, Fendrych was seen drinking by—"

Boruvka glanced at the papers over which he had been dreaming of a trip to Venice, but not with Zuzana—"Lucie Helebrantova, model."

The stout lady laughed scornfully.

"Helebrantova! My dear inspector, that's the same thing!"

"How do you mean, the same thing?"

The lady gave him a mystical smile.

"Oh. I'm afraid that matters which elude the strict laws of logic are not very plain to you."

"They are plain enough to satisfy me," Boruvka frowned. "But unfortunately they do not suffice as proof."

"They don't? And if I tell you that just before that terrible event Marcela confided to me that she was pregnant—"

"To you? You were on such intimate terms?"

The lady shed a tear or two, or rather she simulated weeping by the delicate use of her handkerchief, taking care not to smudge the mascara round her basilisk eyes.

"I was as fond of Marcela as if she had belonged to me. She and Yvonka were great friends. Yvonka is my daughter, all that is left for me from my dear deceased husband," the handkerchief came into play again. "That's why she confided in me. Poor thing she was so upset that—well, I ought not to mention this, but you are a gentleman and you sympathise with others' misfortunes—anyway, she asked me to make certain arrangements for her. She didn't want to go to the commission*, because the father was not her fiancé—"

The lady lowered her lashes, sighing and added:

"Life is hard on women."

The lieutenant cleared his throat.

"In your opinion the father was Fendrych?"

"In hers," declared the lady tragically.

"Isn't it possible that it was Nesetril's?"

"That good-natured fellow?" The lady exclaimed in amazement. "But, inspector, she would not have had to conceal it from him. He would have married her on the spot. He followed her around like a faithful hound."

The lieutenant blinked and shook his head. Something fits and

* A medical commission which deals with applications for abortions, legal in Czechoslovakia.

something doesn't fit, he told himself. How could that woman have known that the murdered girl was pregnant? Girls like Marcela didn't usually boast about that sort of thing. And if she had told the boxer, it was not very likely that she would have requested the manageress to fix her up. But whom could Kralova have learnt it from? Yvonka? Maybe it had only slipped out in the heat of the argument with the boxer.

"So why didn't she saddle Nesetril with the paternity" he asked, "if—according to what you say—she was having intercourse with him at the same time? Would it have occurred to him to dispute his paternity if he was running after her like a faithful hound?" Wait a minute, he answered himself immediately, Nesetril would say that conjugal duties were not desirable during training. Maybe he, and not Hezounkova, was speaking the truth, maybe he denied rather than importuned Marcela, and could easily reckon that the child was not his. Evidently that was what he had worked out. That was logical. But the lady had a more mystical explanation up her sleeve.

"My friend," she said in a melting whisper, "you really are ignorant of the female psyche. Fendrych—she simply succumbed to his spell! That man is a devil—he has an absolutely unnatural power over women—over *some* women—particularly over very young women. Nearly everyone yields to him. And every woman, without exception, hates him afterwards."

"Really?"

"Yes, indeed. Whereas Nesetril—that was real love!" The lady uttered the romantic word with a sugar-coated capital L. "And Marcela was too decent to do a thing like that to that good-natured man, to her kind-hearted bear."

Boruvka cleared his throat and desiring to create an impression by hinting at vast experience, remarked:

"Ehm, I know women from many aspects, but—"

"Ach!" the lady closed her eyes and pressed Boruvka's fingers. "I know you do! A woman feels it. You radiate a sort of, sort of—"

"What?" asked the lieutenant stupidly.

The lady repeated that little interjection and then said:

"Nobility — willpower — goodness — masculinity — I don't know—"

"Ahem—I don't either," muttered the lieutenant uncomfortably.

"But I know! I'd love to have a talk with a man like you some time, and not just about this case. I am alone and as a woman I often feel lost, helpless—you could advise me—"

"Whenever you need anything, turn to us," said the lieutenant. "That's what we're for."

"Ach! Why the plural, dear inspector—or may I call you friend?"

"As you please. So you think Fendrych—"

"Oh let's forget Fendrych—"

The telephone rang. Malek informed his chief that he would be a little late because he still hadn't finished interrogating Marcela's girl friends. The lieutenant told him that it was all right. He hung up and told the manageress that he had been summoned to an important consultation.

The lady rose to her feet. Boruvka was enveloped in a fresh wave of perfume.

"I shall come again. I'll obtain further proof against Fendrych. I shall come very soon. And when we have proved the case against him, we must celebrate it together. Will you promise me that?"

"Yes," said the detective faintly. "Without fail."

The pressure of her hand numbed him. When she had left Boruvka shook his head in wonderment, as though he could not believe his own ears. Or rather eyes, because afterwards he squatted down and looked through the keyhole. The lady was strutting elegantly along the corridor in the direction of the staircase. Suddenly she stopped dead. She fidgeted, laid her hand on her thigh and fumbled with something there. Suspender, surmised the experienced lieutenant. As though in confirmation, the lady pulled up her skirt but dropped it immediately for Sintak had sailed into view. He paused awkwardly and then passed the lady with a deep bow. She looked round, noticed a door on the left and disappeared quickly inside. Boruvka knew that it was the door to the toilet.

Someone coughed behind his desk. He straightened up smartly and turned round. It was the young policewoman. She was wearing the black blouse with the white buttons and was holding a file in her hands. She had entered unobserved from the adjoining office.

"Here are the shorthand notes typed out, comrade lieutenant," she announced standing at attention.

"Put them on the table," said the lieutenant with dignity. and when she had done so and turned sadly to leave, he added: "Oh, wait. Tell comrade Sintak to have Fendrych brought along immediately."

The policewoman looked taken aback. She seemed to be waging an inner struggle. She fixed her large eyes on Boruvka and asked quietly:

"Are you going to arrest him, comrade lieutenant?"

"That's none of your business," he replied with odious arrogance.

The girl hesitated. Then she said quite softly:

"If you want to have him arrested, I think you should wait a little while."

"You do?" he cut in with slimy irony.

"Yes. Because certain facts have come—may come to light—"

"Now look, comrade! Facts have come to light, yes. Facts have just come to light which give me good reason to talk to Fendrych again and in great detail!"

"You think that what Kralova told you about—"

Boruvka was dumbfounded. He succumbed to an incredible and dark suspicion that women really did possess special extra-sensory powers.

"How do you know what Kralova told me?"

The policewoman lowered her gaze.

"I heard it. She—"

"How did you hear it?"

The lowered gaze disposed of the theory about extra-sensory powers.

"Through the door. I—"

"So you were eavesdropping?"

"I wasn't eavesdropping. But your door is not very sound-proof. Every word can be heard."

"When one puts one's ear to the door, eh?"

"No—it's enough to stand by the door—"

"And why were you standing there?"

"I was bringing those reports—"

"So you were bringing reports and at the same time you were standing still, eh? And you were listening all the time?"

"I didn't want to interrupt you."

The lieutenant only snorted angrily. Each preserved an offended silence. After a while the policewoman plucked up courage.

"That Kralova hates Fendrych. That's why she wants to put the finger on him."

"How do you know?"

"It's enough to hear how she talks about him—and see how she tries to sedu—I mean how she tries to influence you—"

"Ah!" the lieutenant flared up as red as a radish. "Feminine logic again, eh? Logic without proofs. Just—simply it's enough to listen in and we know everything! But, dear comrade," he bleated, and the word "dear" stung the young policewoman, "we in the homicide squad cannot be guided by feminine logic! We in homicide have to be guided by Aristotelian logic!"

Boruvka's conversance with the classics left the girl speechless. She had no idea what Aristotelian logic was. She had no idea either that that very week, when Zuzana had turned to her father for help with her homework in political economy (under which subject Mr Nevlidny dabbled in philosophy), the detective had racked his brains for a long time searching for an error in the statement:

Everything that has wings flies.
An ostrich has wings.
Therefore an ostrich flies.

The lieutenant was standing by the window, silent, albeit enraged, looking at the façade of the little church of St Sidonius, and the girl was unaware of the sorry role this repellent saint had played in the lieutenant's changed behaviour towards her. As he did not order her to leave, she summoned up courage once more and said:

"I know that you cannot be swayed be a mere supposition. But there is that rear entrance to the workroom. Anyone could—"

Boruvka turned round threateningly and the policewoman bit off her words.

"Are you meddling in the investigations again?" he cried. Then he caught sight of the white buttons and forgot what he had intended to say. He shut his eyes and remembered what it was. "Yes, anyone could have gone out through the rear door. That is anyone who had got hold of a key. But eight of the employees have keys. And each of them has lots of friends. We shall investigate them, comrade, one by one. But the general order of the day is economy, if you haven't heard. And we have here two very suspicious characters who demonstrably threatened the murdered girl, or rather they pestered her and used her for their own ends, and by one or other or both of whom she is pregnant."

The policewoman was sorely tempted to comment on this gynaecological phenomenon but she was winded by another effusion of the lieutenant's extraordinary erudition.

"*Entia non sunt multiplicanda praeter necessitatem*!" bleated the detective and she asked humbly:

"What does that mean?"

"It means—" the lieutenant groped for words. "It is called Occam's razor."

"He was a murderer, Occam?"

"Occam was a philosopher from—he was a philosopher from olden times."

"I don't understand it," wailed the girl unhappily.

"It means—it means, well, something like we say in Czech: Why do a thing simply when it can be done in a complicated way?"

"Yes. But I still think that it would not be very complicated—or uneconomical—"

Boruvka, uncomfortably near to being caught out trying to pass off as conversance with scholastic philosophy a scrap of classical knowledge trapped in the convolutions of his brain, literally exploded:

"Of course! Feminine logic is not at all complicated! Feminine logic is too much for us poor chaps at homicide! Do you know what, comrade," he raged on, "you'd better ask for a transfer to pick-pocket duty at the White Swan store! I recommend it! There you can keep an eye on women's shopping bags. Your criminological talents will be up to that level. Here you'd soon be introducing telepathy or spiritualism or other branches of feminine logic!"

The girl, for the second time since the previous day, lost patience at this allusion. Overwrought, she snapped:

"Forgive me, comrade lieutenant, but sometimes my feminine logic is necessary when your Aristotelian brand ceases to function!"

She turned on her heel and stalked out of the room without waiting for an order. She intended to slam the door, but at the last moment her courage failed, so she only shut it vigorously behind her.

Boruvka's round face resembled a red wine-skin.

Sergeant Malek entered the office a moment later and his face also displayed a tendency to redness.

"Impudent hussy!" the lieutenant relieved his feelings. "Y'know what she told me? But I'll teach her—"

Malek cut him short.

"I think, Josef," he said icily, "that you should draw a line between official matters and private—," he hesitated, "—private intrigues."

"Private? Me? What on earth—?"

"Don't put on an act! Everybody's saying it!"

"What?"

"You know what," exclaimed Malek roughly, his voice cracking with insane jealousy. He had just tried again to put his arm round the girl's waist and the redness of his cheeks was not the result of his emotional state alone. "That you are deceiving your wife with our young comrade!"

"Well that takes the cake! I—" The lieutenant's whole being rebelled against the injustice of fate. "I've been holding back for a year—and that's all I get—"

"You've been holding back very ostentatiously," remarked Malek sarcastically. "You nag her very obviously over every trifle. It sticks out a mile—"

"But I—"

"Simply, it's rather crude eyewash!"

Eyewash! That was his reward for his superhuman efforts to stick to the path of virtue. This injury stabbed him like a knife. "You're the one to talk, Pavel!" he retorted, deeply offended. "Do you think I'm blind? That I don't see your billing and cooing? That I haven't noticed you whispering together over the typewriter for four days already? Isn't it the pot calling the kettle black, Pavel?"

"Maybe," said Malek. "But I'm single and you're a married man. The father of a family. That isn't exactly what I'd call the new socialist morality."

"Pavel, as God is my witness—"

"There is no God," remarked the sergeant informatively.

This broke Boruvka's spirit.

"There's nothing between us," he croaked, "I swear to you. Pavel—"

"Tell that to the marines," retorted Malek. "But don't get the wind up. You needn't worry. *I'm* a man of character. *I* shan't tell your wife. And now listen. I have the Rosenblum results."

The results proved absolutely nothing, but the lieutenant did not take them in anyway. White buttons, the sergeant's unmasking and the bogged-down case all merged into an amorphous mist of despair, and Boruvka began to contemplate a voluntary exit from this ungrateful world.

Therefore it was a not unwelcome distraction when the stout lady sailed into his office again at three o'clock in the afternoon, accompanied this time by a spotty dressmaker.

"My friend," she whispered sweetly, holding his right hand for a disproportionately long time. "I promised you further proof —and here you have it. What do you say to that?"

Boruvka did not reply.

"What's this all about?" he asked curtly, looking at the witness.

"Tell him, Alenka, what you saw the day before yesterday in the afternoon."

The dressmaker drew a breath and recited as though she had learnt it by heart:

"Marcela Linhartova gave Mr Fendrych the brush-off."

"She slapped his face," the lady smiled. "And what did Mr Fendrych say?"

"He said: 'I'll pay you back, you—'" The witness stopped short.

"Well?"

"He used a rude word," the lady put in. "Alenka would blush to repeat it."

"What rude word? Evidence must be precise and complete!"

"He said—" The witness still could not find enough courage, and before she could bring herself to disclose what shocking thing Mr Fendrych had said to the murdered girl, the door flew open and the gentleman in question appeared in the doorway.

"I beg your pardon," he said.

"What do you want?" thundered Boruvka.

"I was sent for—"

Boruvka recalled that he had given the policewoman orders to this effect in the morning. She had carried them out, and Boruvka could not help feeling that she had done so with a certain amount of malice.

"Oh yes, of course," he said. "Come in."

Fendrych entered, and Boruvka noticed the manageress's face fall. Fendrych was followed by a man of slighter build.

"What do you want?"

"He's my witness," said Fendrych apologetically. "About the beer. He, too, saw me drinking yesterday. I even offered him a swig."

"Why didn't you name him as your witness in the first place?"

"I was so upset it slipped my mind. I only remembered Miss Smetanova and Miss Helebrantova—"

"Naturally!" the lady sneered through clenched teeth. The spotty dressmaker huddled like a frightened ball in the armchair.

"A piece of evidence has come to light which aggravates your position," said Boruvka sternly. "The day before the murder Miss Linhartova slapped your face and you gave utterance to an expression of a threatening character—"

"But I didn't mean it!" groaned Fendrych. "I only . . . how shall I put it? It was only a manner of speaking. I'll explain it."

"In addition the comrade here," Boruvka nodded in the direction of the manageress, "has divulged something which concerns the murdered girl and herself. You had intercourse with her which had unwelcome consequences."

Fendrych sat bolt upright, then glowered at the stout lady.

"I—I always took precautions! Only with a contraceptive," he turned to the lieutenant. "Anyway she's at the time of life when it's no longer—"

The lady coughed.

"How do you mean 'at the time of life'?" asked Boruvka. "Miss Linhartova was not quite twenty-two—"

Fendrych gasped.

"Me? With Linhartova?—But—That's her doing!" he snarled, turning on the manageress, his face black with hatred. "That's her doing, for revenge, comrade prefect! Me and Linhartova—I ask you! Look at me! I chatted her up a bit! I stuck my paw where it had no business! That's why she socked me! But her!" he pointed at the darkening lady. "If you only knew her! She won't leave anything in pants alone! Did she give me a time! In a manner of speaking, you know. It was 'My friend this, and my friend that!' until I yielded. And when I came to my senses and told her to go—to where she belonged—she—oh, you should have heard the scenes! And now she wants to pin the blame on me for that poor girl who was done in by that moronic king kong, that champion of the Republic—the rotten old whore!"

"Well, really!" the lady exclaimed loudly. "You boor!"

The situation rapidly deteriorated into an uncontrollable verbal duel, in which the lieutenant tried vainly to intervene. In the end Malek, aided by the witness, had to drag the enraged designer into the corridor by force.

The lieutenant—with his collar torn—turned to the lady. Her bosom was rising and falling rapidly and the cosmetic façade was blotched by the sweat of agitation.

"I hope you don't believe that degenerate scoundrel, inspector."

"Don't hope!" shouted Boruvka unexpectedly. "I do believe him! It's enough for me to look at you and see you trying to sedu—to influence me—and I know everything! You ought to be ashamed of yourself! The mother of a grown-up daughter! And me, a married man! And out of sheer spite you would have got an innocent man into—"

"I don't know whether *you* behave like a married man," retorted the lady. "I noticed very plainly the young lady who was with you and how you—"

"Don't drag her into this," Boruvka burst out. "Altogether, you take far too much notice of things that don't concern you!

You ought to be ashamed! Such an old frump! I'll tell you this: it doesn't surprise me one bit, not one bit, that Fendrych ditched you! Not one bit!' "

The last words were addressed to the lady's back.

Even if her bosom had heaved with suppressed emotion, the lady had preserved decorum—unlike the lieutenant—and had sailed out of the office like a real lady, which, in fact, she was not. Or was she? Boruvka did not know what to make of ladies.

He mopped the sweat from his round face and collapsed into an armchair. Then he did something which he only resorted to on the rare occasions when he was troubled with nausea. He delved into the bottom drawer of his writing desk, drew out a bottle of "Monastery Secret" liqueur, poured himself out a tot and knocked it back.

During that afternoon he knocked back several more. The case seemed to have lodged in the shallows. The scene with the manageress had disgusted him. Malek's allegation had provoked him to impotent rage. And the policewoman in the black blouse ached like an agonising thorn in his heart, which not even the most skilful surgeon could have extracted.

He dragged himself from the police station through the streets of spring-like Prague, faintly perfumed with a hint of lilac like the year before, and dropped into the Embassy Bar. When he sallied forth, the hint of lilac had perceptibly increased in direct ratio to the mental fog and yearning alcoholic despair towards which the lieutenant had progressed at the bar.

He weaved past the wide, brilliantly lit windows of the self-service store at the bottom of Wenceslas Square and the tuft of hair waggled dispiritedly on his round head. He had left his hat in the Embassy. He felt utterly defeated on all fronts. This was the bitter end. Life—for the fifteen or twenty years he would still toil and moil upon this earth—would offer nothing but disappointments, suffering and pain. He looked with melancholy eyes into the bright and shiny shop and suddenly stiffened. A well-known figure was standing at one of the many counters of tinned food. It had its back to him and was torn between tunny fish in tomato sauce and processed cheese flavoured with vegetable.

The lieutenant hiccoughed—or was it something more like a groan—broke into a trot, tripped, clutched the waist of a smart gentleman in a broad-brimmed hat, muttered an apology and shot round the corner of Wenceslas Square. In a moment he was blazing a trail through the evening crowd in the direction of the counter above which peeped an imposing chignon.

The girl had not yet solved her problem: she was still hesitating between tunny fish and cheese, and a lonely chunk of crusty bread reposed in her wire basket. A wave of tenderness swept over Boruvka. And of profound regret. He approached the girl from behind and addressed her hoarsely:

"Comrade—"

She turned and her face registered startled consternation.

"Comrade—I—you—we—"

"Don't be angry, comrade lieutenant," she pleaded anxiously. "I know you didn't want to have the fingerprints taken. But I thought—"

"To blazes with the fingerprints!" cried the lieutenant desperately. "I—"

"But they proved I was right. Really."

"Comrade!!" groaned Boruvka. "Comrade! Forgive me for shouting at you!"

Afterwards they were sitting—as they were supposed to have done exactly a year before, but had not—in the Tomcat wine tavern, talking about the case. At least ostensibly.

"You were right," he admitted humbly. "Her hatred for Fendrych was written all over that woman's face."

"In any case, he was above suspicion, at least I think so," said the policewoman. "After all, he wouldn't have chosen a time when he might have been required any moment."

Boruvka sighed.

"You're right. I should have discounted him from the start. It must have been the boxer after all. But how on earth did he get through that door!"

The question remained suspended in the air. The policewoman pecked at the fried pork which the generous lieutenant had ordered, thereby preventing her from ruining her digestion with tinned tunny fish.

"Don't be cross," she said, "but I don't think it was the boxer.

It's too subtle for him. To get hold of an accomplice who would phone him, then—"

"Who then?"

The girl looked uncomfortable.

"You know you wanted to ascertain all the people who had a key to the rear door of the workroom—"

"Yes?"

"Marcela Linhartova had one, too."

"I know."

"And—I wanted to tell you but you wouldn't let me get a word in edgeways—"

"I'm sorry," mumbled Boruvka.

"That's all right. It was the small key that was in her bag separately, remember? Not on the ring with the others."

The lieutenant sat upright with a jerk.

"That means?"

The girl nodded and allowed him time to repair his reputation. She was a very unselfish girl.

"That means," said Boruvka, "that—wait a minute—let's say the murderer borrowed it from her—or stole it from her—had a duplicate made and wanted to put the original back in her handbag after the murder—because he knew that it was known that she—I mean Marcela—had one, and he was afraid that a hunt would be made for it—and as a search would start with people who knew her intimately—"

"Yes. But he didn't have time to put it back on the ring with the others, so he just dropped it into her handbag."

They both fell silent. Boruvka thought hard but the remnants of mental fog had not lifted entirely. He said in a disappointed tone: "But the pieces still don't fit together. During the few moments the janitor was distracted by the disturbance in the hall, Nesetril wouldn't have had time to slip through the door at the main staircase, race downstairs, run up the other staircase, unlock the workroom from behind, enter the cubicle—"

"Oh no," the policewoman interrupted him. "And anyhow when the janitor left his desk and went into the hall, Marcela Linhartova was already dead."

Boruvka reddened.

"You're right! I'm— But what about the handkerchief? That

belonged to Nesetril. He couldn't have left it there by mistake. He's a bit slow on the uptake, but—"

"But he's not so stupid as to leave an obvious visiting card behind him," the policewoman completed for him. "It was the handkerchief that gave me the idea that someone was trying to frame Nestril. And then the telephone."

"Telephone?"

"And the mourning card in Marcela's flat."

"That's—" Boruvka did not finish what he had intended to say. He didn't know himself. The policewoman continued:

"Someone called Nesetril to the phone at the very moment the murder was committed or just before. That's why I wanted to have the fingerprints taken from the phone in the hall. Because that's the nearest phone to the scene of the crime—I mean the nearest public telephone."

Sweat beaded Boruvka's forehead. His mental fog lifted.

"And you think—?"

The girl nodded gravely. The beautiful chignon shone magnificently.

"Yes," she said. "The person who phoned is the murderer."

"As a matter of merely formal interest, professor, where were you yesterday afternoon?" Boruvka asked about half an hour later, standing in the angry-looking scientist's doorway.

"Where? At the cinema. Why?"

"Just to complete the record—you didn't keep the little piece of paper by any chance, did you?"

The use of the diminutive reminded Boruvka of the stout lady, therefore he hurriedly corrected himself:

"Your ticket, I mean."

"Wait a moment," said the professor and put his hand into his breast pocket. He drew out a handful of used tickets, and searched among them, frowning. "Here we are. The Blanik cinema, five thirty. 'The Call of the West' was on."

"Oh yes, an interesting film," the lieutenant nodded. "But the short film that preceded it was even more interesting. What was it called? 'The Lonely Child' or something like that. Do you remember? About illegitimate children."

"Yes, something like that," said the professor. "I thought it was rather good."

The lieutenant grew immensely sad.

He was almost ashamed that such an old trick had sufficed to convict a murderer.

Further proof was provided by the professor's fingerprints on the telephone in the foyer of the Rosenblum salon, which the young man in the fingerprint department had taken at the young policewoman's request—as a favour in his own time after work. The murderer had not worn gloves, for this would have looked odd in a public call box on a hot spring day. Also he was over-confident of the subtlety of his plan, and when he returned through the hall after the murder, he had cold-bloodedly replaced the receiver on its rest.

In the fire of cross-examination the scholar collapsed ignominiously and made a full confession. When his cousin had confided her troubles to him, he had seized upon the unique opportunity. He invited Nesetril "for a chat" in Marcela's flat and intentionally provoked him to the loudest possible argument, assuming correctly that the tenant above would notice it. While this was going on, he appropriated Nesetril's monogrammed handkerchief. The boxer was in the habit—Boruvka recalled it retrospectively—of wiping his palms with his handkerchief and leaving it lying around. Afterwards while "consoling" his cousin, Linhart had stolen the workroom key from her. He knew of its existence—his cousin had once lost it and he had had a duplicate cut for her from one which she had borrowed from a friend. On the afternoon of the murder he had listened behind the workroom door where the loudspeaker could be heard broadcasting the programme for the benefit of those behind the scenes. When the time approached for Marcela's entrance in a swimsuit—and the professor knew that she would be alone in the cubicle—he ran downstairs, used the phone in the foyer to have Nesetril called out of the auditorium, ran up the rear staircase to the first floor, checked that the workroom was empty, and from then on everything went smoothly. Fate played into his hands—he did not even have to wait for his cousin as he had originally reckoned. She was just changing in her cubicle.

When Boruvka dictated the report to the policewoman, the girl had to prevent him from—deservedly—attributing to her all the credit for catching the murderer. It cost her a lot of effort to secretly re-style and re-word the report—at home that night—so that it contained the lieutenant's usual sprinkling of Germanisms but also made it clear that Professor Linhart had been unmasked by her beloved chief.

But she derived pleasure from doing it. And her best reward was not the rise in salary of thirty-five crowns a month, strictly in accordance with the scales, which Boruvka recommended, but that almost forgotten tone in which the detective uttered remarks which had no place in the report he was dictating.

"I admire your powers of deduction," he said, for instance. "How logically you arrived at the connection between the mourning card and the motive for the murder—that Professor Linhart wanted to inherit the Austrian factory owner's fortune, because he had left everything to his niece and those two were the only relatives. I call that really logical reasoning!"

"I don't know whether it was logic," replied the girl uncertainly. "I think it was rather the dowry."

"What dowry?"

"Oh, I've got an uncle," said the policewoman. "He's an affluent writer, but otherwise he's quite nice. Josef Kopanec. I'm his only living relative. He's an old bachelor—and he won't be dissuaded, he's so terribly old-fashioned—so he keeps putting money aside for my dowry." She paused and then added significantly: "I've already got fifteen thousand."

"But what connection—?"

"Well, when I saw the mourning card and noticed that the only signatories were employees, no relatives, it occurred to me that perhaps he, too, was a kind uncle, maybe also a bachelor and that maybe he'd been saving up a dowry for Marcela—"

"Excellent!" breathed the lieutenant. Then the thought crossed his mind that however excellent a feat, it could hardly be termed strictly Aristotelian logic. He cogitated. Could it be that there was something in feminine logic—even as far as criminology was concerned?

"But I won't need it anyway," observed the policewoman quietly. The lieutenant started out of his reverie.

"What?"

"The dowry. I'll never marry!"

"What an idea!" exclaimed Boruvka and the knife twisted in his heart. "Such an intelligent and—" he plucked up courage "—pretty girl—"

The policewoman shrugged her shoulders.

"I have no luck with men," she said. "At least not with those I care about. Do I, comrade lieutenant?"

The next day the lieutenant came to the definite conclusion that feminine logic was a closed book to him. He had a visitor, the last person on earth he would have expected.

The stout lady.

Hadn't he mortally offended her? He had called her an old frump, or something like that, he'd forgotten what, in his fury. But something like that, or even worse.

Yet the lady had come; she sat down on the edge of a chair and took out a silver cigarette case.

"Do you mind?" she asked.

He offered her a light. The cigarette shook in her trembling fingers as she lit it. She fidgeted nervously with the cigarette case in her gloved hands.

"I hope, lieutenant, that you will forget what happened here yesterday afternoon. I beg you to do so."

"Oh that was nothing," said Boruvka who after the previous evening would have pardoned even the murderer of his own mother. "Don't let's talk about it."

"I—" The lady choked and the silver cigarette case fell on the floor. Boruvka gallantly bent to retrieve it and laid it on the table in front of her. She took out a dainty handkerchief and blew her nose very faintly.

"I—but I won't detain you. A woman's dreams—especially if she is alone—rarely come true."

The lieutenant murmured awkwardly:

"But, madame, everything will turn—" He did not get any further.

"Thank you," said the lady. "I shall never forget what you have done."

She stood up, picked up her cigarette case, put it into her handbag and turned to leave the room.

The red-faced lieutenant did not know exactly what he had done that deserved her thanks but he gave it only a passing thought. He skipped to the door and held it open for her. When he had closed it, he shook his head and again stooped to peer through the keyhole.

He saw the lady walking elegantly down the corridor, then she looked round and suddenly dived into the toilet.

He straightened up.

Well I'm blowed, he thought. Do women also get the trots from nervousness—or is it her suspender again?

He was at a loss for an explanation.

He found one much later.

X

The End of an Old Tom-Cat

I T W A S A L S O the end of the cats' mating season. That night
a whole quartet gave a concert behind the chimney on the roof of
Lieutenant Boruvka's house, wailing persistently in a melancholy,
yearning fashion and disturbing the lieutenant's sleep.

And at the other end of the city an old tom-cat lay dying.
Painfully. He writhed in terrible paroxysms. He shouted. But
before anyone could come to his aid, he died.

Now—at seven in the morning—Lieutenant Boruvka was standing in front of a disordered double bed on which, clad in a
pair of blue-and-red striped pyjamas, was slumped a huge mound
of human flesh that only an hour ago had still been the Public
Prosecutor Paul Hynais. Now he had become an ugly corpse with
a face contorted by a scowling grimace, very much like the
countenance familiar to a large number of criminals and people
treated as such by the Prosecutor. Only his face was even more
terrifying, and less professional.

Shortly before he expired, the Prosecutor had vomited, and
the remnants of a partly digested supper had soiled the front of
his pyjama jacket, the blanket, and the pillow.

The old police doctor Seifert straightened himself up, his joints
creaking audibly, and he turned to Boruvka with a wry expression on his face.

"Looks like arsenic, but there are some atypical symptoms,"
he said. "We'll have to wait for a lab report."

The young Emergency Service physician nodded eagerly.

"I felt there was something wrong. When the lady phoned us,
I thought at first it would be a case of food poisoning—judging
by what she said—but then—"

"And what *did* she say?"

239

"She said that her husband had stomach cramps, and she was afraid that he'd eaten something that disagreed with him."

Lieutenant Boruvka looked darkly round the bedroom. Apart from the tumbled bed, it could have gone on show. Inside the half-open linen cupboard sparkled piles of accurately folded bed linen tied with pink and blue ribbons. The Prosecutor's suit was on a hanger, his shirt, underclothes, and socks lay in a neat heap on a chair. Over the bed hung a large painting of some procession underneath an impressionistic deluge of red flags. The picture seemed somehow out of keeping with this room, a cold, sombre room gleaming with polished wood and a great deal of chill glass.

"It was all over by the time we got here," the young doctor went on. "The speed with which death had taken place at once struck me as fishy. That's why I sent for you."

"What time was it when Mrs Hynais called you?"

"At five. But I was out seeing a patient."

"So that you arrived here—when?"

"At half past five. And unfortunately that was too late. Only I—," the doctor glanced at the body on the bed, "I doubt whether I'd have been of any help, even if I'd come earlier. What do you say, Doctor?"

Seifert, the old police doctor, nodded.

"I shouldn't imagine you would," he said.

Lieutenant Boruvka remained silent, his eyes still roving the chilly bedroom. Through the window, in the mist of a cold morning, he could see a garden. A very well-kept garden. Apple-trees, cherry-trees, with the first blossoms showing white in the grey mist, stunted trees conscientiously tied to sticks, flower-beds tended by someone who was an expert in gardening. The window was open, and Boruvka heard a woman crying next door.

The wife of the man towering like some monstrous mountain on the dishevelled bed was not crying. She was a small, elderly lady, standing there in the kitchen by the glass door leading to the terrace. She was pale, her ashen, wrinkled face framed by sparse grey hair made striking by a pair of very black and very large, almost childlike, eyes. What those eyes were saying the lieutenant did not know. He could not read them.

"You told the doctor over the phone that you were afraid

your husband might have eaten something that disagreed with him. What did you mean?"

"Well, we'd had minced meat for supper," said the woman in a small, timid voice. "It had been left over from the day before, and so I was afraid that perhaps the meat had gone bad, it was such a hot day yesterday—"

"But you had some of it as well, didn't you?"

"Yes."

"And you felt no ill effects?"

The woman shook her head.

Sergeant Malek went over to the sink and rattled the crockery in it.

"Is this what you used for your supper?" he asked. "You didn't wash up last night?"

"No, I didn't," said the woman. "I meant to do it this morning, but when this happened . . ."

Malek looked at Lieutenant Boruvka, who nodded. Malek then beckoned to Sergeant Sintak, who took several plastic bags out of his case and started filling them with the plates containing traces of the Prosecutor's last meal.

Lieutenant Boruvka took a look round the kitchen. Like the bedroom, it was extremely tidy, the white, old-fashioned cupboard gleaming like a Catholic altar.

"Didn't your husband eat anything else?"

"Not at home," replied the woman hesitantly. "But he liked to take his food in town during the day."

"Can you tell me where?"

"Oh, different places. In the snack-bar at the Alcron, at the Gourmet, in the Film Club—I don't really know all of them. He was very fond of his food, and—"

"Yes?" Lieutenant Boruvka urged her.

"And sometimes he wouldn't want his supper when he came home. Last night he also left a bit. He must've had too much to eat in town again, I suppose. I was annoyed with him about it, but little enough did he care."

Malek gave a discreet cough, trying to catch the lieutenant's eye. But Boruvka only stared out of the window.

"And what happened last night?" he asked gloomily. "Were you with him all the time during the meal?"

"Yes, I was."

"Did he use any pills for indigestion? Did he take any alcohol with his supper?"

"He had some beer," said the woman, pointing to an empty bottle on the kitchen table. Malek picked it up. There was a little beer left on the bottom. Malek handed the bottle to the other sergeant.

"And he *was* in the habit of taking pills. Carried them in his jacket pocket. He suffered badly from indigestion ..."

"How about sleeping pills?"

"No, he slept very well."

Boruvka made a sign to Sergeant Sintak, who went off into the bedroom, where the Prosecutor's jacket was hung up.

"So he had nothing else, apart from the minced meat and the beer?" enquired Lieutenant Boruvka. "Couldn't he have taken something on the quiet, without you knowing about it? You say you were with him all the time?"

"Yes, that's right," replied the woman, and then she hesitated. "Oh—actually I *was* out of the room for a short while, answering the telephone. It was a trunk call, my sister from Liberec."

"How long were you away?"

"Oh, I don't know. Two or three minutes, not more. My sister only wanted to tell me that she'd be coming to see us on Saturday, and she hung up immediately. I got the connection at once. So it probably wasn't as much as two minutes."

"Well, couldn't he have taken something then? Out of the refrigerator, for instance?"

She shrugged.

"I really don't know."

"We'll take a look at the things in the fridge, just to make sure," said Sergeant Malek.

Sergeant Sintak now came back from the bedroom and handed Boruvka a blue phial. Boruvka went up to the glass door of the terrace and read: *Pepsin pancreolan*.

He was gazing at the half-empty phial, lost in thought, when his face was touched by a vivid ray of the sun. He looked up. The garden had cast off the misty shroud, and the white cherry-blossom sparkled like a large flock of butterflies. The rusty spring sun flooded the terrace with light, and a black cat ran across the garden. Boruvka recalled the nocturnal concert, and sighed. Heaven knows, he thought, why there seem to be more and more cats all the time. Is it because people don't have to pay any tax for them? Or could it be that there's something more dignified, some greater mystery and freedom about cats than there is in dogs? Or in people, if it comes to that.

Here there also seemed to be plenty of them. The black shadow was quickly followed by another, brown-and-white in colour, and from somewhere behind the villa came a furious mewing. On the otherwise spotlessly clean terrace one of these nocturnal visitors had left a disgusting memento, which it had in vain tried to hide in the concrete of the floor. They're cleanly creatures all right, thought Lieutenant Boruvka, but still, it's not exactly hygienic to keep cats in the city.

The mewing could be heard again, and then the two cats re-appeared in the garden, flying like two live, twisting projectiles between the trees and over the neat flower-beds before they disappeared from view in the white crown of a cherry-tree. The woman in the villa next door was still weeping disconsolately.

Lieutenant Boruvka sighed, and turned to the Prosecutor's wife.

"When did the first symptoms appear?" he asked.

"Towards morning. He woke me at about half past four and complained of severe pain in his stomach, and so . . ."

Dr Seifert now took over the interrogation, and Lieutenant Boruvka gave himself up to his thoughts.

The ringing of the telephone brought him out of his reverie. The Prosecutor's wife automatically reached for the instrument, but Boruvka stopped her and picked up the receiver himself.

"Hullo?"

There was a brief silence, then he heard a faint female voice which, he could have sworn, belonged to a young girl.

"Can you—can I speak to you? I—I've changed my mind."

When he replied Sergeant Sintak looked up in surprise, for the lieutenant was speaking in an unnatural, hoarse whisper quite unlike his normal voice.

"Yes, go on," Boruvka said.

"You're not alone?"

"No."

"And could you come at nine? Same place as yesterday?"

"All right," replied Lieutenant Boruvka. "But let's say at the Union Café, shall we."

"Yes," said the girl. "The Union Café at nine."

Boruvka hung up.

Sergeant Malek gave him an inquisitive look. Boruvka shrugged his shoulders and turned back to the Prosecutor's wife.

"Tell me, Mrs Hynais, your husband was a Public Prosecutor. Didn't he perhaps get any threatening letters lately?"

It transpired that threatening letters formed a regular part of the Prosecutor's mail, and had especially done so in the fifties. At first, Hynais had handed them over to the police, but as they were all anonymous anyway, and since there was never any attempt to carry out the threats, he had stopped doing that and had unfortunately disposed of the letters by throwing them in the waste-paper basket.

Sergeant Malek did not attach any importance to them, either. Standing with Lieutenant Boruvka by the garden gate in front of the villa as they were about to get into the official car and drive to the Union Café, he said confidently:

"For my money I'd say she did it. And made a pretty amateurish job of it too, I expect. Women just haven't the brains for a really well thought out murder. They may be pretty clever in other ways, but murder, no."

Boruvka knew that the feminine brain his Sergeant had in mind was the one beneath a certain majestic chignon which had only yesterday—the lieutenant had listened behind the door—been the subject of yet another argument between Malek and its wearer. It made her look so awful that she would most probably die an old maid if she did not change her style, Malek had asserted venomously, for he was more than willing to save the girl from such a terrible fate. But she had never shown the slightest intention of invoking the Sergeant's aid in respect of her virginity.

"Sure," said the Sergeant gloomily. "Sure she could've done it. I guess the whole case will boil down to the question of obtaining material proof. What kind of poison was used, how it could have been obtained, and so on. These poisoning cases usually wind up like that."

Boruvka cast a gloomy look at the garden of the next-door villa. An old lady with a tear-stained face was working on the flower-beds. Not nearly so well-kept as the flower-beds in the Prosecutor's garden.

Malek looked at his watch. "By lunchtime we ought to have the lab report."

It was ten to nine.

Three minutes later they were at the Union Café. The place was empty at this hour, the only customer being an elderly man, formerly a Catholic Member of Parliament, who was avidly reading the foreign Communist newspapers. Lieutenant Boruvka sat down at a little table right by the door, concealing himself behind a copy of *Rudé právo*, while Malek seated himself next to a large window with etched flowers in the corners, from where he was able to see the pavement in front of the café and Sergeant Sintak, leaning nonchalantly against a lamp post.

The police car was parked in a narrow side street just round the corner.

At five minutes past the hour a girl came in and looked all round the room. Not finding the man she was looking for, she crossed to a table in the far corner and ordered a cup of coffee. She kept toying with a glove, turning nervously all the time to look at a clock on the wall, thus offering Boruvka a pretty profile.

Looking at her like this, he thought she seemed familiar, but he could not remember why. A moment later, however, the girl herself confirmed that they *had* met before; when the lieutenant laid aside his newspaper, their eyes met and she nodded an embarrassed greeting. Now he realised where he had met her. He got up and crossed over to her table.

"Good morning, Miss Peskova. How are you?" he said pleasantly.

The dancer—she was a friend of the murdered Ester Nakoncova, whose acquaintance Boruvka had made when investigating the Odeon Theatre murder—smiled uncertainly, and shook his proffered hand.

"Oh, thank you. Just the same as ever, I guess."

245

"Waiting for somebody?" Lieutenant Boruvka sat down opposite the girl.

"No. I mean, yes, I am. But I don't suppose he'll be coming now." She cast another glance at the clock.

Boruvka's face grew sad.

"No, you're right. He won't."

The girl turned pale. Her hand flew automatically to her slender throat.

"He—someone gave him away? How did they find out?"

Lieutenant Boruvka fixed a pair of melancholy eyes on her face.

"Tell me everything," he suggested.

The girl burst out crying.

When she sobbed out her story, it turned out to be quite different from what Boruvka expected.

"It was Zdarska who suggested it to me—her sister had a similar spot of trouble, something to do with foreign currency," she explained, amidst tears. "And she said I ought to go and see him. Well, I did, but when I saw what he looked like, I—"

Lieutenant Boruvka nodded understandingly.

"The price seemed too high," he said mournfully.

The girl hung her head.

"That's right. But last night I thought it over and, well, you see, my brother's whole future is at stake. At least, that's how I see it. He's going for an entrance examination to the School of Economics, and if he went to prison now—"

"What's he done?"

"Nothing, Lieutenant. He's just a silly young boy, that's all, you know how it is. He and some pals of his probably had a drop too much, or maybe it was the Big Beat that did it, I don't know—well, anyway, they broke some furniture during a concert at the Cultural Centre and they ran away when the cops turned up. My brother was the only one they managed to nab. But he's only a silly kid, it's not really his fault—"

"You are pretty fond of your brother, aren't you?"

"Well, after all, he *is* my brother," said the girl sadly. "You see, our mother died when he was born, and Father—well, he married again, and so it was I who brought him up. My brother, I mean. Oh, but it's not my fault that he's behaving so stupidly,"

246

she added quickly. "I didn't have enough time to devote to him, that's what it was. . . ."

"Hynais was to appear for the Prosecution against your brother?" Boruvka interrupted her.

"Yes, that's right."

"What did you tell him?"

"I said I'd think it over and let him know."

"And how did he—?," Boruvka was not quite sure how to phrase his sentence; it was a very delicate matter and he did not wish to hurt the girl more than was necessary, "—how did he ask you in the first place? Did he say straight out what he wanted, or did he just hint it?"

Rather to Lieutenant Boruvka's surprise, the girl now raised her head and looked him straight in the eyes.

"He hinted—but in such a way that there could be no doubt about it. See what I mean?"

"Yes, I see," said Boruvka sadly.

"Have you—has he been arrested then?" she asked. "Did it all come out, that business with Olga Zdarska's sister?"

"No, it isn't that."

His answer startled her.

"Oh! In that case, perhaps I oughtn't have—"

"Don't worry," Boruvka reassured her. "You can't harm him now, whatever you tell me."

"Who's going to prosecute my brother's case, do you know?"

"No, I don't know. The only thing I do know is that it won't be Hynais."

"Has he been fired?"

"No, but he won't ever prosecute again, just the same."

"He won't?" breathed the girl.

"No," said Boruvka. "He's dead."

When she had calmed down a little, she gave Boruvka more details, and he learned that her "deal" with the Public Prosecutor had been negotiated in an incredibly matter-of-fact manner. Hynais had agreed to see to it that her brother was let off as lightly as possible, and had even promised to arrange things so that the boy should not be prevented from entering the university.

All this in exchange for the kind of favour women had traded with already in ancient Babylon.

They—the young dancer and the Prosecutor—met at the Film Club, where Hynais had previously had an appointment with a film director and where he then took his dinner. The girl told Boruvka she had lost her appetite as a result of the interview, but the Prosecutor showed every sign of enjoying his meal. She couldn't recall what he had ordered, but she knew there had been a lot of it.

"Never mind," said Lieutenant Boruvka. "We'll find out what it was he ate last night."

"Why, the shameless old tom-cat!" fumed Sergeant Malek as they drove from the Union Café to the Film Club, his indignation making him forget that the friendly relations existing between him and the lieutenant had cooled somewhat lately. "Would you believe it, Joe! I was always fool enough to think that judges and prosecutors were models of integrity—"

"They're only human," said Boruvka. "Like the rest of us. And sometimes it's just a coincidence," he added, "whether you're a prosecutor or anything else."

"Who, Dr Hynais?" asked the waiter at the Film Club. "Sure, he was here all right. He comes here quite often, he acts as a legal adviser on crime films. Last night he sat over there, with Miss Peskova. Yes, he had dinner, that's right."

"What did he order?" Lieutenant Boruvka looked round the restaurant, in which two waitresses were laying the tables for lunch. Through the open serving hatch he caught a glimpse of the kitchen, of a young cook in a tall white cap.

"What did he have? Wait a mo. I remember that the bill was pretty large," said the waiter, thinking. "He had soup with meat balls—steak Tartare—Milanese roast—chocolate cake with whipped cream—beer—and a cup of coffee. That's it."

"What beer?"

"Pilsener. Two glasses of it."

The young cook behind the service hatch leaned out and stared inquisitively at Lieutenant Boruvka.

Rather too inquisitively.

And he was not so young as all that, he was at least thirty.

The lieutenant thought in silence for a while before turning again to the waiter.

"Can you let me have a list of all personnel who were on duty last night?"

The analysis of the contents of the deceased's stomach and intestines showed that he had died as a result of poisoning by tetraethyl of lead. The dose had evidently been a fairly small one, since the poison did not take effect until some ten hours after consumption. If Hynais had been poisoned during his supper at home, that was. With a really small dose, reflected Lieutenant Boruvka, the poisoning might have taken place even earlier, at the Film Club, for instance.

The name of the poison—tetraethyl of lead—awakened some ancient association in the lieutenant's mind. But though he thought hard, he could not remember what it was; all he had was a visual memory of the Prosecutor's black library in that sombre study and, in its bottom corner under the gilded spines of large lexicons, he had noticed several bright-coloured little volumes that did not look like legal literature. He made a mental note to find out what these books were.

He did not carry out his intention, however. The laboratory report gave the result of the analysis of the crockery taken from the kitchen sink as being absolutely negative; they had found no trace of tetraethyl of lead or any other poison.

As a result, Lieutenant Boruvka now concentrated on the list given him by the waiter at the Film Club, and this led to a remarkable discovery. Not from the chemical laboratory but from the Department of Records.

Lieutenant Boruvka found out that a cook, Otokar Hejda, had in 1950 been sentenced to two years' imprisonment for assisting someone to cross the frontier illegally.

The cook on the waiter's list was named Otokar Hejda.

A study of the man's criminal record showed that he had in fact spent a whole ten years in gaol, having been arrested again only two days after leaving prison in 1952. He had hidden the uniform of an Army deserter, who was caught when trying to escape across the border into West Germany. The uniform had been brought to Hejda by the deserter's girl friend, at whose flat the man had changed into civvies. This being Hejda's second similar offence in three years, he this time got a five-year-sentence. He had then got involved in some fracas in prison which, together with an attempt to escape, prolonged his stay behind bars to a total of ten years, and it was only the amnesty that finally set him free, though he still had to do two years in a military labour battalion.

Reading the sad story of Hejda's past, Lieutenant Boruvka felt that behind the dry language of the official documents there lay something more than an ordinary career of crime.

And there was something else.

At both of his trials, the prosecution had been represented by Dr Paul Hynais, and the sentences demanded by him (in both cases the judge had reduced them) indicated that he was a hard and uncompromising character. The case of the poisoned prosecutor was beginning to clear up.

Or was it?

"Good gosh!" exclaimed Sergeant Malek. "From that kitchen you can see perfectly well who's sitting at the tables in the dining-room. So that's it! He's the scoundrel who did it, then."

"Which scoundrel?"

"Why, Hejda of course."

"Yes," said Boruvka mournfully. "If we find proof that he was the poisoner, he'll hang."

"And serve him right!" commented Malek, a staunch advocate of the death sentence, and he spat disgustedly through the open window of the police car. It was late in the afternoon. "Though I guess that old tom-cat was a bit of a lad himself," the Sergeant went on reflectively. "But that's as it may be; we mustn't view him as just an ordinary human being, we've got to keep his social function in mind as well." Malek was in full spate, as if he were lecturing at a political schooling lesson. "And this, if you ask me, is a nasty case of murder aimed not only at the man but at his social position and thus at our social system as such—"

"Yes," Boruvka interrupted him, speaking in his most lugubrious manner, "I'm with you there—in Hynais's case it was a function more than anything else. . . . The only thing is, Paul—"

He paused.

"What?"

"Don't you think it could be taken as a mitigating circumstance? A crime committed while the balance of his mind was disturbed, or at least in a highly emotional state—even if it was a —a social function that struck out at him and not the man—as a man—"

"You are talking in riddles," growled the Sergeant. "Who struck at whom?"

"Hynais, I mean. At Hejda," replied Lieutenant Boruvka.

"Yes, I know," he said a little later, softly and mournfully, to the frowning cook, "you were young and all that, but according to the law it was a crime."

"What would *you* have done?" demanded Hejda, giving the lieutenant a look of hate. "If you'd been a Boy Scout since you were seven and a friend of yours, also a Scout, had come and asked you to help him? And if you'd known the Bohemian Forest inside out, as I did?"

Boruvka left the question unanswered.

"But that business with the uniform," he continued after a short pause. "Surely you could have thought twice about *that*."

The cook's eyes wandered round the kitchen, coming to rest on a large, highly polished cauldron. A black cat's head peeped out from behind the cauldron. But the cook was not really taking in the scene in that spotless kitchen, his mind was elsewhere, and so it was only Boruvka who noticed.

"I did it because of the girl," explained the cook. "What was I to do? She came bursting in one evening—actually it was on the day I got back home from jug. She was desperate, didn't know where to turn. So what was I to do, I ask you. I was twenty-one, and I loved her."

"Oh, it was *your* girl, then?"

"No, she was Vasek's. That's the chap who deserted. But I was madly in love with her. And during those two years in gaol—well, I guess you wouldn't know, but you've got to have something to think about when you're in prison. Especially if you're nineteen."

"The only trouble was, she was the deserter's girl?"

"Well, yes, but I didn't really mind. I was simply in love with her. I wanted to help her. So I hid that uniform."

Hejda looked at the floor for a few seconds, and then he added:

"Oh, I know you won't understand—you've simply had all the luck."

"How do you mean?" Lieutenant Boruvka asked softly.

"You were lucky, not being brought up the way I was, not being a Boy Scout, not believing the things I believed in. That's just pure luck. At the age of nineteen it can't be either your fault or your merit, if you see what I mean. It's just pure chance. Just luck. Oh, but of course, *you* weren't nineteen in those days," Hejda said, and fell silent.

Boruvka did not reply. A little later he asked:

"And that trouble in prison, what was that about? Something to do with illicit distilling of wine, wasn't it?"

Hejda gave a bitter laugh.

"Wine!" he exclaimed. "I like that! I made about a thimbleful, that's all."

"Oh, I see. But why on earth...?"

"Because they needed it to serve Mass with!" said the cook angrily. "No, don't get the wrong idea, I wasn't a Catholic scout or anything like that. I don't care a damn about religion, but in gaol you sympathise with the other fellows, whatever their views. And the priests were eating their hearts out, not being able to serve Mass without the wine. So I made it for them."

"How did you do it?"

The cook grinned.

"I told them to ask their housekeepers or concubines or whatever they are to send them pastry with raisins. We were allowed to receive food parcels. Occasionally, that is. Well, I scooped out the raisins and fermented them, and they had their wine. Or the blood of the Lord, as they call it."

From somewhere at the back of the kitchen there now came sounds as of someone choking. Both the men turned round. On a table at the back stood the black cat, its front paws in a large pan with minced meat, and as they looked the animal backed away frenziedly, vomiting.

"Go on, scram!" shouted Hejda, but before he could take any action the cat had gone, streaking away like a black torpedo.

The End of an Old Tom-Cat

"Shouldn't you be more careful of hygiene in this place?" said Lieutenant Boruvka sternly.

"It's the porter's cat," said the cook by way of apology. "Gets in here through the ventilator shaft, the little beast. I always give it left-overs in that tin in the corner. But of course, it had to go and eat up all that sausage meat, and now it's sick."

Boruvka noticed that the cat's vomit had exactly the shape of the animal's gullet, the food not having had time to reach its stomach.

"This forms in their stomach because they keep licking their fur," said Hejda, holding something he had picked up out of the mess on the table. "That's why every cat is sick now and again."

Lieutenant Boruvka looked and saw a small black ball of cat's fur.

"O.K., let's get back to business, shall we," put in Malek, who had remained silent in the background during the whole conversation between Lieutenant Boruvka and the cook. His voice was harsh and unfriendly. "What did you put the poison in? The steak Tartare or the meat balls?"

"Who, me?" Hejda's eyes bulged with disbelief. "But gentlemen! Comrades! What gave you the idea—why, I wouldn't dream of doing a thing like that! I've had more than my fill of prison, I don't ever want to go back there again!" There was terror in the man's eyes now. "Why should I put my head in the noose? You can't believe I'd do a dumb thing like that! Gentlemen! Comrades!"

Lieutenant Boruvka suddenly gave a jump, making Sergeant Malek look at him in astonishment.

The lieutenant turned away from them as in a trance and started out across the kitchen like a sleepwalker.

"What's up, Joe?" Sergeant Malek called after him, but Boruvka made no reply, walking out of the door, across the restaurant, and down the stairs, where he instructed Sergeant Sintak, who respectfully awaited his orders, to tell Malek that he had been taken ill and had gone to see a doctor.

Then he vanished in the growing darkness of the city streets, on which the light haze of a May frost had again fallen.

*   *   *

253

Lieutenant Boruvka did not go to see any doctor. He strode, lost
in mind—and his thoughts must have been of a melancholy
nature, for his round face was like a despondent full moon—
through the narrow alleyways of the Old Town, in which the
first drinkers' songs could already be heard coming raucously
from the beer cellars. On top of the pantile roofs, beneath that
other, less melancholy moon, feline bridegrooms raised their
black and pink snouts to the scented night. And from behind a
chimney discharging smoke towards the starry sky, a green-eyed
bride looked out enticingly. The lieutenant was carried by the
gay evening crowd to the Little Square, and he stopped in front
of the illuminated windows of the big hardware store in the old
house called *U Rottu.* For a few moments he stood hesitating by
the window displaying gardening tools, then he made up his mind
and entered the shop.

He reappeared some ten minutes later with a small parcel
wrapped in brown paper under his arm and taking a tram number
11 he drove through the early spring evening to the residential
district of Vinohrady.

It was completely dark by the time he reached the Prosecutor's
villa, but there was a full moon, and so the low ivy-covered front
of the house was well visible, mysterious and silent in the quiet of
the deserted street.

Lieutenant Boruvka did not ring. Cautiously, like a burglar, he
looked to right and left and then, with surprising agility in view
of his bulk, he climbed over the fence.

He found himself in the well-kept garden, which glittered with
dew-drops. Taking great care not to make any noise, he circled the
sleeping villa. There was no light in any of the windows. The
lieutenant went as far as the terrace, stretching there before him
at eye level like the grey surface of some concrete lake.

He pulled out his handkerchief, stretched out his right hand,
and picked a small unsavoury something up from the surface of
the concrete lake, wrapping it carefully in the handkerchief.

Still he did not return the way he had come, nor did he ring
the bell by the gate. On tiptoe he crossed the garden to the fence

dividing it off from the garden of the neighbouring house and, with the same agility as before, climbed over.

He stopped in front of a freshly dug flower-bed in one corner of the garden. As he hesitated, his round moon face assumed a sorrowful expression. The lieutenant sighed, and started unwrapping his brown-paper parcel. In the quiet of the night the paper cracked loudly. He drew out of it an Army field shovel, which gleamed with oil in the white light of the moon.

Boruvka set to work.

It did not take him long. Very soon the sharp edge of his shovel came up against something soft. Regardless of his fine, light-coloured suit and of the likely comments of his wife when she discovered its condition, he knelt on the ground, laid aside the shovel and scraped away at the earth with his hands.

He worked carefully, almost gently.

His brows contracted gloomily as he caught sight of something in the fresh soil. A soft, striped fur. A tom-cat. An old fat moulted tom-cat was lying there in the damp spring earth, lying on his side, his mouth open as though he had died in terrible, painful convulsions.

An expression of extreme sadness appeared on the lieutenant's face.

Carefully, almost gently, he lifted the dead creature from its grave and wrapped it in the brown paper.

He forgot the shovel, leaving it behind on the flower-bed.

"But where did she get hold of the poison?" queried Sergeant Malek. "After all, tetraethyl of lead—"

Without a word Lieutenant Boruvka handed him a small book. An old, much-handled paperback with a bright cover. "I found this in their library," he said. "Open it at page 151."

The Sergeant looked distrustfully at the title—*The Roman Hat Mystery*—and at the name of what appeared to be some dubious American author: Ellery Queen. He started reading on the page indicated by the Lieutenant, and his face grew longer as he read:

"What would I do if I needed the poison for the commission of a crime and wished to leave no trace?" asked Ellery.

A fleeting smile crossed the Professor's lean face.

"Tetraethyl of lead can be extracted from ordinary petroleum."

"Petroleum!" cried the Inspector. "How could it be traced?"

"That's just the question," said the poison expert. "I can buy petroleum anywhere I like, go home, and distil tetraethyl of lead in a very short space of time and with very little effort."

"Doesn't that mean, Doctor, that Field's murderer must have had laboratory experience—that he knew something of analysis?" enquired Ellery hopefully.

"Not at all. Anybody possessing a domestic still can obtain this poison without leaving a trace. Tetraethyl of lead has a higher boiling point than the other components of the liquid. All you have to do is to distil the lot to a certain temperature, and what is left is your poison."

Sergeant Malek finished reading and laid the book aside.

"There you see, Paul," said Lieutenant Boruvka sadly rather than ironically, "sometimes it pays even for the criminologist to read detective novels."

That was the end of the case of the old tom-cat. The analysis of the cat's vomit which Boruvka had picked up on the terrace of the Prosecutor's villa, as well as of the remnants of food in the animal's stomach bore out the presence of tetraethyl of lead. Nature had tried to save the cat, but the retching reflex had not proved strong enough. The cat had dragged itself home, to the kitchen of the villa next door, and there, under the bed of its old mistress, it died.

It was she, the old widow, whom Boruvka had heard weeping so disconsolately when he arrived at the villa to investigate the Prosecutor's death. And it was she who had been working in the neglected garden next door—or so the lieutenant had thought. In actual fact he had witnessed the lonely funeral of the old tom.

The Prosecutor's wife confessed without showing any sign of contrition. Her motive had been a simple one: she hated her husband. She could no longer put up with the mental cruelty she was constantly subjected to, she knew all about his infidelities, as well as about various other things, and she had finally made up her mind to act.

Before going to bed she had carefully washed her husband's plate, which she then smeared with sauce and sprinkled with pieces of minced meat. Needless to say, with minced meat that had not been tainted with the tetraethyl of lead.

But fate had been unkind to her. While they had been at supper, the phone rang, and she had gone out of the room for a couple of minutes to talk to her sister in Liberec. The Prosecutor, who had already eaten well and plentifully in town, had made use of her brief absence to throw the remaining half of his portion out on the terrace.

At that very moment the old tom, whom the ancient urge of all flesh had lured out into the sweet-scented spring night, happened to be passing by.

The cat stopped. Although in his animal brain he heard the call of a different instinct, he decided not to ignore this unexpected treat.

And thus the cat and the Prosecutor came to share the poisoned food.

A full moon sailed across the sky, quartets of cats sang on the Prague rooftops, and Lieutenant Boruvka could not sleep.

And in the low, ivy-grown villa an old tom-cat expired before the ambulance came.

XI

His Easiest Case

A CLEAR THUMB print, magnified to gigantic dimensions and resembling an abstract cloud, was suspended on the projection screen, and the four men in armchairs sat as though transfixed.

Then the youngest of them, a good-looking, tanned, dark-haired young man, stood up, and went over to the armchair in which a chubby man was huddled, his round face shining like a pale lantern in the dimness of the projection room.

The young man opened his mouth to say something, hesitated, raised his hand as though to strike the man in the armchair, let it fall, hesitated again, then turned and strode briskly out of the room.

He slammed the door behind him.

The grave-like silence of the room deepened.

A tall man, with grey-flecked hair, sitting in the middle of the group, cleared his throat and said:

"To suggest it might have been a mistake is—"

"Is out of the question!" the bald man on his left completed the sentence for him. "For as long as fingerprinting has been fingerprinting two identical prints of different thumbs have never been found. Apart from that there is a very clear and distinctive scar on this thumb."

The grey-haired man coughed again and turned to the man with the face of a waning lantern.

"You still claim, comrade lieutenant, that you have never been there? Is—isn't it more likely that you have forgotten?"

The other man coughed too and reiterated hoarsely:

"No, I've never been there, comrade superintendent." He

258

added—and he could have bitten off his tongue before he finished the sentence: "I'd certainly remember that."

In the darkened projection room his chalk-white face coloured slightly.

"So, comrade sergeant, run through the exact course of the investigations once more," Superintendent Kautsky commanded the tanned young man, rubbing his forehead wearily.

"At eight five yesterday we received a call from the writer Josef Kopanec, State Prize—no, not a Prize Winner," recited Sergeant Malek promptly. His face was tautened into sharply-hewn granite features. "He reported that he had gone to visit his niece, our comrade, and found her unconscious. Everything allegedly testified to a murderous assault. We reached the place at eight eight. The address is Number Eleven VI Second of May Street. A one-room flat. The young comrade was lying on her stomach on the floor, the murder weapon was sticking out of the nape of her neck: a meat chopper. Dr Seifert ascertained that the comrade was still alive, so we took her to hospital immediately."

The sergeant lapsed into silence. In his mind's eye he relived the scene which had moved even his relatively immovable heart the day before. The meat chopper was projecting from the nape of the neck, in the middle of the object which he had once declared would cause the owner perpetual maidenhood—the majestic chignon. It had cleft the adornment and the two parts hung limply on either side of her head, matted with blood. Blood gleamed like a terrible halo round the girl's head on the blue carpet, and the fat writer was standing in a corner of the room weeping unrestrainedly.

"And otherwise? Were there any signs of a struggle?" asked the superintendent.

"No. The blow had obviously been delivered in a treacherous manner and quite unexpectedly." Malek returned to the present. "A tray with two cups of coffee was lying on the floor a few paces away. Spilt of course. From this I deduce that the murderer was known to the comrade. He had come on a visit, the comrade prepared him some refreshment and as she was carrying it to the table, the murderer brutally and treacherously struck her from behind with the meat chopper and fled."

"Wait a minute," the superintendent interrupted him. "You said—"

"I take it back!" declared the sergeant. "I meant it this way: he didn't flee. First he carefully wiped all the door handles and all the glass, china and chrome objects so that we did not find any fingerprints. Only on the toilet door handle," he cleared his throat, adding: "And only that one."

"How do you explain that?"

Malek drew his brows together, saying icily:

"In my opinion it testifies to two things. The murderer was a professional. He knew the danger that fingerprints constituted for him, and with regard to the circumstances—being on a friendly visit—he couldn't work in gloves. He was obliged, therefore, to remove all possible traces after the crime. And secondly: when he had removed them, he remembered something he had left in the toilet or he simply went cold-bloodedly to use the lav and as he touched the handle with his hand wrapped in a handkerchief, his thumb got free—maybe he had a hole in his handkerchief—and left a print on the handle. That's why there is only one print and a thumb print at that, and no other fingerprints."

"A professional, you say," growled the superintendent. "But this isn't America, for Pete's sake! We don't have professional murderers here, at least as far as I know. Nothing like that has ever been reported to me—"

"I didn't mean a professional murderer," said the sergeant coldly, and paused for effect. "I mean a professional on murderers."

The superintendent passed his hand over his forehead again wearily.

"I still can't believe it," he cried unhappily. "You assert that he and the comrade—it's never been reported to me—"

He stopped.

The sergeant nodded vigorously.

"She was in love with him," he said. "And he took advantage of her. Maybe he got her into a situation—I mean a woman's situation in which he needed to silence her—or they simply quarrelled over it—"

He fell silent because he himself could not believe it. The superintendent stood up and began to pace up and down the room. He had been working in the criminal investigation bureau for a long time and he knew that everything in the world was possible. At least as far as crime was concerned. And he knew too that things were always more complicated than they appeared when presented by one individual. Even when the individual was unbiased. And the sergeant's stony expression indicated that this individual was far from unbiased.

The superintendent came to a standstill and looked sharply at Malek.

"And you—" he snapped. "Didn't you like the comrade?"

The tanned young man's face darkened. He did not reply.

"Well?"

"Yes, I did," croaked the sergeant. "And that's why I'll get him, however improbable it seems."

The superintendent narrowed his eyes.

"She was not well disposed towards you, was she?"

Malek stood as rigidly as a statue, then he shook his head very slightly.

"But you tried, didn't you?"

"Yes," replied Malek stiffly. "But Bubble had better luck than I did."

"Who?"

"Lieutenant Boruvka."

"That's his nickname?"

"Yes."

"It's never been reported to me," said Kautsky. "Anyway I dislike comrades calling each other by disrespectful nicknames," he declared sternly, and resumed his pacing of the office. He stopped at the table and picked up an enlarged photograph of the lieutenant's thumb.

"No other fingerprints at all were found on the handle?"

"No. Only a small part of another print on the inside. Obviously also Boruvka's. Karal is still working on it."

Kautsky walked round the table and sat down in the armchair.

"So send Bub—Boruvka to me."

But the lieutenant was not to be found. His name was given out three times over the internal loudspeaker system, and in the end they got really worried. They searched the attic and the cellar, all the shafts and nooks on the premises. They phoned the lieutenant's home, until it occurred to Malek that Zuzana Boruvkova might be denying her father's presence, and he went to see for himself. There he behaved with no consideration whatsoever. He peered into every corner, he even opened cupboards, and then at last he took pity on the distracted Mrs Boruvkova. By way of reassurance he informed her under the seal of official secrecy that her husband had disappeared and there was a justified suspicion that he had been abducted by foreign intelligence. This piece of information failed to calm Mrs Boruvkova.

He enquired about Boruvka at the Ministry of the Interior's club which the lieutenant never frequented, and at the Waldek coffee lounge where the lieutenant used to meet old schoolmates from the grammar school he had attended in K., then he returned to the police station and announced that the lieutenant was missing.

As anyone experienced in crime detection knows, the disappearance of a person suspected of murder cannot be interpreted otherwise than as an admission of guilt.

And if the murder is a crime of passion, it is usual to start dragging the surrounding ponds and rivers. Therefore, just before noon that day a boat of the river security force set out on the Vltava. The crew were armed with nets and long poles with hooks on the end.

The haul was a dead loss. They did not net the expected corpse.

They could hardly have done so. It was sitting where Sergeant Malek—outstanding more for his methodicalness than astuteness —had not dreamed of looking. In room Number 13 of the surgical clinic beside a bed occupied by a pretty, pale girl whose small face was dwarfed by an enormous dressing of white gauze and plaster. She was unconscious. The lieutenant was crouching by her bedside, seemingly engrossed in melancholy thought.

He was not thinking.

Memories were chasing through his mind. And in all of them this pale girl with the monstrous turban figured.

He sat there for a long time. Doctors entered, felt her pulse, shrugged their shoulders at the mute, despairing question in the lieutenant's eyes, whispered orders to the nurses and left. The nurses administered injections and left. The lieutenant remained.

They found him there at five o'clock, when it finally dawned upon Malek where to look. They took him off to the police station. Malek forgot to call off the river security squad, so they went on dragging the river to no purpose all night.

In the meantime, Kautsky questioned Boruvka. The lieutenant spoke in a hollow, broken voice, such as no one ever remembered hearing from him.

"I don't know who it was," he said. "A woman. She phoned me just before five, saying that it was very important."

"Why didn't you tell her to come and consult us at the police station?"

"I did. But she made me promise to meet her privately, stressing that it was a matter of life and death—" Boruvka paused, "—and a lady's honour."

"And you swallowed it," Kautsky nodded glumly. "Our knight in shining armour! At least you see now that chivalry doesn't pay in the crime business."

"Or he invented it," said Malek maliciously. "An unknown woman, a meeting in the rose garden in Stromovka park; he waits there for an hour, no one comes—and in the meantime some one attempts to murder his mistress! Tell that to readers of crime fiction, not to us!"

Boruvka turned despairing eyes on his young colleague.

"Don't speak of her like that, Pavel. She wasn't my mistress."

"Oh no!" Malek curled his lip scornfully.

"Wait a minute, comrade," the superintendent silenced him. "We have no reason to disbelieve the lieutenant—"

"What do you mean, no reason?" Malek rudely interrupted his most senior superior. "The young comrade was in love with him —everyone knew that. She was seen with him at least once at the Tomcat." This revelation caused Boruvka to wonder at the sergeant's ability as a sleuth. "Last week, after the Rosenblum case, he proposed a rise of thirty-five crowns a month for her, and before that they were seen flirting together while they were writing out a report. Against all this can be set only his claim that at the critical time some mysterious, unknown woman invited him to Stromovka park and he waited for her alone without witnesses for an hour. And his fingerprints are found in the murdered woman's flat. If it were anyone else, we'd have arrested them ages ago. What do you mean we have no grounds for suspicion?"

"Calm down, comrade," said Kautsky. "In any case, you too have been seen flirting, or rather attempting to flirt, with our young comrade. You have even, or so it has been reported to me, taken her in the police car and during the discharge of official duties placed your arm around her waist and she—"

"But *my* fingerprints are not on her door handle!" snapped Malck. "*I* have never been in her flat in my life!"

The superintendent glanced at Boruvka. But the lieutenant was gazing blankly into space, his face a study of astonishment, incredulity and grief.

Someone knocked at the door. Kautsky opened it. Karal, the fingerprint expert, was standing in the doorway.

"Yes?" asked the superintendent.

"I have the second imprint, comrade superintendent," said Karal quietly and peeped into the room. "That impaired one on the inside of the handle. We've identified it."

"Well? Go on."

Karal peeped into the room again and whispered:

"Could you step into the corridor for a moment?"

When the superintendent had complied and shut the door behind him, Karal announced as though he himself could not believe what he was saying:

"It is an imprint of Sergeant Malek's index finger."

"My fingerprint! Ridiculous!" exclaimed the sergeant indignantly. "It's a mistake!"

"There has never been a case of two people having identical fingerprints," the superintendent pointed out quietly. "It seems you were both lying."

"I wasn't!" yelled Malek. "I swear it! And I have witnesses! The comrade never allowed—I've never set foot in her flat! On my word of honour!"

"And you?" Kautsky turned to Boruvka.

The lieutenant jerked himself out of his reverie.

"Yes," he said.

"That means you withdraw your previous statement that you have never been in the comrade's flat?"

"No, no. I was thinking of something else. And my guess will probably turn out to be correct. Could we have the fingerprints projected once more?"

"Certainly," replied Kautsky.

They took their seats in the projection room again. A strange, surrealistic cloud with a distinctive scar darkened the screen.

"Yes," repeated the lieutenant glumly. "Look at the edges."

"They are smudged," said Karal. "Obviously when the would-be murderer tried to wipe the handle—" He stopped short.

"You are right," said the lieutenant sadly. "And he tried extremely carefully. Look: the fingerprint is impaired on all sides. And there at the bottom right-hand corner is part of another print."

"That's too small," said Karal. "With the best will in the world we cannot identify that."

"It won't be necessary," said Boruvka. "I only want to say that the murderer took great care to wipe off all the prints except mine, so that only mine would be left."

"You mean to say—" the superintendent began.

"Of course," the lieutenant nodded sadly. "That print got there *before* the handle was wiped, not *after*."

Kautsky looked wonderingly at Boruvka, then at Malek.

Malek red and puffed up with anger, choked:

"That only proves that you were there in her flat! It doesn't refute anything."

"Then it would, of course, prove that you too had been there," remarked Kautsky in perplexity.

"But I haven't been there!" squawked Malek. "He has! He used to visit her! He was seen! That is—he wasn't seen—but his print is there with its distinctive scar!" he concluded desperately.

"Oh no, Pavel," said Boruvka. "I wasn't there. And neither were you."

With these words he rose to his feet and silently left the room.

In the girl's one-room flat he looked long at the lavatory door handle and then at the bathroom door handle. They were next to each other and they were both brown. And yet—when he scrutinised them closely—he ascertained that there was a difference in the shades of brown.

From his pocket he took out a handle which he had unscrewed from outside the door that divided the lavatory from the washroom at the police station. Its shade of brown corresponded exactly with the shade of the door handle of the girl's WC.

He grew terribly sad.

About an hour later he was still very sad, sitting in his office where a week before Fendrych, the dress designer, had tried to prove his innocence.

"That's why you dropped your cigarette case at the police station," Boruvka told the stout lady seated opposite him at the table strewn with samples of material and business correspondence. "You knew that I'd pick it up for you, and that you'd have my fingerprints. For comparison. On the way from my office you went to the toilet, locked yourself in and changed the handles on the inside door. When you were there the first time, you went to the toilet to do up your suspender and you noticed the kind of handles that were there. During your second visit you brought an extra handle with you in your handbag. At home you compared all the fingerprints. You are an intelligent woman and your sister's husband is a judge. It was no problem for you to study the fundamentals of fingerprint comparison. Besides, I have a scar on my thumb which even a layman could not overlook. And then you wiped off all the other prints and left only mine there.

"And finally," the lieutenant continued, "you changed the handles in the girl's flat. And all because—"

He lapsed into silence. The lady looked him in the eyes and her own were full of hatred.

"Because you had insulted me," she said. "In the deepest way a man can insult a woman. Because—". She paused and then hissed: "Because you gave me the brush-off!"

"But why did you want to take the young comrade's life—she wasn't to blame in any way?" asked Boruvka who was extremely naïve in some respects.

The lady grew livid.

"Because you didn't give *her* the brush-off!" she hissed. "Do you understand?"

The lieutenant grew sadder than ever before in his life. For at no other time in his life had somebody else's mistake affected him so profoundly.

At nine o'clock in the evening the girl's eyelids fluttered and two large black eyes looked out at the world. At the hospital world. The lieutenant's heart thudded. The doctor who was standing over the sick girl sighed with relief.

The black eyes wandered over the white ceiling, then they looked about and alighted upon the detective's face. A faint smile flitted across the small face under the monstrous turban. Her lips moved.

"Comrade lieutenant—"

"Excellent!" cried the doctor. "So you can have a good meal now, young lady. You're over the worst of it!"

"Do you know what saved her?" the doctor asked the radiantly happy Boruvka. "That chignon!" He chuckled. "You know, I often think what ridiculous things women contrive for themselves —it must have taken her at least half an hour every day to do her hair—but it so happened that it was well worth her while. If it hadn't been for that monstrosity on her head, the chopper would have penetrated her brain! But she stuffed that chignon with a filling made of foam rubber—what do women call them, a toupée or something, probably something else, I don't know. It doesn't matter. Anyway that ridiculous thing saved her life. And I'm glad of it," he said, examining the X-ray photograph of a hideous skull. "So young and pretty; it would have been a pity to lose her."

Entirely engrossed in the photograph of the unsightly skull, in reality concealed by a skin-thin layer of beauty, he did not notice that the expression of almost sinful bliss had deepened on the lieutenant's round face.

"That's marvellous!" the policewoman crowed the following afternoon. Sitting up in bed, she turned her wide seductive black eyes on the shy lieutenant, and wondered whether the turban did something for her. "That is, it's terrible, of course, but it's wonderful how cleverly you worked it out! But that's because, comrade lieutenant, you are so well-educated and such an expert on women."

She did not mean it ironically.

"Me?" the lieutenenat asked wonderingly. "Never! I can't make them out at all. But they have always—somehow been my undoing."

The policewoman dropped her eyes. But the lieutenant hadn't meant it in that sense.

"I had to leave my former profession on account of them." He spoke as though he were reading from a cadre questionnaire, for in the girl's presence he was afflicted even now with attacks of meteorological conversation and official terminology. "I was originally a gym master, but—"

The girl—a trifle disappointed—turned to him again, saying in a surprised tone:

"I didn't know that!"

"I know. I don't boast of it to anyone. But it's a fact."

"Tell me about it, please. Please do!" she begged.

Boruvka being lost, so utterly lost that not even St Sidonius could have saved him, had he been at hand, began to relate the following story:

XII

Crime in a Girls' High School

"IT WAS A long time ago," he sighed. "More than—" he reflected "—more than eighteen years ago. And it began that day—it was a Wednesday, I think. Yes. On a Wednesday morning in the staff-room. Except for Mr Kote, who had been given permission to attend his grandmother's funeral at Caslav, we were all assembled there at a quarter to eight precisely, as required by our headmistress, Ivana Krulisova, whom the girls, and off the record we teachers too, called Ivana the Terrible. Partly on account of her looks—she may have been a woman, but she bore a strong resemblance to a bulldog—partly on account of her soap-box speeches in which she ranted against imperialists, revisionists, *kulaks*, cosmopolitans and class enemies altogether. In essence she was actually a kind Czech soul in a Czech body nourished on buns and dumplings, and the girls (and we too) knew it and took advantage of it. Ivana the Terrible was terrible only in theory. About a month before, while we were sorting out the Fourth Form girls to be allowed to sit for the matriculation examination, we had come across one who was unmistakably a *kulak*'s daughter from a twenty-five-hectare farm. For three days Ivana had gone about like a lost soul and finally she had harangued us in the staff-room about Makarenko whom she confused a bit with Lysenko, talking about heredity, the well-known bourgeois pseudo-science, and how, according to Soviet genetics, characteristics are not inherited but acquired through education, and concluded this whole scientific diatribe with a metaphor about a young tree being pliable. The result: the *kulak* girl from the twenty-five-hectare farm was placed under the patronage of the school CSM* group and allowed to sit for matric.

* The Czechoslovakia Youth Union.

269

"But that's only by the way, you know. So, there we were in the staff room, and Chocholousova Jana from IVA was sitting there, snivelling because someone had stolen her notebook in which she had an envelope containing 5,200 crowns in old currency, the sum having been collected for the school outing to the Moravian-Caves district. The day before, she had left it in the geography study where she had been helping Mr Kote check the CSM membership cards, and when she had gone back for it at half past six, it wasn't there. Oh dear, oh dear, five thousand valid Czechoslovak crowns, what was she to do?

"We were standing dutifully sobered by the gravity of the situation. Ivana the Terrible grew pale and red alternately; her maternal heart visibly bled for Chocholousova Jana. With my bandaged right hand, which I had cut the previous evening with the bread knife, I was trying hurriedly to write up my notes for my PT lesson with IB, not having had time the day before. I was camouflaging my activity with *Rude Pravo* so that Ivana would not spot me. The other teachers were standing around like Braun's statues at Kuks chateau in manifold postures according to their dispositions. Mr Semerak, rigid in a double-breasted jacket, as though it had been a swaddling band, announced drily:

"We'll have to call the police."

But Ivana the Terrible objected, so we did not phone for the police. She delivered a tub-thumping oration in the staff-room on confidence in our girls, and the school's unblemished reputation, followed by another tub-thumper in the gymnasium, into which our 236 pupils were crammed, on the theme: "In a socialist society we do not crack the whip at people!" The gist of this was that the thief who had made off with the notebook and the money would realise that our society gave everyone a chance to reform in the appropriate institution, and would own up honourably. No one came forward, of course. Idealism was and remains an absolute fallacy.

At nine o'clock we were sitting in the staff-room again, dutifully even more sobered, and Mr Semerak suggested phoning the security police at Pardubice.

Before Ivana the Terrible could deliver her third homily of the

day, this time against employing the services of the security police
in our school, standard bearer for a record salvage collection,
there was a knock at the door and Ivana called out:

"Come in!"

Three Fourth Form pupils entered: Chocholousova, Prochazkova and Klimova. Chocholousova with a nose as red as a
carnation, Prochazkova, chairwoman of the school branch of the
CSM, and Klimova, Chocholousova's best friend, a pretty
eighteen-year-old brunette with a delightful bust in a white
blouse.

"Here you are, comrade headmistress, here's Klimova,"
hiccoughed the bereaved Jana.

"What!" cried Ivana. "You, Klimova? I'd never have thought
it of you—"

"No, no!" the chairwoman of the CSM cut in, "Klimova
didn't steal the money. But her brother used to be a private
detective in Prague."

So it happened that the former private detective arrived at our
girls' school at noon. He was now a waiter. He did not start
work until the evening, and so he had come from Pardubice in
under two hours in answer to our telegram. With his brown skin
and eyes like coals of fire he looked like a Sicilian in an Italian
film. He sported a trim moustache and a hat with a striped bow.
He did not remove this on entering the room, but merely
touched the brim with three fingers in the manner of a man of
the world. He uttered a curt greeting: *"Cest praci!"** In reply to
the blushing Ivana's diffident hints that he would be compensated
for his efforts-er-in the interests of the school's reputation-er-
privately, because the school, being a state institution could not-
er-pay anyone in a private capacity . . . he waved his hand in a
magnanimous gesture and declared that he would conduct the
investigation for nothing in defence of his sister's honour.

This floored us momentarily because so far no one had suspected Klimova of theft—after all she was Chocholousova's best
friend—but Ivana explained to us afterwards that the comrade
had meant it collectively, in the sense that the honour of the
school was at the same time his sister's honour.

* "Honour to work!" The Czechoslovakia Communist Party greeting.

And so the former private detective, Jaroslav V. Klima, set to work.

He started off right at the scene of the crime, in the geography study. He invited me, IVA's class teacher to attend the investigations, and firmly dismissed the others, including Ivana the Terrible, decreeing that the school should go about its normal business.

Then he sent for Chocholousova.

She came in, sat down on the edge of the chair as timidly as a church mouse, and the rays of the March sun, penetrating the besmeared window, lent her eyes and nose a carmine hue.

Opposite her Private Detective Klima straddled a chair, the back of which he had turned towards her, rested his elbows on the arms and pushed his hat to the back of his head. Then he unbuttoned his jacket. I expected to catch sight of a revolver in a holster under his armpit, but he apparently carried it in some other place.

"Well now!" he barked sharply and Chocholousova jumped so that she nearly fell off her chair.

"It's all right, just tell the comrade here what happened yesterday," I soothed her.

Jaroslav V. Klima hissed with dissatisfaction and threw me an angry look.

"I am in charge of the investigation," he snapped, and turned to Chocholousova:

"O.K., shoot!"

Chocholousova launched into a faltering narration.

She explained that she had discovered her loss only after reaching home, just before half past six. She had turned round immediately and run back to school. She wanted the caretaker to lend her the key to the staff-room where the keys to all the studies were kept (they had originally hung in the caretaker's lodge, but the alert and vigilant spirit of Ivana the Terrible had roamed as far as there) but the caretaker had declared that there was a mighty big interest in the geography study that day, and despite his poor health, had accompanied her personally to the staff-room and from there to the study. But they had not found anything in the study.

Jaroslav V. Klima listened to the narration frowningly. When the girl had finished, he asked her:

"Do you ever find yourself in—sort of states?"

Chocholousova glanced at him timidly.

"What kind of states?"

"You sort of have the feeling that you are not you..."

Chocholousova said nothing to this.

"A sort of split, you know—a split consciousness—"

While putting these questions, the ex-private detective did not take his hypnotic eyes off the girl. She shivered and squeaked:

"I don't know."

"Aha," observed the detective significantly. "Interesting."

I could see that we were going to have fun with Jaroslav V. Klima.

Then he told Chocholousova to say after each other quickly any words that came into her head. For a long time nothing came into her head; then she finally produced this chain of association: skirt—shoes—Bata*—crisis—capitalism—and Jaroslav V. Klima looked at me significantly. He then asked her if she preferred cats or dogs, and finally he borrowed a notebook from me, tore a sheet out of it, made an irregular blot on it from Mr Kote's bottle of red ink and asked Chocholousova to tell him what it conjured up in her mind.

"I don't know," said the girl sadly.

"What sort of feeling do you have?"

Chocholousova was silent.

"None?" suggested J. V. Klima.

"None."

"Look at it carefully."

The girl looked at it carefully. She said uncertainly:

"It looks like—"

"Yes—?"

Jaroslav V. Klima raising his eyebrows slightly, squinted at me again.

* The leading pre-war Czech shoe manufacturer.

"Like—," whispered Chocholousova, "well, like a sort of —blot."

"That will do," said the detective tersely.

After various similar psychological experiments, he finally asked her if she had noticed anything suspicious in the study.

"When we were inside, it seemed to me—," said Chocholousova, "—but I don't know."

"I must warn you that you are testifying as though you were under oath," the private detective reminded her sternly.

"I don't know for sure." The pupil writhed on her chair. "But it seemed to me as though someone was running downstairs."

Jaroslav V. Klima stood up, hooking his thumbs into the armpits of his waistcoat. The March sunshine lit up his narrow, small-featured face, and he commenced to pace up and down the study. Then he turned to the girl at lightning speed and fixed his piercing eyes upon her.

"Were they men's footsteps or women's?"

"I—I don't know—" replied Chocholousova in confusion. "I think—perhaps—both—"

"Interesting," remarked the private detective thoughtfully, drawing a breath through his teeth. "Very interesting! You may go."

"Are you interested in psychology?" he asked me when we were alone.

I shook my head.

"I am," said Jaroslav V. Klima. "It is very important for a criminologist. And in this case the psychological factor will obviously be decisive. I used several psychological tests on the interrogated person. They told me a lot."

I asked him what they had told him.

"I'll keep that to myself for the moment," replied the private detective. "Keep your eyes open. The case is beginning to clear up."

Then he sent for the caretaker.

"What did you mean by the words 'there's a mighty big interest in the geography study today'?" he demanded sternly.

"Because Celbova from IIIA had been there before Chocho-lousova," said the caretaker. "And she made such a fuss about it that I had to go there to see for myself."

J. V. Klima's voice rose to a thin falsetto:

"What?"

"Whether the key had really been lost."

It appeared that about six o'clock Celbova had borrowed the staff-room key from the caretaker. She was head of the CSM puppetry group, who had given a performance that afternoon at a local nursery school. Celbova had wanted to put the sack containing the puppets into the geography study. The caretaker had lent her the staff-room key but she had returned in about five minutes asserting that the study key was missing from the board in the staff-room, that the geography study was locked and someone seemed to be moving about inside. She even thought she had heard a muffled cry of pain. By nature an extremely argumentative man, the caretaker had spent ten minutes in dispute with Celbova, reiterating his view, regardless of what she had to say, that Mr Kote had left for Caslav and no one else had any business in his study. As far as the key was concerned, he was of the opinion that Celbova had suffered a mental blackout, because none of the pupils had borrowed the staff-room key from him and all the staff had left ages ago. He had immediately proved his blackout theory, because when he had finally gone to the staff-room with her, the key to the geography study was hanging in its usual place. The sack of puppets was then tidied away, the study was locked, Celbova was chided and the caretaker returned to his lodge.

No sooner had he settled down comfortably to his evening pipe than Chocholousova had swept in like a tidal wave and the expedition to the geography study had been repeated. In this respect the caretaker's testimony tallied exactly with Chocho-lousova's. The caretaker too thought he had heard footsteps hurrying down the stairs.

Jaroslav V. Klima, however, did not attach any importance to the footsteps. Instead he muttered to himself thoughtfully: "Celbova. Hmm."

And he sent for Celbova.

He learnt from her precisely what he had learnt from the

275

caretaker, and in addition he ascertained that the smudged blot reminded her of a cloud, that she preferred cats to dogs, that she had splitting headaches from time to time but that she did not suffer from a feeling of split personality, and elicited from her the following chain of associations: man—woman—brigade—daddy—a good hiding—which, after the pupil had left, he confessed was not quite clear to him.

"Did you notice her lips?" he asked me. It was impossible not to notice them. Celbova was the school beauty queen.

"Turned down at the corners," remarked Jaroslav V. Klima gloomily. "Indicates a weak personality. That woman suffers from an inferiority complex. She is capable even of committing a crime to compensate for this feeling."

He drew a pipe from his pocket and began to fill it, with an owl-like expression.

The turned-down corners of Celbova's lips were caused, of course, by the permanently disdainful expression which she used as a deterrent against importunate would-be acquaintances from the neighbouring technical college. But I did not inform Jaroslav V. Klima of this. In any case he would have rejected such an unpsychological explanation.

"And now," he announced, "we'll examine the scene of the crime."

He stood up and went towards the door. His black eyes scanned the room keenly while he veiled himself in a cloud of smoke. His gaze rested on the locked cupboard, to which only Mr Kote had a key; the desk, adorned with a mass-produced bust of a statesman, which flies had used for the same purpose as they had the famous portrait of a certain sovereign*; on the wide armchair in which Mr Kote, an elderly gentleman, habitually snatched forty winks instead of writing up his lesson notes when he had a break. He also scrutinised the large map of the Republic on the right-hand wall, the picture of Emil Holub† fleeing from cannibals on the left-hand wall, and the stained window, behind

* The portrait of Francis Joseph, Emperor of Austria–Hungary, hanging in Palivec's pub U Kalicha in Jaroslav Hasek's famous book, *The Good Soldier Schweik.*
† Czech explorer.

which stood a half-empty bottle of milk. Then suddenly, without warning, he did a knees full bend and peered under the armchair.

"Aha!" he crowed, looking up at me significantly from his fish-eye view. "The criminal always makes a mistake. That is the golden rule of detective work."

Then he straightened up and crossed to the armchair; he hitched up his trousers, spread a red handkerchief on the floor, knelt down on it and groped under the armchair. His thin face reddened with exertion, then he bared his yellow teeth in a satisfied grin which made his pitch-black moustache bristle.

He stood up and stretched his hand towards me with the palm upwards.

The March sun fell on his palm.

On it lay a woman's black suspender.

"Yes, the criminal always makes a little mistake," declared Jaroslav V. Klima, stuffing the suspender into his pocket. "Where does Celbova live?"

"But that hasn't got anything to do with the money!" I exclaimed in astonishment.

"You think not?" Jaroslav V. Klima retorted, his voice heavy with irony. "I think so. Turn it over in your mind."

All the way to Celbova's lodgings I turned it over in my mind thoroughly, I might almost say feverishly. But I could not discover any connection between the suspender and the theft of funds intended for the Fourth Form outing.

The private detective announced curtly to the landlady who opened the door to us:

"Police!"

Pushing her aside, he entered the house. The landlady looked startled, but as she knew me, she calmed down a bit and showed us into her two tenants' bedroom.

It had formerly been a bedroom for a married couple and was dominated by a wide double bed with a canopy. At the sight of the bed Jaroslav V. Klima raised his eyebrows again.

"Does Celbova sleep in this bed?"

"Yes, sergeant," replied the widow.

"Alone?"

"With Miss Karvasova. They both lodge here."

"Interesting," remarked the private detective. "Look, have you ever caught them sleeping in the same half of the bed?"

"Oh yes, often, sergeant," replied the widow promptly.

Jaroslav V. Klima bestowed on me another of his significant glances.

"The young ladies don't usually heat the room in the winter," the landlady went on, "and so towards morning they snuggle together for warmth."

"For warmth, you say?" the detective repeated sarcastically, and then sent the landlady out of the room.

"Did you notice?" he turned to me. "Lesbian leanings. Quite clear. It is often linked with a predisposition towards theft. The case is taking on a much clearer shape."

He looked round and went over to the chest of drawers. He took a pair of pigskin gloves out of his pocket, drew them on ceremoniously and then carefully opened the top drawer. He systematically rummaged through all the drawers. I stood apart, finding it distasteful to assist at such intimate sleuthing among my pupil's underwear. J. V. Klima worked quite efficiently on his own, and after a fruitless twenty-minute search straightened up with a satisfied expression and turned to me smiling.

"Nothing!" he declared triumphantly.

"Perhaps she hid the money somewhere else."

"I wasn't looking for the money," he informed me scornfully. "That is doubtlessly well hidden somewhere *outside* this house. *That* won't escape us. I was looking for a black suspender belt with one suspender missing."

The connection between a suspender belt and the lost suspender was clear to me, but the connection between the belt and the theft remained a mystery.

"There are two possibilities," said Jaroslav V. Klima. "Either she discovered the loss of her suspender and disposed of the belt as an incriminating object, or—"

He looked at me triumphantly.

"Or?" I breathed nervously.

"Or she is wearing it!" he said. "A well-known trick. The *corpus delicti* in the most usual place. Do you know The Case of the Purloined Letter by Edgar Allan Poe?"

I had to admit that it had not occurred to me. I would have

pointed out a third possibility, that the suspender was part of a belt belonging to another pupil, but Jaroslav V. Klima was so obviously convinced of the iron logic of his deduction that I had not the heart to spoil his pleasure.

We returned to the school.

In the square we ran into Klimova's landlady. The private detective—for the first time that day—took off his hat with a ceremonial flourish and gravely enquired first of all after the good lady's health and then about his sister Lucie's conduct. At the second question the landlady's face clouded.

"Unfortunately, Mr Klima, Lucinka has changed lately."

"How do you mean?" asked the detective sternly.

"She is keeping secrets from me," replied the landlady who evidently was one of the loquacious members of her species, "and she tells me lies."

Jaroslav V. Klima frowned.

"Oh, does she?"

"She's told me several times," said the landlady, "that she was going to see a friend or attend an English lesson, and I found out afterwards that she hadn't been either at her friend's or at her English lesson. Like yesterday. When I asked her where she'd really been and reminded her that you'd asked me to keep a maternal eye on her as it were, she only tossed her head and said, just imagine, that she's of age and it's none of my business!"

The private detective glowered to the maximum possible degree. He pressed the landlady's hand gloomily and firmly, saying:

"I'll come and see you towards evening, madam. And then I'll deal with her. Never you fear! Now I have some important work to do. Good-day!"

We continued on our way to the school in silence. The private detective gazed sombrely in front of him and then he suddenly addressed me:

"Have you, as her teacher, noticed anything about my sister?"

I shook my head.

"Have you seen her with any men?"

"No," I said. "She strikes me as being a very self-controlled girl. She is making good progress at her lessons; she is interested in gymnastics—"

The Mournful Demeanour of Lieutenant Boruvka

Jaroslav V. Klima seized me by the hand as he had the land-lady. "If you should ever see her out with a fellow, take her home immediately and report it to me. I'll settle the matter with her. With both of them. I give you full powers."

'But—" I attempted to object, but the private detective did not allow me to get in a word edgeways.

"I am responsible for her to our deceased mother of immortal memory. On her death bed she entrusted Lucie to my care and protection. If she should lose her innocence, I'd kill her and her seducer too!"

His black eyes flashed and again I was reminded of an Italian film. His black moustache bristled. A shiver ran down my spine. We found ourselves at the school and the private detective stopped short. There was an overgrown garden at the back of the school; in front of it the road forked. The left fork led to the main entrance, the right led round the garden to the back and farther on to the old part of the town.

"The garden," said Jaroslav V. Klima. "Is here any other entrance to the school?"

I hesitated. Then I replied:

"Yes. From the garden. But there is a fence all round the garden and there is no gate in it."

"Interesting," remarked the detective. "Let's go!"

Instead of going to the main entrance, we turned to the right. We walked slowly along by the fence and Jaroslav V. Klima rapped it with his knuckles. We soon found ourselves in a narrow lane between the fence and the black wall of an old rope-plaiting workshop. The sun was hidden by clouds and the lane was dark and clammy. It lay in cool shade and there were rust-coloured patches on the fence where the wood was crumbling from dampness.

The private detective stopped at one of them. He laid his hand on the plank and pushed it lightly. Then he turned to me, his black eyes shining with triumph.

"The garden *has* got a back entrance," he exclaimed. He seized the two adjacent planks with both hands and drew them apart. The triangular space revealed a view of the neglected school garden, a jungle of ferns. The private detective squeezed through the gap and swore wrathfully. I crawled through after him. He

was standing up to his knees in ferns and pressing his right hand
to his lips.

"What's the matter?"

"I scratched myself," he hissed. "Damn it!"

He stooped down, lifted a greenish mossy stone from under the
ferns, went back to the fence and after several blows bent a
dangerous blood-covered nail which had been sticking out of the
plank. Then he looked round. A lightly trodden path led from the
gap in the fence through the ferns.

"They escaped this way," stated the private detective, pulling
his red handkerchief out of his pocket and wrapping it round his
hand.

"Who?" I breathed.

"The criminals."

I was silent for a moment. I tried in vain to sort out in mind
the ideas that were obviously guiding his reasoning.

"You—you no longer suspect Celbova?" I asked.

He grinned.

"On the contrary. More than ever. Doesn't that path say anything to you?"

I looked at the path. It led to the back entrance of the school
building, which was not kept locked. It was hardly discernible.
I really didn't know what it said to Jaroslav V. Klima. It definitely didn't say anything to me that could be connected with
the theft of money from the geography study and the leader of
the puppetry group.

I shrugged my shoulders.

"You lack the ability to deduce from plain clues," sighed the
detective. "And yet it's as clear as daylight. The thief had an
accomplice."

He looked at me with a long-suffering expression.

"Elementary, my dear sir," he exclaimed. "Celbova borrowed
the staff-room key, got hold of the study key, appropriated the
notebook and the money, handed them over to her confederate
who came by this path," he pointed to the track through the
ferns. "Then she locked up and went to the caretaker with the
story about the key from the study having disappeared. An alibi,
you follow? In the meanwhile the accomplice was hiding on the
floor above. When the caretaker went to the study with Celbova,

the confederate—or confederates—fled downstairs and left the school by the *back entrance across the garden*," he concluded.

How did Celbova know that the money was in the study? And why did the accomplices hide on the floor above when they could have gone down at the same time as Celbova and escaped by the back door which could not be seen from the caretaker's lodge? These questions sprang to my mind but I regarded it as unfitting to influence the great detective in his deductions.

Klima said:

"I shall need an assistant."

"An assistant?"

"Yes. It will be necessary to discover which pupil from the two top forms is wearing a black suspender belt with one suspender missing."

Strewth, I thought, and the very idea took my breath away.

It must have taken Ivana the Terrible's breath away too, because she reddened a little and her mouth dropped open. Klima stuck to his guns. In the end the task was entrusted to the twenty-two-year-old English mistress, against whom semi-disciplinary proceedings had recently been held because she had modelled in the nude for a local artist notorious for drunkenness and modernism.

The examination was conducted behind the closed doors of the Fourth Form classroom. In the meantime I was sitting in the geography study with Klima who was expounding his reflections.

"In our line a man must possess a particularly well developed ability to reason logically," he remarked thoughtfully. "Logic is everything. And then psychologic. That too is everything. Psychologic and logic, and mainly noticing even apparent trifles. A talent for observation. That is everything. When I was still working at the Karlik detective agency, the boss used to entrust the most complicated cases to me. Of course they were mostly sexual crimes, not theft and things like that." He lapsed into silence. I knew what sort of sexual crimes private detective agencies were concerned with. I wondered whether extra-marital intercourse was classified as a crime in our penal code. "And that's another thing," mused the great detective. "Behind every crime is *sexus*. I shouldn't be surprised," he said, taking the black suspender out of his pocket, "if it were at the back of this theft."

He turned the suspender over in his hand, looking at it with obvious relish.

Suddenly he executed one of his unexpected lightning movements. He twitched as though he'd been bitten by a viper and held the suspender up in front of his eyes. Then he groped feverishly in his pocket and drew out a magnifying glass, a standard magnifying glass nearly four inches in diameter. He examined the suspender through it, hissing:

"Well, I'll be damned!"

I jumped.

"What's the matter?"

"Look here!"

I looked through the magnifying glass. On the underside of the metal part of the suspender a trademark was engraved, clearly legible under the glass:

MAIDENSHAPE CORSETS
Pat. reg. USA

The detective's eyes sparkled.

"Get it?"

"No, I don't."

Jaroslav V. Klima leapt out of his chair.

"But it's as plain as a pikestaff, my dear sir! The net around the criminal is tightening! We have an ideally narrowed circle of suspects!"

And he rushed out into the corridor.

There we ran into the English mistress.

"Well?" asked Klima.

"Nothing," replied the mistress.

"Excellent!" exclaimed the private detective. "That was to be expected," he turned to me. "If we were to rummage among the tins in the town rubbish dumps, we would undoubtedly find a black suspender belt with a missing suspender somewhere. But it won't be necessary to conduct such an arduous operation. Let's go!"

And we went to the staff-room.

*　*　*

Ivana the Terrible looked at the black suspender through the magnifying glass and paled. The detective watched her with an eloquent smile.

"Well? What do you say to that?"

Ivana dropped into a chair, turned on Jaroslav V. Klima horrified eyes of folk tale, forget-me-not blue and gasped:

"Espionage!"

"Nothing of the sort! There's no need to alarm yourself," the detective waved his hand. "It only proves one thing: the owner of the belt has relatives abroad. American goods are not sold here. Show me the cadre dossiers!"

These dog-eared, highly confidential papers brought a terrible revelation that left even Jaroslav V. Klima speechless. A careful examination disclosed that from the cadre point of view ours was a jewel among schools, for out of our 236 pupils only one had relations abroad:

Lucie Klimova.

We froze into immobility round the staff-room table, engulfed in a painful silence. Me, Jaroslav V. Klima and Ivana the Terrible. Jaroslav V. Klima's Adam's apple shot up and down his thin throat. Ivana was red in the face. I looked askance at the fateful box headed *Relations Abroad* in Lucie Klimova's cadre questionnaire, and read:

Clara Paese—aunt	
Isabella Francesco—aunt	
Lucia Petrinelli—aunt	
Mariucca Franconi—aunt	
Cesare Franconi—uncle	New York, USA
Benito Franconi—uncle	
Carlo Franconi—uncle	
Emilio Franconi—uncle	

I glanced quickly at the box headed *Parents: Father: Vaclav Klima, musician; Mother: Marie Klimova, née Franconi, deceased.*

That explained her brother's Italian mores. And his Italian eyes.

A shiver ran down my spine.

Jaroslav V. Klima sat motionless, slowly turning purple. Ivana fixed her eyes on him and I read sympathy in her expression. She cleared her throat and said:

"Perhaps there's some mistake, comrade—"

But the private detective leapt up as though he had been stung by a wasp.

"It's no mistake! *Porco Dio!*" he yelled and banged his fist on the table in a most undetectivelike way. "My own sister! Where is she? Where is she?"

He looked round wildly as though he expected that Lucie Klimova might be hiding in the staff-room. Then he riveted his attention on the door. He headed for it, shouting inarticulately. Ivana made an ineffectual attempt to stop him but Klima dodged her and rushed toward the door. It opened and an embarrassed gentleman holding a brief-case stood in the doorway. The detective collided with him at full tilt and brought them both to the ground.

The gentleman was the first to recover. He sat down on a chair.

"I beg your pardon," he said, holding out his hand to the half-stunned Jaroslav V. Klima. "My name's Kote. I must apologise. A regrettable misunderstanding has arisen. The money is in my possession."

"*Porco Dio!*" yelled Klima.

"I found it in the study as I was leaving," Kote explained humbly. "Please forgive me. I have caused a great deal of unpleasantness, but I had no time to ascertain whom the money belonged to, therefore I locked it in my safe so that it should not get lost. I intended to mention it to the caretaker on my departure, but somehow—I forgot—"

Jaroslav V. Klima was staring at the teacher as though he were an apparition.

"Thank heavens!" cried Ivana the Terrible joyfully. "That's taken a weight off my mind, comrade Kote."

The detective babbled:

"So no money has been lost?"

"No it has not, unfortunately—or rather fortunately," stuttered Kote in confusion and retreated a step from the detective. Jaroslav V. Klima went a perceptibly deeper shade of purple. He suddenly thrust his hand violently into his pocket, leapt towards Kote, seized him by the tie with his right hand and dangled the black suspender in front of his eyes with his left hand.

"And what does this mean?" he shrieked, his voice cracking.

"I—I have no idea," stuttered Kote, endeavouring to free his tie from Klima's grip with his two white, chubby hands. Klima's black eyes rested on those white, pasty hands which had probably never wielded any implement heavier than a pen, and something seemed to strike him. He looked at them for a long time. Then he looked at me. A shiver ran down my spine. Jaroslav V. Klima's black eyes travelled from my face to my bandaged hand.

My heart missed a beat. Jaroslav V. Klima executed the last lightning move of the day and the staff-room was illuminated with a beautiful galaxy of red, blue and green stars.

"You must have got the point—", Lieutenant Boruvka hesitated and then, for the first time during the whole period he had known her, he called the policewoman by her Christian name, "—Eva. Jaroslav V. Klima has been quite a good, conscientious and agreeable brother-in-law, except that he persisted in keeping the promise he had made to his dying mother concerning his sister, even after Lucie got married. He dogged my footsteps for many years, seeming not to trust my moral principles."

The lieutenant sighed and gave the policewoman an awkward smile.

"A fortnight after the case of the black suspender his sister's honour was saved by me in St Lawrence's Cathedral in K. But it didn't save me as a teacher. I had to leave the school at K, and a chance occurred—through a friend from my army days—and perhaps I was a little impressed by Jaroslav V. Klima. After all, he had solved the case, although it was different from what he had been led to expect. I handed in an application to the police force—scoundrels are supposed to make the best policemen—the founder of our profession, the famous Vidocq, was actually an escaped galley slave."

He lapsed into silence. The girl gazed into blankness, into the unknown. The lieutenant thought sadly that the case of the black suspender had not cheered her up. Controlling his emotions, he adopted a light tone again:

"It turned out to be true in my case too—I remained with the homicide squad and I can't say I haven't managed to get to the bottom of something here and there. I hope, though, you haven't formed a bad opinion of me. I was young then, you know, although I was a teacher, and I was bewitched by her grey eyes. They were set in a black frame—she had pitch-black eyelashes, you know." Boruvka was lost in reverie. "All her family have black or grey eyes, and all in such pitch-black frames. I'll show you a photograph some time, if you are interested."

He glanced at her uncertainly, but the girl's own eyes, also black, also framed with black lashes, still gazed into space.

The lieutenant sighed.

"Well, to finish the story. Simply: Lucie was my pupil; we could not meet in public. K was too small a town for that. There was only the geography study, where my colleague Kote had a wide couch for his afternoon nap. That evening when Lucie was supposed to be at her English lesson, and Celbova began to rattle the door handle, we naturally panicked a bit and hastily restored ourselves to a civilised state. That's when Lucie lost her suspender. I had just managed to lock the door and hang the key in the staff-room when I heard the caretaker returning with Celbova. So we hid on the floor above, and when the two of them were in the study, we ran downstairs and out through the back across the garden, which was the way we used to get into the study secretly. Being in a hurry, I cut my hand on that nail that was sticking out, on which Jaroslav V. Klima afterwards scratched himself. That's the only falsehood I resorted to while telling you this story, Eva. It wasn't the bread knife. It was the nail. Well," sighed Boruvka, "nine months later—I was already slogging with the squad—Zuzana was born."

"But—" the policewoman demurred.

"What?" The large, forget-me-not blue eyes in the round moon face, above which the disobedient tuft of hair stood up, were fixed questioningly on her. It was an amusing story but the girl did not appear to be amused. She looked at Boruvka and felt sorry for him. He was no longer young. She suddenly understood the deep, infinite sadness which was ineradicably engraved on the lieutenant's face, and she too grew sad.

"What were you going to say—Eva?" asked Boruvka quietly.

"Nothing," she sighed, near to tears. "Only—only you must be very proud of Zuzana. She is a very pretty girl."

A smile flitted across Boruvka's face.

The girl had lied. She had been about to say something quite different. But now in the depths of her heart she knew for sure that she would never tell the lieutenant how very improbable it was that a grey-eyed woman and a blue-eyed man should have a daughter with eyes as green as a cat's.

Prague 1962–1965